BY MORGAN LLYWELYN
FROM TOM DOHERTY ASSOCIATES

1949

1949

A Novel of the Irish Free State

Morgan Llywelyn

FORGE®

A TOM DOHERTY ASSOCIATES BOOK

NEW YORK

1949: A NOVEL OF THE IRISH FREE STATE

Copyright © 2003 by Morgan Llywelyn

This book is printed on acid-free paper.

A Forge Book
Published by Tom Doherty Associates, LLC
175 Fifth Avenue
New York, NY 10010

www.tor.com

Forge® is a registered trademark of Tom Doherty Associates, LLC.

Library of Congress Cataloging-in-Publication Data

Llywelyn, Morgan.
    1949 : a novel of the Irish Free State / Morgan Llywelyn.—1st ed.
        p. cm.
    ISBN 0-312-86753-0
    1. Ireland—History—1922—Fiction. 2. Women Revolutionaries—Fiction.
3. Single Mothers—Fiction. 4. Women farmers—Fiction. I. Title: Nineteen forty-nine. II. Title.

PS3562.L94 N49 2003
813'.54—dc21

                                                          2002032525

First Edition: March 2003

Printed in the United States of America

0 9 8 7 6 5 4 3 2 1

For
Micaela Jordan Winter

Acknowledgments

The author owes a great debt to the numerous Irish men and women who have contributed to this novel by sharing their time and their memories. There are too many to thank them all by name, but without them it would have been impossible to construct a picture of Ireland during the Thirties and Forties.

Two in particular, however, deserve special mention. Donncha O Dúlaing made me aware of the drama of radio broadcasting in the early days of the state, and described for me in detail those small things which history books never tell. Douglas Gageby, writing about his father-in-law, Seán Lester, introduced me to an almost forgotten but heroic Irishman who played an important role on the international stage at a crucial time.

History is slippery. Different people remember events in different ways. The best anyone can do in trying to reconstruct a past time is to piece together a fabric composed of many memories. Each of the novels in this series contains true fragments from hundreds of lives, vividly and generously recalled for the author and then interwoven into the fabric of the story.

Thank you all, so very, very much.

Dramatis Personae

Fictional Characters (in order of mention):

Ursula Jervis Halloran: Born approximately 1910 in Dublin. Foster child of Ned and Síle Halloran.

Henry Price Mooney: Born in Clare in 1883, and Ella Rutledge Mooney, his wife, born in Dublin in 1890. Daughters Isabella and Henrietta.

Edward Joseph Halloran, "Ned": Born in Clare in 1897. His parents drowned in the sinking of the *Titanic*.

Norah Daly: Ned's spinster aunt; his mother's sister.

Kathleen Halloran Campbell O'Shaughnessy: Ned's older sister in America.

Frank Halloran: Ned's older brother.

Lucy and Eileen Halloran: Ned's younger sisters. Eileen married Lucas Mulvaney in 1929.

Tilly Burgess: The Mooneys' housemaid.

Finbar Cassidy: Born in Donegal in 1905. A civil servant in the Free State government.

Felicity Rowe-Howell, "Fliss": Ursula's English roommate at Surval Mont-Fleuri.

Madame Dosterschill: Ursula's German teacher.

Heidi Fromm: Ursula's Austrian classmate at Surval, who marries Stefan Neckermann, a Swiss botanist.

Cedric Rowe-Howell: Felicity's brother, a pilot for the Royal Mail Service.

Louise Kearney Hamilton: Henry Mooney's cousin, and her husband **Hector Hamilton,** the painless dentist.

Lewis Baines: Cedric Rowe-Howell's friend, the son of Donald Baines from *1921*.

Robert Averitt, Malcolm Weed, and E.G. Bletherington: Foreign correspondents.

Muriel Baines: sister of Lewis Baines.

Magnus Leffler: Swiss obstetrician.

Finbar Lewis Halloran, "Barry": Ursula's son, born April 6, 1939.

Gerry and George Ryan: hired men at the Halloran arm in Clare.

Michael Kavanagh: son of Kathleen O'Shaughnessy's chauffeur.

Barbara Mooney Kavanagh: daughter of Michael and Isabella Kavanagh, born 3 May 1947.

Historical Characters

Aiken, Frank (1898–1983): Armagh-born Irish nationalist; revolutionary, and politician. Commandant of the northern division of the IRA in 1921. Appointed as minister for defense by de Valera in 1932; minister for external affairs 1951–54 and 1957–69; Tánaiste 1959–69.

Attlee, Clement (1883–1967): Leader of the British Labour Party.

Avenol, Joseph (1879–1952): French-born secretary-general of the League of Nations until 1940.

Blythe, Ernest (1889–1975): Northern Protestant born in County Antrim. Joined the Irish Republican Brotherhood; organizer for the Irish National Volunteers; spent the 1916 Rising in prison; elected as a Dáil deputy for North Monaghan in 1918; minister of trade and commerce in the first Dáil; Free State minister for finance, and for posts and telegraphs; director of the Abbey Theatre.

Brennan, John: Pseudonym of Sydney Czira, writer and broadcaster; a sister of Grace Gifford Plunkett (see following).

Brennan, Robert (1881–1964): Revolutionary, author, and diplomat; commanded six hundred Volunteers in Wexford during the Easter Rising; under the first Dáil Brennan was responsible for establishing the Department of External Affairs; opposed the Treaty; one of the first directors of the *Irish Press;* Irish minister to Washington during World War II.

Bóru, Brian (941–1014): Born near Killaloe, County Clare. Prince of the Dál gCais; king of Munster; became Ard Rí (High King) of all Ireland in 1002. Died defeating the Vikings and their allies at the Battle of Clontarf in 1014.

Byrne, Alfie (1882–1956): Member of the Dáil; served three years as member of the Seanad; was lord mayor of Dublin for a record nine successive years.

Byrne, Donn (1889–1928): Novelist born in New York of Irish parents, but raised in Armagh.

Chesterton, Gilbert Keith, known as G.K. (1874–1936): English critic and author of verse, essays, novels, and short stories.

Clandillon, Séamus (1878–1944): Born in County Galway. Irish language scholar, civil servant, and devotee of traditional music; became first station director and later director of broadcasting at 2RN.

Clarke, Kathleen (1878–1972): Born in Limerick of a revolutionary family. Married Thomas Clarke.

Clarke, Thomas James (1858–1916): Born on the Isle of Wight. Joined the IRB in Dublin in 1878; served fifteen years in British prisons for his revolutionary activities; emigrated to America; returned to Ireland and opened a newsagency and tobacconist's shop in Parnell Street; was the first signatory of the Proclamation of the Republic; fought in the 1916 Rising; executed by the British.

Collins, Michael (1890–1922): Born in County Cork. The son of a self-educated farmer; went to London at sixteen, where he worked in the civil service; joined the IRB in London; returned to Dublin to take part in the 1916 Rising as aide-de-camp to Joseph Plunkett; imprisoned by the British; member of the Supreme Council of the IRB; minister of home affairs and then minister of finance in the first Dáil; negotiated the Anglo-Irish Treaty in 1921; commander in chief of government forces in the Civil War; killed at Béal na mBláth on 22 August 1922.

Connolly, James (1870–1916): Born in Edinburgh, Scotland, of Irish immigrant parents. Trade union organizer; dedicated socialist; signatory of the Proclamation of the Irish Republic; organizer of the Citizens Army; commandant-general of the Dublin forces during the 1916 Rising; executed by the British.

Cosgrave, William Thomas (1880–1965): Born in Dublin. Joined Sinn Féin; elected to Dublin city council in 1909; joined the Irish Volunteers in 1913; served under Eamonn Ceannt at the South Dublin Union during the 1916 Rising; minister for local government in the first Dáil; supported the Treaty; first president of the Executive Council of the Irish Free State, 1923–32; lost the general election to Fianna Fáil in 1932; helped found the Fine Gael Party in 1933; retired from politics in 1944.

Costello, John Aloysius (1891–1976): Dublin-born lawyer. Served as attorney general 1926–32; joined Fine Gael in 1933; represented the government at the League of Nations; became taoiseach in 1948; declared the Irish state a republic during a press conference in Canada that same year.

Czira, Sidney née Gifford (1889–1974): A sister of Grace Gifford Plunkett; wrote under the pseudonym "John Brennan."

Daladier, Édouard (1884–1970): Premier of France who signed the Munich Pact, ceding the Sudetenland to Germany.

de Gaulle, Charles-André-Marie-Joseph (1890–1970): French soldier, writer, and statesman. Became a brigadier general in 1940; elected president of the French Republic in 1958.

de Valera, Eamon (1882–1975): Born in New York City. Raised in County Limerick; taught mathematics in Blackrock, County Dublin; joined the Gaelic League and studied Irish with Sinéad Flanagan, whom he subsequently married. Was sworn into the IRB by Thomas MacDonagh; joined the Volunteers in 1913; commanded the third battalion of the Dublin Brigade during the Rising; imprisoned by the British. Sinn Fein TD for Clare; president of the first Dáil 1919–21; president of the second Dáil 1922; rejected the Anglo-Irish Treaty; president of the executive council of the Irish Free State 1932–37; spearheaded the Constitution of 1937; taoiseach 1937–48, 1951–54, 1957–59; president of the Republic of Ireland 1959–73.

de Valera, Vivion (1910–1982): Born in Dublin. Eldest son of Eamon de Valera. Scientist, lawyer, businessman, and politician; managing director of the *Irish Press* 1959–81.

Dillon, Geraldine Plunkett (1891–1986): Sister of Joseph Mary Plunkett; mother of novelist Éilis Dillon.

Eden, Anthony, First Earl of Avon (1897–1977): British foreign secretary 1935–38, 1940–45, 1951–55, and prime minister 1955–57.

Emmet, Robert (1778–1803): Dublin-born member of the United Irishmen. Hanged by the English for attempting a Rising.

FitzGerald, Desmond (1888–1947): Born and raised in London. Joined the IRB in 1914; organized Volunteers in Kerry; fought in GPO in 1916; director of publicity for first Dáil Éireann; editor of the *Irish Bulletin*. Supported the Treaty; Free State minister for external affairs 1922–27; minister for defense 1927–32); senator 1938–42. Father of future taoiseach, Garret FitzGerald, and architect Desmond Fitzgerald.

Franco, Francisco (1892–1975): General and leader of the Nationalist forces that overthrew the Spanish Democratic Republic in the Spanish Civil War, 1936–39. Subsequently dictator of Spain until his death.

Gallagher, Frank (1898–1962): Cork-born journalist. Cofounder of the *Irish Bulletin*; first editor of the *Irish Press*; deputy director of 2RN in 1935; director of the government information bureau in the Fifties.

Goebbels, Paul Joseph (1897–1945): German-born minister for propaganda in the Third Reich.

Healy, Timothy Michael (1855–1931): Nationalist M.P. who in 1890 had bitterly opposed the continuance of Charles Parnell as leader of the Home Rule party; in 1922 was appointed first governor-general of the Free State.

Hempel, Edouard: German Minister to Éire during the war years.

Hitler, Adolf (1889–1945): Born in Austria. Leader of the National Socialist Party (Nazi) from 1920–21; dictator of Germany from 1933. He assumed the twin titles of Chancellor and Führer in 1934. He rearmed Germany ostensibly to take back the territory lost under the Versailles Treaty, then set out to conquer the continent. His "new order" called for indiscriminate extermination of whole peoples.

Hobson, Bulmer (1883–1969): Born in County Down of Quaker parentage. Founded a number of organizations including the Ulster Debating Club and the Protestant National Society; cofounded the Dungannon Clubs and Fianna Éireann; joined the IRB; was a founder member of the Irish Volunteers; opposed the Easter Rising; supported the Treaty and became an official in the Revenue Commission in the Free State.

Hoover, J. Edgar (1895–1972): Director of the United States Federal Bureau of Investigation from 1924–72.

Hughes, Séumas: Séumas O hAodha: Officer in the Volunteers; fought in Jacob's Factory during the Rising; secretary to Cumann na nGaedheal; announcer for 2RN.

Hugo, Victor (1802–1885): French poet, dramatist, and novelist.

Huxley, Aldous (1894–1963): English novelist and social critic.

Hyde, Dr. Douglas (1860–1949): Born in County Roscommon. Scholar and writer, cofounder of the Gaelic League with Eoin MacNeill, named as first president of Ireland in 1938.

Joyce, William (1906–1946): Born in New York. Propagandist known as Lord Haw-Haw who broadcast from Nazi Germany during World War II. In 1945 he was arrested by the British who executed him for treason. Originally buried in Wadsworth prison, his body was reinterred in Galway.

Kiernan, Dr. Thomas. J. (1897–1967): Dublin-born diplomat and author. Ph.D. in economics at London University; married to ballad singer, Delia Murphy; inspector of taxes in 1919; joined the staff of the Department of External Affairs; became director of broadcasting at 2RN in 1935; ambassador to Australia in 1950; later served as ambassador to West Germany, Canada, and the United States.

Larkin, James "Big Jim" (1876–1947): Born in Liverpool to Irish parents. Trade union leader and international activist; instrumental in founding the Irish Transport and General Workers Union; denounced the Treaty; founded the Workers Union of Ireland; three times elected to the Dáil.

Lauri, Lorenzo (died 1941): Cardinal and papal legate of the Roman Catholic Church from 1926 until 1941.

Lemass, Seán Francis (1899–1971): Born in County Dublin. Joined the Volunteers in 1914, originally serving in de Valera's company; fought in the GPO in 1916; escaped deportation and went back to school; as a member of the Dublin Brigade he accompanied Collins's assassination squad on Bloody Sunday and took part in killing British agents. He subsequently opposed the Treaty; was appointed minister for industry and commerce by de Valera in 1932; during World War II held crucial post of minister for supplies; became taoiseach in 1959.

Lester, John Ernest "Seán" (1888–1959): Born in County Antrim. Member of the Gaelic League, the Dungannon Clubs, the Irish National Volunteers; was sworn into the IRB by Ernest Blythe. News editor on the *Freeman's Journal*; in 1923 went to work for Desmond FitzGerald publicizing the work of the Free State; in 1925 was put in charge of correspondence for the Department of External Affairs; in 1929 was appointed Irish representative to the League of Nations; named high commissioner for Danzig 1934–36; assistant secretary-general of the League of Nations 1936; last secretary–general of the League.

Lie, Trygve (1896–1968): Norwegian politician and diplomat; first secretary-general of the United Nations, serving from 1946–52.

Lloyd George, David (1863–1945): Welsh-born British prime minister from 1916–22; conducted the negotiations with Ireland for the Anglo-Irish Treaty that concluded the War of Independence and set off the Civil War.

Lynch, Liam (1893–1923): Born in County Limerick. Member of Supreme Council of the IRB; chief of staff of the IRA during the Civil War.

MacArthur, Douglas (1880–1964): U.S. general who commanded the southwest Pacific theatre in World War II.

MacBride, John, Major (1865–1916): Born in Mayo. Member of the IRB; married Maud Gonne in 1903; did not join the Volunteers but on Easter Monday, 1916, offered his services to Thomas MacDonagh and was second-in-command in the Jacob's factory garrison; executed by the British.

MacBride, Maud Gonne (1866–1953): Born in Surrey, England. Famous beauty who inspired W. B. Yeats; founder of revolutionary women's society called Inghinidhe na hEireann; married John MacBride in Paris but the marriage failed; Maud returned to Ireland in 1917 and was actively involved in republican endeavors; opposed the Treaty; organized the Women's Prisoners Defence League.

MacBride, Seán (1904–1988): Son of Maud Gonne and John MacBride; born in Paris, educated in France and Ireland; accompanied Michael Collins to the Treaty negotiations as his personal aide; served for a time as chief of staff of the IRA; called to the bar in 1937, he defended a number of prominent Republicans; disillusioned with Fianna Fáil, MacBride founded Clann na Poblachta in 1946; became minister for external affairs in coalition government of 1948; involved in many international organizations; chairman of Amnesty International 1973–76; won Nobel Peace Prize in 1974; Lenin Peace Prize in 1977; American Medal for Justice in 1978.

MacDermott, Seán (1884–1916): Born in County Leitrim, Ireland. National organizer for Irish Republican Brotherhood; member Military Council IRB; one of the signatories of the Proclamation of the Republic; executed by the British.

MacDonagh, Thomas (1878–1916): Poet, college professor, and revolutionary; one of the signatories of the Proclamation of the Republic.

McLellan, "Mac": Doorman at 2RN during its early years.

MacNeill, Eoin (1867–1945): University lecturer and historian; cofounder, with Douglas Hyde, of the Gaelic League; first president and chief of staff of the Irish National Volunteers.

McQuaid, John Charles (1895–1973): Born in County Cavan; entered the Holy Ghost novitiate; ordained in 1924; president of Blackrock College; appointed Archbishop of Dublin by Pope Pius XII.

MacRory, Joseph (1861–1945): Roman Catholic primate.

MacSwiney, Mary Margarite (1872–1942): Elder sister of Terence MacSwiney, lord mayor of Cork who died in British prison on hunger strike. Member of Sinn Féin; taught school for a number of years until dismissed in 1916 for supporting the Rising; in 1920 was invited to testify in Washington before an American commission investigating conditions in Ireland.

Marconi, Guglielmo (1874–1937): Physicist and inventor, awarded the Nobel Prize for Physics for the development of wireless telegraphy. His father was Italian, his mother was Irish, a daughter of Andrew Jameson of the brewing family. Marconi's first wife also was Irish: Beatrice, daughter of the 14th Baron Inchiquin.

Markievicz, Constance (1868–1927): Born Constance Georgina Gore-Booth in London. Her mother was an English aristocrat; her father owned large estates in Ireland, where she was raised. After studying art in Paris she married Count Casimir Markievicz of Poland. Later she became deeply involved in the Irish trade union movement and then the struggle for independence. Cofounder with Bulmer Hobson of Na Fianna Éireann. Member of Cumann na mBan and the Citizen Army. Second-in-command to Michael Mallin in Saint Stephen's Green during the 1916 Rising. While in an English prison she became the first woman to win election to the British Parliament but never took her seat there. Subsequently she served in the Irish Parliament as the world's first minister of labor.

Moloney, Helena (1884–1967): Actress, trade unionist, feminist, Republican; became a member of Inghinidhe na hÉireann in 1903. Joined the Citizen Army and took part in the attack on Dublin Castle in 1916.

Mosley, Sir Oswald (1896–1980): English politician. In 1932 he founded the British Union of Fascists. A great admirer of Hitler, he was interned after the outbreak of World War II, as was his second wife, Diana Guinness, née Mitford.

Murphy, Seán: Irish ambassador to France during World War II.

Mussolini, Benito (1883–1945): The youngest prime minister in Italian history, and the first of Europe's Fascist dictators. In 1936 he formed a Rome-Berlin Axis with Adolf Hitler. The Italian resistance movement eventually was responsible for Mussolini's capture and execution.

Ní Ghráda, Mairead (1896–1971): Secretary to Ernest Blythe in the first Dáil; woman's organizer for 2RN, also in charge of children's programming and a station announcer.

O'Brien, Sir Donough Edward Foster (1897–1968): Sixteenth Baron Inchiquin; descendant of Brian Bóru.

O'Brien, Vincent (1870–1948): first musical director and conductor of the Radio Éireann Symphony Orchestra.

O'Casey, Séan (1880–1964): Dublin-born playwright; largely self-educated; joined the Gaelic League and learned Irish; was for a time secretary of the Citizen Army.

O'Connor, Rory (1883–1922): Born in Dublin; fought and wounded in the 1916 Rising; director of engineering for the IRA during the war of independence; opposed the Treaty; was one of the leaders of the Republican garrison in the Four Courts during the Civil War; captured and executed by the Free State.

O'Conor, Owen Phelim (1870–1943): The O'Conor Don; promoted by the Gaelic Monarchist Party in 1937 as potential King of Ireland.

O'Duffy, Eoin (1892–1944): GOC and then chief-of-staff in the Free State army during the Civil War; appointed commissioner of the civic guard in 1922; sacked by de Valera in 1933; developed the Blueshirts as a quasimilitary organization; elected president of Fine Gael party in 1934.

O'Hegarty, Patrick Sarsfield (1879–1955): Cork-born; member of the Irish Republican Brotherhood; postmaster with the British civil service until dismissed for his revolutionary activities; author of *The Victory of Sinn Féin*; secretary of posts and telegraphs 1922–44.

O'Higgins, Kevin Christopher (1892–1927): Born in County Laois; Sinn Féin T.D. in the first Dáil Éireann; supported the Treaty; became minister for economic affairs, then minister for home affairs; largely responsible for the establishment of the Garda Síochána as an unarmed force; vice president of the Executive Council and minister for justice and external affairs in the Cosgrave administration.

O'Kelly, Seán T. (1882–1966): Born in Dublin. Member of the Gaelic League; member of the IRB; founder member of Sinn Féin; aide-de-camp to Pádraic Pearse during the Rising; envoy to Paris Peace Conference. First elected to the Dáil in 1918; opposed the Treaty; founding member of Fianna Fáil in 1926. When Fianna Fáil came into power in 1932 he became vice president of the Executive Council; later minister for local government and public health, then minister for finance. Second president of Ireland 1945–59.

Pearse, Pádraic (1879–1916): Born in Dublin of an English father and Irish mother. Educationalist; poet; barrister; member of the Gaelic League; founder of Saint Enda's School in Rathfarnham; chief author and signatory of the Proclamation of the Republic; president of the provisional government of the Irish Republic; commander in chief of the Republican forces in 1916; executed by the British.

Plunkett, Grace Gifford (1888–1955): Widow of Joseph Mary Plunkett.

Plunkett, Joseph Mary (1887–1916): Poet and revolutionary; one of the signatories of the Proclamation of the Republic; executed by the British.

Pius XI (1857–1939): Original name Ambrogio Damiano Achille Ratti. Elected to the papacy in 1922.

Pius XII (1876–1958): Original name Eugenio Maria Giuseppe Giovanni Pacelli. Elected to the papacy upon the death of Pius XI in 1939.

Rommel, Erwin (1891–1944): German field marshal known as the Desert Fox; commander of the Afrika Korps in World War II.

Roosevelt, Franklin Delano (1882–1945): Thirty-second president of the United States. As a young New York lawyer in 1919, Roosevelt had once been employed by Eamon de Valera to circumvent laws that could stop the Irish from selling Dáil bonds in the United States.

Russell, George "AE" (1867–1935): Born in County Armagh. Author, editor, and poet.

Ryan, Frank (1902–1944): Born in County Limerick. Fought on the Republican side in the Civil War; editor of *An Phoblacht*; founder member of Saor Éire; a Republican pressure group; took a party of 200 Volunteers to Spain to fight on the Republican side in the civil war; was captured and sentenced to death, a sentence later commuted to thirty years' imprisonment.

Shaw, George Bernard (1856–1950): Born in Dublin. Comic dramatist, literary critic, and socialist; winner of the Nobel Prize for literature in 1925.

Skeffington, Hanna (Johanna) Sheehy (1877–1946): Born in County Cork into a Fenian family. Married Francis Skeffington in 1903.

Stalin, Joseph (1879–1953): Secretary-general of the Communist Party of the Soviet Union; became premier of the Soviet Union in 1941 and ruled as dictator until his death.

Steinbeck, John (1902–1968): American novelist; won the Pulitzer Prize for *The Grapes of Wrath*.

Truman, Harry S. (1884–1972): Thirty-third president of the United States.

von Hindenburg, Paul (1847–1934): The son of an aristocratic Prussian officer, he commanded German land forces during the Great War; elected as the second president of the Weimar Republic in 1925. Under duress by the National Socialists he appointed Hitler as chancellor in 1933.

Wells, H. G. (Herbert George) (1866–1946): English novelist, journalist, sociologist, and historian.

Wilson, Katie Gifford: a sister of Grace Gifford Plunkett.

Wilson, Thomas Woodrow (1856–1924): Twenty-eighth president of the United States.

1949

Chapter One

FLAMING in the western sky were the banners of a salmon and gold sunset. Birds sang themselves to sleep in the hedgerows; shadows flowed like water across the hills of Clare.

As the gray stallion galloped up the lane toward home, a startled blackbird exploded from a gorse bush. The horse shied violently but the girl on his back merely laughed. "Heart of a lion, you," said Ursula Halloran.

Reining the stallion to a halt, she stroked his neck. He pawed the ground and snorted with belated courage. "Easy, *Saoirse*,* stand easy now." Until he was obedient to her will she would not allow him to move forward.

Caught in a bubble of time, they waited.

WHEN she was a toddler in the Dublin tenement district, Ursula had been known as Precious. Applied to a scrawny waif with huge blue eyes staring out of a pinched little face, the name was ironic. Irish slum children were far from precious in 1914.

Eleven years—the last five spent on a farm near Clarecastle—had wrought a transformation in the girl. The pale hair of infancy had given way to a heavy mane the color of oak leaves in autumn. Healthy freckles were spattered across glowing cheeks; puberty had brought a hint of gray to her eyes. Her smile revealed excellent teeth, a rarity among the Irish.

Early malnutrition had left its mark, however. She would always be too

*Irish for "Freedom." Pronounced *Sayr-sha*.

slender. The angular planes of her face did not conform to the current fashion for feminine beauty, though in old age they would be magnificent. They might have been carved from the stones of ancient Ireland.

In her imagination Ursula never pictured herself as a mythic warrior queen. Her models were living patriots: Maud Gonne, the passionate revolutionary who had inspired W. B. Yeats and personified Caitlín Ní Houlihan, the eponymous spirit of Ireland, in his most famous play. Or Constance Markievicz, the fearless rebel countess who had turned her back on rank and privilege to fight beside the men in the Rising of 1916.

Ursula kept a scrapbook devoted to the countess.

The beauty of those famous women meant nothing to her. It was their inner fire she sought to emulate. When country lads followed Ursula with their eyes she thought they were seeing her as she saw herself. Heroic in her heart.

THE blazingly yellow blossoms of the gorse smelt like coconut. Atop a hillock in the adjacent field stood a solitary thorn tree; one of the fairy trees enchanted when Ireland was young. The white lace mantle that was its springtime glory had almost gone. When a breeze set the last few petals adrift, bereft branches clawed the sky with empty fingers.

Ursula felt an inexplicable connection to Ireland's ancient magic, as if time were a curve without beginning or end and some remnant of druidry slumbered in her blood. *But there is a new magic now*, she thought. *Invisible waves of power are racing through the air. Uncle Henry says they will change the world.*

His letter in her pocket was like an unexploded bomb.

She slipped one hand into her woolly jacket and withdrew two envelopes. The flap of one had already been torn open. Taking out the letter, she strained to reread Henry Mooney's typewritten words in the fading light.

20 May 1925
Dear Ursula,
I hope this finds you well. Ella and I are in good form, considering everything, and our little Isabella is a blessing in these troubled times. For such a wee mite she certainly has a mind of her own. She reminds me of you in that respect. You must come up to Dublin to see her. <u>Soon</u>.

The deliberate emphasis was disturbing. Newspapermen like Henry never underlined words.

His letters to Ursula invariably included commentary on political events, an interest they shared. This time he wrote sourly: "The partition of Ireland is a disaster, even worse than the Act of Union that forcibly joined this country with Britain. Partition stranded thousands of supporters of the Union within the Irish Free State. But that was the price the Unionist Party was willing to pay to cut off a portion of the north from the rest of the island and turn six counties into what they call 'a Protestant state for a Protestant people.'

"As you know, Protestants in the south are not discriminated against. Sadly the same is not true for the Catholics who now find themselves stranded in the north. The government of the Free State—most of them Catholics themselves—has abandoned these unfortunate people to their fate. Mobs describing themselves as 'loyalist'—meaning loyal to the king of England, I suppose—are attacking them with impunity.

"Have you heard of the B-Special militia in Northern Ireland? It is composed of Protestants who belong almost without exception to the Orange Order. The B-Specials have undertaken to solve the problem of sectarian violence in the north by the simple expedient of eliminating the Catholics. According to the latest figures I've seen, over six hundred have been killed in the last couple of years. Ten thousand have lost their jobs and twice that number have lost their homes.

"In the dictionary I once gave you is the word *pogrom*. Look it up. You will find that originally a pogrom was the organized massacre of Jews in Russia. It now describes what is happening to Catholics in the north. When we began the struggle to free this island from foreign domination, who could have foreseen it would turn out this way?"

Henry's letter concluded, "Next month I shall be off to London for a few days. I hope to sell a feature article on the British Broadcasting Company, which is about to liquidate as a private corporation and go public. I have mixed feelings about broadcasting. As a print journalist I am committed to the written word, yet I predict that one day all communications will be carried on radio waves. Wireless transmission will change the world, Little Business."

Ursula smiled at Henry's use of the old pet name. No one else ever called her Little Business.

On the back of the letter was a postscript in his wife's graceful handwriting. "You really must come soon. We have something to discuss which cannot be put into a letter. Henry wanted to travel to Clare to talk to you, but I would not allow it. I was afraid for him. You understand."

I do understand, Ella, Ursula thought sadly as she tucked the letter back into its envelope. *There would be trouble if Uncle Henry came to the farm.*

The Irish Civil War, which some called the War of Brothers, was only two years in the past. The wounds to the Irish soul were still bleeding.

Gathering the reins and clucking to her mount, Ursula sent him forward at a trot. A gentle blue twilight soon enfolded them. When they reached the long lane off the Ennis road Saoirse pricked his ears and broke into a headlong gallop, eager for his bucket of oats.

The stallion was kept in the barn at night. By the time Ursula unsaddled him, rubbed him down and fed him, the pungent smell of lamb stew was drifting across the walled farmyard between the kitchen at the back of the house and the barn.

Ursula gave her horse a parting caress, rubbing her cheek against his silky neck. Sitting on a stile was considered enough amusement for teenage youngsters in rural Ireland. But Ursula Halloran had a horse.

Saoirse raised his head from his oat bucket long enough to nicker after her as she closed the barn door.

With boyishly long strides, Ursula crossed the farmyard to the house. Her own stomach was rumbling with hunger. Yet she paused for a moment before going in.

Framed by the open top of the half door was a familiar picture. At a large kitchen table covered with an oilcloth sat a lanky, dark-haired man, sipping a glass of *poitín*. An old woman as plump and soft as a buttered scone was cooking a meal on the black iron range set in the mouth of the cavernous fireplace.

Every evening Ned Halloran and his Aunt Norah repeated this scene. Every, every evening. As predictable as the tick of the clock on the wall.

Radio waves can travel to faraway places, Ursula thought as she gazed into the kitchen, *places where people live different lives. Exciting lives. Things happening. If I could ride on radio waves . . .*

When she entered the room, Ned Halloran and his aunt looked up in anticipation. Ursula could light a room with the candlepower of her smile. Tonight, however, she merely gave a preoccupied nod. "I'm back, Papa."

"What's wrong?" Norah Daly asked sharply.

"Nothing's wrong."

"Did ye call at the post office?"

"I did of course. There was a letter from Kathleen in America." Ursula dug into her pocket and produced the two envelopes, dropping the unopened one onto the table.

"What's that other one?" Ned Halloran wanted to know.

"Just a note for me, Papa." She stuffed it back into her pocket.

The look he gave her was a dagger of green glass. "From where?"

"Dublin."

"Dublin." He spat out the word.

"Don't be starting on the girl," the old woman admonished.

"All I said was Dublin, Aunt Norah."

"It was how you said it. I'll have no rows in here."

Ned's cleft chin jutted at a dangerous angle. "I'll fight where I like."

The old woman left her cooking for a moment to pour an additional inch of *poitín*, colorless as water and potent as fire, into his glass. "Wrap yourself around this now and don't be making trouble."

She returned to the range and thrust a long-handled spoon into the pot. A critical sip, a shake of the head. "There's no flavor to this lamb at all. Frank butchered it too young, so he did. Chop another onion or two," she said to Ursula, "and would you ever make some dumplings?"

Ursula hated cooking. "Can't Lucy and Eileen make the dumplings?" she asked hopefully. Ned Halloran's sisters liked to cook. Or so they claimed.

Norah Daly pushed a lock of gray hair back from her forehead with one liver-spotted wrist. "Eileen's walking out with her latest young man and Lucy's gone down the fields to fetch Frank for his tea. He'd not eat otherwise. The poor crayture works all the hours God sends. Unlike some not a hundred miles from here," she added, shooting a narrow glance at Ned, "who waste their time drilling with the Mid-Clare Brigade."

"I think Papa's very brave to remain active in the Irish Republican Army under the circumstances," Ursula said. "It's almost as bad as it was after the 1916 Rising, except now it's other Irish men, instead of the British, who're jailing our patriots. What Papa's doing is more important than milking cows and planting cabbage. He's fighting for the Republic that was stolen from us."

Norah retorted, "Don't be preaching Republicanism to me, girleen. Did I not join *Cumann na mBan** meself? But that was then and this is now. Do ye not read the newspapers? They're beginning to print *Republican* with a small *r*."

"Changing a capital letter to lower case doesn't mean a thing."

"Our side lost the war, Ursula!" Norah cried in exasperation. "The IRA

*League of Women; Republican organization that played an active role in the 1916 Rising.

Volunteers were ordered to bury their weapons! The Free State government is perfectly within its rights to arrest those who won't accept its authority. I agree with your Uncle Frank. He says we should be planting crops that fill the belly instead of filling the churchyard."

Ned Halloran picked up his glass and the letter from America and strode from the kitchen. The stairs creaked. A door slammed overhead. A furious fist thudded against a wall. Again and again and again.

There was no more political talk in the kitchen. Ursula took a sulphur match from the box beside the range, and, clenching the matchstick between her teeth to keep her eyes from tearing, she began chopping onions.

After a time Norah said, "What was in Henry's letter?"

Ursula removed the match. "Only the usual Dublin *goster*.* He sent you his love, though."

The old woman's face pleated into a smile. "He's not the worst in the world, is Henry. He's almost as dear to me as my poor dead sister's children, may God a' mercy on her. It's a terrible thing entirely, this quarrel between Henry and your father."

"Half the families in Ireland aren't speaking to one another," said Ursula. "The Civil War's too recent."

"You think that's the trouble?"

"What else could it be?"

Norah did not answer. Difficult questions were best ignored.

There was a scraping of feet outside. Frank, the oldest Halloran, balding and bony, clomped into the kitchen. "Stones in the high field wanted clearing," he said. Thanks to a new set of badly fitted false teeth, he spoke with a whistle. He hung his cap on its customary nail and dropped wearily onto a chair. The farm was killing him. Wearing him down, demanding more than he had to give. Although he hired men to help with the work they never stayed very long. In the end Frank felt it was all up to himself.

His father had sown and planted according to the stars in the sky and the phases of the moon. In those days the farm had flourished. On the death of his parents, the land had come to Frank as the oldest son. He dismissed his father's theories as "pagan airy-fairy" and would have nothing to do with them. Month by month and year by year, the place was slowly failing and he did not know why.

In his secret heart Frank hated the farm.

His sister Lucy followed him into the room. A sober, stolid child, she had grown into a sober, stolid woman, with thick eyebrows and a graceless body. Lucy was the second of three Halloran daughters. Kathleen, the family

*Chat; small talk

beauty, had married a prosperous American and was living in New York. Eileen, the last born, was a dimpled flirt who was expected to make a good match locally.

No young men took Lucy walking out. People said of her, "She won't have a man on foot and the men on horses pass her by."

Few options were open to rural spinsters. If she did not emigrate Lucy could either become a shop assistant in town, or serve as unpaid labor on the family farm. Lucy disliked farm life, but she had no taste for shop-keeping either and lacked the desperation to emigrate.

If—as seemed increasingly likely—Frank remained a bachelor, and the widowed Ned did not marry again, upon their deaths the farm would pass to Lucy. By that time she would be long past childbearing. Ironically, she would have plenty of suitors then—feckless men looking for a woman of property to support them.

Of all those in the Halloran household, only Ursula truly loved the land. She was the one who walked the fields in every season, examining the condition of soil and crops, checking on walls and fences, pausing often just to look. To gaze out across hills and fields, feeding her soul with their silent poetry.

Yet for reasons everyone understood and no one talked about, the farm would never be hers.

"There's a letter from America," Norah said while Lucy poured a cup of strong tea for Frank.

"From Kathleen? Where is it?" The hands that reached for the cup had the soil of Clare ground into their creases. When Frank was younger those hands had been renowned for their skill with the fiddle. Local lads and lasses had thronged to the crossroads dances where he played, and there was a *seisiún** in the Halloran house almost every week.

After Frank inherited the farm the music in him had died of neglect. He owned a wind-up gramophone but rarely played it. He never went to dances anymore, nor encouraged fellow musicians to come to the farmhouse for a seisiún. Aside from trips to the Ennis market or Clonroad Fair he only left the farm to go to Mass. A letter from his oldest sister was an event.

"Ned's after taking Kathleen's letter," his aunt told him. "He's in one of his moods, so leave it with him for now. Ursula has a letter from Henry Mooney, though."

"Is someone ill in Dublin? The babby?" Frank always expected bad news.

"They're all in good form," Ursula assured him, "though Isabella's hardly

*Traditional music session.

a babby anymore. She'll be three this autumn and I have yet to see her. They're urging me to visit them in Dublin."

"Ned won't let you go," Frank said.

"I'm too old to need his permission."

Lucy gave her a look. The two got along well enough, but a glimmer of jealousy was surfacing between them. "How old are you then?" Lucy asked maliciously.

Ursula responded as she always did to a challenge, with sparkling eyes and a rush of color to her cheeks. "Old enough to travel! Let me remind you that I went up to Dublin on my own for Henry and Ella's wedding. And I'll go now if I choose, with or without Papa's permission."

Lucy exhaled sharply. "You wouldn't defy your own father!" But she knew otherwise. Lucy and Eileen Halloran were the products of a highly conservative rural society. Ned's daughter was made of different clay.

With an exasperated sigh, Norah Daly turned from the range. "Leave it be. I told you before; I want no rows in this house. Was the war not bad enough?"

"Which war?" Ursula asked. "The one we won or the one we lost?"

Next morning, the ticket agent at the Ennis railway station greeted the girl warmly. Everyone knew Ursula Halloran. Her father had fought the British from the General Post Office in 1916. In Clare there were no better credentials.

Chapter Two

"So you sneaked off to Dublin without telling anyone." Henry Mooney chuckled. "I did that myself, first time I came up to the Big Smoke."

"You always said it's easier to apologize afterward than to ask permission beforehand."

"That's a motto for newspaper reporters, Ursula," Ella chided, "not an excuse for bad manners."

They were sitting in the parlor of the Mooneys' semi-detached Georgian villa in Dublin's Sandymount Avenue. The couple were a study in contrasts. Henry, in his early forties, was well built in spite of rounded shoulders and a tendency to slouch. His eyes were enmeshed in laugh lines. His deep, calm voice with its west-of-Ireland accent elicited confidences. Even strangers trusted him.

Born into the upper levels of Dublin society, Ella Rutledge Mooney was a strawberry blond with dark amber eyes and a hand-span waist. Her anglicized enunciation identified her as a member of the Protestant Ascendancy, the propertied class in Ireland. Some mistook Ella's finishing-school manners for hauteur—until they saw her smile and fell in love, as Henry had done, with her dimples.

Earlier this evening they had taken Ursula upstairs to visit little Isabella in the nursery, under the watchful eye of Tilly Burgess, the Mooneys' housekeeper. Tilly was a necessary part of the household. Like other women of her class, Ella had been brought up to marry, not to cook and clean. Besides, Tilly was the only person who could control the headstrong Isabella. The child's parents were too doting for discipline.

Now as they sat in the parlor, Henry asked Ursula, "How do you like my beautiful daughter?"

"She really is beautiful. But why did you call her Isabella? Doesn't the Church want children to be given saints' names?"

Ella said, "Since we married we've drifted away from organized religion. Henry's Roman Catholic..."

"Backslid Roman Catholic," Henry interjected.

"And I was raised Anglican," Ella went on imperturbably, "but we've seen so many difficulties caused by... well, we both love the same God and that's good enough for us.

"When the baby was born with dark hair and eyes I thought she looked rather Spanish. Henry wanted to name her for me but I hated the idea. I didn't want to become 'Big Ella,' or worse yet, 'Old Ella.' So I suggested Isabella as a compromise. It's a lovely Spanish name and ends in Ella. Of course Henry's called her Bella ever since. You know how he is about nicknames."

"There's not a drop of Spanish blood in my daughter," Henry asserted. "One of my ancestors was a Welshman, that's where she got her coloring. Children carry the history of their forebears like chapters in a book, if one knew how to read them."

Ursula stiffened. "What are you trying to tell me, Uncle Henry? Is there something I should know?"

Obfuscation and circumlocution were traits the Irish had developed to an art form over the centuries. Talking around something rather than addressing it directly was a survival mechanism, a way of avoiding confrontation. Ursula Halloran was the exception. She asked straight questions and wanted straight answers.

Her bluntness caught Henry off-guard. He had not meant anything in particular by the remark. "I... mmm... was just making conversation, Little Business."

"But you had some urgent reason for wanting me to come to Dublin. What was it?"

Henry slumped in his seat. "I'm thoroughly browned off with this country, if you must know. Sick of living with a sword hanging over our heads. The Civil War hasn't really ended. Former comrades-in-arms are shouting at one another in Dáil Éireann,* accusing old friends of being traitors and murderers. Government agents are scouring the countryside for illegal arms

*Irish Parliament.

and decent men and women are being charged with treason. I can't bear to see what's happened to this country."

Ursula said hotly, "It's the fault of this hateful Saorstát Éireann the Anglo-Irish Treaty lumbered us with. Irish Free State indeed! What's free about it? We're still within the Empire. We have a British governor-general who has to sign our legislation before it can become law, and the government is run for the benefit of big business and big farmers, just as it was under British rule.

"Remember Pádraic Pearse's vision of the Irish Republic, Uncle Henry? 'A non-sectarian society where the poor and the old will be cherished and the hero and the poet alike will have honor.' That's what we fought for. If Pearse's Republic were restored everything would be all right."

Henry was touched by the ardor of the young that admitted no obstacles. "Life isn't that simple, Little Business." From his waistcoat he took a silver pocket watch. "This stopped the other day. You might say, wind the watch and everything will be all right." He wound the stem. Nothing happened.

With his thumbnail Henry opened the back of the watch and held it out to show Ursula. "See those tiny cogs and gears? They're totally interdependent. One bent wheel and the entire mechanism can break down. Irish society is like these watchworks, which is why the simplistic approach has never worked here and never will. If we had the Republic tomorrow we would just have a new set of problems."

"Our politicians could sort things out if they didn't have any British interference," Ursula declared.

"Politicians." Henry gave a snort. "Like most revolutions, ours devoured its most imaginative leaders. What's left to run the country is a different breed. Cautious to a fault, most of 'em. They've retained the British administrative machinery because that's all they know, so we're lumbered with the same old colonial policies we fought so hard to be rid of. The only real difference I can see is that Cosgrave's banned divorce in the Free State rather than continuing to allow it under the British model. But he's a devout Catholic anyway, so that's hardly surprising."

An elbow in his ribs made him break off abruptly. "Stop editorializing," Ella rebuked him. "This is supposed to be about Ursula."

"You're right, Cap'n, as always." With an effort, Henry redirected his thinking. "Little Business, there are some ... mmm ... some arrangements we'd like to make for you before we go."

"Before you go! Go where?"

"America."

"Why ever would you want to visit America?"

"We won't be visiting. We're emigrating."

"You can't!" Ursula's eyes widened in alarm. Henry Mooney had been part of her life for as long as she could remember. Henry and the Hallorans had once lived in the same Dublin rooming house. He had been her papa's best friend and her mama's confidante: the person they turned to in times of trouble.

When the other adults were too busy, Henry had always found time for Ursula. He had read the newspapers with her and answered her ceaseless questions. When he bought a typewriting machine he had showed her how to use it. He had taken her to her first horse-riding lessons, and after she and Ned went to live on the farm in Clare, Henry had even given her Saoirse.

"You can't leave Ireland!" she repeated.

"I never expected to," Henry said. "I thought I would spend my life as a Dublin journalist and that was fine with me. Oh, the pay wasn't great, and most newspapers had a pro-British policy because they knew which side of their bread was buttered. But I could accept that.

"Then came 1916. When the authorities insisted that public opinion was against the rebellion, Dublin newspapers dutifully reinforced that view. They printed near-hysterical editorials claiming the leaders of the Rising were hoodlums and psychopaths.

"After those same leaders were executed, the public learned who and what they really were. Poets, schoolteachers, a leading trade unionist—decent, highly principled men, every one. Men who thought the freedom of this country was worth dying for."

Ursula's eyes blazed. "It is," she whispered ardently. The memory of those days came pouring over her like a wave; the drama and terror and exhilaration she had only half understood at the time.

Henry continued, "As you may recall, the mood of the country changed almost overnight. I was one of the few reporters who chronicled the groundswell for independence. It may be conceited, but I'd like to think the articles I wrote for the *Irish Bulletin* helped give Ireland the courage to fight on until the battle was won."

He was referring to the outlawed Republican newsletter that had been the only paper during two years of government censorship to document, day by day, the full story of the Anglo-Irish war: Ireland's desperate War of Independence.

"For a moment we almost had it all," Henry said. Pain cracked his deep voice like a fissure in oak. "With the people solidly behind them, Michael Collins and the IRA fought the almighty British Empire to a standstill. I was damned proud of them. Sorry about my language, Ella, but I *was* damned proud of them, damn it!"

"Yet when the army split afterward, over the Treaty, you supported Michael Collins against the Republicans like de Valera and Papa," Ursula reproached him.

"Both sides wanted the same thing, an independent Ireland," said Henry. "They just differed on how to get it. Mick Collins believed the twenty-six-county Free State was the best deal we could get at the time. The British government was willing to annihilate the Irish people to avoid giving us total independence."

"Why?" Ursula demanded to know. "I've never been able to understand that."

"You should pay closer attention to the international scene," Henry told her. "Setting Ireland free would have had global implications for the empire at a time when Britain was engaged in a life-and-death struggle to hold onto India and Egypt. Those ancient lands wanted to regain their independence too, and they were a lot more valuable to the Crown than Ireland.

"Mick knew that partitioning this island would create a running sore. He only signed the Treaty because the British threatened to pour two-hundred thousand fresh troops into Ireland immediately if he didn't."

Chapter Three

G OD love Michael Collins," sighed Henry, "he didn't know the British were bluffing. Most of their army was demobilized after the Great War. The troops who'd fought Mick and the IRA had been thoroughly demoralized by the experience, and the British hardly had anyone left to send over here. A few thousand at the most. Our lads would have wiped the ground with them and got our country back with no strings attached. But Lloyd George and Winston Churchill outfoxed us and the chance was missed."

"De Valera wouldn't have made that mistake," Ursula said.

Henry shook his head. "Dev's a realist. In spite of what you may want to believe, he would have bowed to the inevitable too. Instead he sent Mick to London to take the fall for him. If Mick had lived, I'm convinced he would have got the other six counties back in time. He fully intended to dismantle the Treaty brick by brick."

Ursula lifted her chin. "Papa says the Irish Republican Army is all the Catholics in Northern Ireland have to defend them against the Protestant mobs. He says the Free State is too much under the British thumb to do the honorable thing and—"

"Whoa!" Henry held up his hands. "I know that speech, I hear it almost every day. That's what I mean about a sword hanging over our heads. Unfinished business, unfinished violence. Men who still want, still *need*, to fight. The lust for blood just under the surface.

"During the Civil War I saw things I'll never forget. Appalling things that shook my faith in my fellow man. As long as I stay in this country those images will keep coming back to me, like some terrible nightmare I can't wake from.

"Besides, I have to make a living. As a freelance journalist I can no longer do that here. I can't sanction a lot of the things the Free State is doing, nor write the propaganda they want. I need to make a fresh start somewhere else."

Henry's face gave no hint of the many nights he had lain awake, talking in the darkness with Ella. Agonizing over a decision.

"I'm hoping to buy a small business in America," he went on. "A country newspaper or maybe a printing shop. Thanks to the *Bulletin* I have a lot of contacts over there and I've learned of several opportunities already."

Ursula appealed to his wife. "Surely you don't agree with this. How can you move thousands of miles away from your family?"

"Henry and Bella are my family now," Ella replied with her golden-brown eyes fixed on her husband's face. "My relatives are decent, tolerant people, and when I married Henry they accepted his being a Catholic. But they also are members of what you call the landlord class, Ursula. They firmly believe the 1916 Rising was an act of treason and they have never been comfortable with Henry's Irish nationalism. Since the new Land Commission took over so much of their property for redistribution to their tenants there are certain...stresses." She gave a delicate shrug, as if those stresses were inconsequential. "Sometimes the only way to deal with family problems is to distance oneself from them."

"I know about family problems," Ursula said. "They can hurt worse than anything. Papa is the best man in the world, but after Mama died...and then the Civil War...well, he's just not himself anymore. He carries on long conversations with Mama at night. My bedroom is next to his and I hear him talking as if she were right there with him. Sometimes he gives great deep sobs that would break your heart. If I knock on the door he shouts at me to go away. Next day he may seem all right, then suddenly he'll be angry over nothing. That's why we can't keep hired men on the farm for any length of time. They're afraid of him."

Ned Halloran's mental condition, which had become increasingly obvious in Ursula's letters, was a matter of grave concern to Henry. There was nothing he could do for the man he had loved like a brother, any more than he could turn the clock back to that brief slice of time when Ireland had called herself a republic. All he could do was try to shield Ursula from witnessing the breakdown of the man she adored.

He cleared his throat to draw her attention. "About those arrangements

I mentioned, Little Business. Since the Great War new opportunities are opening for women. They're entering the sciences and politics and—"

"Countess Markievicz was the first woman in the world to become a minister of labor," Ella cut in as if they had rehearsed this.

"I know all about that, I have the newspaper articles in my scrapbook. She was a heroine of the Rising," said Ursula.

"Con's war record didn't qualify her for a cabinet post," Henry pointed out. "Her political assets were intelligence and energy. They are priceless—and you have both. But you do need an education."

"I am educated. Papa taught me out of his old schoolbooks. English grammar and Irish and Latin and mathematics—"

"Textbooks alone," Henry interrupted, "aren't an adequate preparation for life. Your father studied with Pádraic Pearse, but Pearse is dead and no other school in Ireland is providing the sort of curriculum he offered at Saint Enda's. For a comparable education you would have to go abroad. Are you interested?"

"You mean go to school in England?" Ursula straightened indignantly. "Not for anything! The English murdered Mr. Pearse and Mr. Connolly and it's God's miracle they didn't murder Papa too. I hate them all."

Henry and Ella exchanged glances; the speechless conversation of two people who understood one another perfectly.

"Not England, dear," said Ella. "We've discussed this at some length. As your own words just revealed, we feel that you need to acquire a larger worldview."

"Are you talking about going to a university on the Continent? I don't have the academic qualifications."

"I know, dear. Instead, we propose to give you a year or two at a private school in Switzerland. They accept students on rather a different basis. My recommendation should help; I went there myself, as did my mother. And you will enjoy the journey: a sea voyage to France and a train to Switzerland," she added, cannily appealing to the girl's adventurous spirit.

The full import of what they were saying began to sink in. "You can't afford to send me to a private school abroad," Ursula told Henry.

"Agreed. It will take every shilling I have to set us up in America. Ella has a fortune in her own name, though. I swore before we married that I would never use a penny of it to support my family and I shan't, but . . ."

"But I've persuaded him to let me do this for you," Ella finished. "The money's no good to me otherwise, it's just sitting in the bank."

Her hand reached out and found Henry's reaching for her. They sat looking expectantly at Ursula.

•   •   •

SOMETIMES she knew. Simply knew what was fated to happen. Did not need to question herself or agonize over decisions, but knew with irrevocable certainty, as if the future and its secrets were spread out before her to read like the pages of a book. Pages inscribed with wind and rain and wisdom.

When she was little, Henry Mooney had called Precious 'fey,' unwittingly identifying a part of her which predated flesh and blood.

On the train ride home Ursula mentally rehearsed the way she would broach the subject to her father. Henry's involvement would create difficulties at first, because of the quarrel between himself and Ned, but Ned Halloran had received his education at Saint Enda's through the help of a mentor. Surely she could make him appreciate the symmetry of a similar opportunity for her.

Surely.

THE battle when it came was savage. Like most important events, it took place in the kitchen.

Ned Halloran roared so loudly he frightened the hens scratching in the yard outside. "I forbid it, Ursula! Get that idea out of your head right now. You're not to write to that man or even mention his name. Not ever again. He wants to steal you from me but he won't get away with it this time. He won't get away with it this time!" Ned shook his fists in the air as if he could not control them.

Dismayed, Ursula stepped back. "You don't know what you're saying, Papa. Uncle Henry's always been your friend."

"My friend!" Ned's laugh was hollow. "That's how little you know. Listen here to me, you're never to go back to Dublin, ever. I demand your promise."

"I won't promise, Papa. I can't be living my whole life on this farm."

"And why not?"

"Because there's nothing for me here."

"Your family is here. *Ar scáth a chéile a mhaireas na daoine.*"

" 'People live in one another's shelter,' " Ursula translated. "That's just an old saying, it doesn't mean anything. Besides, this isn't my family." Her fingers clenched tightly around her thumbs, a habitual reaction to stress. Now that she had to fight she realized how much she wanted the prize. "I'm an orphan," she said flatly.

A muscle twitched in Ned's jaw. "You're no orphan. Síle may be dead but I'm still your father and I'm telling you . . . ."

"You can't tell me what to do!" she lashed back. "And you are *not* my father. You never allowed anyone to talk about it in my hearing, but do you think I don't know? I was a foundling you rescued from the Dublin streets. I don't belong to anyone but myself!"

In the emotion of the moment Ursula's words were not a cry of grief, but a declaration of independence.

The stunned look on Ned's face told her she had gone too far.

She laid her hand on his arm and softened her voice, soothing him as she would a difficult horse. "Please, Papa, see me as I am. I'm not a child anymore. I'm at least sixteen, maybe older. And you always say I'm intelligent. Surely you understand that I don't want to spend my life working on a farm I'll never inherit because I'm not really a Halloran. I'd rather go out into the world and see what it holds for me."

Ned's tense features eased in sympathy. She thought she was getting through to him. Then she added, "Uncle Henry's offering me the opportunity to do just that."

Something shifted in his eyes. "Leave me for *him*, will you?" Ned thundered. "I'll see you dead first!"

Chapter Four

HENRY Mooney met a badly shaken Ursula Halloran at Kingsbridge Station. Her eyes were red-rimmed.

"You have a lot of luggage," Henry remarked as the porter lifted her suitcase and a stack of boxes from the railway carriage.

"I brought everything I own, even my saddle. Everything except Saoirse." She looked as if she was about to cry again. "Oh, Uncle Henry, he gelded him!"

"He did what?"

"Papa took the hired men and a butcher knife and locked the barn door on the inside and . . ." Her voice broke. ". . . and gelded my horse. I heard him scream!

"You know how I'd fought to keep Saoirse a stallion. They said a girl couldn't manage one but I proved they were wrong. He was so proud and grand and he trusted me, Saoirse *trusted* me. Papa always said trust was the cement that held us all together. Now how can I ever trust *him* again? After . . . after he . . ."

Her shoulders were shaking, though whether with grief or fury Henry could not tell. "I'm sorry," he said, aware it was insufficient. "Is the horse all right otherwise?"

"He's alive, but he'll never be the same. Why did Papa do that? I don't understand. And something else. He accused you of trying to steal me and said he wouldn't let you get away with it 'this time.' What was that supposed to mean?"

Henry suddenly made himself very busy with the luggage. " 'Fraid I can't tell you," he muttered. "Run out to the street and find a taxicab, will you? Tilly's waiting tea for us."

The Mooneys tried to convince Ursula the break with Ned was only temporary, but she would not be comforted. "You didn't see him. He even spoke of killing me."

Henry struggled to keep the shock he felt from showing in his face.

Ursula went on, "Frank and Norah insisted I leave as soon as I could and come up to you. If you'd seen my horse standing there in the barn with his head hanging, and the blood still running down his legs . . . I couldn't bear to be in the same house with Papa after that."

"You are welcome here for as long as you like," Ella assured her.

Letters were written to Switzerland, applications made, a sum of money sent. All that remained was for Ursula to obtain a passport. But passports required documentation.

Henry Mooney had friends on both sides of the philosophical chasm that now existed. "There's a young fellow in the Department of External Affairs who owes me a favor," he told Ursula. "We'll get your passport, don't worry."

FINBAR Cassidy surveyed his desk with distaste. As the most junior member of the passport section, he was given the bulk of the routine work. By staying in the office until almost eleven the previous night he had managed to clear most of it. Now a fresh stack of files awaited him. Miss Lynch's doing, no doubt.

He sighed, raked his fingers through his crisp red hair, looked around vaguely in hopes Miss Lynch had at least brought him a cup of tea, saw none, sat down, lit a cigarette, and was just opening the first file when a sour face framed by frizzled gray curls peered around the door of his office. "There's someone called Henry Mooney outside, with a woman he calls his niece. Claims you'll see him without an appointment."

"Ah, thank you, Miss Lynch. Send him in. And could you bring us some tea?"

"Mmmph." The door closed.

When it opened again, Henry Mooney stood there with a woman. A very young woman with blue-gray eyes that lanced straight into Finbar Cassidy's soul. Without waiting to be introduced she said, "Since this is a department of government I suppose you're pro-Treaty. I'm a Republican myself. And do you have to smoke that cigarette? I hate the smell."

Cassidy was nonplussed. "I . . . ah . . . yes. I mean . . ." He ground out the cigarette in a cracked saucer. "It's good to see you again, Mooney. Say, is this really your niece?"

Henry chuckled, evading a direct answer. "Allow me to introduce you. Ursula, this is Finbar Cassidy, whom I helped get out of a scrape some time back when he . . . well . . . that's of no consequence. Finbar, meet Ursula Halloran. She is a young person of strong convictions, but I'm sure you won't hold that against her. She needs a passport in order to go to school abroad, and I told her you could fix her up."

"We can, of course. I assume she has the necessary documents?"

Henry thrust his hands into his trouser pockets and rocked back on his heels. "Mmmm, she does and she doesn't. You may recall a little explosion some time back in the Four Courts. Ursula's birth cert blew up with the other records in there. But she was born and reared in Dublin, and she does have her Confirmation cert, of course."

"I see." Cassidy had heard this before. "The bombardment of the Four Courts was mighty convenient for some, Henry. As a result of the Civil War people have been leaving these shores in droves, and you have no idea how many are claiming their documents were lost in that explosion."

"Thousands of documents were lost," Henry affirmed. "I was there that day and saw scraps of paper blowing like snow all over Dublin. You can't deny people their legal status over a little inconvenience like that."

"Not if they have other suitable authentication, of course."

"Suitable authentication. God's garters, you sound like every British bureaucrat I ever met. Damn it, Finbar, this is Ireland and this girl is as Irish as yourself or myself! The bishop who confirmed her knew who she was. And I vouch for her, isn't that good enough?" Henry leaned his knuckles on the desk and thrust his face into Cassidy's. "I vouched for you when those six IRA lads caught you in that laneway, didn't I?"

5 September 1925

Dear Uncle Henry,

I arrived at Surval Mont-Fleuri on Thursday. Surval is what they call a "finishing school"; something I had not realised before. If I had, I might have refused to come. Now I am here I shall make the best of it. Obviously you think this is something I need, and it is rather an adventure.

Europe is astonishing. I have already seen ever so many people whose coloring and features are unlike ours. I never realised before that there is a recognisable Irish "look," but there is. That was my first discovery and it did not come from a textbook.

The school consists of a big country house rather like an Ascendancy mansion, set on the heights of Montreux with splendid views of Lake Geneva, which the locals call Lac Léman. (The language spoken in this part of Switzerland is French.) The lake is almost periwinkle blue and is framed by vineyards and mountains. Steamers buzz across its surface like so many black-and-white flies.

The walls of the school are covered with portraits and landscapes in gilded frames. The furniture is so highly polished you can see your face in it. The students' bedrooms are quite plain but the reception rooms are desperately grand. The furnishings in just one of them would support the inhabitants of a Dublin tenement for life.

Meals are served in a vast dining room with crystal chandeliers. The cooks are Swiss, so everything is oily or fatty or flavored with seasonings I do not recognise. I do not like it very much. Madame says my palate needs to be educated, but at least she does not make me clean my plate. We are always supposed to leave food on our plates to show that we are used to having enough to eat. (And myself coming from an Ireland with terrible memories of the Famine!)

The table napkins are folded to look like flowers. We are supposed to look like flowers too. We wear one frock in the morning, another in the afternoon, and then dress for dinner. I suppose this is to show that we are used to having plenty of clothes.

I am sharing a room with a girl called Felicity Rowe-Howell. As you can tell from her double-barreled name, she is English, so I suspect our relationship will be anything but felicitous.

The girls here range in age from fourteen to twenty-two years. Several are displaced royalty with titles that ceased to be meaningful after the Versailles Treaty redrew European boundaries. One is even a princess. (I told her I was a Republican but she did not seem to understand what that meant.) We have a White Russian whose parents barely escaped the Russian Revolution, and a pair of blond twins from Florence (they are very elegant and actually paint their faces!), and the daughter of a Czechoslovakian diplomat, and an Austrian whose father was an Olympic skier, and a Turkish girl who was born in a harem.

Some of the girls complain because we have to make our own beds. Even the princess must. Madame says it is good for our character. (I must have lots of character already because I have always made my own bed.) We do not wash our own clothing, though. A number of laundresses are employed because a lady never does washing.

European languages are compulsory, so I am taking both French and German. My Latin will help me with French. Only two other girls are studying German since the Germans are still under a cloud because of the war. Our teacher, Madame Dosterschill, is a gentle, cultured woman. Her eyes twinkle when she makes little jokes in German. It is difficult to equate her with the savage Boche who slaughtered so many of the Irish at the Somme. I have to hold two quite contradictory images in my head.

Some of my other courses are art, music, etiquette, and deportment. We practice walking around with books from Surval's library balanced on our heads. I tend to stop and read mine when no one is looking.

Did you know it is considered vulgar to use contractions in everyday conversation? Papa taught me not to use them in letters, but I do not know if I can eliminate them when I speak. I would not sound like me.

The best thing that happens in boarding school is receiving parcels from home. Please tell Ella the clothes she bought for me are perfect. (Meaning they are what everyone else is wearing.) The short skirts are the latest style but are not really practical in a cold climate. I suppose I shall get used to them. Perhaps my skin needs to be educated too.

We are encouraged to observe our own religious practices, which are diverse, as you can imagine. The Italians and I go down to the village for Confession and Mass, always accompanied by a member of the school staff. Madame allows no girl to step outside the gates without a chaperone. Catholic Ireland is no stricter than Surval.

However on some weekends students are taken to Paris, Prague, Munich, or Florence, to absorb the culture. There is an extra charge for these trips. I hate spending more of Ella's money when she has been so generous already, but oh, Henry! Just think of seeing Prague!

As soon as I leave school I shall get a job and pay back every penny.

Would you please send newspapers from home to read in my room at night so I don't have to talk to this wretched Felicity person? I am particularly hungry for current news and feature articles. But send the minutiae too, even the advertisements.

Love,
Ursula

When he finished reading Ursula's letter Henry folded it up and put it into his pocket to share with Ella. "Deportment indeed," he chuckled to himself. "What will they make of a girl who strides out like a boy and says what she thinks?"

The following day he went to Glasnevin Cemetery. Dark yews weeping. Tombstones like rows of crooked teeth. Henry made his way to the Republican plot and walked back and forth, reading the names. O'Donovan Rossa. Cathal Brugha. Erskine Childers. Thomas MacDonagh's wife Muriel.

John O'Leary—of whom Yeats wrote—"Romantic Ireland's dead and gone, it's with O'Leary in the grave."

Síle Duffy Halloran.

Here he stopped. Uncovering his head, Henry stood holding his soft trilby in both hands. For a long time he did not move. Then he slowly sank to his knees. "I'm doing my best, Síle," he whispered to the listening earth.

16 October 1925

BRITAIN, BELGIUM, FRANCE, AND GERMANY SIGN MUTUAL SECURITY PACT
Former Enemies Vow Never to Fight Again

14 November 1925

IRISH REPUBLICAN ARMY CONVENTION VOTES SUPREME AUTHORITY TO ARMY COUNCIL

10 December 1925

DÁIL SANCTIONS BORDER AGREEMENT
Eamon de Valera Claims Agreement Enshrines Partition and Abandons Tens of Thousands of Northern Catholics

Chapter Five

10 December 1925

Dear Uncle Henry,

This has been my first autumn away from home, though I am not sure what I mean by "home" any more. Clare seems so far away. Switzerland is beautiful, very neat and clean, with astonishing mountains, yet I long for golden fields at harvest time, and the way the mist turns the hills of Clare to fawn-coloured velvet. I even miss our gray bleak winters, when it rains for weeks and the turf smoke from the fireplaces permeates everything. Not neat, not clean, but home.

Papa never answers my letters. Aunt Norah writes that he forbids my name to be mentioned at the farm. Since you and Ella will be sailing for America in April, I cannot think of the Sandymount house as home, either. I am hanging in space like a star.

That sounds self-pitying but I do not mean it that way. I am grateful for this opportunity. I am making friends and wonder of wonders, I am even learning to ski. My instructor says I am fearless. My favorite companion on the slopes is the Austrian girl, Heidi Fromm, who allows me to practice my execrable German on her.

There are also stables here, and horse riding, but it is not the same as being with Saoirse. I brought his bridle with my things and hung it on the wall of my room. Other horses seem like poor imitations.

Thank you for inviting me to spend Christmas with you and Ella. I appreciate the offer, but the sight of your packing cases would make

me too sad. If I do not see you preparing to leave it will not be so
real for me.

THERE was another reason for her reluctance. Ned Halloran's parents
had gone down with the *Titanic*, a tragedy that nearly claimed his life as
well. Young Precious had learned the details by eavesdropping on adult
conversations. When Ned spoke of "the dark sea, waiting"—an image that
would haunt him all his life—the horror in his voice had a profound effect
on the listening child.

Years later, when Ursula boarded the passenger steamer that would carry
her to the Continent, her stomach had clenched in unexpected panic. The
girl who prided herself on her physical courage had spent the trip suffering
from alternate bouts of terror and nausea.

Never again, Ursula had promised herself then. *If I ever get back to Ireland
I'll never take another sea voyage!*

Her letter to Henry continued:

Congratulations on your achievement, it must be wonderful to realise
your dream! Imagine buying a newspaper of your own, even if it is
in some place called Muleshoe, Texas. (Are you sure you have that
name right?)

The Finola lingerie Ella sent to me has already arrived. The silk is
very beautiful, I never had anything so fine. I am writing a proper
thank-you letter to her, and another to Tilly for the warm knitted
vests she sent to me. The vests are less fashionable but much more
practical.

My small box of presents for all of you will go out tomorrow. My
roommate has promised to post them from London. Felicity is not
nearly as awful as I expected. She is a hearty girl whom everyone calls
Fliss. She describes herself as "jolly hockey-sticks," which is English
slang. Although Madame does not approve I am collecting colorful
foreign phrases. They are like salt in the stew.

Fliss says her family is solidly Tory (her father is a former M.P., a
"backbencher") but she calls herself a liberal. She says liberalism is the
wave of the future and is quite happy to discuss politics with me.
Although we have very different points of view, I am learning to
debate without arguing. Madame is teaching me to be "deeplomatic."

Fliss has bought me Shakespeare's tragedies for Christmas and I
am giving her a collection of his sonnets. We did not compare notes
ahead of time, so it came as something of a surprise to discover we

both chose Shakespeare. We actually have rather a lot in common. In addition to an interest in politics, we gorge on chocolate when we can get it, are terrified of Madame, and love horses. The Rowe-Howells have stables at their country place in Sussex and Fliss invited me for the holidays, but I declined. The truth is, while I enjoy the Bard of Avon I am not prepared to enjoy England.

I shall spend Christmas at Surval. The school stays open through the holidays because the parents of some of the girls park them here like bicycles while they socialise. There are more ways to abandon a child than to leave it in the street in Dublin.

Over the holidays I plan to make a few shillings by tutoring the younger girls in basic French. Just since September I have become almost fluent, and I am even better at German.

"Our girl's finding her feet," Henry told Ella when he finished reading the letter. "It isn't easy, but she's always been a tough little scrap."

His wife put down her sewing. Her loving eyes scanned his face. "You miss her very much, don't you?"

"I do of course. I've known her almost as long as Ned has. If I'd been in Bachelor's Walk that day I might have been the one who found her," he said wistfully. Thrusting his thumbs into the pockets of his waistcoat, he rocked on the balls of his feet, thinking. "Cap'n . . . how would you feel about taking Ursula to America with us instead of Tilly?"

Ella drew a deep breath. "If that would make you happy, let's."

Henry's heart leaped—then slowed. He, who knew every nuance of her voice, detected a reluctance of which she was not consciously aware. When Ella fell in love with him she had accepted his Irish nationalism as part of the package. She had even agreed to raise their children in the Catholic faith. But adding to their family a militant rebel who had carried messages—and probably guns—for the IRA would not be easy for her. Ella might even see the younger woman as a potential rival.

Out of love for him, Henry's wife already had stretched her emotional resources to the limit. To ask for more would be cruel. "Forget I even suggested it," he said briskly. "I don't know where I get such notions; the girl's much better off where she is. We're going to live in a small Texas town in the middle of nowhere. You and I shall have each other, but what would there be for her? Besides, if she was living in America how could she make things up with Ned?"

"Do you think they will reconcile?"

"They will of course. He loves her dearly and she idolizes him. Ursula's a bit of a hero-worshipper and Ned Halloran's always been her hero. He may have lost the run of himself, but I know how strong he is. One of these days he'll pull himself together and want his daughter back. If I've taken her away to America he never will forgive me."

"What are the chances of his forgiving you anyway?"

"Two, I suppose," Henry replied sadly. "Slim and none."

15 June 1926

Dear Uncle Henry,

How exotic Texas sounds! Imagine all of you living in a timber house—except people there call it a "frame" house, you told me—with the prairie wind blowing clouds of red dust while poor Tilly struggles to hang the washing on the line. You were wise to take Tilly with you. I do not know how Ella could manage without her. From what you tell me, it takes both women to cope with Bella.

Have you seen any Red Indians? The postcard you sent me of the Comanche chieftain called Quanah Parker is very handsome. His mother was a white woman, it says on the back. I wonder if any of us is all one thing or the other. I have started thinking about that lately. You have some Welsh blood, and I, well, who knows what I am. Irish, that's all.

Europe in the wake of the Great War is a bit like Ireland but on a larger scale. New borders and old grudges. My German teacher explained that her country has suffered ruinous inflation ever since the war as a result of the huge reparations forced upon it by the Versailles Treaty. Unemployment is extremely high. Many people blame their problems on the Jews and the Communists. It is hoped the League of Nations will admit Germany in September, which at least will give the Germans a forum for expressing their grievances.

Did you know that the English novelist H. G. Wells was the first to suggest a league of nations? I have begun reading his books. The early ones, such as *The Time Machine*, are wildly imaginative, but he makes me think and I like that. I am going to purchase his *Outline of History* as soon as I can.

Speaking of money—since Ella so kindly made the offer, I should like to stay here for one more year. Do not misunderstand, I still get homesick. Last night I dreamed I was in the barn with Norah Daly, helping her with the milking. (Do you remember how she always put her finger into the froth of the milk afterwards, and sketched the sign of the cross on the cow's side?) After next year I am determined to come home. Ireland is waiting for me like a promise.

Henry Mooney took off his hat as he entered the house and sailed it across the room to land atop the hat rack; the polished brass hat rack brought all the way from Dublin. "How do you like my one parlor trick?" he asked his wife as she came with open arms to meet him.

Ella tilted her head back and looked up at him, laughing. "You ask me that every night, sweetheart."

He gave her a squeeze, being careful not to press too hard against her swelling belly. "Is the little one comfortable in there?"

"You ask that too. And he is."

"Are you so certain it's a boy?"

"Don't you want a boy?"

Henry chuckled. "Not necessarily. I love being surrounded by women. Speaking of women, I had a letter from Ursula today. Says she'd like to stay at Surval for one more year."

"I thought she might." Ella's dimples danced. "In another year she will be quite a polished young woman. What then for her?"

"Mmm ... I've been thinking about that, Cap'n. I'll arrange for her to talk to some people I know in Dublin, people who can give her employment that will stimulate her mind. If we leave it up to her, who knows where that reckless streak might take her?"

"Still spreading your wings over her, aren't you?"

He chuckled. "Trying to."

"Do you think there's any danger of war breaking out in Ireland again? You keep up with the situation over there; what's happening?"

Taking his silver pocket watch from his waistcoat, Henry wound it thoughtfully. "Remember that the Sinn Féin* Party fractured after the Anglo-Irish Treaty," he told his wife. "Sinn Féin flatly refused to serve in the new Dáil with treatyites. That split Irish nationalism right down the middle. Militant Republicans on one side and parliamentarians on the other.

"The Republicans continue to deny the legality of partition and demand an independent thirty-two-county Irish nation. Personally, though, I think the Irish Republican Army's a spent force. The war's over, so who are they going to fight?

"W.T. Cosgrave and his pro-Treaty Cumann na nGaedheal† Party are running the country now, and they aren't warriors. Businessmen and large landowners, most of them. That's not to say they aren't decent men, they are. I know Cosgrave; I even interviewed him a couple of times."

"Is he as handsome as Michael Collins was?"

*Ourselves Alone.
†Society of the Irish.

Henry smiled at his wife's romantic imagination. "He has close-set eyes and an egg-shaped head, Cap'n. Not very dashing, I'm afraid, but looks aren't everything or you wouldn't have married me." Before she could protest he went on, "Fortunately Cosgrave also has a steely determination, and he's going to need it.

"For one thing, he has very few resources to work with. Britain gave the Protestants in the north the lion's share of industrial development. The rest of Ireland was seen as nothing more than England's larder and deliberately kept ignorant of industrialization. This means the Free State is economically very vulnerable in today's world. I don't envy Cosgrave the job of trying to turn things around, but thanks to his temperament he'll probably make a better fist of it than Dev would."

"Eamon de Valera will never accept the Free State," Ella said.

"Don't be so sure. Dev's a Republican but he's also a born politician. From what remains of the IRA he's drawn the nucleus of a new political party to challenge Cumann na nGaedheal. By contrast with Cosgrave's businessmen and large landowners, Dev's party comprises ordinary working men and women; the plain people of Ireland who won our freedom in the first place. Dev intends to fight for the Republic by using the governmental structures of the Free State he despises. He's calling his new party Fianna Fáil.*

"He may have shot himself in the foot, though. You'll recall he refused to accept the oath of allegiance to the British crown. That was his main objection to the Treaty; he thought the oath was a more crucial issue than partition. But because the Free State has dominion status all members of the Dáil have to sign the oath. Dev's made it policy for his new party to refuse. He won't modify his principles for anyone. So even if they're elected, members of Fianna Fáil must abstain from taking seats in the Irish Parliament.

"Although Cosgrave fought in the Rising most of his cabinet are parliamentary nationalists. *They* won't try to take the north back at gunpoint. They'll reason with the British, or bargain with them, or just accept what's been done even if they don't like it. So my answer to your question is . . . there'll be no more war in Ireland. In my considered opinion."

He chuckled. "Sorry I'm so long-winded, Cap'n. You should know better than to ask a journalist a question. Let's just say I'm cautiously hopeful. War does seem to be the human condition, though. Thank God Europe at least is pacified!"

*Soldiers of Destiny.

20 November 1926
IMPERIAL CONFERENCE IN LONDON ANNOUNCES
ESTABLISHMENT OF BRITISH COMMONWEALTH OF
NATIONS
Commonwealth to include the dominions of Australia, Canada, Irish Free
State, Newfoundland, New Zealand, and South Africa. Nonindependent
status of India remains unchanged.

Chapter Six

THE young woman who left the train at Westland Row wore a snug cloche that covered her bobbed hair. Two years of bleaching with lemon juice and glycerine—a complexion treatment Madame insisted upon—had faded her freckles to invisibility. Men cast admiring glances at the slim, silk-stockinged legs revealed by her knee-length skirt. Women noticed the continental cut of her lilac-colored spring coat.

Ursula Halloran was a different person from the girl who had left Ireland two years earlier. She had arrived at Surval with the blinkered viewpoint of an island dweller and a full set of prejudices she believed to be truth. In Europe she had encountered other people's prejudices, other people's truths.

"All human skin," she had once remarked to Felicity Rowe-Howell as they stood at their easels in art class, mixing flesh tones on their palettes, "is some variation of brown. Creamy-beige or pinky-beige or yellow-beige or bronze or mahogany or ebony. Considered objectively, there's not much difference between any of us."

Fliss had laughed. "Try and tell that to my father. He believes we English are vastly superior."

Ursula tensed imperceptibly. "Do you agree with him?"

"I never really thought about it," said Fliss, putting down her brush. "Some of us are downright ratty. My brothers view women as little more than an exotic form of masturbation."

Ursula had struggled to conceal her shock, but in time she grew accustomed to Fliss's risqué remarks. Some of the European girls at Surval were much more explicit.

They unwittingly had made Ursula aware of the childlike innocence of the Irish.

As she emerged from the train station in Dublin, Ursula raised one gloved hand to shade her eyes from the spring sunshine. There was none. The air smelt of recent rain and rain to come.

She stood still for a moment, feeling Ireland seep back into her pores. An Ireland lacking the luxuries Europeans took for granted and many of the basic amenities as well. Ireland with its fixed ideas about good and evil, Celt and Saxon, Catholic and Protestant. Republican and Free Stater.

A rank of taxicabs was waiting at the curb. Ursula signaled to the lead driver. "Number sixteen, Middle Gardiner Street," she directed.

"Would you not walk from here?" the man asked in surprise. "You'd have to carry them suitcases but it would cost ye nuthin'."

Ursula smiled. "I prefer to take a cab, thank you. And will you please go the long way 'round?"

"How long, miss?"

"West along the quays as far as Smithfield Market, then back to Parnell Square, then over to Middle Gardiner Street."

He said dubiously, "Do you know where you're going at all?"

"I do know," she assured him.

"It'll cost ye," he warned.

As they drove through the familiar streets north of the Liffey, Ursula recalled the city sounds of her childhood. Iron-shod hooves ringing on cobblestones as carriages and jaunting cars and heavily laden drays competed for space. Bicycles hissing along. Tram bells clanging. Small boys shouting raucously, drunks bellowing as they emerged from pubs, neighborhood women calling to one another from open doorways.

Street traders crying, "Coal blocks!" "Dublin Bay herrins!" "Five oranges for tuppence!" "Rags bones and bottles collected!" Organ-grinders with hurdy-gurdys. Veterans of the Great War busking on corners, playing fiddles and tin whistles or singing the ballads of an earlier age.

Now, Ursula observed, the horse-drawn vehicles were slowly giving way to automobiles. Otherwise it appeared to be the same northside Dublin she had always known. Pungent and rowdy and idiosyncratic. A place where many people lived and died impoverished; where tuberculosis and enteritis and typhus cast long shadows. How strange that it had changed so little, when she had changed so much!

The postwar era was a time of grinding poverty for Dublin's lower classes. Infant mortality was endemic. The poor had no sanitation; they fetched their water from communal outdoor taps and survived on little more than cabbage and potatoes, or bread with a bit of dripping. The pawnbroker was almost a member of the family. Men's suits were pawned on Monday and reclaimed in time for Mass the following Sunday.

Short-term survival, not long-term economic recovery, was the preoccupation of the Free State government. During the Civil War roads and bridges had been destroyed and numerous buildings burnt, doing great damage to the infrastructure of the country. Much of Dublin waited to be rebuilt. It was hard to know where the money would come from. As a result of its dominion status within the commonwealth, the government looked with increasing desperation to Britain.

The cab driver called, "Here we are, miss. Sixteen Middle Gardiner Street."

As Ursula unsnapped her handbag to pay him, a fading trace of perfume, foreign and exotic, wafted into the air. Two Vincent de Paul nuns in their butterfly headdresses were walking past. They glanced at Ursula, then swiftly dropped their eyes.

Hector Hamilton, Painless Dentist proclaimed a hand-lettered card in the window facing the street. The redbrick house was not as large as Ursula remembered. The front door with its Georgian fanlight was not as tall, nor the polished brass knocker as high. And had its facade always been so grimy with coal dust?

But when the door swung open, the cry of welcome was familiar. "Precious!" shouted Louise Hamilton as she gathered the young woman into her arms.

"Everyone calls me Ursula now," gasped the girl, half-smothered against the older woman's capacious bosom.

Laughing, Louise relaxed her embrace. "Except my cousin Henry. When he sent your things over here he labeled them *Property of Little Business*. I stored them for you in the attic. As soon as you wrote you were coming, I dusted them off and put them in our best room. Here, you," she called to the waiting taxi driver, "will you ever bring those suitcases inside?"

"You shouldn't have gone to any trouble for me, Louise. I don't want to dispossess one of your regular lodgers."

"Sure and you won't. Since I married Mr. Hamilton I don't do much in the way of lodgings anymore, not the way I used to when you and Ned and Síle lived with me. How is your dear father anyway?"

The girl said casually, "I haven't heard from him for a while."

Louise sniffed. "Too busy to write letters, I suppose. The government's still arresting Republicans; I'd be very much surprised if our Ned's not among them one of these days. But enough of that." She put one arm around Ursula's waist. "Come through and I'll make you a nice cup of . . . my, you certainly are thin!" Drawing back, she gave Ursula a critical look. "You never did have a pick on you, but I thought once you grew up you would fill out a bit."

"I'm not thin, it's my clothes. Ella insisted on my having the latest fashions while I was at Surval, and the style now is to flatten the bust and give a boyish figure."

"God between us and all harm, why would a woman do that? You'll be wanting some decent dresses straightaway."

"I'll make do with what I have, Louise. From now on I shall pay my own way and I can't afford to buy any more clothes."

"No woman should be seen with her knees peepin' out," the other insisted. "You'll never get yourself a husband that way."

"I'm not looking for a husband," said Ursula.

As soon as she was settled into number 16, she set out to reacquaint herself with the city of her birth. She took long walks up one street and down another. Dublin was a walking city.

The deprived areas north of the Liffey had not changed from her earliest memories; poverty was still poverty. But there were signs of change elsewhere. The Free State government was housed in one of the great symbols of the old imperialism, the splendid Ascendancy mansion called Leinster House. As the new nation worked to establish its identity, symbolism was important.

Dubliners had felt a profound sense of shock when the cast-iron pillar-boxes used for posting mail were repainted from British red to Irish green.

HENRY Mooney sent Ursula a personal letter and four envelopes in a brown paper parcel. Each envelope contained a letter of introduction from himself, recommending "Miss Ursula Halloran, of Clare and Dublin" for employment.

Sitting on the bed in her room, she spread the envelopes out like playing cards. "Begin with P.S. O'Hegarty," Henry had instructed. "If you make a good impression on him you shall not need the other three. I have known P.S.—that is what everyone calls him—for years. He has written several books on Irish subjects, which explains why his language is a bit flowery.

P.S. used to be a postmaster with the British civil service. When they found out he was a member of the Irish Republican Brotherhood they dismissed him. After the War of Independence he took the pro-Treaty side, and now he's the secretary of the Department of Posts and Telegraphs, with a lot of jobs in his gift. Some of his opinions may get up your nose, but I trust your teachers at Surval have taught you better than to blurt out your politics on first acquaintance."

The Department of Posts and Telegraphs was temporarily housed in Dublin Castle while the General Post Office, destroyed by British artillery during the 1916 Rising, was being rebuilt. For seven centuries the sprawling complex known throughout Ireland simply as "the Castle" had been the seat and symbol of English domination. Now it contained the government of the Irish Free State.

To Republicans, the Castle was still occupied by the enemy.

As Ursula Halloran approached the wrought-iron gates opening into the Upper Yard, her thoughts, whatever they might be, were concealed behind a facade of impeccable poise. Her felt hat was from Kellett's, the leading Dublin milliners; her white gloves were spotless. The mauve suit she wore turned her eyes to a mysterious smoky gray.

"I have an appointment with Secretary O'Hegarty," she told the guard. "Would you be so kind as to direct me to his office?"

In Ireland people were labeled by their accents, which identified both their birthplace and their station in life. This young woman's precise diction was beyond the guard's ability to categorize, but her self-assurance was convincing. With a respectful salute, he passed her through the gate.

Patrick Sarsfield O'Hegarty was a bespectacled, square-faced man with a tightly trimmed moustache. Meeting Ursula at the door of his office, he bowed her in with the courtesy of his generation and held a chair for her.

She handed him the letter of introduction. After a perfunctory reading he dropped the letter atop a pile of other papers on his desk. "My old friend Henry Mooney seems to think you would be an asset to the civil service," O'Hegarty remarked in a lilting Cork accent. "We're receiving applications by the score but we'll always look at someone special."

Ursula dazzled him with a brief smile before dropping her eyes. The gesture conveyed the message that she was someone special, but too modest to say so.

O'Hegarty studied her in silence for a few moments. "Well, well. I suppose you'd best tell me about yourself. Your people are from Dublin and Clare, I understand?"

Sitting with an erect back and her hands neatly folded in her lap, Ursula gave him a creatively edited version of her family history. Obfuscation could be learned.

"You're very well-spoken," he observed. "Where were you educated?"

"For the past several years I've been studying on the Continent," she replied smoothly, "specializing in languages. I am fluent in both French and German. And Irish of course. *An bhfuil Gaeilge agat?**"

"I come from an Irish-speaking family," O'Hegarty told her with obvious pride. "I'll arrange for you to take the civil service examination as soon as possible. The exams are competitive, but with your background you should have no difficulty in winning a place, Miss Halloran." He hesitated. "It is 'Miss'? To join the civil service these days a woman must be unmarried or widowed, you know."

"I have never been married. Nor do I have plans to be."

He dropped his chin and peered at her over his glasses. "You aren't one of those gunwomen, are you?"

"Gunwomen?"

"Females playing a role God never intended for them. Sadly, many of the women who helped the Volunteers during the War of Independence enjoyed the excitement in a most unfeminine way. All that swashbuckling went to their heads like strong drink. They took to first-aid, drill, and guns, and thought of nothing else. They were all but unsexed. One might say their mother's milk blackened to gunpowder."[1]

Ursula said nothing. Her gloved hands were neatly folded in her lap. Only a sharp eye would have noticed that her fingers were clenched around her thumbs.

"To the gunwomen the Truce was an irritation and the Treaty a calamity," O'Hegarty went on, warming to his topic. "In the Civil War the gunwomen fought more fiercely against their fellow Irishmen than they ever had against the Tans.† In 1923 the Free State government held over three hundred females in Kilmainham Gaol, ranging in age from twelve to seventy.[2] All rabid Republicans."

"How interesting," Ursula said, as if the matter were of no interest.

"What are your own feelings about the Civil War, Miss Halloran?"

"Having political opinions is unfeminine," she replied. Hands in lap. Eyes demurely cast down.

"Well said! We must find a position suitable for such an intelligent young

---

*Do you speak Irish?

†The "Black and Tans"; military irregulars sent by the British to suppress revolution in Ireland through terror and intimidation.

lady. Did Henry tell you I'm overseeing the Free State Broadcasting Service? Not that I approve of wireless broadcasting, mind you. A waste of valuable funds on a fad, if you ask me."

Trying to conceal her excitement, Ursula said, "You did say I speak well."

"Only the male voice is really suitable for broadcasting," O'Hegarty stated flatly. "I suppose there's no harm in women presenting programmes intended for other women, but the female voice lacks *gravitas*. There are a couple of clerical openings in the Dublin station, however. Would you consider one of those?"

When she nodded, he went on, "The director over there is Séamus Clandillon. Clandillon recently made some unauthorized appointments, including his own daughter and Grace Gifford's sister Katie[3]—one of those gunwomen I spoke about—and he's been ordered to get rid of both of them. My department will supply his staff from now on. If you pass the civil service examination, I can guarantee Clandillon will take you."

Chapter Seven

DR. Douglas Hyde had inaugurated the new broadcasting service from Dublin the previous year. Officially it was the Dublin Broadcasting Station, but the public preferred to use the call letters, 2RN—a clever pun on "to Erin." Originally 2RN was only on air from 7:45 until 10:30 each evening. As time went by those hours were extended. Urgent news was broadcast immediately.

Although dedicated to providing an Irish voice for an Irish people, station policy was to avoid any semblance of the raging political debate that had plunged the country into civil war.

The 2RN studio was in Little Denmark Street, off Henry Street. An employment exchange occupied the ground floor of the building. The porter at the door directed Ursula up a crooked, poorly-lit stairway to the first floor, where she entered a dingy room crammed with tables, stools, packing boxes, and unidentifiable electronic equipment. A piece of carpet black with ground-in coal dust was laid over the linoleum floor.

Trying not to brush against anything, she edged sideways into the room. A middle-aged man with his shirtsleeves rolled up and a cigarette tucked behind his ear was crouched over a table, fiddling with a large black box and muttering under his breath. He glanced up distractedly. "You are?"

"Miss Ursula Halloran. I've been sent from Posts and Telegraphs."

"You want the office, one flight up. This is the control room, studio's through that door."

"What's behind the screen?"

"A sort of waiting room for guest performers."

A red light was burning over the door to the studio. Ursula could hear music inside. "Can I listen in to the program?" she asked hopefully.

"They're only rehearsing for tonight. There's a pair of headphones in the men's toilet that will pick up what's coming over the microphone, but I'm afraid that's all I can offer."

16 May 1927

Dear Papa,

As of yesterday I am gainfully employed! I have taken a clerical position with 2RN. Fortunately Uncle Henry once taught me to use a typewriter. Although I am a bit rusty I shall practice like mad. In a few days I shall be handling routine correspondence as well as doing the filing. The staff here is small and everyone is expected to perform multiple tasks. Even though I am not very good at it, they have me making the tea. (Perhaps if I make it too bitter they will assign the job to someone else.)

Séamus Clandillon, the station director, has an abrupt manner, but one has to admire him. He works incredibly long hours, doing everything from general administration and directing programs to recruiting talent. Both he and his wife are professional singers. During the station's inaugural broadcast they volunteered to go on air and sing if one of the scheduled performers failed to appear.

Mr. Clandillon suffers from gout, and often takes off his shoes in the studio and walks around in thick socks. Do you suppose Aunt Norah could suggest one of her country cures for his condition? It would certainly put me in his good books.

The highest-ranking woman at the station is Mairead Ní Ghráda. When Ernest Blythe was minister for trade and commerce in the first Dáil—the Republican Dáil—Mairead was his secretary. Now she is the woman's organiser at 2RN. Is that not an odd title? She is in charge of children's programming, and also a library of gramophone records from which she selects music to be played over the air. Because I know a little something about music thanks to my education at Surval, she said I could help her.

Another person whom I like very much is the announcer, Séumas Hughes. He prefers to be called *Séumas O hAodha*. You must know him; he was the first person to sing "The Soldier's Song" in public, at a Volunteers' concert. During the Rising he fought in Jacob's Biscuit Factory under the command of Thomas MacDonagh. He begins each transmission by saying in beautiful Irish, *"Se seo Radio Bhaile Atha Cliath agus Radio Corcaigh."**

For now the broadcasts are of very low power, but one day people all across the country will be able to listen to the wireless. You and Frank should buy a crystal set for the farm. They only cost a few shillings and you can put one together yourselves. Then you can hear the news almost as soon as it happens, and you can imagine me here in the Dublin station, thinking of you.

Your loving Ursula

There was no reply.
There was never a reply.

WORKING at 2RN was like acquiring a new family; a lively family in which something exciting was always happening. Ursula never missed Mass on Sunday, but otherwise most of her waking hours were spent at the broadcasting station. Or thinking about broadcasting. Concentric waves spreading out like brave soldiers carrying urgent messages. Ireland listening. Herself at the heart of the excitement.

Upon receipt of her first pay packet, she counted out the small sum to the last ha'penny. Her only extravagances would be buying books—used ones, of course, from the many used bookshops in Dublin—and sending her clothes to a commercial laundry. Her European wardrobe would have to last a long time. She could not afford to submit fashionable frocks to the tortures of the copper boiler in the back yard, and Louise's brutality with a flatiron.

Mairead Ní Ghráda had recommended two laundries, the Magdalen and the Swastika, both of which had vans to collect and deliver. Work at the Magdalen was done by "fallen women" whose priests or families had turned them over to the nuns of the Holy Saints Convent.

Ursula chose the Swastika Laundry. Named for an ancient form of cross, it had no unpleasant connotations.

Taking out a dog-eared notebook in which she had kept an itemized account of the money Ella had spent on her, Ursula read the daunting total. Twice. With a sigh, she put the remainder of her wages, together with the

---

*"This is Radio Dublin and Radio Cork."

account book, into a large envelope that she deposited in the traditional Irish savings bank: under the mattress.

ONE of 2RN's proudest claims was the presentation of running commentaries on sports events before the BBC was able to do so. In May the station scored a real scoop by announcing that Charles Lindbergh's plane had been sighted over Ireland on its record-making flight from New York to Paris. Aside from such events, daily programs paid little attention to the news. That was left to the print media. Everyone read the newspapers.

2RN produced live dramas featuring some of the stars of the Abbey Theatre, and was building its own orchestra. It also presented comedy sketches, a children's hour, an Irish language program, and rebroadcasts from abroad.

Guest artists were willing to work for "next nothing" because they enjoyed the novelty of broadcasting. This was fortunate, because the station suffered from a chronic lack of funds. Constant requests for additional money, or for the payment of outstanding bills, were sent to the Department of Finance. Composing the letters became Ursula's responsibility. If no senior member of staff was available she signed them herself, writing U. Halloran in a forceful hand.

The atmosphere at 2RN was friendly and informal. Members of staff worked all hours, often coming in on their day off to lend a hand. When a live drama was broadcast, the guest artists and even the door porter helped with the sound effects. Ursula was shown how to pound her thighs with cupped hands to reproduce the rhythms of a galloping horse, and pour dry rice into a folded paper at just the right speed to simulate everything from a light shower to a downpour of rain.

The general election on the ninth of June was a topic of great interest at the broadcasting station. Ursula listened avidly to what everyone had to say, but kept her opinions to herself. Most of the time.

The Cumann na nGaedheal Party won forty-seven seats in the Dáil. An energetic campaign spearheaded by Eamon de Valera and Constance Markievicz won forty-four places for Fíanna Fail, compared to twenty-two for Labour and only five for Sinn Féin. But since the Soldiers of Destiny still abstained from taking the oath, they could not take their seats.

On June 22 the Dáil assembled without the abstentionists, though several smaller parties were represented.

W.T. Cosgrave of Cumann na nGaedheal was overwhelmingly reelected as president of the executive council.

Ursula posted the details to Henry Mooney. "The Republicans are letting the Free Staters win by default," her letter mourned. "The Free State appropriated the symbols of the Republic—the tricolour flag, the green army uniforms, the Dáil—but the government they represent is just business as usual under different management."

THE ship that took Ursula's letter to America also carried Eamon de Valera. He was going to raise money for his new political party.

IN July a story broke that no one expected. The illusion of a peaceful summer Sunday exploded in a hail of gunfire.

Chapter Eight

THERE was no broadcast that Sunday until 8 P.M., when a musical program was scheduled. Station employees tended to drift in to Little Denmark Street during the day, however, to help set up the studio for the orchestra. Ursula was just taking off her hat when Séamus Clandillon thrust a piece of paper into her hand.

"Thank God there's someone here who can type! Give me a news script, we have to go on air as soon as possible."

Ursula stared in disbelief at the scribbled note. All her fingers turned to thumbs. She wadded up and threw away three sheets of paper before producing a script Séumas Hughes could read into the microphone. Clandillon was in such a hurry he did not check the script, but ran downstairs to the studio with it.

"Stand by for a special bulletin," Hughes announced, his voice cutting through a crackle of static. "Dateline Dublin, July tenth. Kevin O'Higgins, the minister for justice, has been assassinated. Details are sketchy, but it appears O'Higgins was gunned down in Booterstown as he was walking to Mass at his local church. Witnesses report the ambush was carried out by several men in a waiting car.

"O'Higgins, it will be remembered, was the man who ordered the execution of Erskine Childers. During the Civil War Minister O'Higgins presided over the executions of seventy-seven Republicans, including Rory O'Connor, who had been the best man at his wedding."

Within moments of the broadcast Clandillon loomed over Ursula's desk. "Who told you to write that?"

"Why, you did," she replied, wide-eyed.

"I never told you to add the part about the executions."

"Is it not true?"

"It is true, but that's not the point. We can't have staff editorializing."

"Did I do that?"

"You know you did."

"Séumas didn't have to read it out."

"You knew he would."

Ursula pushed back her chair and stood up. "Please don't reprimand him." Lifting her chin, she gave the station director a level look. A stony, challenging, Ned Halloran sort of look. "I accept full responsibility for the wording of the bulletin," she said.

"What makes you think I'm going to reprimand him? Just don't do anything like this again, Miss Halloran. Whatever our personal opinions may be, this is the Free State Broadcasting Service and the government pays the bills. No Republican propaganda is allowed."

"Only pro-Treaty propaganda?"

Clandillon bit his lip to keep from smiling. "Hold your whisht,"* he advised.

LATER Mairead Ní Ghráda told Ursula, "You had it wrong, you know."

"Sorry?"

"About the seventy-seven who were executed. Ernest Blythe was in cabinet at the time, and he claims the number was actually eighty-four or eighty-five."[1]

Ursula drew a sharp breath. "Why is that not generally known?"

"A lot of things happened during the Civil War that will never be generally known," the older woman said.

THE men who had shot O'Higgins escaped. They melted into the city without being identified. It was later claimed they had been IRA men on their way to a football match, and just happened to see O'Higgins in the street.

According to the slain man's wife his dying words were, "I'm going to sit on a damp cloud with Mick Collins and play a harp."[2]

The assassination of Kevin O'Higgins burst like a thunderclap over the

*"Be silent."

Irish political scene. O'Higgins, arguably the most dynamic, powerfully intellectual individual in the new government, had been considered the "strong man" of the Free State regime. His late friend Michael Collins had referred to him as "the Balls." O'Higgins had seen himself as Collins's successor and refused to let anything intimidate him. He had been fully aware the IRA hated him, but had never doubted he was doing his duty.

Some of the staff at 2RN loudly condemned the murder. Others remarked that he had got what he deserved. Séumas Hughes never said anything to Ursula about the wording of the news bulletin, but the following day when he passed her on the stairs, he winked at her.

The murder had taken place in broad daylight in full view of a number of people. Yet no one seemed able to identify the assassins or explain how they had escaped.

In a letter to Henry Mooney, Ursula exulted, "The murderer is murdered, that's one for our side!"

She wrote the same thing to Ned Halloran, but she did not post that letter. She no longer sent any letters to him, because having them go unanswered was too painful. She kept the unposted letters in a box under her bed. Addressed, "Dear Papa," they became an informal journal that no one would ever see.

MEN who visited 2RN on business could not help noticing the vivacious young woman with the dazzling smile. The unmarried ones asked her out. Her answer was always the same, delivered in tones of polite regret. "Thank you, I'm very flattered. But it's just not possible at present." Without actually saying so, she left would-be suitors with the impression that she was seeing someone else. Their feelings were spared and she did not have to lie.

She told her journal the truth. "Dear Papa," she confided. "I have no intention of getting involved with any man. I have my reasons."

URSULA maintained a lively correspondence with a number of her former classmates from Surval. Heidi Fromm, who had married a Swiss botanist named Stefan Neckermann, wrote, "We are dividing our time between Munich, where my husband lectures at the university, and Kenya, where he is compiling the definitive index of native plant life." She sent Ursula a large map of Kenya and a colorful description of life in the Crown colony.

"I can learn more about the world from my friends than I ever did from a geography book," Ursula remarked to Louise one afternoon.

The older woman looked up from preparing a hearty dinner of Dublin coddle.* "Why should you care what's happening in other countries? Sure we have enough troubles of our own. I'll be in trouble meself if I don't give Mr. Hamilton a nice pudding tonight. How do you feel about rhubarb and custard?"

Five days later the wireless carried a story that had a more profound effect on Irish emotions than the O'Higgins murder.

In or out of government, Constance Markievicz had been a tireless worker for Republican causes. Her intractable idealism was an inspiration to many. A member of the standing committee of Sinn Féin, she had presided at the inaugural meeting of Fianna Fáil in 1926 and served as a member of the national executive.

That same winter there had been a severe coal shortage in Dublin. Madame Markievicz had exhausted herself arranging for fuel for the poor, even driving into the mountains to pile her car with turf to distribute to the tenements.

By 1927 her friends had begun commenting that she looked very worn. She had campaigned hard in the general election, helping to secure the large turnout for Fianna Fáil and winning a seat in the Dáil for herself—one she could not take up because of de Valera's policy of abstention.

Shortly afterward she went into hospital for an emergency appendectomy. Following a second operation, her family were called. Her estranged husband, Count Casimir Markievicz, rushed from Warsaw to Dublin to be at her bedside—summoned by a message broadcast on the wireless.

When Séumas Hughes read the news bulletin on July 15, he made no effort to keep the emotion out of his voice. "At one-thirty this morning, Constance, Countess Markievicz, aged fifty-nine, answered the Last Post. She was the founder of Na Fianna Éireann,† took an active part in the 1916 Rising, was imprisoned numerous times by the British, was the first woman to be elected to the British Parliament but refused to take her seat, was elected to the first Dáil Éireann as a member of the Sinn Féin party and served this nation as minister for labor from 1919 to 1921. At the time of her death she was a member of Fianna Fáil. Funeral arrangements will be announced later."

Hughes's voice broke on the last sentence. Within the radio station men and women, whatever their politics, were crying openly.

---

*Potato, bacon, and sausage stew.
†The Warrior Band of Ireland, a national scouting organization.

That night Ursula took out the scrapbook she had kept on the countess and leafed through its pages. Her eye fell on a newspaper clipping referring to a lecture to the Irish Women's Franchise League, in which Constance Markievicz had urged women, "Dress suitably in short skirts and strong boots, leave your jewels in the bank and buy a revolver. Take up your responsibilities and be prepared to go your own way depending for safety on your own courage, your own truth and your own common sense."

The Free State government refused to allow Constance Markievicz to lie in state in any of the civic buildings. Her body was taken to the pillar room of the Rotunda Hospital instead. Across the street from the site of Tom Clarke's former shop where much of the Rising had been planned, and flanked by an honor guard composed of Fianna boys in full uniform, the rebel countess lay at peace at last. Thousands of Dubliners filed by her coffin to say good-bye.

On the seventeenth of July a huge funeral procession wound its way to Glasnevin Cemetery as had the processions of so many heroes before. The coffin was wrapped in the Irish tricolor and heaped with flowers. Eight additional vehicles were required to carry more wreaths and flowers. The cortége took over two hours to pass the short length of O'Connell Street.

Tens of thousands turned out to honor Constance Markievicz: members of the Ascendancy, writers, artists, feminists, Republican politicians (there was no official representative from the Free State), Fianna boys, IRA Volunteers, and veterans of the Citizens' Army. Jim Larkin and what appeared to be the entire trade union movement mingled with the men and women of the slums, mourning the loss of their most devoted and unselfish champion.

In the crush of people lining the route was Ursula Halloran. When a white rose slipped from the masses heaped upon the coffin and fell into the road, she darted forward and seized it, thrusting it into the bosom of her frock. All day she was conscious of it against her skin.

Eamon de Valera had come home in time to deliver the funeral oration at Glasnevin. Taller by a head than any of the men around him, his long, horselike face gaunted by prison and hollowed with experience, he spoke in a slow, solemn voice. People held their breath to listen. This was de Valera himself! A hero from a time already passing into myth.

He concluded, "The world knew Constance only as a soldier of Ireland, but we knew her as colleague and comrade. We knew the kindliness, the great woman's heart of her, the great Irish soul of her, and we know the loss we have suffered is not to be repaired. It is sadly we take our leave, but we pray high heaven that all she longed for may one day be achieved."[3]

With Constance Markievicz was buried the military uniform she had worn during Easter Week, 1916.

THE photograph dominating the front page of the *Clare Champion* had been taken from the roof of the General Post Office in Dublin, which was still undergoing reconstruction. Risking life and limb, the photographer had crawled out onto a narrow ledge to capture a picture of the Markievicz funeral cortége. A sea of people filled O'Connell Street in either direction, overflowing into every side street.

Ned Halloran sat with the newspaper spread in front of him. He was unaware of being in his bedroom in the farmhouse in Clare. Part of him had returned to 1916 and the GPO. As it did every day, his mind presented him with kaleidoscopic visions of the defining event of his life.

He had a hundred memories of Madame Markievicz. The most indelible was the last: marching off on Easter Monday morning to fight for Ireland in St. Stephen's Green.

Gone to join a larger army now.

The army of the Dead.

Síle.

Ned leaned forward, trying to make out the faces of the people in the street. Was one of them Síle? Were she and little Precious in that crowd? They must be. Must be. Nothing could have kept them away.

In the upper corner of the paper was a photograph of Constance Markievicz in her youth. A tall, slim, regal beauty, arrayed in the trappings of wealth and privilege. She had turned her back on all of it. Gone off to help the poor, to help poor Ireland.

Ned touched the paper with his fingers. Touched the dead face. But it was not dead. How could it be dead when he was staring into those living eyes?

She's still alive somewhere, he thought. They all are. Somewhere out there in the peopled dark.

Síle. Pádraic Pearse. Joe Plunkett. Thomas MacDonagh.

Síle.

Abruptly he stood up. "Wait for me," he said. "I'm coming."

Chapter Nine

IN his newspaper office in Texas, Henry Mooney had learned of both deaths by way of the telegraph. He immediately wrote to Ursula, "If it were possible I would come back for Con's funeral. She was the greatest woman I ever met.

"As for Kevin O'Higgins, whom you called a murderer, you must not make assumptions when you do not know all the facts. Exercise a little moderation.

"Remember that men on both sides of a battlefield view themselves as patriots. I happen to know that Kevin's father was killed by the IRA during the Civil War. His son was devoted to him and took his death very hard. Understandably, Kevin became convinced that physical force republicanism was the greatest danger to the Free State. As the minister for justice it was his duty to protect the nation from its enemies, and to that end he did his best.

"We must grieve for Kevin O'Higgins and for every man and woman lost to violence."

The rebuke in Henry's letter stung Ursula. She did not want moderation. She wanted passion.

With the death of Kevin O'Higgins, W.T. Cosgrave's main rival on the political scene was gone. Only Eamon de Valera remained a threat. Cosgrave cannily introduced the Electoral Amendment Act, which required every parliamentary candidate to sign an affidavit agreeing to put his name to the oath and take his seat if elected. This meant abstentionists could not even run for office.

The ground was cut out from under de Valera.

• • •

T HE broadcasting station closed down for lunch. Ursula often ate her mid-day meal in Wynn's Hotel, which since 1916 had prided itself on being "part of the Republic." Great deeds had been planned there by the leaders of the Rising. The paneled interior of the hotel, restored since a disastrous fire during the Civil War, hummed with history. Many Dubliners could not afford a hotel luncheon yet wanted to eat in refined surroundings, so Wynn's accommodated them by turning a blind eye on the source of their food as long as they purchased a beverage—usually a cup of tea.

One August afternoon Ursula entered the hotel restaurant carrying her customary lunch: two bacon sandwiches prepared by Louise and wrapped in brown paper. When the last crumb had been eaten and the brown paper folded along its creases and saved for reuse, she ordered a second cup of tea that she sipped very slowly, using up the minutes. Then she left the dimly lit sanctuary of Wynn's and walked back to Little Denmark Street.

The sky was radiant but there was a hint of early autumn in the air. A tingling crispness, as tart as the first bite of an apple. Blue haze trapped in the tops of the trees.

Ursula forgot the posture drilled into her at Surval, the hours spent gliding across polished floors with a book balanced atop the head, and stepped out with an athlete's ardent stride, long-legged and free.

If I were in Clare I would be riding Saoirse this very minute. Galloping across the fields with autumn coloring up around us like a tapestry. Or meandering along a little boreen with the reins lying loose on his neck, and himself and myself like one creature. . . .

Her pace slowed; her inward eyes gazed upon private vistas. People brushed past her but she did not notice them. Her heart thudded to re-membered hoofbeats.

When she reached the broadcasting station, the door porter greeted her with, "Welcome back, Miss Halloran. Ye took your time, but sure, on a grand day like this who could blame ye?"

"Are the others back already?"

"They are indeed." He gave an exaggerated wink.

"Have you been drinking, Mac?" she asked suspiciously.

"Not yet, but I'll be stocious tonight. Legless. Carried home on a door."

"You mean you plan to get drunk?"

"Stocious!" he repeated. "I'm going to toast the Chief until the pubs close." Winking again, he held the door for her. "Trot inside now."

"Why are you being so mysterious, Mac?"

He grinned. "Ye'll know soon enough."

Ursula found her colleagues in gales of laughter.

"Och, that Dev's a cute hoor!" exclaimed Séumas Hughes, mopping his eyes.

"What's he done now?" Ursula asked.

"He knew he'd either have to give up politics altogether, or find a way to take the oath in spite of his scruples. So de Valera wrestled with his conscience ... and as usual, Dev won. Off he goes to Leinster House this morning, appears before the clerk of the day, and announces—in Irish—that he's not giving any promise of faithfulness to any power outside of the people of Ireland. The clerk says he doesn't care about that; all he requires is de Valera's signature in the Dáil record book. He opens the book and indicates where Dev is to sign. Below the oath.

"Then—and this is the rich part—Dev sees the Bible lying beside the open book. He promptly removes it to the far end of the room and tells the clerk, 'You must remember I am taking no oath.' Being careful not to look directly at the open record book, he takes a sheaf of papers from a folder he brought with him and sets them down so they cover the wording of the oath entirely. Then he signs his name.[1] He'll be able to claim he didn't know what he was signing!"

Mairead Ní Ghráda laughed so hard she had hiccups.

The next morning de Valera arrived up at Leinster House with a flock of Fianna Fáil delegates. Standing on the steps in front of a battery of reporters, de Valera declared that the oath was merely an empty political formula. Then he marched his followers inside to sign the book. Fíanna Fail took their seats in the Dáil the following day.

Ursula gleefully wrote in her journal, "Dear Papa, the Republican star is rising again!"

A few days later Ursula received a disturbing letter from Norah Daly. "Your father's after leaving the farm, Ursula. When I looked in his wardrobe his clothes were gone, not just his Volunteer uniform, but everything. If he comes up to Dublin please let us know. We are worried about him."

I should have kept posting those letters, Ursula thought with a pang of guilt. *Given him something to hold on to. But how could I? It would be like begging. I don't know if he read those I did send. He probably wadded them up and threw them on the fire.*

As she walked to and from work, she searched the faces in the street. *He could be anywhere. Henry used to say he was a will-o'-the-wisp. Next to*

Michael Collins, Ned Halloran was the most slippery of all the Volunteers. Per-
haps he's gone to the north. That's it. That is just what he would do. Gone north
to defend our people.

Nevertheless she kept watching for Ned.

She had always searched passing faces. Hoping—fearing—to find one
that looked like her face.

OVER four years had elapsed since the official end of the Civil War, yet
the unresolved conflict continued. Dublin rang with gunfire in the night.
Men from both sides were tumbled into unmarked graves down the country.
Increasingly disillusioned with militarism, the public, encouraged by the
government, put the entire blame on the IRA. There was little or no criticism of government forces. The attitude was, "Sure we voted for that
crowd, didn't we?"

Playwright Seán O'Casey, who originally had been a member of the Irish
Republican Brotherhood, became one of republicanism's most outspoken
critics. The man who once wrote in fury of the English, "These men ramped
over the land for hundreds of years; shot, hanged the leaders of the Irish
who wouldn't agree with them, and jammed the jails with the rest,"[2] had
been embittered by the Civil War. His hatred for the IRA now exceeded
his hatred for those against whom they had rebelled.

O'Casey's postrevolutionary trilogy, *The Shadow of a Gunman, Juno and
the Paycock*, and *The Plough and the Stars*, deliberately restricted the revolution to the filth and decay of the Dublin slums. The nationwide impulse
for freedom was ignored. Republican characters were depicted as repellent
and morally bankrupt. According to O'Casey it was not the rebels who were
dying for the ordinary people, but the ordinary people who were dying for
the rebels.

After a controversial beginning the plays became hugely popular.

Ursula refused to attend any of them.

In November a concert featuring the newly christened Radio Éireann
Symphony Orchestra, conducted by musical director Vincent O'Brien, was
given in the Metropolitan Hall. A reduced price of one shilling was available
for the working classes, who were allowed in first. "Upper class" tickets
were sold at an increased price.[3]

At Surval Ursula had acquired a taste for classical music. On the appointed evening she went to the concert hall straight from work. As she

waited to purchase her ticket, she automatically scanned the faces of people walking past.

One of them paused, then grinned. Most Irish women dropped their eyes when confronted with a man's gaze. Ursula smiled back.

When the young man whipped off his hat, crisp red hair rose from his scalp like a forest fire. A wholesome, pleasant, open countenance, with brown eyes sparkling amid a face full of freckles. "Miss Halloran? Do you not remember me? Finbar Cassidy from the passport office?"

"I do of course. I'm surprised you remember me, though."

"Oh, I'd never forget you," he assured her. "What are you doing here?"

"I'm going to the concert. Our orchestra is playing a Beethoven symphony tonight."

" 'Our' orchestra?"

"I'm employed by the Dublin Broadcasting Station," Ursula said proudly. "Are you interested in classical music yourself?"

"I'm a brand new convert," Cassidy assured her. He dug in the pocket of his Crombie overcoat and pulled out his wallet. "Will you be my guest?"

"I pay my own way, thank you."

"Surely a young lady like yourself . . ."

"I pay my own way," she repeated. Then she smiled. "But I'll save a seat for you next to mine, if you like."

Her smile was amazing. Finbar luxuriated in it for a moment while every other thought skittered from his mind. Recovering himself, he bought a program at the door to share with her. As they sat in their brown plush seats their arms almost, but not quite, touched. From time to time she glanced at him covertly. He whispered, "They're quite good, I think."

"I think so too, but I'm prejudiced."

"As I recall, you're a girl of strong prejudices."

Ursula was about to take offense until he laughed out loud. Then her own effervescent laughter bubbled up.

"Ssshhh!" hissed someone behind them.

With an effort they controlled themselves. They dare not look at one another for fear of laughing again.

When the performance ended Finbar invited Ursula to a café near the hall for hot chocolate. Remembering her aversion to smoking, he left his cigarettes in his pocket.

She studied his face across the table. Beneath the fiery hair was a wholesome, open countenance, with warm brown eyes and blunted features, as if a finer face had been drawn and then partially rubbed out. Only his ears were distinctive. Instead of being rounded at the top they were almost pointed, like a faun's.

Finbar Cassidy was one of the plain people of Ireland. The native Gaels who had suffered conquest and humiliation and impoverishment until the mere fact of survival was a miracle. All that remained of an ancient race of warrior kings.

Ursula opened the conversation with a classic Irish question. "Where are your people from, Mr. Cassidy?"

"Finbar, please. My father's fathers have fished the coasts of Donegal for generations. Before that they were farmers in Fermanagh until Cromwell drove them out and planted Protestant settlers on their land. My mother, God have mercy on her, was a MacMahon my father met at the fish market in Galway. She claimed descent from Brian Bóru, but sure, everyone in Ireland does that."

"How do you know so much about them?"

"Once the sun sets, there's not much for fishermen to do but mend their nets by the fire and tell stories. And what's more interesting than stories about one's own family?"

Ursula took a sip of her chocolate. Dabbed her mouth with a napkin. *Stories about one's own family. Exploring the roots that go back . . .*

Finbar intruded on her reverie. "Suddenly you seem far away. What're you thinking?"

"Nothing."

His quick grin flashed amid a blizzard of freckles. "I never met anyone less likely to be thinking nothing."

Young ladies at Surval were taught to respond gracefully to compliments from young men, but Ursula Halloran would never be comfortable with compliments. Sometimes she did not even recognize them. "Be assured that I am in the habit of saying what I mean, Mr. Cassidy," she said tartly.

His brown eyes begged forgiveness. "I do apologize, Miss Halloran. I have a talent for wrong-footing myself with you, it seems." He reached for their handwritten bill. "I'll pay this and then take you home, if you'll allow me. Or is that something you would rather do for yourself too?"

Chapter Ten

LOUISE Hamilton put her hands on her hips in disgust. "What good did learning them fine manners do you? You should have invited that young man into the parlor, Ursula, and him after bringing you in a taxi on such a cold evening. I made sticky toffee pudding earlier," she said unnecessarily. The smell of burnt sugar lingered on the air. "You could have offered him some instead of slamming the door in his face."

"I did no such thing, Louise. I just didn't ask him in."

"And why not? A nice young man with a pensionable job. It's time you were thinking of your future, as Mr. Hamilton remarked just the other day."

"When I was a little girl," said Ursula, "I dreamed I would marry Uncle Henry."

"That's all very well, since he's not really related to you. But he's taken so."

"He is," Ursula acknowledged tonelessly. "Henry is taken."

ACCORDING to the 1926 census the Free State had the highest proportion of unmarried people in Western Europe. More than 50 percent of those between twenty-five and forty would spend the rest of their lives single. Mass emigration and a stern Catholicism that condemned sensuality and forbade sex for any reason other than procreation within marriage were largely responsible.

．　　　．　　　．

FINBAR Cassidy was not easily discouraged. At the weekend he called on Ursula and invited her to the cinema. She meant to refuse, but it was simpler just to say yes. *We've already attended a concert together. What harm can there be in going to a film?*

Outside the theater Finbar bought her a vanilla ice cream and teased her about a smear of cream on the end of her nose. Ursula's smile was so magical it made his heart leap.

Yet in unguarded moments he glimpsed a lurking sadness in the girl.

A fortnight later he accompanied her on a tour of Dublin's museums. The various collections were much as the departing British had left them, only shabbier. The government had no money to spare for items it deemed nonessential. It pained Ursula to see Ireland's cultural heritage gathering dust. *We wrested our treasures out of the lion's paw . . . for this?*

Afterward they paused in St. Stephen's Green to rest. Sitting upright on a park bench with her hands folded and her eyes downcast, Ursula reminded Finbar of a grave, quiet child who expects the worst.

He resolved to make her smile more. From then on, whenever they went out together he regaled her with jokes and funny anecdotes. When she laughed he felt as if she had given him a present.

URSULA found Finbar as comfortable to be with as an old friend, but he was also, she concluded, an amiable lightweight who never entertained a serious thought. She could not imagine him being willing to die for Ireland.

Finbar Cassidy did not compare to the pantheon of heroes in her heart.

When he asked Ursula to go to Mass with him she declined. Attending Mass with a young man implied a possible future together, and there could be none. After that she was always busy when he invited her out. Eventually he stopped calling.

MOST single Irish women—and a surprising number of married ones— were ignorant of the mechanics of reproduction. But Ursula had spent her adolescence on a farm. When neighboring farmers brought their mares to Saoirse for breeding, she had held the stallion's lead shank because no one else could control him. She had watched him mount his mares. Watched the plunging hindquarters, the thrusting, giant phallus. Smelt the heated musk. Felt passion vibrate down the lead shank into her hand.

And wondered . . .

SOMETIMES Ursula took out the only picture she had of Síle Halloran, a photograph of herself and Ned together. Called a "cabinet portrait," the glossy sepia print revealed two young people uncomfortable at the camera's scrutiny, leaning against one another as if for support. When they were together a golden circle seemed to surround them, shutting everyone else out.

Ned had changed almost beyond recognition since that picture was taken. But Síle Halloran was frozen in time. Solid cheekbones. Eyes slanted like a cat's. A wide, sensuous mouth.

The little girl called Precious had overheard someone say, "That Síle's a man's woman and no mistake."

A man's woman.

ON Saturday afternoons Ursula's female contemporaries went to the cinema together to weep over the latest romance from Hollywood. In the evenings they met at one another's homes for card parties and sandwiches filled with Galtee cheese and sliced celery. Mostly they talked about their husbands' faults—or about finding husbands.

Ursula accepted one or two such invitations, struggled to conceal her boredom, and never went again.

Instead she began attending the meetings of Dublin's Republican women, making friends among the generation that had taken an active part in 1916. Women like Geraldine Plunkett Dillon, Helena Moloney, and Kathleen Clarke. The gunwomen, as P.S. O'Hegarty called them.

Their dreams were Ursula's dream; they spoke a language she understood.

In her journal the adult Ursula wrote: "Maud Gonne's marriage to John MacBride collapsed. Constance Markievicz separated from her husband. There are women who need something larger than marriage. I am one of those women."

I am one of those women.
Ursula Halloran was consciously inventing herself.

5 January 1928
STALIN EXILES KEY OPPOSITION FIGURES
Joseph Stalin now holds all reins of power in the Soviet Union

Chapter Eleven

2RN extended its range of offerings. As the small orchestra expanded there was more music than ever, although no songs relating to the Great War were played. They were perceived as "British"—or as too painful to the sensibilities of Irish people who had lost menfolk in that war.

Other programs included Spanish for beginners, vocal impressions of famous people, and information about the care of animals. A debate between George Bernard Shaw and G.K. Chesterton was rebroadcast courtesy of the BBC. Mrs. Sidney Czira, another of Grace Gifford's sisters, presented a popular series entitled *The Ballad History of Ireland* under the pseudonym of John Brennan. She had been a contributor to the station since its very beginning.

In May of 1928 Seán T. O'Kelly spoke heatedly in the Dáil about John Brennan. Her contract for broadcasting had been broken because one of her letters was published in the newspapers. The letter expressed her political opinions, O'Kelly said, which were not the same as his, but he strongly disapproved of depriving her of part of her livelihood for simply expressing her opinion.[1]

Ursula volunteered for every job that came up within the station and offered numerous ideas for new programs. Other women were presenting cozily domestic radio shows. *Drawing and Painting for Children* was one of 2RN's most successful offerings. Ursula's suggested programs were intended for a wider audience with a more international view. To buttress her position she quoted the editor and poet George Russell, better known as AE: "Nationalism in every country requires a strong admixture of internationalism to prevent it becoming a stupefying drug."

Séamus Clandillon listened patiently to her arguments. Ursula had a sense of being patted on the head, like a child who has done a clever trick but is not allowed to take part in grown-up conversation. Her suggestions were not accepted.

Instead she was moved to the front of the office to greet visitors with her smile.

WE are going to have a new Republican newspaper in a year or so!" an excited Ursula wrote to Henry Mooney. "You should have stayed in Ireland. Eamon de Valera and several of his supporters intend to establish a daily called the *Irish Press*. They are offering share subscriptions in all the Dublin papers except the *Irish Independent*, which refused to accept the advertisement.[2] I pawned Saoirse's saddle and bought five shares myself. Your Little Business is now a woman of property."

ON the thirtieth of July, 1928, the Irish tricolor was raised for the first time at the Olympic Games in Amsterdam. Competing in the hammer throw, Dr. Pat O'Callaghan became the first citizen of an independent Ireland to win a gold medal in the Olympics.

When the news reached Ireland, Ursula Halloran, who hated all domestic chores, sewed in her room all night with the door locked. When she was satisfied with the result she folded a heap of fabric, wrapped it in brown paper, and slipped out of the house shortly before dawn.

Dubliners on their way to work that morning were greeted by a banner on the front gates of Trinity College, bastion of Anglicized education. Made of white cloth trimmed in green-and-orange ribbon, the banner proclaimed in bold letters: "Congratulations Pat O'Callaghan, first Olympian of the Irish Republic!" The banner was torn down, but not before a number of people saw it.

HECTOR Hamilton bought a wireless set for number 16, and Louise installed it in a place of honor in the parlor. The wet battery had to be carried to a garage for recharging. Fourpence was set aside for this purpose, saved in a jam jar on the mantle until required.

Ursula hurried home from work each day to join Louise and Hector in front of the set. While the women watched, Hector fiddled authoritatively with the cats-whiskers antenna. They crowded close to him to share the sounds leaking from the headset, which he controlled by virtue of being the man in the house. Sometimes the crackle was so loud nothing else was audible, but on rainy evenings Ireland's despised weather was an excellent conductor. Then there could be a few hours of magic.

The evening broadcast opened with a stock exchange list, brief news bulletin, and weather report. Few in Ireland knew anything about the stock exchange, but everyone was obsessed with the weather. News was the station's weakest element. Information was haphazardly gathered from the Dublin evening papers and BBC broadcasts.

At the start of one evening's program in late May it was announced that the governor-general, Tim Healy, would be giving a talk on air later. Ursula made a wry face and stood up to leave the room.

"Where are you going?" asked Louise.

"I want to be well away before Healy starts talking. He's nothing but a puppet of the British."

"Well, I want to hear him," declared Hector. The dentist was an unprepossessing little man teetering on the far rim of middle age, a compulsive talker who had discovered that the wireless gave him additional topics for conversation. When he had patients helpless in the chair, he could hold forth as never before.

Ursula left the room, muttering under her breath, *"Is binn béal ina thost."**

Healy did not speak that night after all. The news ran over time; even the weather would be cut short. "Ursula, come back and hear this!" Louise called up the stairs.

Ursula returned to the parlor. Hector gave her the headset just as Séumas Hughes said, "Gangs of loyalists in Belfast are putting Catholic neighborhoods to the torch. Early this morning a young mother who fled from her blazing home with her infant in her arms was stoned in the road. To the accompaniment of taunts and jeers from the loyalists, the child was battered to death together with its mother."

Ursula related his words verbatim to the other two.

"Monsters!" gasped Louise.

"Hooligans," said the more temperate Hamilton, "who are an insult to the name of loyalism. I cannot believe His Majesty would ever condone ..."

---

*Sweet is the sound of the silent mouth.

Incandescent with anger, Ursula whirled around and ran back up the stairs.

In one corner of her room was a carefully loosened skirting board. Behind it, chiseled into the plaster, was a recess. She eased the skirting board away from the wall and reached into the recess. Her fingers touched the reassuring surface of a Mauser semiautomatic.

The gun had once belonged to Síle Halloran, who had purchased it to replace a Luger confiscated by the British. When Henry Mooney set off to report on the War of Independence, Ursula had sneaked her mama's pistol into his luggage to keep him safe.

Henry had never spoken of it to the girl, never even mentioned he had the gun or guessed where it came from. But when he packed Ursula's belongings and sent them to number 16 while she was in Switzerland, he had included the Mauser.

She knelt on the floor for a long time, holding the gun. Turning it over and over in her hands. Fascinated by its singularity of purpose.

If I had stayed with Papa in Clare I could be wherever he is now. We would be fighting together to protect our people.

She had no doubt that Ned Halloran was in the north. Once she could have found him easily. As a wild young girl who galloped her horse across Clare with vital messages tucked into her knickers, she had been a trusted part of the IRA communications network. Between then and now lay a stretch of years. Both Ursula and Ireland had changed. The old contacts were broken.

If she asked Clandillon for time off he would give her a few days. But even if she could find Ned, he might not want her with him. She recalled all too well their last meeting. Ned Halloran was unpredictable, capable of violence.

It's a risk worth taking.

Ursula's spirit leaped from her body and ran out into the street brandishing a pistol.

Her body did not follow. Her physical self remained in the room.

She felt like a piece of paper being torn in two.

At last she put the Mauser back into its hiding place. For a long time she stood at the window, gloomily staring down at the street. A fine mist had begun falling. The mellow light of street lamps glinted on timeworn cobblestones. Walking along the pavement was a member of the Garda Síochána* doing his rounds.

*Civic Guard.

The Garda Síochána had been developed from the Royal Irish Constabulary, which was disbanded in 1922. Many members of the RIC were on the organizing committee of the new police service. There was no mention of "Royal" in the title. This was to be a new police force for a new Ireland. Although some civilians joined, preferential recruitment had been given to members of the Free State army. After the Civil War the *gardai*, or guards, were distributed throughout the country to keep the peace of the fledgling state.

Their uniforms were totally distinct from those of the old RIC. They consisted of fitted tunic and trousers of navy blue worsted woven in Ireland, with a stiff collar, snug leather belt and smart cap that bore no resemblance to the intimidating spiked helmet of their predecessors.

The largest change was in the matter of weaponry. It was felt that Ireland had suffered far too much from the consequence of armed force. With some reluctance the late Kevin O'Higgins had created a separate department known as Special Branch that was trained in the use of firearms, but they were to be employed only in exceptional situations. Ordinary members of the Garda Síochána were unarmed.

Feeling eyes upon him, the young garda in the street looked up. He could see Ursula silhouetted against the gaslight in her room. He paused long enough to touch the brim of his cap to her, then went on his way.

Her eyes followed the man until he vanished into a pool of night between the street lamps. *What sort of courage,* she wondered, *must a man have to face the darkness without weapons?*

Chapter Twelve

IN October of 1928 the broadcasting station moved into quarters in the General Post Office, which was still undergoing restoration. The new home of 2RN boasted three studios instead of one, and enough offices for an expanding staff. The doorman, "Mac" McClellan, met everyone from delivery boy to government official with a cheery greeting and a comment on the weather.

Although the improvement in space was dramatic, there were drawbacks. Entry was on the Henry Street side and uncomfortably close to the constant babble of the open-air market in Moore Street. When the windows were opened for ventilation, noise came boiling in. Because the station shared facilities with the post office, the one small lift to the upper storeys was always crowded. The ride was accompanied by a high-pitched screech of machinery reminiscent of a fingernail on a slate.

Visitors emerging on the third floor found themselves in a long, bleak corridor lined with offices. The walls were painted in flat shades of cream and gray that swallowed the light. At the end of the corridor a private staircase led to the broadcasting studios on the floor above. For acoustic purposes, the ceilings of the studios were hung with heavy draperies made from old army blankets.

The station had a distinctive, institutional smell. "Rather like burnt dust," was the way Ursula described it in a letter to Felicity.

Fliss wrote back, "How I envy your career! My days are an endless round of boring social events where I only see the same boring people. I long to meet someone different. Right now I'm stalking Sir Oswald Mosley, the new Labour MP. He is wonderfully unpredictable, having changed political parties at least twice. He is making speeches in Parliament advocating socialism, which my father insists would destroy life as we know it. Sir Oswald's wife Diana is one of the famously gorgeous Mitford sisters and was married to one of the Guinnesses—the Irish brewing family, you know. Are they friends of yours?"

The Guinnesses with their Georgian mansions and their English titles and their fine airs? Friends of mine? Hardly, Fliss. I've never even tasted the stout they brew. Ladies don't drink stout. Ursula frowned. *I wonder why not?*

On her way home from 2RN she went into the nearest pub and ordered a pint of Guinness. The bartender was embarrassed for her. He meant to refuse until he got a good look at her eyes.

He pulled the pint.

Ursula drank it.

She left the pub with dried foam clinging to her upper lip and did not bother to wipe it away.

THE station's limited newscast announced that the government planned to establish a volunteer defense force. The regular Free State army would be reduced to 5,000 men. These would act as instructors for the new recruits—who would *not* be members of the Irish Republican Army.

HENRY Mooney was convinced that taking his family to America had been the right decision. His financial situation had improved dramatically. Ella's style and grace made her welcome in the best social circles. Their two little girls, Isabella and Henrietta, were thriving. America was good for all of them. Henry was even thinking of taking out citizenship.

"This is an amazing country," he wrote to Ursula, "truly the land of opportunity. The stock market has gone through the roof and everyone, myself included, is heavily invested in stocks and shares. At first I was too cautious to do more than take a little flutter, but when the money began rolling in I bought more. I can afford to be *flaithiúlach** now. I can do those things for my family which I have always wanted to do."

To illustrate his letter, Ella had drawn a caricature of herself swathed in jewels and attended by a coterie of servants.

*lavish, generous.

. . .

At year's end an attempt was made to reconcile the various shades of out-of-power republicanism and create one cohesive political voice. Representatives from the IRA, Sinn Féin, Cumann na mBan, and the Republican left gathered in Dublin, where the long-awaited constitution of the Irish Republic was unveiled.

The document had been drafted by Mary MacSwiney, sister of Terence MacSwiney, the late lord mayor of Cork who had died on hunger strike in a British prison. The Republican constitution promised liberty, equality, and justice for all citizens, free universities, health insurance, unemployment compensation, pensions for the elderly and disabled, and a housing scheme for the underprivileged.[1]

In effect there were now two diametrically opposed governments on offer for Ireland. And two armies.

When the text of the Republican document was published Ursula added it to the box of newspaper clippings she was collecting. As soon as she had time, she meant to start a new scrapbook.

Ursula was outraged when a spokesman for the Free State used 2RN to denounce the Republican conference and its delegates. He sneered at their constitution and rejected their efforts to create a political dialogue. "While in the city these dangerous individuals shall be kept under the closest observation," he assured his listeners.

"Our people are being demonised," Ursula wrote in her journal. "If I were station manager I would never have let him in the door!"

A few days later a collection of books including works written by Victor Hugo and George Bernard Shaw were burned in County Galway on the order of the bishop of Tuam.[2]

Book burning, the deliberate destruction of ideas, was anathema to Ursula. She expected some member of government would come to Henry Street to speak up against this outrage.

None did.

In a dark mood she took herself to the pub which had served her first pint of Guinness, and ordered another.

. . .

Tension was growing between the IRA and the Cosgrave administration. There were numerous reports of illegal Republican drills and marches. More than one treatyite down the country had been shot by shadowy men who vanished into the night. Nervous cabinet members suggested the Republicans might try to seize power by force.

Two issues of *An Phoblacht*, the major Republican newsletter, were suppressed by government order. Members of its staff were arrested. In spite of this, de Valera went ahead with his plans for the *Irish Press*.

Ursula Halloran celebrated the New Year by redeeming Saoirse's saddle from the pawnshop.

In the first month of 1929 W.T. Cosgrave and Desmond FitzGerald, the minister for defense, went on a tour of the United States to encourage support for the Free State government. As a parting salute, 2RN played an hour-long program of American popular music, including jazz.

Listeners flooded the station with letters of complaint. When Ursula came in to work she found them piled on her desk with a note: Please answer these at once.

After reading the first dozen she sought out Séamus Clandillon. "Every one of these letters refers to Catholic values," she told him, "and a number of them are from the clergy. The archbishop of Tuam condemns jazz as the 'mesmeric rhythm of sensuality.'[3] We're being accused of corrupting the innocence of Irish youth! Can you believe it?"

Clandillon's expression was glum. "At Mass our parish priest condemned the broadcast in the strongest terms. And me with my whole family sitting there. The wife was not best pleased, I can tell you."

"How am I supposed to answer these complaints?"

"Tactfully. Apologize for upsetting them, and give the impression—without actually saying so—that we are, as always, in complete agreement with the Church."

Ursula looked disgusted. "I'll feel like a perfect hypocrite. Are there any other impossible jobs you'd like me to do while I'm at it?"

"I'm sorry to put you in this position. But I'll make it up to you," Clandillon promised.

A few days later he told her the station was going to use one of her program suggestions: a biographical sketch about Guglielmo Marconi, the developer of wireless communication, focusing on his connections with Ireland.* "Would you like to submit a sample script?" Clandillon offered. "Give us some interesting details about his Irish wife, that's what the women would like to hear."

Ursula worked all night on the script, writing, rewriting, staring into space looking for the perfect word or phrase, wadding up the paper in impatience and starting again.

She was dismayed to admit to herself, as gray dawn light filtered into the room, that perfection was not possible. But she had done the best she could. As she gave the script to Clandillon, she said, "Mr. O'Hegarty once told me I have a good speaking voice. May I read this on air?"

He scanned the pages. "I'm afraid not."

"But women are presenting programs all the time. You're even letting Mairead Ní Ghráda be relief announcer."

"Only when Séumas Hughes is unavailable. You're missing the point, Ursula. What you have written is a scholarly piece employing an impressive vocabulary. It isn't suitable for a female presenter."

"It's *my* vocabulary and I'm a female."

He shook his head. "I'm sorry. We'll take the piece though, and pay you for it."

She could no longer hold her temper. "I understand entirely! There is a certain 'place' for women in Ireland, and we won't be allowed to step outside it. We might as well stay home and have babies. That's all you really want us to do, isn't it?"

"Surely you know me better than that. I have to operate within the limits imposed on me, Ursula; we all do." He gave her a wan little smile. "The revolution's over, you know."

Writing to Henry, Ursula complained, "You once assured me that new opportunities had opened for women. Perhaps so, but not in Ireland. The other day I read an article in *The Voice of Ireland*. The author—a woman herself, I am ashamed to say—claimed that 'the over-involvement by women in politics has led to the neglect of sweeter and more pressing matters.[4]

"What has gone wrong, Henry? We served as equals with the men during the revolutionary years. Now we are being relegated to menial positions again."

Henry responded, "Ireland is still living in the last century, an era when women were to be cherished and protected. I am old-fashioned enough to

*See *Dramatis Personae*.

subscribe to that philosophy. But America has opened my eyes to what is possible for people who accept no limits on their ambition. Do not let anyone put you in a box, Ursula.

"I have done some expanding myself. After a considerable amount of soul-searching I have sold the newspaper and purchased a small printing company in Dallas. Advertising leaflets, calling cards, headed notepapers. 'Quality a Specialty' is our motto.

"Ella never came right out and said she was unhappy in Muleshoe, but her joy at living in a city again is obvious. We are building a new house with six bedrooms and the latest in electric lighting.

"Ella plans to have redbud and dogwood trees lining the approach to the house, and crepe myrtles and snowballs and many other shrubs I never heard of before. Yesterday we ordered a set of wicker rocking chairs. On hot summer evenings we shall sit on the veranda and drink iced tea and watch the fireflies twinkle on and off like stars."

WHEN Henry thought of Ireland it was usually Ursula's face he saw. He was unaware that his letters had begun to sound like those of a rejected sweetheart trying to impress a lost love with his current situation.

THE majority of IRA Volunteers were survivors of the Black and Tan reign of terror that had ended with the War of Independence. The Volunteers had obeyed the order to dump their weapons after the subsequent Civil War, but some had never demobilized emotionally. They believed the Republic was still to be won and were actively soliciting aid from America. This took the form of cash for operating expenses—and weaponry such as Thompson machine guns.

Although the Cosgrave administration was deeply concerned, Republican sympathizers in the Dáil turned a blind eye to this activity. During a heated parliamentary exchange in Leinster House one of de Valera's T.D.s, Seán Lemass, accurately if imprudently described Fianna Fáil as a "slightly constitutional party."[5]

ON the fifth of February, 1929, Eamon de Valera was arrested on the border of County Armagh and taken to Belfast jail for infringing an order prohibiting him to enter Northern Ireland. W.T. Cosgrave personally made representations to the Northern Ireland government seeking his release, but de Valera was forced to serve a token sentence.

11 February 1929
BENITO MUSSOLINI SIGNS TREATY WITH POPE PIUS XI CREATING VATICAN STATE

Chapter Thirteen

RECOGNITION of the Vatican's independent sovereignty was hailed by Irish Catholics for its religious significance. To others it was simply a political development.

Following the Treaty, southern Protestants had found themselves in a new Irish state proud of its nationalist and Catholic credentials. Although they did not suffer from discrimination as did Catholics in the north, they were uncomfortably associated with the former British regime.

A large number moved to England. Far fewer moved to Northern Ireland. Those who remained had personal or business ties inextricably linked with the south and could not imagine leaving. They negotiated the difficult path into a new Ireland by becoming increasingly Irish in thought and outlook.

But they did not read Catholic newspapers and they did not light candles for Mussolini.

EILEEN Halloran was a great worry to her family. Since the age of sixteen she had kept company with one young man after another. Again and again Norah Daly had predicted marriage, only to be disappointed. Had Eileen been on the Continent, she would have been envied for her popularity. In Ireland she was a liability. People were talking.

So Ursula could imagine the relief with which Norah Daly wrote in March, "Eileen has agreed to marry Lucas Mulvaney from Quin. The wedding will take place on the twenty-third of this month."

The sudden announcement was a surprise. A betrothal of at least a year was customary. Nor could Ursula recall any of Eileen's suitors who was named Mulvaney. *Unless he was one of those lads she used to meet at dances. She always did attract the handsome ones.*

"What good news, Aunt Norah!" she replied by return post. "I shall ask for Friday and Monday off so I can attend the wedding. I am sure you have put notices in the *Clare Champion*, but please put them in the Belfast and Derry newspapers as well. Perhaps Papa will see them."

THE train rattled over the tracks; tracks blown up during the War of Independence, then barely patched before they were blown up again during the Civil War. In their fractured iron they bore the scars of a fractured nation.

No one mentioned the condition of the tracks. A sort of national amnesia was underway. The revolutionary decade that had won a limited degree of freedom from Britain was being dismissed from the consciousness of the Irish people in an act of emotional self-preservation. They were willing to settle for what they had, flawed and incomplete as it was.

The terrible poverty that afflicted cities and towns existed in the country too, though it was not as immediately obvious. People with a little bit of land were able to subsist on what they could grow. Starvation had not been a problem in rural Ireland since the Great Famine. However, vast numbers of people still lived in dilapidated cabins innocent of sanitation. They had no money, but worked through the barter system. Their lives were little changed from the lives of their great-grandparents. Under British rule they had possessed no more than they had now.

But now they were free.

FRANK met Ursula at the Ennis station with the farm wagon, a high-sided vehicle pulled by two shaggy draft horses. "The county council's tarring the Ennis road and they're letting people buy the empty barrels for next nothing," Frank said, "so we'll collect some on the way home. They have all sorts of uses."

Eying the filthy wagon, she gestured ruefully at her good beige coat. "Could you not have brought the pony and trap?"

"We put the pony down before Christmas," Frank told her as he tossed her small suitcase into the wagon bed.

"Poor Tad! Did he break a leg?"

"He was too old to be of any more use," the man said. Country people were not sentimental about animals. He added, "I could drive that horse of yours if he would pull a cart, but he won't accept a harness."

"Saoirse's a saddle horse," Ursula said indignantly.

Frank scowled. "Can't ride him either; he goes wild if anyone tries. He won't pull a plough, and thanks to what that fool brother of mine did, we can't stand him at stud to the local farmers anymore. So there's that bit of income gone. Divvil a soul will buy him now, not even a tinker."

Ursula folded her fingers tightly over her thumbs. "Let me remind you that you can't sell Saoirse anyway, Frank. He's mine." She kept her voice calm. Frank could be as stubborn as Ned. If she argued with him, he might wait until she had gone and then sell the horse anyway. It was best to change the subject. "Have you heard anything from Papa?"

"Not a sausage." Frank flapped the reins at the plough horses, who broke into a shambling trot. "It's just as well," Frank went on. "This wedding is cursed enough without Ned blowing in like the east wind."

She gave him a quizzical glance but he said nothing more.

Norah Daly insisted on welcoming Ursula to the farm with a brimming mug of heated milk and sugared bread, a childhood treat known as "goody" that the young woman had long since outgrown. She consumed it obediently, however, and forced an appreciative smile.

Norah then took Ursula upstairs to her former bedroom and firmly closed the door behind them. In an urgent whisper the old woman said, "Before you see Eileen I have to warn you. She's showing."

"Showing? You don't mean . . . is she . . ."

"She is," Norah affirmed, crimson with shame. "Weddings should be in May, but this one won't wait any longer. Thanks be to God he's marrying her at all." The old woman's thin lips closed over her disapproval as tightly as a farmer's purse.

There were none of the celebratory trappings Ursula had expected for the wedding. No crowd of neighbor women helping with the cooking and baking, no sheets and quilts being aired on fences and hedgerows, no small children taking up the stones that marked the borders of the path to the house and scrubbing them to pristine whiteness to welcome guests.

No guests; only the families of the bride and groom.

"Don't say anything," Eileen hissed to Ursula when they met in the kitchen. "I can't bear it if you say anything." There was a new, sullen set to her mouth. She was as plump as ever; plumper. But her youthful freshness was gone.

"I wasn't going to say anything, Eilie, except I hope you'll be very happy."

"Happy. How can I be happy when I've got meself trapped?"

"Is Lucas Mulvaney that fine-looking lad who plays the tin whistle? Lots of girls would think you're lucky."

"Lucas is forty years old and as ugly as lye soap," Eileen contradicted. "And he's never played music in his life. He works in a slaughterhouse."

Ursula raised her eyebrows. "He owns an abattoir?"

"I said he *works* there. Lucas sluices the killing floor after the cattle are slaughtered." Her words began to rush over one another, anxious to get it all out at once. "He lives with a whole rake of brothers and sisters on a rented smallholding that's good for nothing but growing rocks. That's why he was willing to marry me. Frank arranged it."

"But is Lucas not the . . ." Ursula's glance dropped to Eileen's swelling waist.

"He is not! You think I'd let myself be tumbled by the likes of him? The scrapings from the bottom of the barrel?" Tears rose to flood level in her eyes.

"Then who?"

"God!" cried Eileen. Her voice shivered like glass about to break. "The child is God's and I'm the Virgin Eileen!"

URSULA found Saoirse turned out in a distant field, barely surviving on the exhausted grass of late winter. Oats were no longer being grown on the farm. The horse's ribs resembled the timbers of a wrecked ship; his protruding hipbones formed a hat rack. When she called to him the gray horse threw up his head and stared for a moment, then broke into a trot. By the time he reached the gate he was galloping.

Ursula gathered his big head into her arms and baptized it with her tears. "I'm sorry, *a stor,** so sorry. I didn't know, I thought they would take care of you."

Her sense of betrayal was acute.

THE wedding was held in a side chapel as cold and dark as bog water. Father Durcan had refused to conduct the ceremony in the main church. The bride's loosely fitted frock was gray wool trimmed with Limerick lace.

---

*"My darling."

The groom was distinguished by profuse sweating and a fat neck that overflowed his collar like pudding spilling out of a basin.

Eileen's family kept an anxious eye on the bride, who had been teetering between depression and hysteria. The Mulvaneys were in better spirits. One of theirs was marrying up.

Afterward the party adjourned to the Halloran farm. There was no wedding feast. Norah Daly shooed the rowdy Mulvaney clan into the parlor, from which she had removed all breakables except Frank's small collection of records, stacked beside the gramophone to provide a salubrious atmosphere. Tea would be served to the women. The men expected something stronger.

The priest did not join them. Even the confessional had not extirpated the stain of Eileen's prenuptial fecundity to his satisfaction. "Father Durcan will be quick enough to urge Eileen to have scores of babies now that she's married, though," Lucy remarked as she and Ursula were slicing fruitcake and putting the kettle on the boil.

The half-door creaked to announce a latecomer arriving. Glancing up, Ursula gasped. "Papa!"

They stared at one another across the debris of the past.

"Papa," Ursula repeated. Softly. Not a plea, but an invitation to cease hostilities.

A muscle tightened in Ned Halloran's jaw. "Came for the wedding," he said as if every syllable hurt him.

"I hoped you would."

Ned was thinner than ever and his mop of black curls had turned to grizzled gray wire. A livid scar zigzagged from his sharp cheekbone to his left temple. His right ear was crumpled like wadded paper. As he gazed at Ursula a green fire ignited in the deep hollows of his eye sockets: an intense beam that searched and scorched.

When Lucy spoke they were both startled, so intense had their focus been on each other. "Ned Halloran, it's about time you surfaced! Poor Aunt Norah's been worried threadless. Every morning she's off to Mass to pray for you."

Ned turned toward his body toward Lucy without taking his eyes off Ursula. "Is she now." His voice had a knife edge.

"She is, ye ungrateful git," snapped Lucy.

"And you," Ned addressed Ursula in the same hard tone. "Do you pray for me too?"

Her clenched fists clutched her thumbs in the effort to keep her voice steady. "At Mass I light a candle for you. And before I go to bed I ask God to keep you safe."

Lucy gave a sudden sob. "I was afraid you were killt!"

Ned bounded forward and gathered his sister into his arms. She buried her face against his chest. Over her head, Ned's eyes met Ursula's again. "Precious?" he whispered.

When he opened his embrace to include her, she flew to him.

That was how Norah found them when she entered the kitchen. "What's keeping you with the . . . merciful hour! It's yourself!"

"It is myself," Ned agreed gravely.

His arms opened again.

"He's back!" Norah shrieked. "Come here everyone, our Ned's home!"

Hallorans and Mulvaneys surrounded Ned and carried him off to the parlor like a trophy. He was seated in Frank's favorite chair. A glass of Frank's favorite whiskey was put into his hand and refilled as soon as he took a drink. Norah ran back and forth between parlor and kitchen, urging food upon him and giving him anxious little pats to assure herself that he was, indeed, home.

If things were different, Eileen would have resented his stealing the limelight at her wedding. Under the circumstances it was a blessing.

Generations of rural inbreeding had given the Mulvaneys vacuous, interchangeable faces. Male and female alike were staring at Ned in openmouthed awe. *At least they have enough wits to recognize a genuine hero when they see one,* Ursula thought. Then she noticed a strange expression on Frank's face. He watched his younger brother with something akin to hatred.

Resolutely apolitical, Frank had never involved himself in Ireland's struggle for independence. He had stayed on the farm and done his best to support the family. No one had ever said thank you. No one had ever looked at him the way people were looking at Ned now.

After a few minutes he muttered about needing to tend to the livestock and left the house.

No sooner had Frank gone than the Mulvaneys began firing questions at Ned. "Were you in the north?" one of Lucas's brothers demanded to know.

"Could be." Gazing down into his glass, Ned swirled the whiskey like a fortune-teller examining tea leaves.

"Did ye shoot any Prods up there?" A female Mulvaney clasped her hands together under her receding chin and waited for gory details.

Ursula found their avidity unnerving. "Can't you see he doesn't want to talk about it?"

But the interrogation went on. "Who was with you?" "Any boys from Clare?" "What weapons had ye?"

Ned took a long drink and stared off into space.

His questioners persisted. "Did ye kill any o'them dirty loyalists? You can tell us, we're family now."

Norah lost her temper. "Go away out o'that! We're after having a wedding, there'll be no talk about killing. Lucy, give these men another wee drop before they die of thirst."

By the scruff of its neck the conversation was dragged to other topics. For an hour the Hallorans listened to the Mulvaneys complaining about their lot in life: their unproductive land, their avaricious landlord, their unrelenting bad luck. Then they went home with their pockets stuffed with chocolate biscuits and Norah's sausage rolls. Ursula saw one of the men hide a bottle of Frank's whiskey under his coat just before he nipped out the door.

The parlor filled with evening shadows. Getting to his feet, Ned paced the room, pausing from time to time to glance out the window.

"What's wrong with you at all?" Norah asked him.

"I don't like to sit still. Is Frank not back yet?"

"I didn't hear him come in."

Ned continued pacing. Ursula followed him with her eyes.

The newlyweds were to spend their wedding night in the Halloran house. Norah had cleaned and aired the large front bedroom. Her best red-and-white quilt was on the bed. Although Eileen postponed the moment as long as she could, the couple retired early. When they had gone upstairs the parlor filled with an embarrassed silence. Words sank like stones into a bottomless pool.

As soon as Frank came in, Norah prepared the house for the night. She put the few remaining scraps of food into a bucket for the pigs, tidied up the kitchen, banked the fires. A small lantern was placed beside the kitchen door to light the way to the outdoor privy, the earth closet, in its shed. The family took turns making the short journey.

When Ursula's turn came she placed the lantern on the small shelf beside the wooden seat before she sat down. The familiar pungent odor of the privy enveloped her. Wavering lantern light danced on the rough plank walls. This too was familiar. She recalled the way she used to create shadow plays to amuse herself.

The splintery wood divided one large shadow into two separate figures.

Lifting the lantern, Ursula manipulated the light until the two halves came together again. Suddenly they reminded her of animals mating.

A lance of heat ran up her spine.

FRANK Halloran was waiting at the kitchen door to take the lantern from her hand. He did not meet her eyes.

When she heard Ned enter the bedroom next to hers, Ursula slipped out of bed. Her bare feet remembered the strip of Turkey carpet on the floor. Nose and toes and fingertips, the farm was imprinted upon her. Her place and not her place. She had no place as she had no father.

She knocked on the wall. "Papa? It's me. May I talk with you a while?"

There was no reply.

She filled her stoneware washbasin with water from the matching pitcher and scrubbed her face. The water was bitterly cold. *I should have thought to bring up heated water from the kitchen.* She recalled winter mornings when she had broken the ice in her washbasin with the handle of her hairbrush.

Climbing into bed, Ursula snuggled under the covers. After a while she realized she was listening for Ned's voice, for his agonizing one-sided dialogue with Síle.

Ursula went to the wall and knocked again. "Papa?"

A flurry of small, unidentifiable sounds was followed by silence. Then Ned called, "Come in if you wish."

He met her at his door. He was still dressed, though Norah had left a fresh flannel nightshirt on his bed. "Are you not sleepy?" he asked.

"Not yet. There are so many things I wanted to ask you, but I didn't think you wanted to talk in front of the others."

"I don't, Ursula."

Ursula. Not Precious anymore.

"Did you get any of my letters? I used to write to you every week, from Dublin, from Switzerland . . . I wrote to you when I went to work at the broadcasting station . . ."

He went to the locker beside his bed and opened a drawer. "I kept your letters here."

The drawer, she noticed, was now empty. "You read them?"

"Of course."

"But you didn't answer them."

"I didn't answer them."

Why not? Oh Papa, why not? Part of her wanted to scrape the scab off the wound; clear her conscience by assigning all blame for their quarrel to him; vilify him for what he had done to Saoirse. But that would break the thread reconnecting them. Tenuous cobweb connection composed of loving memories rather than blood.

"I'm sorry, Papa," she said. She hoped he would reply in kind, but Ned Halloran had always been stubborn.

Someone has to give and I can do it. "I'm so sorry," Ursula reiterated. "Please say you forgive me."

The skin around his eyes tightened until he—almost—smiled. "If you carry a lamb long enough it becomes a sheep. I don't want to carry a sheep on my aching back for the rest of my life."

Ursula gave a relieved laugh. "Then will you forgive Henry too?"

The shutters closed in Ned's face. "That's different."

She shied away from the subject. "I noticed you were reluctant to talk with the Mulvaneys."

"Never tell people more than they need to know, that's a rule of the IRA. Eileen's in-laws don't need any information about me."

"Do I?"

"It would be safer if you had none. I don't want you involved with that anymore."

"Will you at least tell me if you were in the north?"

"I was of course. I was needed there."

"Is it very terrible? We hardly get any news from across the border."

"The government doesn't want you to know," Ned replied. "It's an Irish solution for an Irish problem: ignore it and it will go away. Cosgrave and company think that's the only way to maintain peace with Britain." His lips curled in a contemptuous sneer. "Peace. With Britain. Translate that as 'keep knuckling the forelock and bending the knee and perhaps they'll let us keep our poor fractured country, as much of it as we have by His Majesty's grace and favor!'

"I'll give you an example of what life is like in the north, Ursula. The first Christmas I spent there, myself and another Volunteer stayed in a Republican safe house in Belfast. A shabby tenement, as bad as anything you'd see in the slums of Dublin. That's all that's available for Catholics up there.

"Our host's old father and mother came up from the country for the holidays; all of us crammed together in the one small house. The family had not eaten turkey in years; the younger children had never tasted one. Their father had been out of work for five years. A fine, decent, able-bodied man, but no one would hire him because he was Catholic. His family had a feast that Christmas, though. I liberated a strutting big tom turkey from a poultry yard in a Protestant neighborhood and we polished that bird's bones.

"It was a treat to see the faces around the table. Smiling, laughing even. Grease on their chins and eyes full of stars. After the children had been put to bed the adults had a little celebration of their own. When country people come up to Belfast to visit their relatives, they like to play cards and drink whiskey and speak Irish. Irish is still spoken in the north, to some extent. But not for much longer."

"Why?"

"Because at any moment, day or night, the door may crash open and a loyalist gang comes in shouting and roaring, breaking up the furniture." Ned's voice sank deep in his chest and one eyelid twitched. "If they catch anyone speaking Irish they beat them to death."

Intuition warned Ursula what was coming.

"That Christmas night," said Ned, "fifteen men broke into the safe house. My guard was down, I admit it, so what happened was my fault. But I'll never let my guard down again. They battered us with clubs and rifles until no one had enough strength left to fight back, then they tore the place apart. They left one old woman and three men dead. The bastards thought I was dead too, but I'm hard to kill. They practically tore my ear off with a blow from a rifle butt, though. I'm deaf on that side now."

Ursula felt sick to her stomach. "What did the police do about it?"

Ned gave a bark of harsh laughter. "The Royal Ulster Constabulary? There was no point in sending for them, not for a Catholic family. They might arrive a day or two later and have a look, but in the finish-up, nothing would be done and no charges filed."

"Are there no Catholics in the police force up there?"

"A few, but they do as they're told. The RUC belongs body and soul to the loyalists. It's their private army. All our people have is the IRA: me and those like me. I memorized the faces of the men who murdered my friends that night. We've taken out two of them already and we'll get the others. Sooner or later."

His voice was ice. His eyes were ice. "Is Mulvaney responsible for Eileen's trouble?" he asked abruptly. "Or was it someone else?"

He would kill the man without thinking twice! Ursula realized. "I don't know, Papa. Surely you wouldn't . . . I mean, Lucas is her husband now, and . . ."

"He'd best be good to her then," Ned grated.

There were so many things she wanted to say to him: stepping-stones to carry them back across the quagmire to earlier, happier times. But those times had been shared with her Papa, not this frozen, bitter man.

Perhaps tomorrow in the daylight it would be easier. She started toward the door.

"Where are you going?"

"To bed, Papa. I'm tired, and you must be too."

"I'm never tired," he said brusquely. "Did Frank come in yet?"

"He did of course. You were there, don't you remember?"

Ned's eyes were, briefly, blank. "Remember?" He raised one hand and stroked his forehead. "Of course I remember."

"Does your head hurt? Is the old wound bothering you?"

"My head never hurts."

She knew he was lying. "Is there anything you need?"

"I have everything I need."

She could not leave it at that. "Even when you're . . . away? What do you do for money, Papa? I worry about you, you know. How do you live? The IRA can't afford to pay the Volunteers."

"Kathleen sends me money." He did not elaborate, but Ursula was not surprised. Kathleen in America was a dedicated supporter of the Republican movement.

With an effort, Ned roused himself enough to add, "Go to bed now, it's way past time. And lock your door. Be sure to lock your door."

His words surprised Ursula. There had never been locks on any door in the house.

Just before she left the room she turned and looked back at Ned standing there in his rumpled clothes, his face pale with weariness. "I love you," she said.

That blank look again. Then, "I love you too, Síle," he replied.

URSULA thought she would never go to sleep. She kept waiting for the sound of his voice in the next room. Eventually she sank into a fuzzy grayness, then slid deeper into a darkness broken by kaleidoscopic dreams. She was awakened by a pounding on the door downstairs. The front door, not the kitchen door that people habitually used.

Ursula threw a shawl over her nightdress and went out onto the landing. From the top of the stairs, she strained to overhear Frank's conversation with the midnight callers.

"Is Edward Joseph Halloran here?" an unfamiliar voice was demanding to know.

Ursula stiffened. She had heard that tone, if not that voice, before. When she was a little girl living in Louise Kearney's lodging house, the British had come for Ned and sent him off to prison in England; a prison from which he returned a changed man.

"Why are you looking for him, Constable?" Frank Halloran asked.

"We have an order for his arrest."

Ursula ran to Ned's door and scratched at it urgently. "Papa, the police!" she hissed.

No answer.

She returned to the top of the stairs. Within moments, the constables could be heard searching the rooms below.

Norah and Lucy, both still in nightdress, joined Ursula. "Are you ear-wigging again?" Lucy asked. "I thought you'd outgrown that habit."

Ursula pressed a finger to her lips. "Keep your voice down. The constables are here, looking for Ned."

"Bastards," Norah muttered.

Ursula turned to the old woman. "Who told them he was here, Aunt Norah?"

"I don't know. There are informers everywhere."

One of the constables started up the stairs. Seeing the three women huddled at the top he said, "I'm sorry, ladies, but I'll have to ask you to step aside. We have information that a wanted man is hiding here."

Ursula said, "We aren't the sort of people who hide."

He gave her a surprised look. "English, are you?"

"How dare you insult me!" She deliberately raised her voice to alert Ned. "Don't members of the constabulary recognize an educated Irish accent when they hear one?"

The constable—he was very young and obviously embarrassed—ducked his chin. "I'm sorry. I . . . step aside, please. We don't any want trouble."

Her eyes blazed. "You'll have plenty of trouble if you try to take anyone out of this house tonight!"

Anger roared through Ursula like a forest fire. It felt wonderful. The war had come to her now; her opportunity to do battle. She had a vision of herself springing upon the constable, knocking him backward down the stairs and pummeling him with her fists.

He read it in her eyes and hesitated. "I'm just following orders, miss."

"Let it be," said Norah Daly, laying a firm hand on Ursula's arm. "You'll just make things worse, girl."

Ursula was trembling from head to foot.

"Let it be!" Norah commanded.

The young constable edged past, watching Ursula warily from the corner of his eye.

Chapter Fourteen

WHEN the constable knocked on the door of the large bedroom Lucas Mulvaney shouted, "Can't a man have no peace on his wedding night?" The constable opened the door and thrust his head inside, then backed out, looking more embarrassed than ever.

Ursula's bedroom was across the hall. The door was ajar. A glance showed no one inside but the constable examined the room anyway, including looking under the bed.

The next door was closed. Ursula held her breath.

The young constable rapped the door with his knuckles. No response. When he knocked harder the door swung open. The room was empty, the bed stripped. No trace of Ned Halloran remained.

The constables spent a long time searching the house but found nothing. A search of the barn and outbuildings yielded the same result. At last they apologized and left.

When they had gone Lucy flung open the door of the big bedroom. "Lucas Mulvaney, put your clothes on and get out of this house right now!"

Eileen cried, "What are you talking about?"

"One of your husband's wretched relatives informed on my brother."

"Now Lucy," Norah said, following her into the room, "we don't know that."

"Of course we do. Who else even knew he was here? Get out you!" she shrieked at Lucas. "Leave here tonight and don't come back! You're lucky I don't take the shotgun to you. We shoot informers."

"What about me?" wailed Eileen.

"Go with him! You married this maggot, that makes you a Mulvaney too. I don't want either of you in my parents' bedroom for another minute. You can sleep in the parlor until dawn, but after that I don't want you anywhere near this farm. Ever."

When Frank appeared in the doorway, Eileen threw out her hands imploringly to her brother. "Are you going to let this happen?"

He did not respond. His face was closed and hard.

Ursula went into her room and closed the door.

By the time she came down to breakfast the couple had gone. No one mentioned either of them. Conversation centered on the weather and the farm chores. Norah and Lucy argued about making pickles.

Ned had once told Ursula that the ancient bards punished those who broke the law by ceasing to remember them. They were expunged from tribal memory. Denied heritage and birthright.

Ursula returned to Dublin on Monday afternoon to find a long letter from Felicity awaiting her. She took the letter upstairs and curled up on her bed to read it before she even unpacked. She wanted something to distract her from a black mood.

At the end of the letter the English girl mentioned a new British airmail service that would serve India, Egypt, Palestine, and Iraq. "My brother Cedric is one of the pilots they have recruited from the Royal Air Force. Do you remember when airmen seemed so glamorous? In the Great War they duelled in the sky like knights of old. Now flying aeroplanes has become a job like any other. Silly old Cedric is quite blasé about it, but he is blasé about everything. I am the only true enthusiast in my family. Perhaps I shall learn to fly and become an aviatrix."

Although regular air services had not yet been established in Ireland, civilian adventurers had been taking to the air since 1910. At one time an Irish woman, Mrs. Elliot Lynn, had been the only woman in the world to hold a commercial pilot's license.[1] Britain's Royal Air Force had stationed squadrons at Baldonnel Aerodrome, southwest of Dublin. During the War of Independence Michael Collins had hoped to capture one of their planes to "disturb the Black and Tans in their strongholds."[2] Now the Irish Air Corps, a part of the national army, was based at Baldonnel.

Flying machines, mused Ursula, gazing out the window at a Dublin sky heavy with coal smoke. *Electricity, radio waves . . . not so long ago, people would have called all those things magic.*

She imagined herself togged out in a helmet and white silk scarf, swooping through the clouds like an eagle.

I wonder if I would be airsick the way I was seasick.
Somehow she did not think so.

WHEN Ursula received her next pay packet, she asked how soon she might expect a rise in wages. Clandillon said, "I didn't realize how valuable you are until we had to do without you for a couple of days, but I'm afraid we can't afford to give you any more money. Perhaps you'd like to present a program of household hints on air instead?"

"Housework is nothing more than penal servitude for women," Ursula replied scathingly.

Clandillon raised his hands in mock horror. "Don't shoot! I didn't mean to insult you."

The weather changed abruptly; Ursula gave him a smile so radiant he blinked. "You can make it up to me," she suggested. "Let me present a program of international news highlights. I correspond with people in both Europe and America, so I have plenty of sources."

Clandillon shook his head. "We get adequate information through the BBC news service."

"We do not! The BBC reports whatever serves British interests and that isn't always the true picture."

"Then let's just say the public does not want to hear a female voice giving hard news, Ursula."

"Mairead does the news and I never heard of anyone complaining."

"Mairead is not only our relief announcer, but an old friend of the minister for finance. We need his goodwill, such as it is," Clandillon pointed out.

That night Ursula took the envelope from beneath her mattress and carefully counted the contents. Ella's money. *If I save for twenty years I'll never be able to repay her, not on my salary. Henry's wealthy now. They don't need this.*

Yet it was a debt of honor. Drilled into her by Ned Halloran, honor, integrity, and courage formed the bedrock of her scrupled soul.

Ursula sat on the floor, holding the envelope. Remembering a rake-thin gray horse in a barren field. A heavy head pressed against her body. Trusting her.

She spilled the contents of the envelope onto the floor and divided them in half.

2 April 1929

Dear Aunt Norah,

I am enclosing a postal order for some money and shall send more every month. Please use this to purchase oats for my horse. See that he has two full measures every day, and a warm bran mash once a week in cold weather. His hooves are to be trimmed every two months. If Frank refuses, remind him that Saoirse is mine. Frank has no rights in the matter.

She narrowed her eyes, looking down at the words she had written. Then she added, "If he still refuses, tell him I know what he did. If anything happens to Saoirse I will tell Papa."

She did not know if her guess was correct; she hoped it was not. But even if Frank was not the informer, surely he had done some thing, some time, which he would not want Ned to know.

Everyone had sins.

Blackmail was a sin.

On Friday Ursula went to Confession, fully intending to expiate her crime. As she sat in the pew with her eyes on the confession box, waiting her turn, she hesitated. Then she got up and left the church. She could not have explained why.

A few days later the broadcasting station received a pair of important visitors. One was Ernest Blythe, for whom Mairead Ní Ghráda had worked in the first Dáil. Blythe, an ally of the late Kevin O'Higgins, was the minister for finance. His rapidly receding hairline, round face, thick lips, and imperious stare, were familiar to the Irish public from newspaper photographs. He was notorious for having cut the already miniscule pension of the nation's elderly. A great public outcry had followed, but Blythe was not the sort of man to be moved by either hostile or constructive criticism.

IRISH nationalists had believed prosperity would almost immediately blossom as soon as British rule was gone. But the economic fabric of the country had been destroyed. The British government had used southern Ireland almost exclusively to produce food for England. Industrial development was concentrated in the northeastern six counties. With this region lost through partition, the new nation had no industrial base upon which to build.

In the struggle to make the Free State financially viable, Cosgrave's cabinet was waging a virtual campaign against the unproductive elements of society. For the poor, the aged, and the unemployed, Saorstát Éireann was a far cry from Pearse's Irish Republic. Yet there was little choice. The government was trying to build a state from the rubble of dreams.

Accompanying Blythe was a man whom he identified as "my boyhood pal, Seán Lester." Lester was a neatly dressed, dark-complexioned man of average height, with intelligent eyes. Like Ernest Blythe he was in his early forties and spoke with a northern accent. But while the autocratic Blythe held himself apart from the lower-echelon employees, Lester had a greeting for everyone.

He showed a genuine interest in the operation of the broadcasting station. Mairead conducted a tour of the facilities for his benefit. They paused by Ursula's desk. "Ernest and Seán and I are going out for a meal later," Mairead said. "Would you join us to make an even number?"

"Please do," Lester added, smiling down at Ursula.

"Where are you going?"

"Have you a suggestion?" he asked.

"Wynn's Hotel."

Lester chuckled. *"Ceart go leor."**

UNTIL that afternoon Ursula's only communication with Ernest Blythe had consisted of writing letters seeking funds for the station. As she sat across a table from him, the minister for finance muttered, "Halloran, Halloran. Ursula Halloran?" He turned to Mairead, seated on his right. "Is that young woman U. Halloran, by any chance?"

"Guilty," Ursula said.

He swung around to give her a basilisk stare. "You certainly do write a forceful letter."

She refused to be cowed. "Not forceful enough, apparently. You keep refusing our requests."

Like the sun rising over a frosty meadow, Ernest Blythe smiled. "I like this one," he remarked to Mairead.

Ursula decided she hated him. Not because he was pro-Treaty; not even because of his past association with Kevin O'Higgins. But because he spoke of her in the third person as if she were not in the room.

She dropped her eyes to conceal a flare of antipathy.

*"Right enough."

Chapter Fifteen

SEÁN Lester was sensitive to undercurrents. Waiting until Mairead and her former employer were engaged in reminiscing, he said softly, "Ernest isn't as bad as some people think, Miss Halloran. I've known him since we were boys together in Antrim, and he was my best man when I married Elsie."

"That's nice," murmured Ursula, stirring her soup. Carrot and parsnip. Not enough salt. She briefly surrendered to her old habit of earwigging; eavesdropping shamelessly on the conversation across the table. Mairead glanced up and met her eyes; smiled.

Why should she not use her friendship with Blythe to get a promotion? Ursula asked herself. *I got my job through my friendship with Henry. That's how the world works, isn't it?*

Even if it's not fair.

Seán Lester was saying, "Things haven't always been easy for Ernest. When he was barely fifteen he had to go to work as a clerk in the Department of Agriculture under the old British administration. But he's always thought of himself as Irish. Did you know he's the first northern Protestant to become a government minister in the south? He's very proud of the fact, he even likes to be called Earnán de Blaghd."

Ursula broke off a piece of bread and buttered a small portion. "It takes more than using an Irish name to make one an Irishman."

"Ernest's done a lot more. He joined the Dungannon Clubs that Bulmer Hobson founded in Belfast to unite young Protestants and Catholics in the effort to achieve independence for Ireland. Some say the Dungannon Clubs inspired Arthur Griffith.[1] Eventually, of course, they were absorbed into Sinn Féin."

Ursula ate slowly, listening to Lester make a case for Blythe. His loyalty to a friend impressed her.

Lester said, "Ernest and I were both members of the Gaelic League—he learned Irish from Sinéad Flanagan, who is de Valera's wife—so he recruited me for the Dungannon Clubs as well. The membership was never very large, but always ardent. You should have seen us: students and clerks and shop workers dreaming of overthrowing the British Empire! Have you ever heard of the Irish Republican Brotherhood?" he asked abruptly.

She frowned as if trying to remember. "The IRB? Is that not a secret organization?"

Lester gave her a shrewd look. "I suspect you know very well what it is. Anyway, Sean O'Casey invited Ernest to join the IRB. He went to the Kerry *Gaeltacht** to improve his spoken Irish and became an organizer for the Irish Volunteers. He was imprisoned by the British for his activities, so he did not get to fight in 1916."

Ursula leaned forward eagerly. "My Papa fought in the GPO with Pearse and Connolly."

A spark kindled in Lester's eyes: the ember that smoulders though the raging fire is extinguished. "Did he now? I joined the Volunteers myself, Miss Halloran. I was sworn in by Seán MacDermott, who was another friend of mine, but I didn't take part in the Rising. I was with Eoin MacNeill at his house[2] when he canceled the orders; I thought there would be no Rising." He stared into the middle distance. "And now here we are in Wynn's Hotel." Obviously the significance was not lost on him.

"Here we are indeed." Ursula glanced across the table at Ernest Blythe, who was still engaged in conversation with Mairead. He did not seem nearly as interesting as the man sitting beside her. She turned the full force of her smile on Seán Lester. "Tell me more about yourself."

He made a self-deprecatory gesture, a gentle wave of long, elegant fingers. "I'm no one special."

"Please."

"Well . . . in 1923 Desmond FitzGerald asked me to help publicize the Free State. He wanted to give the new government the best possible image while it was getting up and running. After a couple of years the publicity office closed, and I was put in charge of correspondence for the Department of External Affairs. That's what I've been doing ever since. Until now, that is."

---

*Irish language-speaking area.

"Your job isn't who you are," said Ursula, "any more than mine is me. *Who* is Seán Lester?" Folding her hands beneath her chin, she held his eyes with hers.

He was not accustomed to talking about himself, but it would have taken a surly man indeed to resist the flattery of her focused attention. "I was born in Carrickfergus," Lester said, trying to decide what she might find interesting. "My father was a grocer. And we were Methodist," he felt impelled to add. In the north one was always identified by religion. It was claimed that a Jew in Belfast had been asked, quite seriously, if he was a Protestant Jew or a Catholic Jew.

"When I was a boy my family moved to Belfast, to a house in the Ormeau Road," Lester continued. "My formal education concluded with two years at Methodist College, and in 1909 the *Portadown Express* hired me as a trainee reporter. It was not a happy experience for either of us. Portadown is a stronghold of the Orange Order, and I'm afraid I was not as diplomatic as I should have been in expressing my views. When I left the *Express* in 1911 they gave me excellent references, but . . . anyway, I changed employers several times after that, as one Unionist editor after another discovered that I sympathized with Ireland's desire for independence.

"In 1913 I went west and joined the staff of the *Connacht Tribune*. By that time Ernest had sworn me into the local IRB. I fell in love with the west of Ireland, but the best place for an ambitious journalist was Dublin. So eventually up I came to the city. Again I found doors closed in my face because of my politics. Fortunately Arthur Griffith gave me work on some of his publications, and even helped me get a job with the *Freeman's Journal* as news editor."

"You must have known my Uncle Henry!" Ursula exclaimed. "Henry Mooney? He published articles in the *Journal*."

"There was no better journalist in the business," Lester assured her, "and a man of great compassion. You're fortunate in your relatives."

"Henry's not really my uncle, it's more of a courtesy title."

"Having Henry even as a courtesy uncle speaks well for you. Tell me how it came about." Lester listened intently while Ursula sketched out her life for him. Instinctively she felt she could trust Seán Lester—though she did not go so far as revealing her tenement origins.

She never did that.

Blythe's voice cut through their conversation. "What are you two talking about with your heads together? You look like conspirators."

Lester replied, "This young woman was telling me about her schooling in Switzerland. Did you know she speaks French and German? Your broadcasting service has a real prize here, Ernest."

Ursula felt a blush flood her throat and cheeks. Blythe was looking at her curiously. "Is that true, Mairead?" he asked.

"It is true. We're very proud of Ursula at the station."

"But not proud enough to give me a rise in wages," Ursula said under her breath, just loud enough for Lester to hear.

When Mairead resumed talking with Ernest Blythe, Seán Lester asked Ursula, "Are your wages so small, then?"

"It's not just the size of the pay packet. Civil service employees who come straight into broadcasting without working in some other department first are classified as temporary. We have no security of employment and no pension rights."

"I see. Would you be interested in a better paying job?"

Her imagination went galloping off unbidden. With more money she could bring Saoirse east and put him in a livery stable in Dublin, and ride him every day, and . . .

She reined in her thoughts. "I love working in broadcasting, Mr. Lester."

"If we're going to be friends, I hope you'll call me Seán. And if you ever change your mind about the job I hope you'll contact me. I'm going to need people like you. Irish people with a knowledge of French and German are mighty thin on the ground."

"In External Affairs?"

He laughed. "Oh, I'm out of that now. Didn't you know? I've just been appointed Irish representative to the League of Nations."

While Ursula was staring at him in astonishment, Blythe said, "Do you have your wallet on you, Seán?"

"I do of course." Lester stood up and reached into his pocket.

"Good, you can pay for lunch. It wouldn't do for a man with his hand on the government purse strings to look like he's spending some of that dosh on himself."

11 April 1929

Dear Henry,

Recently I was invited to a luncheon party that included Seán Lester, whom you will remember from the *Freeman's Journal*. He has been appointed to represent Ireland at the League of Nations, and thanks in part to my connection with you, he offered me a job when he gets settled in Geneva. Perhaps he was just being polite, but he did insist that we exchange addresses.

I am flattered by the offer, Henry, and I shall certainly respond if he writes to me. But I cannot accept. There is too much to keep me here.

With the exception of the Mooneys, everyone and everything she loved was in Ireland. Besides, she dreaded traveling on a ship again. Her stomach cringed at the thought.

One final reason was more persuasive than any other. Ursula Halloran had taken part in the birth pangs of the nation. The dream of a noble republic had been replaced by grim survivalism, but she still believed things could be made to come right.

Síle Halloran had always said things could be made to come right.

And Constance Markievicz had counseled women, "Take up your responsibilities and be prepared to go your own way depending for safety on your own courage, your own truth and your own common sense."

Ursula meant to stay and fight for the Irish Republic with whatever means came to hand.

A few days later Seán Lester and his family departed for Switzerland. True to his word, as soon as he was settled in Geneva Seán sent Ursula his new address. "We have a nice flat at 43, Quai Wilson, overlooking the lake and with a splendid view toward Mont Blanc. It is serving as both home and office for now, and a bit crowded," Lester wrote, "but Elsie and I would be delighted to have you stay with us for a while. You could observe the situation firsthand and see if you would be interested in joining my staff. We have several good people already and it promises to be a congenial group. Do at least think about it."

How could I not? But my place is here.

In June there was a ceremonial reopening of the GPO. Ursula joined the crowd that gathered in O'Connell Street. Staring at the reconstructed building. Hearing the echoes of the gunshots and the boom of artillery. Pressing fingers into the bullet holes that still pocked the stone columns of the portico.

Here. It happened here.

Something deep inside her longed for it all to happen again. And herself to be part of it.

Chapter Sixteen

To give the Irish Free State a stronger international identity, the government opened diplomatic relations with the Vatican. France and Spain were powerful Catholic nations, both of whom had a history of conflict with Protestant England. Ireland was deliberately courting a connection with them through the Church.

The sixteenth of June marked the beginning of countrywide celebrations to mark the centenary of Catholic Emancipation. On the twenty-ninth there was an eclipse. Ireland was still in festival mood and although clouds obscured the sight in many parts of the country, people made the eclipse an excuse to dance the night away.

Henry Mooney had taught the small Precious to dance, waltzing her around and around in Louise's parlor to gramophone music, while she stood on the tops of his feet. Ned and Síle had danced too. But only with each other.

Now Ursula stood in her window gazing down at the exuberant crowds in Gardiner Street. All the women seemed to have men with them.

Who wants to dance anyway? she asked herself wistfully.

Finally she went to the pub and ordered a pint of Guinness. The bartender knew her by this time. It was not uncommon for her to drop in on her way home from work and order a pint. One pint, never more.

And, as he remarked to the owner of the pub, she always drank it like a lady.

· · ·

ON the twenty-ninth of July W.T. Cosgrave officially opened the Ardna-crusha Hydroelectric Station in County Clare. He predicted that Ireland would now begin to grow industrially. With the coming of hydroelectric power to the west, rural electrification might be possible within ten years.

In August Séumas Hughes informed listeners, "Yesterday the first Free State airmail service to the United Kingdom was inaugurated, flying from Oranmore Aerodrome outside Galway to London's Croydon Aerodrome.[1] And for those of you with an interest in European affairs, the name of the combined Serbo-Croat-Slovene kingdom has been changed to Yugoslavia."

"We're extending broadcasting hours and there's some talk of hiring an-other announcer," Ursula said one morning at breakfast. "I could do the job if they would give me the chance."

From behind his copy of the *Irish Times*, Hector remarked, "You should concentrate on getting yourself a husband."

"Getting trapped, you mean. I refuse to be defined by my relationship with some man."

"Where do you get such ridiculous notions?" Hector put down his news-paper. "Is there something wrong with you, that you turn your back on the highest honor a woman can receive?"

Look at him, thought Ursula. *Smug as a cat in the sun. The sort of man who was content to be dominated by a foreign king, and believes men have every right to dominate women.*

Excusing herself, she left the table.

Later she asked Louise, "How could you have married an aspiring Brit?"

Pleating her apron between her fingers, the older woman said softly, "I was growing old alone, Precious. Please God you never learn what loneliness can do to a woman."

Almost every day thereafter the subject of Ursula's marriage was broached at number 16. Louise dutifully supported her husband on the issue. At last Ursula announced she needed to live closer to the broadcasting sta-tion, packed her things and moved out.

Since number 16 was only a short walk from Henry Street, Louise saw through the pretext but wisely said nothing.

"That girl will come to no good," Hector Hamilton predicted.

Ursula found a furnished room above a greengrocer's shop in Moore Street. A weather-beaten blue door opened onto a gaslit stair that led up to a cramped warren of rental accommodations. The landlady, who was bent almost double with the degenerative bone disease that afflicted many elderly Irish women, had a beaky, avaricious nose and a voice that could slice meat.

"Pay every Friday and don't be takin' no men upstairs," she stipulated. "This is a daycent house."

Instead of a wardrobe to hang clothes in, Ursula would have a piece of rope angled across a corner and concealed by a limp curtain. Hygienic facilities consisted of a rusty cold-water tap and a shared toilet on the stair landing. Yet the room was luxurious compared to the nearby tenements, which had no running water and only a single privy in the yard to serve a dozen or more large families.

As soon as Ursula moved in she borrowed a hammer from one of the shopkeepers in Moore Street and drove a nail into the wall opposite her bed. There she hung an old bridle of Saoirse's. Every morning when she opened her eyes, it would be the first thing she saw.

Next she put up shelves to hold her growing collection of books, including Ned's textbooks from Saint Enda's, Irish poetry, French plays, and German philosophy. Her latest purchase was a secondhand copy of *Ann Veronica*. This early novel by H.G. Wells, with a heroine who rejected conventional marriage, had inspired generations of feminists.

Ursula searched the room until she found a floorboard that could be lifted. The area beneath became a secret repository for the Mauser—and, carefully pressed between two pieces of pasteboard, a dried white rose.

Her room was only a two-minute walk from the broadcasting station. She emerged every morning into the cheerful bustle and excitement of the Moore Street market, where every stallholder soon learned her name and shouted a greeting. Her flashing grin was their reward.

IN October Séumas Hughes was promoted to assistant station director. Mairead Ní Ghráda became the full-time announcer. Although an Irish speaker, she opened each day's transmission simply with "Station calling, Dublin 2RN."

23 October 1929
BLACK THURSDAY
Wave of Panic Selling Hits U.S. Stock Market

29 October 1929
WALL STREET CRASHES!
Stock Prices Fall $14 Billion
Nationwide Stampede to Unload Shares

Chapter Seventeen

On the day the American stock market collapsed eleven speculators committed suicide and hysterical crowds gathered in Wall Street. The reassurances of bankers and brokers were not believed. An unprecedented spree of easy money and overconfidence had come to an abrupt end. Countless investors saw themselves facing ruin.

Within hours shares began to fall dramatically in London as well. The repercussions spread outward in concentric circles of despair until a pall of financial disaster encircled the globe. Even in Ireland, which had little direct experience of stocks and shares, people huddled around the wireless, listening anxiously to the latest reports, worrying about sons and brothers who had gone to the States to make their fortunes.

2RN advertised for a news editor. "Male, of course," as Ursula said scornfully.

In Washington the new president, Herbert Hoover, asked Congress for extra funds for a massive federal construction program to create jobs for the millions who were suddenly out of work. A proposed £42 million public works program was announced in London, but Tories and Liberals alike agreed it would be too little, too late.

More suicides were reported.

"Dear Henry," Ursula wrote, "Are you all right? Did you lose any money in the panic? Please send me a letter as soon as possible. I am worried."

Henry wouldn't do anything foolish, she assured herself. *He has too much common sense.*

She waited with growing anxiety for a letter that did not come.

.   •   •

IN November a new dirigible piloted by an Irishman flew along the east coast of Ireland on its first trials.[1] Ursula went out into the street to gaze up at the sleek airship floating over Dublin in immaculate silence.

Magic.

"Sorry?" A man on the footpath was looking at Ursula quizzically.

I must have been thinking out loud. "I said *magic*," she repeated, indicating the silvery shape overhead.

"Not at all. Don't you know how it works? The whole thing's full of gas, y'see, and . . ." Removing his cap and tucking it under his arm, he explained his own version of the aerodynamics of airships. His tone was that of one instructing a very small child.

"You're very kind," Ursula murmured when he finished. "But I'm afraid I couldn't possibly understand. I'm only a woman."

Still no letter from Henry. She wrote again, with *Urgent* printed large on the envelope.

AT the end of November the new Savoy Cinema was opened by W.T. Cosgrave. The theater's first offering was a documentary film entitled *Ireland*, produced by the government. After carefully counting and recounting the coins in her purse, Ursula joined the queue to buy tickets. A cold drizzle was falling. She turned up the collar of her coat.

"Still standing in line, I see," remarked a voice behind her.

She spun around to gaze up into Finbar Cassidy's warm brown eyes. Her spirits lifted on an unexpected tide. "Will you join me?"

"I'd much rather stay out here in the rain freezing to death," he said. "But sure, we can't let you go in alone." He offered his arm.

Ursula had changed, he noticed. The planes of her cheekbones were sharper and the line of her jaw was leaner, but her smile still raced his heart.

There was a thrill of excitement as the house pianist played a thundering overture. The film itself proved to be thinly disguised Free State propaganda. Had she been alone Ursula would have walked out halfway through. Finbar was not impressed, either. "They're trying to convince us that everything's wonderful when the dogs in the street are howling about the depression," he said. "*Ag duine féin is fearr a fhios cá luíonn an bhróg air.*"

" 'The wearer best knows where the shoe pinches,' " Ursula translated. "I didn't know you spoke Irish."

"The language isn't as popular as it used to be," he said. "After independence Gaelic language and culture underwent a massive revival, but enthusiasm is beginning to fade now. I think it's been promoted too hard. A lot of people want to think of themselves as modern, whatever that is, and resent being pushed back into the past.

"I'm Gaelic from topknot to toenails, me, and proud of it. I learned Irish before I learned English. But I'm also a civil servant, so I trim my sails to the prevailing wind. One must do that in government.

"Sometimes, though . . ." he dropped his voice to a confidential whisper, "sometimes I think we'd be happier with no government at all. Anarchy's better suited to the Irish character."

As he had intended, Ursula laughed. "I can't quite picture you as an anarchist, Finbar."

"There's a lot about me you don't know. I'm an amazing man entirely. Going to run for office one of these days." He ran his thumbs under the lapels of his jacket. "Do you fancy me as a T.D.?"*

Ursula thought he was still teasing. "Representing the anarchist party, I assume?"

Finbar shook his head. "Joined Cumann na nGaedheal a while back." Suddenly she realized he was serious. "Cosgrave's doing his best under incredibly difficult circumstances. He's established an excellent police force and is trying to return the country to normal, God help him. Besides, he looks like the manager of a dry goods store and I find that refreshing after all those Republican characters swaggering around in trench coats and slouch hats."

Ursula bit her lip but said nothing.

After the cinema she let Finbar walk her back to her lodgings. On the stoop she hesitated. This was not Gardiner Street, with Louise waiting to offer a prospective suitor a glass of whiskey and an apple cake baked in a bastible with hot coals on the lid.

"I'm afraid I can't invite you in," Ursula said. "I only have a furnished room upstairs and no gentlemen are allowed above the ground floor."

"I'll forgive you if you'll promise to come out with me again."

When Finbar invited her to a pre-Christmas party in his office she accepted.

The Free State government consisted almost entirely of young men thrust into a situation for which nothing had prepared them. They were learning as quickly as they could, usually from the mistakes they made. Those in

Teachtai Dála, or parliamentary delegate.

External Affairs thought of themselves as diplomats in training. Quick-witted and articulate, they specialized in stimulating conversation.

Ursula thoroughly enjoyed the evening.

Later she lay in her bed staring up at the ceiling, envisioning a map of Europe superimposed over the cracked plaster. New political movements were sweeping from country to country. Communism, fascism, and resurgent nationalism were shaping the postwar world. Ursula could almost feel the energy crackling across the Continent.

Its own revolution over, Ireland was tame by comparison. The drama was elsewhere.

Finbar Cassidy joined the exodus of city dwellers who traditionally returned to their families for Christmas. He traveled to Donegal; Ursula went to Clare.

She was startled when she saw Norah Daly. The old woman had grown frighteningly thin; her clothes hung on her body like a dress on a wire hanger. Her only explanation was, "I just don't have the appetite I used to."

"If something's wrong with you, Aunt Norah, use the money I send for Saoirse's oats and go to the doctor."

Norah shook her head. "No need. No need at all."

When Ursula leaned on the gate and whistled, the gray horse came trotting toward her across the meadow. He looked well-nourished. His coat, though winter shaggy, had been recently brushed, and his hooves were freshly shod.

But he was no longer a stallion. Some things could not be healed.

NEXT morning Ursula walked the fields, saddened to observe they had not been properly tidied after the harvest. Frank had left too much stubble and too many broken stalks. Field walls had stones missing. The lower pasture needed draining and the earth gave off a boggy, sour smell.

Ned Halloran arrived at the farm two days before Christmas, bringing the traditional gift of a box of lemons and oranges. He was more gray and grim than ever, but at least he was home. For a little while. Like a bird perched on a branch, he seemed about to fly away at any moment.

Eileen and her husband made no appearance at the farm. No one mentioned them. They had ceased to be.

The talk around the table was mainly about the farm and the worsening economic situation. One evening Norah produced a letter with a foreign stamp on the envelope. "This arrived in the post today. From Kathleen. She and her husband have been estranged for a long time, you know, and now—"

"Estranged?" queried Ursula. "I should have thought they would be divorced by now. Is there not divorce in America?"

Norah was shocked. "Our Kathleen's a good Catholic! But her marriage is over anyway, so it is. That husband of hers lost a lot of money in the crash and has killed himself."

The Hallorans exchanged looks around the table. "She's better off without him," Ned said at last.

"God forgive you," Norah breathed.

"It's true. Alexander Campbell was a domineering man who made her life a misery. Pass the cream, will you?" He sniffed the proffered jug suspiciously. "Has this turned?"

"What will Kathleen do without a husband?" Frank wondered aloud. "Will she be wanting to come home?" Behind his eyes Ursula saw the sums already being done, the careful calculation of the cost of another person on the farm.

Norah shook her head. "The girl wasn't left penniless, thank God. When they separated Mr. Campbell gave her a settlement in her own name, and she tells me she had the good sense to invest in property rather than shares."

"She can make a new life for herself," Lucy remarked enviously. "Ned, was there not some other man she liked very much? Some American?"

Ursula turned toward Ned. "The priest who married you and Mama was an American, and I overheard you telling Mama that he was a close friend of Kathleen's. Is he the—?"

"Not a priest!" cried Norah, throwing up her hands in horror. "Our Kathleen would never!"

"You remember too much," Ned growled to Ursula in an undertone. He told the others, "Ursula was just a wee child at the time. She misunderstood."

She nodded meekly. "I'm sure I did, Papa."

Lying in bed that night, she heard Norah's words echo in her mind. *"That husband of hers lost a lot of money in the crash and has killed himself."*

Before Ursula returned to Dublin she posted another urgent letter to Henry Mooney from the Ennis post office. She rode into town on Saoirse, aware that she was trying to recapture a time forever lost.

But for a little while it came back. Clean wind off the western sea; little fields nestled within the embrace of low stone walls; the road ahead bracketed by a pair of gray ears.

·   ·   ·

ON the second day of the new year the All-India National Congress over-whelmingly passed Mahatma Gandhi's resolution demanding complete independence from Britain. "They won't get it," Ursula predicted gloomily. "And even if they do, the British will have some nasty trick up their sleeve at the end, like partitioning the country before they leave."

Chapter Eighteen

3 January 1930
Dear Ursula,
I apologize for not writing sooner. I dislike sending bad news. I did lose money in the crash, quite a lot in fact, but not to worry. With Ella's love and encouragement I will get through this. At least we have our health and each other. Many people are worse off than we are.

Thank you for telling me about Kathleen. Although I never met the lady I shall send her a letter of condolence, for Ned's sake.

When time allows and I am not rushed off my feet playing catch-up, I shall write a good long letter and tell you everything. Until then, do not forget

Your Henry

As the year progressed the world was caught in the grip of the Great Depression. Ireland suffered along with everyone else.

From the start of independence some of the Anglo-Irish had simply pretended that 1921 never happened and nothing had basically changed. Their interests remained limited to bridge games and golf and watching rugby at Lansdowne Road, or to the racecourse and the hunting field. The more thoughtful Irish Protestants, however, felt themselves to be genuinely Irish and resented being called "West Brits." They took a sincere interest in building up the new state and were a valuable asset.

Yet none of them could escape the consequences of the economic collapse. Members of the landed gentry who had been forced to sell the bulk of their estates after the War of Independence found that what remained would not support their Big House lifestyles.

Ordinary farmers were having a struggle. Cattle and sheep prices fell drastically as former export markets dried up. Butter and bacon no longer could be sold abroad.

In urban areas salaries were cut and unemployment levels soared. Anyone with a job held on to it with fierce determination. Women in office work comprised less than 2 percent of the paid labor force.[1] Everyone told Ursula how lucky she was to draw a pay packet every week.

In childhood she had accepted poverty as the norm. Ireland was poor, the people she knew were poor, that was just the way it was. Money was not discussed because no one had any.

Until the depression, Ursula had never thought of the lack of money as a negative force sufficient to crush the soul. But in America people were jumping out of windows because they had lost their money. And in Dublin, if people were not talking about the depression, they were carrying it in their eyes.

URSULA began sending a monthly postal order to America. The envelope was addressed to Mrs. Henry Mooney. The accompanying note read simply, *Thank you.*

THE high point of 1930 was the election of the Irish Free State to the Council of the League of Nations.

Ursula immediately sent a letter of congratulations to Seán Lester. He replied, "I am grateful that you remember me. Your cheerful letter brought a breeze off the Liffey into this stuffy office, so please do keep writing. I promise to keep you apprised of events here. Soon we will be busier than ever. Ireland will hold in turn both the presidency of the Council and the acting presidency of the Assembly." Lester did not repeat his offer of a job, however. The Free State government was penurious when it came to External Affairs.

FINBAR Cassidy called occasionally to take Ursula out for a meal or to the cinema. She accepted because he never pressured her. And he was amusing.

But in the small hours of the morning when she could not sleep, she felt as if invisible walls were climbing higher around her. Penning her in.

• • •

DURING the decade that followed the Great War no one had wanted to be reminded of its horrors. As the depression bit deep, the war acquired a perverse popularity. Memoirs, novels, and plays on the subject proliferated, competing with one another to match the black mood of the public. Bookstores offered large displays of *All Quiet On the Western Front*, *A Farewell To Arms*, and T.E. Lawrence's runaway bestseller, *Revolt in the Desert*.

Conversely, since the Civil War interest in Irish culture was waning. Traditional music was no longer popular and even the language movement was in decline. The government was not encouraging the Celtic Revival that had inspired the leaders of 1916.

Christmas 1930 was very bleak.

In 1931 Winston Churchill remarked in the House of Commons that under the Statutes of Westminster Ireland could, at any time, legally repudiate every provision of the Anglo-Irish Treaty of 1921.[2] There was no reaction from the Free State government—which the Treaty had brought into power.

One or two newspapers repeated Churchill's words on the inside pages, but they were not mentioned on the wireless.

URSULA once again approached Clandillon. Experience had taught her that a man could be straightforward about what he wanted but women must be circumspect. "The Dáil is criticizing us for playing too much highbrow music," she told the station director.

He sighed. "Tell me something I don't know." Ursula noticed that his feet were clad only in woolly socks. It was a bad day, his gout was bothering him.

"They also say the station is costing too much. My latest request for funds got nothing but a sharp remark about the depression."

"I'm not willing to take a smaller salary to help Posts and Telegraphs balance their budget," Clandillon grumbled. "My wife ..." He sat down heavily and began massaging his legs.

Ursula said brightly, "If there's too much classical music, might we not cut a bit of it and have a longer news program? Include a little analysis of what's happening abroad. Quote the latest from Winston Churchill, for example. If we expanded the news department we might get more advertising revenue." She treated him to one of her smiles.

Clandillon's eyes glinted with a sudden vision of possibilities. "More advertising revenue?"

"To help us become self-supporting. Of course," Ursula murmured, "that's just an idea."

"We only have one news editor," Clandillon said slowly, thinking through the ramifications, "and he sometimes doubles as a part-time sound technician. We could hardly handle any expansion of the news department."

"Is there any reason why we couldn't employ an assistant editor?"

He slumped in his chair. "You know the reason. We can't afford it."

"Suppose . . ." Ursula looked toward the ceiling as if seeking inspiration, ". . . just suppose we had someone in-house already who would take on the additional work without expecting higher wages? At least until the advertising revenue picks up?"

1 June 1931

Dear Henry,

Your Little Business is now assistant news editor at 2RN! I am increasing my correspondence with friends abroad and will be grateful for any newsworthy nugget from America. Hard news only, please. No social items, no household hints or cookery. I intend to monopolise the international end of things and leave domestic news to the senior editor. I also am going to make a point of personally thanking the newsreader after a good programme. No one bothers to do that, but I know I would appreciate it if I were newsreader.

I have been given a battered (but new to me) desk and filing cabinet, plus access to the telephone. My salary is increased to the princely sum of three pounds ten shillings a week. Best of all, I am relieved from tea-making duties.

Ursula added her small pay rise to the sum she put aside to repay Ella.

In her next letter from England Fliss wrote, "I finally arranged to meet Sir Oswald Mosley through a mutual acquaintance. My father would be furious if he knew. Sir Oswald is the most remarkable man, Ursula. Even his physical appearance is striking: very tall and elegant. He commands attention wherever he goes.

"Sir Oswald has left the Labour Party in order to form a new socialist political party. He is full of ideas that will shake this stodgy country of ours to its foundations. Can you believe it, he actually disparages his title for having no meaning? I think that's very courageous."

One Saturday afternoon while she and Finbar were having lunch at Flynn's in Fleet Street, Ursula mentioned Mosley.

Finbar frowned. "From what I've heard of the man, he's an out-and-out Fascist, Ursula. Your friend would be well advised to avoid him."

"Mussolini is a Fascist and the pope seems to think he's all right."

Finbar's eyes twinkled mischievously. "Pope Pius and Benito Mussolini have something in common."

"They're both Italians, you mean?"

"More than that. Each man wields supreme authority in what amounts to a totalitarian state, firmly opposed to communism and laisser-faire capitalism alike."

"Is that supposed to be a joke? What would the priests do if they heard you calling the Church a totalitarian state?"

"I was teasing and you know it. Roman Catholicism and the nation of Italy are both conservative but there are crucial differences. The pope represents centuries of theological thought. Mussolini is a former socialist who switched to the far right simply because that was the only route to power in Italy after the war."

"So he's an opportunist. That's no crime."

"Mussolini's not just an opportunist, Ursula; he's a dictator. And there's no such thing as a benevolent dictator. The breed is notoriously self-serving."

"We'll never have a dictator in Ireland anyway," she said confidently. "In a republic, supreme power is held by the people."

"This isn't a republic," Finbar reminded her.

7 August 1931

Dear Ursula,

Your promotion is good news. (No pun intended.) Congratulations. It is heartening to hear that someone is doing well these days. Things are not so good here. I finally had to let my employees at the printing company go. It was very hard, because they have families too.

God bless Tilly Burgess, who is willing to go on working for us even though I cannot offer her more than room and board. Tilly is doubly necessary now because Ella has insisted on coming in to help me run the business. "One must work with what one has," the Cap'n says. You should see her sitting at a desk with little Henrietta on her lap while she does the paste-ups.

On the fifth of September Mrs. Margaret Pearse, the mother of Pádraic and Willie, ceremonially started the presses rolling for the first edition of the *Irish Press*.

On that same day Ursula wrote to one of the blond Florentine twins she had known at Surval, inquiring about Benito Mussolini.

The Italian girl described Mussolini as a man of striking physical presence and almost hypnotic charm. She wrote, "In 1919 Mussolini founded a movement called *Fasci di Combattimento*, named for the symbol of ancient Roman authority. During the civil unrest that followed the end of the Great War the people had become very disillusioned with their leaders. The government was corrupt from top to bottom. Mussolini and his Fascists urged the appointment of a dictator who was energetic enough—and ruthless enough—to make a clean sweep of Italian politics.

"At the height of a huge general strike in 1922, Mussolini and his personal militia, the Blackshirts, brought down the government. That October Mussolini became the youngest prime minister in Italian history and promptly set about stabilizing the national economy.

"His speeches are almost like conversations with the people and we love it. We ask questions and he answers, sometimes he even makes jokes. With the army behind him and the people at his feet, Mussolini will create another Roman Empire. He is Il Duce;* our new Caesar!"

20 October 1931
IRA OUTLAWED
Saorstát Éireann Declares Irish Republican Army an Illegal Organisation

*The Leader.

Chapter Nineteen

THE lessons of the Irish Civil War had not been lost on the men now in government. By declaring the IRA illegal, the treatyites hoped to pull the Republicans' teeth. The nation could allow only one army within its borders and that army must be apolitical, giving its allegiance to the Free State rather than to any individual.

This was the opposite of the ancient Irish custom whereby warriors swore themselves to their chieftain.

FINBAR Cassidy was in love with Ursula. He never spoke of it, never even hinted. He was glad she was willing to go out with him at all. For now, it was enough to be friends.

For now.

Centuries of abusive landlordism had left the Irish with a passion for owning their own homes. As she lay dying of tuberculosis, Finbar's mother had extracted a promise that he would not marry until he could afford to buy a house for his wife. On a civil servant's income that was still years in the future. So when he was with Ursula, Finbar tried to behave as if a priest were looking over his shoulder.

Ursula was a puzzle to him. She never spoke of her childhood. From her passport, Finbar knew that her parents were Ned and Síle Halloran. When he tried to learn more about them she was evasive. "My mother was murdered by the Tans. I don't like to talk about it. Aside from that, I was an ordinary child and my parents were ordinary parents. There's nothing more to tell."

He was not sure he believed her, but mystery was part of her attraction. Everything about Ursula attracted him. The way she moved could make his groin heat embarrassingly. When she thought no one was watching, her stride lengthened into a lovely bold swinging walk such as Eve might have employed in the Garden; the walk of a creature natural and free.

It was more than mortal man could bear, watching her walk like that.

URSULA was thankful that Finbar seemed content with a platonic relationship. Yet occasionally she could not help wondering if he even found her attractive.

One Saturday afternoon she lowered the blinds, stripped off her clothes, and studied her reflection in the discolored pier glass in the corner of her room. *I really am too thin. Those protruding collarbones make me look like a starved bird. But at least my bones are straight and I have good teeth.*

No one could tell I was a tenement child. My parents could be anyone. Anyone.

15 November 1931
Dear Henry,
Our mutual friend Finbar Cassidy hopes to stand for office in the next general election. Unfortunately Finbar belongs to Cumann na n-Gaedheal, so he will not get my vote. I have joined Fianna Fáil.

Ursula began compiling biographical information on de Valera and doling it out to the announcer in judiciously selected snippets. Only successes, never failures. By polling day, listeners to 2RN would believe that Dev could walk on water.

YOU know my feelings about Irish politicians," Henry Mooney wrote to Ursula, "but the political route is the only viable one now. If we continue to employ violence we are no better than those who have used violence against us for so many centuries. And that means they win. They will have made us into themselves."

As 1931 wound down electioneering got underway in earnest.

"If my party nominates me as a delegate to the Dáil, will you campaign for me?" Finbar asked Ursula.

"For a treatyite? Under no circumstances."

He laughed. "I knew your answer before I asked."

"I might run for office myself some day," she remarked with elaborate casualness. "I've been thinking about it."

"I'm afraid you won't get much encouragement."

"Why not?"

"You're a woman," Finbar said bluntly.

"What! Why, women were the backbone of Sinn Féin! And when Dev founded Fianna Fáil, Countess Markievicz and Tom Clarke's wife and Pádraic Pearse's sister were part of the Executive Committee."

"That's as may be, Ursula, but Irish politics is becoming more conservative because Ireland's becoming more conservative. It's a man's game these days. Besides, if the IRA puts its muscle behind Dev there may be violence in the general election."

She lifted her chin. "Do you think I'm afraid?"

"I don't think you're afraid of anything," he said with unconcealed admiration. "But I would feel better if you're not involved."

Ursula snapped, "I'm not living my life to make some man feel better."

LONG before the general election, tempers boiled over. De Valera's *Irish Press,* which had begun publication the previous September using funds from America, printed stinging editorials that only slightly fell short of calling Cosgrave and his supporters traitors.

Cosgrave fought back. A Cumann na nGaedheal election poster depicted de Valera being marched along by a gun-carrying member of the IRA, with the caption *His Master's Voice.*[1]

Members of the two parties had fistfights in the streets.

FINBAR Cassidy was not selected by Cumann na nGaedheal to stand for the Dáil. "It's just as well," he breezily assured Ursula. "An aspiring politician should never succeed the first time he seeks office; it's bad luck. The dogs in the street know that."

In reality the pain of rejection bit deep, but he was determined not to show it. He had to live up to Ursula. He knew her better than she realized. Ursula ardently desired nobility of the soul. Her flame scorched everyone who came in contact with her. If he fell short of what she subconsciously demanded he would be discarded without hesitation.

WHEN the party manifestos were published it was obvious that Cumann na nGaedheal was campaigning for the retention of the status quo. Fianna Fáil was proposing sweeping constitutional, economic, and social changes. Both parties claimed to have the support of the Church.

"Surely God can't be on both sides," Ursula remarked to Geraldine Dillon one Saturday afternoon. Geraldine, with a husband and growing children as well as a full calendar of social obligations, had little free time. On rare occasions she was able to meet Ursula in the Gresham Hotel for afternoon tea.

Geraldine had ordered Earl Grey with no milk. She took a critical sip before committing herself to drinking the entire cup. The late Joe Plunkett's sister was a woman of strong opinions, and one of those concerned the proper brewing of tea.

Satisfied that the beverage met her requirements, she asked, "Why can't God be on both sides, Ursula? God is on the side of all humanity. That's what Joe believed."

"People say your brother was a mystic," Ursula replied. "It must be wonderful to have faith as strong as that." She envied Geraldine, who had known them all. Plunkett, Pearse, Connolly, MacDonagh, MacDermott, Clarke, Ceannt . . . the slain leaders of 1916, whose faith in God and Ireland had carried them to their deaths with unflinching courage.

FIANNA Fáil was gaining the upper hand in the God-is-with-us stakes. Because the Church condemned secret societies, Fianna Fáil election posters proclaimed, *Freemasons Vote for Cosgrave's Party. You Vote for Fianna Fáil. They are to God and Erin True.*

A seemingly tireless Eamon de Valera campaigned throughout the Irish Free State. Wearing a flowing black cloak and mounted on a white horse, de Valera swept into country towns escorted by a cavalry of Volunteers mounted on horses with tricolor ribbons braided into their manes.

The IRA flocked to support him. Their idealism had been curdled in their bellies by the actions of their former comrades, and they saw Dev as a new broom that would sweep away the Free Staters once and for all.

In the cities de Valera led torchlight processions accompanied by a Volunteer honor guard. Men and women wept as he summoned the ghosts of the Rising in his speeches. He spoke in a slow, grave monotone that lacked oratorical brilliance, but he did not have to be an orator. He was saying the words they wanted to hear.

The "de Valera Show" drew huge crowds and was mentioned in almost every news broadcast. When complaints were received from Cumann na nGaedheal, Ursula made certain that Cosgrave was mentioned just as frequently—in boring recitals of bureaucratic business that had listeners turning off the wireless.

Meanwhile, she collected every newspaper item she could find about the campaign. She was not above taking discarded newspapers out of rubbish bins to obtain clippings, though she never did it if anyone was watching.

There were rumors that should de Valera win, he would be prevented from taking office by force.

On Monday Ursula did not return to the broadcasting studio after lunch. She joined Helena Moloney and the other Republican women who were marching up and down Dame Street carrying placards emblazoned with de Valera's face and party slogans.

That night over thirty thousand Dubliners attend a final preelection rally. Eamon de Valera made a point of thanking as many of his supporters as he could, including Ursula Halloran. He only spoke with her for a few moments, but he did say, "I knew your father, he was a fine man."

The use of the past tense gave Ursula a start. "He's still alive!"

"Of course, of course." Dev's long face was ravaged with fatigue. "You're working at 2RN, I believe?"

"I am."

"I understand I have you to thank for those helpful preelection broadcasts. Once we're in office I hope you will come to see me."

De Valera moved off to speak to someone else, leaving Ursula rooted to the ground. *Eamon de Valera! Thanking me personally!* She thought she would burst with pride.

Election day, the sixteenth of February, was a Tuesday. That morning Ursula did not tumble into her bed until dawn. Hoarse from singing rebel songs, red-eyed from cigarette smoke, so overwrought she could not fall asleep, Ursula eventually dragged herself back into her clothes and went off to vote as soon as the polling station opened.

On the seventeenth of February the *Irish Press* triumphantly announced: FIANNA FÁIL TAKES 72 SEATS, CUMANN NA NGAEDHEAL 57. WE'RE IN!

Those who had been vanquished in the Civil War had just swept their way into power.

The rigors of the election campaign took their toll on de Valera. For a week he was unable to meet anyone. But when the Dáil assembled on the ninth of March, he entered Leinster House accompanied by his son Vivion, who was carrying a pistol.[2] Some of his colleagues were also carrying revolvers. De Valera's tense face and watchful eyes reminded observers of the IRA commandant of 1916.

Members of the *Irish Press* staff in the gallery jokingly remarked that the reason Dev looked so worried was his knowledge of Vivion's marksmanship.

There was no assassination attempt.

W.T. Cosgrave declined to stand for the presidency of the Executive Council. His closest associates said he simply did not want to return to open warfare in the Dáil.

When Eamon de Valera was nominated for the office his winning margin was higher than anyone had predicted. At the age of fifty, the onetime mathematics teacher, gunman, and rebel, was head of Saorstát Éireann.

Bonfires were lit on the Aran Islands. Pope Pius XI sent de Valera a message of congratulation.

The following day all IRA prisoners were released by government order. Shortly thereafter the banned Republican newspaper, *An Phoblacht*, resumed publication.

"De Valera is the best hope we have for getting back what the Treaty cost us," Ursula said to Finbar as they shared a hasty lunch in Flynn's a few days after the election.

He put down his cheese sandwich. "That's like saying the Devil is our best chance of heaven. The leaders of the Rising sacrificed their lives in hopes of creating a democratic republic, but you can forget about democracy if Dev lets the IRA gain sufficient strength. He and the Army Council will rule the country between them, and then God help us."

Ursula said icily, "The IRA is the true army of Ireland. Every bit of freedom we have now, they won for us."

"I just think—"

"I know what you think." Standing up, she took some money from her purse and threw it on the table. "This is for my lunch."

Finbar rose when she did but then sat back down. His eyes followed her to the doorway, where she disappeared into a dazzle of afternoon light. "This isn't going to work," he muttered under his breath. "This is never, ever, going to work."

He had been brought up to believe it was unmanly to show emotion. For once he could not help it. Pushing his half-eaten sandwich aside, Finbar laid his forehead down on the table.

The other patrons of the café politely averted their eyes.

Chapter Twenty

POPE Pius XI declared the Virgin Mary to be Queen of Ireland and selected Dublin to host the next Eucharistic Congress. It was to be held during the last week of June 1932, to commemorate the 1500th anniversary of Saint Patrick. A committee was appointed to organize the huge event. The first year under Eamon de Valera would be a mighty reaffirmation of the Catholicism of the Free State, as well as demonstrating just what the new nation could accomplish.

Meanwhile de Valera set about implementing his election promises. His first act was to cut his own salary and that of his government ministers. To Ursula's intense pride he sent the announcement direct to her at 2RN, in an envelope addressed in his own hand.

"Decent but frugal living is to be an Irish watchword," he wrote. Ursula made certain he was quoted exactly. De Valera was creating a new identity for the new nation; one corresponding to his own interpretation of the character of the people. Ursula approved. She understood frugality.

Within a fortnight of taking office de Valera suspended the military tribunals that had tried and executed Republicans, then nominated Frank Aiken as minister for defense. Aiken had succeeded Liam Lynch as chief-of-staff of the IRA after Lynch was shot by Free State forces. Yet his heart had not been in civil war. Frank Aiken had no blood lust.[1]

Seán Lemass would be the new minister for industry and commerce. De Valera kept the external affairs portfolio for himself but named a Cumann na nGaedheal man as minister for justice. The shrewd political move placated some of his most vociferous opponents—for a time.

De Valera's announced plans for government came as a thunderbolt. He intended to abolish the oath of allegiance to the British Crown, introduce protective tariffs, and withhold payment to the Royal Exchequer of the land annuities.

Land annuities were loans that had been made by the British government to Irish tenant farmers, in order to facilitate the purchase of their holdings. The annuities were doubly hated. Many thought the interest rate charged amounted to usury, while almost everyone felt the injustice of having to borrow money to buy back lands that had belonged to their forefathers for a thousand years.

Of all de Valera's plans, the withholding of annuities cut the deepest. In effect he was declaring economic war on Britain. It was the sort of grand gesture his admirers expected of the Chief.

Ursula's soul ached to perform a grand gesture. She thought of Helena Moloney and the other women who rescued the broken lead type that had printed the Proclamation of the Republic. They had used it to reprint the Proclamation in time for Easter 1917—and brought a steeplejack over from London to raise the tricolor on the tallest flagpole in Dublin, defying the furious British authorities.

The women always had been the staunchest Republicans.

WHEN Ursula Halloran was personally summoned to de Valera's office to receive the text of his latest announcement, she felt as if all her Christmases had come at once. *Oh Papa, I wish you were here to see this!*

It would be Ursula's first visit to the hub of power. She did not know just what to expect, but when she saw de Valera's office she was not surprised.

The room was awkwardly proportioned, the ceiling too high for the limited floor space. Tiny blisters in the paint on the walls revealed underlying damp. In keeping with Dev's policy of frugality there were no curtains on the tall windows. The glass panes radiated the cold. A thick carpet, the only touch of luxury, failed to muffle the sound of a clock that struck the quarter hours with a jarringly loud chime. Prominently displayed were a statue of Abraham Lincoln and a copy of the American Declaration of Independence.

The tall, thin man behind the desk glanced up when Ursula entered. At that moment a telephone on the desk rang. He carried on a brief conversation in Irish, put down the receiver and half-rose from his chair to extend his hand.

"Miss Halloran? It was good of you to come."

"I appreciate your thinking of me."

"I have been giving a great deal of thought to broadcasting recently," de Valera said. "The wireless is proving to be a most satisfactory way of communicating with the people." As usual, he spoke in slow, measured tones. The folds of his face were draped into somber lines.

Must he look so lugubrious? Ursula asked herself. *I wonder if that expression frightens children.*

"Therefore," de Valera was saying, "we have authorized the erection of a high-powered radio transmitter at Athlone, which will be capable of receiving a live broadcast from the pope in Rome and transmitting it to the Eucharistic Congress in Dublin."[2]

"That's wonderful!" Ursula responded—thinking not of the religious aspect but of the excitement of a more powerful transmitter.

The man behind the desk smiled. "I am glad you agree." When he smiled his whole face changed; rearranged itself, became kind and human and almost endearing. "We are grateful for your support in the past and trust we may continue to rely upon you."

"You can of course!" she promised. *De Valera trusts me, Papa!*

Opening a desk drawer, de Valera took out a manila folder and handed it to her. "Then please have this announcement broadcast this evening."

As soon as Ursula was back at her own desk she read the typescript she had been given by de Valera. Twice.

According to this latest announcement, de Valera was going to retain Cosgrave's anti-divorce legislation permanently. He also addressed the Censorship of Publications Act, originally devised to criminalize Republican propaganda. De Valera was reassigning the censorship board to the protection of public morality.

Ursula gave the announcement to the newsreader; she had no choice. She listened to the subsequent broadcast with misgivings.

I hope this isn't as repressive as it sounds.

Dev's announcement greatly pleased the Church hierarchy. Once they had denounced republicanism. Now they praised Eamon de Valera.

Although he had marked Ursula out as an important broadcasting connection, de Valera did not encourage the advancement of women in politics.

At Fianna Fáil meetings they were once more relegated to what Ursula thought of as "tea-serving." That, and approving whatever the men said. There were increasing mutterings among the Republican women who had supported him so strongly.

The mutterings grew louder when a law was passed preventing the hiring of married women as teachers. Soon it was expanded to the whole civil service.[3]

Although Ursula and Finbar still met from time to time, he avoided any mention of politics. He was afraid of saying something that would cause a permanent break between them. Republicanism was Ursula's center of gravity. Finbar had no trouble with the philosophy; it was the gunman lurking in the shadows that he rejected.

Books were Ursula's refuge. Sometimes she would close one and stare off into space, repeating a favorite phrase as someone else might smell a rose in a garden. She loved beautiful words, the grace of language. When several of her favorite books were condemned as obscene by the government censors, she grumbled to Finbar, "They want to pretend there's no such thing as sex in Ireland."

He had never heard any nice girl use the word *sex* before. "Why are you complaining?" he asked. "I didn't know you had any interest in the subject."

"I simply don't have time for that sort of thing."

"Other people do," he said quietly. "Married people."

She gave an elaborate shrug. "Good enough for them."

In spite of his best efforts he was losing ground with her, and he knew it.

Fashionable shops in Grafton, Dawson, and Dame Streets, whose clientele were predominantly members of the Ascendancy, continued to display the Union Jack on every important date in the English calendar. On the third of June the shop fronts blazed with celebratory flags and banners for the birthday of King George V.

That night many were torn down. No one saw it done. No one had the slightest idea who the culprits might be.

In late June the entire Catholic world seemed to be coming to Ireland for the Eucharistic Congress. Temporary buildings had to be erected to accommodate the overflow of pilgrims. One hundred and twenty-seven special trains were laid on to bring people to the city. Special Masses were held in churches throughout the countryside so that everyone could take part in the triumphant celebration of the Eucharist.

Dublin was *en fête*. Ropes of flowers and colored bunting disguised peeling shop fronts and decaying tenements. Shrines decked with more flowers were set up in almost every street. A replica of the round towers found at many ancient monastic sites was erected in Dame Street. The air rang from morning to night with the sound of choirs practicing. Five thousand priests, one hundred sixty bishops and eleven cardinals from forty countries arrived, adding their numbers to twenty thousand Irish clerics.[4]

2RN undertook a week of outside broadcasts beginning with de Valera's official welcome for the papal legate, Cardinal Lorenzo Lauri, on the twentieth of June. A squad of the newly formed Irish Air Corps flew in the formation of a cross over the ship carrying Cardinal Lauri as it sailed into Kingstown Harbor. Subsequently Rev. John Charles McQuade, president of Blackrock College, hosted a lavish garden party at the college in the legate's honor.

McQuade had been a friend of the de Valera family since 1928, when their son Vivion was a student at the college. At de Valera's suggestion, McQuade's invitation list was sent to Ursula well in advance.

"Special guests at Blackrock," the 2RN newsreader breathlessly informed listeners, "will include our own Cardinal MacRory, Cardinal Hayes of New York, Archbishop Dougherty of Philadelphia, and Archbishop O'Connell of Boston, plus a number of leading ecclesiastics from many nations. Such a distinguished assemblage has never been gathered in Ireland before."

Following the party, newspapers were filled with photographs of de Valera's Soldiers of Destiny being warmly greeted by the hierarchy of the Roman Catholic Church.

A candlelit Mass for men only was held in the Phoenix Park. The following evening the Mass was celebrated for women. On Saturday one hundred thousand children marched to the Park through intermittent rain to offer up the Holy Sacrifice.[5] Little girls in white dresses and white organdie headpieces, surreptitiously comparing ruffles and ribbons. Little boys in white sailor suits, their high spirits controlled by stern parental adjurations.

The climax of the celebrations was a Pontifical High Mass in the Phoenix Park on Sunday. When Finbar asked Ursula to attend the event with him, she accepted. It was predicted that the crowd in the Park would number over a million people—twice the normal population of Dublin. A slightly-built woman would need a male escort.

For the occasion Ursula chose a lightweight frock of sprigged muslin in a shade of ice blue so pale as to look white, and a broad-brimmed summer hat. White cotton gloves and the first new shoes she had bought in years completed her ensemble.

Sunday dawned cloudless and bright; high summer. By the time Finbar called for Ursula, only foot traffic had a hope of getting through the crowded streets. As they walked toward the Phoenix Park they were caught up in a tidal wave of humanity. Men, women, and even small children were fingering their rosaries and praying audibly as they moved forward. "Hold onto me," Finbar warned Ursula, "or you'll be carried away entirely."

They were swept through the Park gates without any chance to speak to the welcoming priests waiting on either side. The crowd inside was even larger than the one in the streets. Fifteen acres of parkland were tightly packed with humanity giving off great quantities of body heat. The air turned steamy.

Steel bowls filled with water had been placed at intervals throughout the Park to restore anyone who fainted.

Jockeying for position, moving only a few steps at a time, Finbar steered Ursula toward the white marble colonnade where a glass-sided dome shielded the high altar. The vast multitude gave way grudgingly. Ursula's dress was soon damp with perspiration. Her eyes were dazzled, her head beginning to throb. She could feel a blister rising on her heel: punishment for her extravagance in buying new shoes she could not afford.

"Here comes the procession now!" someone cried.

Ursula protested, "I can't see a thing."

"Here, I'll lift you up." Finbar's hands clasped her waist before she could object. With a grunt of effort, he thrust her toward the sky.

She gazed out across a sea of worshipers. Women wearing bridal white with veils, their snowy purity punctuated by fathers and husbands in their best Sunday suits. Laborers in caps. Tenement dwellers in rags. But their best rags, their cleanest rags.

As the procession paced solemnly forward, the ecclesiastics in robes of scarlet, purple, and gold stood out like princes.

At the heart of the procession was a silk canopy embellished with tassels. Ursula saw Eamon de Valera himself carrying one of the poles. He towered above the other supporters, causing the canopy to dip and waver precariously above the head of the papal legate.

Near the colonnade a sound crew from 2RN was waiting to broadcast the Mass to the nation. Ranged on either side of the altar was a choir composed of five hundred men and boys in dark red robes and white surplices. To the front an army honor guard stood at rigid attention. The overwhelming impression was of sanctity and might in equal measure.

In the breathless heat the scene shimmered like a vision of heaven.

Finbar's arms were trembling. He let Ursula slide down until he could brace her body against his chest with his arms tightly wrapped around her hips. Through the thin fabric of her sweat-drenched frock she felt the warmth of his body.

"Can you still see?" he asked. She did not answer. He would not be able to hear her anyway. A chorus of nine hundred children had begun an exultant paean to Mary. This was the prelude to the *Panis Angelicus*, which would be sung by the world-renowned Irish tenor, John McCormack.

People swaying in an excess of emotion, music soaring . . .

Finbar's body against hers . . .

He lowered her to stand on her own feet. Pressed against him. With his arms still around her.

Neither of them moved.

Before the liturgy began a shiver of anticipatory exultation ran through the crowd. Ursula closed her eyes.

The great crowd murmured, breathed, took on a life of its own. Life in the sun. In the Park, in the Garden . . .

In the kitchen of the Halloran farmhouse, as in most homes in Ireland, was an oil-lit Sacred Heart lamp. From spring through autumn a small vase of flowers always stood beneath it. When Ursula lived at the farm one of her duties had been to change the water every day and replace the flowers when they wilted. She had never questioned a ritual that was as much a part of life as eating or sleeping.

The liturgy of the Mass was the same. She did not need to hear the Latin the priests intoned; it was carved on her bones.

Mass was a mighty river in which they were a million tiny little droplets glistening in the sun. Flowing together toward God.

Kneel. Stand. Give the responses.

Finbar behind me. Still touching me. Still touching. Flesh and spirit joined . . .

She felt his hands on her waist again. Touching her as lightly as a butterfly's caress.

The sacrament continued, carrying them toward God.

Finbar's hands slowly eased along her ribs until they reached the sides of her breasts. Ursula's entire consciousness concentrated in the tiny area of flesh touched by his fingers. She should pull away at once. She should turn around and slap his face.

She did not move.

His breathing grew ragged. His hands slipped farther forward. Cupped the soft swell of her breasts.

Until that moment Ursula had never known that her breasts ached to be touched. Never known that it would bring a profound sense of completion to her whole being.

Eyes still closed, she leaned back against Finbar Cassidy.

Her nipples were painfully erect. Her body knew exactly what it wanted him to do. She made a tiny movement that brought her nipples into contact with his searching fingers. He gave a gasp.

No one noticed. The pair of them could have died where they stood and no one would have looked around, enthralled as the great crowd was with the moment and the Mass.

Enthralled, Ursula let Finbar explore the uncharted topography of her heart.

A blare of trumpets sounded. "King of Kings!" thundered the chorus. "Lord of Lords!"

As it had done when Saint Patrick celebrated the Mass all those centuries ago, a bell signaled the moment of transubstantiation. The bread and wine of the Eucharist were transformed into the actual body of Christ. A million heads bowed. A million fists beat a million breasts.

The congregation as one turned its eyes toward the altar.

In the silence one could hear the wings of seagulls overhead, on their way to the sea.

FINBAR'S face was flushed. "Are you all right?" he asked in a choked whisper. "I never meant to—"

"I'm all right." *Don't ruin it by saying anything, Finbar. Please don't!*

THE estimate of a million people in the Park had been, if anything, conservative. When the Mass was concluded, the huge crowd formed itself into a giant procession. Men and women marched together, alternately praying and singing as they slowly left the Park and made their way toward O'Connell Bridge. Thousands of spectators lining the route joined in the hymns and prayers. Many adults had tears of joy streaming down their cheeks.

"Christ Himself is here with us," a ruddy farmer was telling anyone who would listen. "I saw him with me own two eyes. He came down out of the sky as a white dove."

Ursula's entire body was ablaze with heat. It lay bog-thick in her throat, choking her.

Appalled by his own temerity, Finbar was afraid Ursula would never speak to him again. He took a firm grip on her arm and let the crowd carry them to O'Connell Bridge, where another altar was set up. There a final blessing was given to the people as evening shadows lengthened.

At the foot of the bridge another crew from 2RN was conducting interviews. They recognized Ursula and waved her over. "Say something to the nation, Miss Halloran," a man urged, thrusting the microphone into her face. "Tell us what this experience means to you."

My first time on the wireless. Now's my chance. But the heat, the crowd . . . Finbar touching me . . .

"I'm speechless," she blurted.

Her interrogator smiled. "I am certain that would apply to tens of thousands today. Thank you so much for your insight, Miss Halloran." He turned away to interview someone else, leaving her furious with herself.

"Would that be Miss Ursula Halloran by any chance?" A man stepped forward from the crowd on the bridge.

The handsomest man Ursula had ever seen.

Chapter Twenty-one

A tall man with a neat moustache and sharply cut features. His eyes were sky blue. When he removed his hat his hair gleamed gold, like wheat in the sun.

"You *are* Miss Halloran?" His upper-class English accent represented everything Ursula had schooled herself to hate.

Yet his deep, mellifluous voice resonated in her bones.

"I don't believe we've been introduced," she said faintly.

"My name is Lewis Baines." He held out his hand. "I've heard Felicity speak of you many times and I must say, her description fits you perfectly."

"You know Fliss?"

"We're great chums. Our fathers were at Cambridge together and her brother and I served together in the war. When Felicity heard I was coming to Dublin, she insisted I knock you up."

"Sorry?"

"You know, call on you. Are you unfamiliar with our English slang?"

Ursula drew a deep breath to steady herself. *A voice like that should be registered as a lethal weapon. He makes ordinary words sound like poetry.* "Forgive me, Mr. Baines; of course I know what the phrase means. My train of thought is a bit derailed just now, that's all."

"I found the Mass quite moving myself," Baines acknowledged, "though only as an observer. I've been covering the Congress for the *Daily Mail* in London."

"You're a newspaperman?"

"A foreign correspondent, actually, but it's more a hobby than a profession. Something to do whenever I want a spot of travel. A cousin of mine owns the paper so I'm always assured of an assignment."

"My Uncle Henry bought a newspaper in America a few years ago." *What am I thinking about at all! Imagine me showing off for an Englishman!*

Finbar Cassidy cleared his throat in the manner of a man who had cleared his throat before and no one noticed.

Ursula gave a start. "Oh, I *am* sorry. Mr. Baines, this is Finbar Cassidy. Finbar, may I introduce . . ."

"Howd'youdo," said Finbar. He and Lewis Baines locked eyes in instant antipathy. "I'm sorry, Mr. Baines, but I need to take Miss Halloran home. She's had an exhausting day, what with the heat and the emotion and so forth."

Baines made a gallant little bow. "Quite, old fellow. By all means take care of her. Miss Halloran, will you permit me to call on you when you've recovered a bit? Tomorrow evening, perhaps? I have your address, Felicity gave it me. She neglected to include your telephone number, though. Perhaps—"

"Many of us are not on the phone," Finbar interjected.

Baines gave him a penetrating look. "I see."

Ursula said, "You don't see at all, Mr. Baines. I should like it very much if you would call on me tomorrow. I shall be home from work by seven if that's convenient. Good day." She shook his hand again, then turned and walked away. With an athlete's ardent stride, long-legged and free. Both men followed her with their eyes.

After an awkward moment Finbar muttered, "Excuse me," and hurried after her.

When he caught up with Ursula she would not look at him. "How dare you do that!" she hissed out of the side of her mouth.

"Do what?"

"You know what I mean. Have I ever said or done anything that would give you the right to imply to Mr. Baines that you and I share an address?"

"I did no such thing, Ursula."

"My mother could smell a lie at fifty paces and so can I," she said. "I'm going home. You can walk with me or not, just as you like."

"But I thought we were going to have a meal."

"I'm going home now," said Ursula Halloran.

THE following day was a Monday, but the spell cast by the events of the preceding week lingered. People went to work as in a dream. Ursula's thoughts kept drifting; she had to snare them like rabbits. She did remember to congratulate the outside broadcasting teams on a job well done, and one of the men replied, "You're the bright spark around here for sure, Miss Halloran."

That evening Lewis Baines called to take her to dinner. He brought Ursula a box of violet creams from Fortnum & Mason's, and had booked a table at Jamet's.

Dublin's premier restaurant was almost empty, a sure sign of the times. There were fresh flowers on the table and new candles. The heavy silver flatware gleamed. The handwritten menu was three pages long. Lewis studied the much shorter wine list, then summoned the headwaiter. After a conversation punctuated with French phrases, a dusty bottle of a superior vintage was produced from some hidden cache.

Whatever Lewis Baines did was marked by total self-assurance. Ursula had never seen anyone so at home in his own skin. Sitting at ease in Dublin's most expensive restaurant, he might have been at home in his own parlor. *Drawing room,* she mentally corrected. *He would have a drawing room, not a parlor.*

Ursula had never been to Jamet's, but fortunately Surval had prepared her for dining in luxurious surroundings. The school also had equipped her with rules for a variety of social situations, including dinner with a man one did not know well. *Begin with neutral pleasantries. Then seek mutual acquaintances. Find a subject of interest to both of you for general conversation. Avoid unpleasant topics.*

And try to control the butterflies in your stomach, Ursula admonished herself as Lewis began to talk to her in his mesmerizing voice.

The conversation opened with a discussion of American jazz, after which Lewis related several anecdotes about Fliss and her brother Cedric, who was now a pilot with the Royal Mail service, then moved on to the subject of aviation in general. Not once did he mention the depression. His glance never wandered around the room. The moment Ursula's glass was empty he summoned the waiter with the lift of one eyebrow.

Ursula never mentioned her work at 2RN. She only wanted to listen. Over cheese and biscuits, Lewis described a few of his experiences as an aviator during the Great War. Thrilling battles in the skies. Tiny planes duelling thousands of feet above the earth. Pilots on both sides saluting one another before opening fire.

Forgetting herself entirely, Ursula leaned forward with her elbows on the table. When Lewis flew his hands through the air to demonstrate aerial acrobatics, her eyes sparkled. "How I envy you! Are you still flying now that the war's over?"

"I have a little plane of my own, a DH Moth. She's in Bristol now but I might fly her over one of these days and take you for a ride. In fact, you should have a pilot's licence, Ursula. You'd make a fine aviatrix."

"Oh, I've thought about it," she lied airily. *If feeding a horse is expensive, what must it cost to take flying lessons?*

Lewis locked her eyes with his. "Don't just think about it. At the end of life one only regrets what one did not do. I once sat in a plowed field holding my copilot's head in my lap after we'd crashed. He was dying and we both knew it. He said to me, 'I never walked on a beach barefoot, Lew. Not once. And now it's too late.' "

Lewis took out a silver cigarette case from which he extracted a black Turkish cigarette. "You don't mind, I trust," he said, without waiting to see if she did. The waiter hurried forward to light it for him.

Ursula thought the cigarette smelled like burning tar. But she did not complain.

THE full moon slipped through ragged cloud like a coin falling through a hole in a pocket. As Ursula stepped out of the taxicab, a sudden wash of moonlight illumined the sculpted face of Lewis Baines.

"Thank you for a lovely evening," she told him.

He gave another of his courtly little bows. "If I didn't have to return to London in the morning, we would do it again tomorrow night. But we shall meet again. I promise."

Bending down, he took her face between his two hands and kissed her. Slowly and very thoroughly.

Without saying anything more he walked her to her door, and waited until she was safely inside before going back to the taxicab.

Ursula stood with her back against the closed door. Eyes closed.

I promise.

Chapter Twenty-two

ON Friday evening Ursula went to Confession.

One should always begin with the worst sin, she believed. Once that was out of the way the priest would find it easier to forgive the others. But which was the worst sin? Letting Finbar touch her body? Or letting Lewis put his tongue in her mouth?

Her flesh remembered. How vividly her flesh remembered!

ANONYMOUS in the shadows of the confessional box, the priest listened through the grille as she struggled to describe her experiences. Even with her educated vocabulary the words did not come easily. Irish women simply did not say such things.

"You allowed a man to put his hands on you? At *Mass?*" The priest's outrage hissed through the grille.

"I did, Father." *No point in lying about it. God sees everything. You can't lie to Him.*

Ursula waited with bowed head while the priest chastised her savagely. The blame was not ascribed to Finbar but to herself, the female, the weak vessel. "You have been an Occasion of Sin, young woman!" When the tongue-lashing was over the priest heaped her with penances.

How long will it take to say ten decades of the Rosary every day for a week? How many can I do before I go to work? I'll have to get up earlier.

A waspish voice snatched her thoughts back. "I said, have you anything else to confess?"

"I . . . er . . . let a man kiss me, Father. And . . . and put his tongue in my mouth." Ursula did not bother to add that she had enjoyed it. *Enjoyment* was a word one dare not use when speaking of sex.

"The same man, I assume?"

"A different man, Father."

"You shameful and perverted creature! The devil has his mark on your soul, young woman. If you continue in this way you are in great danger of being excommunicated."

W HEN Ursula escaped the confessional box she did not kneel in a pew and pray. Instead she left the church and walked aimlessly through the streets of Dublin. She had much to think about. Henry Mooney always said the best way to think was to take a long walk.

What's so terrible about kissing? Married men and women do it all the time. Ned and Síle certainly did; I saw them.

And touching . . . Finbar touched my breasts but it did me no harm. I'm still a virgin. That's the most important thing to the Church, isn't it? Virginity? Like Mary's?

A deep and stubborn anger was rising. *I refuse to believe we did anything wrong. It was just a moment's pleasure for both of us. Pleasure as simple and thoughtless as enjoying the sun. How can that be so evil that God might turn his face from me forever?*

Is it God? Or the Church?

Walking with her head down, watching her feet on familiar cobbled pavement, Ursula let her thoughts follow untrodden paths. For the first time she questioned a theology that condemned the very pleasures which God had built into the human body. Was such condemnation not, in itself, a perversion?

And yet, and yet . . .

Her thoughts and her feet rambled on.

Catholic Ireland does have a very special magic. Luminous occasions of innocence and beauty. Benediction, May Altars, First Communion. The sacrament of the Eucharist. The exalted way one feels, partaking of the body of Christ.

Ursula paused in her walk. She was standing in front of a church in one of the most impoverished areas of northside Dublin. *Catholic Ireland also has a God who must be bargained with; a condemnatory God who sells indulgences for money. Those who can afford it least give the most. Tenement women spend money that should buy shoes for their children in order to buy their parents out of purgatory. Meanwhile the bishops wear gold embroidery.*

Is this what Christ intended?

There was more than one version of Irish history. The one sanctioned by the Church described an unbroken continuum from Saint Patrick to present-day Catholicism. The Faith as it always had been and always would be. Unchanged and unchangeable. World without end amen.

But in dusty, forgotten tomes in secondhand bookshops Ursula had read a different story.

New forms of Catholic devotion had been introduced into Ireland in the nineteenth century. These displaced the earlier tradition, a tolerant and peculiarly Irish blend of Christian and pre-Christian, Celtic and Norman. The new version of Catholicism was solidly Roman. The clergy and the religious orders now owned the Church that originally had belonged to its people. The laity had become merely supplicants.

Although it stressed the importance of family values, the Church replaced the home as the center of life. Rituals traditionally performed by women, such as publicly mourning the dead, were taken over by a patriarchal priesthood. Through the Requiem Mass the priests had appropriated death, but they were biologically unable to appropriate birth. So they found another way to marginalize women. Irish women were given the cult of the Virgin to identify with—a pure, unquestioning, submissive woman whose innocence was not soiled by sexual intercourse.

Virgin Mary, Queen of Ireland.

Ursula longed for the serenity of absolute faith. *Why do the priests make it so hard?*

SHE heard nothing from Finbar Cassidy for almost a week. Then one evening he was waiting for her when she left the broadcasting station. Standing on the pavement with his hat in his hands. "Have you forgiven me?" he asked.

She gave him an innocent stare. "Forgiven you? For what?"

"You know."

"Do you mean for being so rude to Mr. Baines? I have not; it was quite unforgivable."

"I'm talking about what happened in the Park."

She tilted her head to one side as if trying to remember something of absolutely no consequence. "What happened in the Park, Finbar?"

"Please, Ursula! You know exactly. It's haunted me ever since. I have to know I'm forgiven."

"If that's so important, I can't understand why you've waited until now to ask."

"I wasn't sure you'd see me."

"So you ambushed me?"

Prodded past endurance, Finbar lost his temper. "You're such a Republican I thought you would appreciate an ambush!"

Ursula gave a soft laugh and linked his arm with hers. "There's nothing to forgive."

Finbar felt dazed.

DEAR Ursula," Fliss wrote. "Perhaps I should have warned you that Lewis Baines was coming to Ireland, but I thought it would be fun to surprise you. Is he not a Greek God? We girls are all crazy about him. You must have made an impression, though. At a house party last weekend Lew said he's planning to visit Ireland again soon."

I promise. I promise.

Ursula hoped for a letter from Lewis but none arrived. Days turned into weeks, weeks became months. She wanted to write Fliss and ask about him but her pride would not allow it.

FINBAR was now kissing her when he left her at her door. Kissing her softly on the lips with his mouth closed. She would allow him to embrace her, but she always stepped back as soon as the kiss ended.

He thought she was afraid. He was afraid himself, and dare not try to go any farther.

Ursula never alluded to the incident in the Park. If Finbar did, she changed the subject. Yet sometimes he caught her looking at him in a strangely speculative way. Her smoky blue-gray gaze drifted over his face. His body. Those eyes mesmerized him. They held him pinned like a moth skewered to a cork.

An evening with Ursula left Finbar shaken. He tried to rein in his imagination where she was concerned; sometimes he swore to forget her. Then he would find himself walking up to the weather-beaten blue door again and know he was doomed.

26 September 1932
EAMON DE VALERA GIVES INAUGURAL SPEECH

Irish Leader Becomes Chairman of the Assembly of the League of Nations

22 October 1932
PIONEERING FLIGHT FROM BALDONNEL TO BERLIN VIA LONDON
Businessmen Hope to Establish Regular Air Service

16 November 1932
PRINCE OF WALES OPENS STORMONT
New Home for the Northern Ireland Parliament

Chapter Twenty-three

NED Halloran propped his rifle against a tree and slumped down beside it. He tried to recall a time when he had not felt weary, weary to the marrow of his bones.

New Year's Day, 1933. Soon the Americans would swear in a new president, Franklin Roosevelt. But the same old problems endured in Ireland. Between Northern Ireland and the Free State was an unpoliceable border of some 320 miles, meandering through woodlands and farmlands, cutting right through houses in some cases, the major destabilizing force on the island. Men like Ned roamed both sides of the border fighting an undeclared war.

A few hours earlier there had been gunfire from the direction of Crossmaglen, a County Armagh border village. "Hold your position here, Halloran," the O/C had ordered as the other men moved out in that direction, "in case we need you to cover our retreat."

Ned resented being left behind though he understood the reason. Sometimes, as now, a headache would leave him half-blind with pain. His hands shook so badly he could not hold his weapon steady. "You ought to go home for a while, lad," the O/C had advised just this morning.

That, thought Ned, was part of the problem. He was not a lad anymore. He no longer awoke clear-headed and full of energy. Waking had become a painful, incremental process. Sounds would gradually intrude into his dreams, letting reality flood in. When he could avoid it no longer he would pry open his eyelids and wait for his vision to clear. Then he must force his reluctant body to move.

After a night spent sleeping on damp ground under a hedge, the rats of arthritis gnawed at his joints. Old man, he called himself privately. Old man, though he was not quite forty.

He felt sixty.

But there was work to be done in the north and no one else to do it. Only the IRA. The *real* army. Simultaneously trying to protect the northern Catholics and find some way to win back the amputated Six Counties.

South of the border some of the IRA were running far too wild, getting their own back against the treatyites who had persecuted them. Former government officials were assaulted.[1] Garda stations were attacked when the police tried to intervene. Law and order was breaking down. There was a rumor among the Volunteers—there were always rumors—that the military tribunals that de Valera had disbanded might be reestablished.

"If this is an army," Ned muttered to himself, "we should act like one. That includes you, Halloran. On your feet. Stand at attention." He hauled himself up and waited.

More gunfire. Closer. The imperative crack of sound that focuses the mind and freezes the heart.

Four men came running up. Four from a squad of five. "Where's Patsy?" Ned wanted to know.

The O/C shook his head. "He's facedown in a ditch back there. We ran into a whole company of B-Specials. They don't give a donkey's arse what happened to the village, but they were damned glad to get us in their sights. We'd best split up and make a run for it before they catch up with us."

Ned reached for his rifle. "I'm not willing to leave Patsy! We can make a stand right here, fight them off and then go back for his body. We can—"

"We can't. It's a whole company of the bastards, I'm telling you, and they mean business. Use your head, Halloran. If you stay here and die you won't be any good to the cause except as another martyr, and Christ knows we've plenty of them already."

When Ned still hesitated the exasperated officer reached for his rifle. "If you're determined to die, I'll take this. We're short enough of them as it is."

Ned's fingers tightened on the weapon. He would not disobey orders, but he could not give up the gun.

ON January thirtieth, at the age of forty-three, Adolf Hitler became chancellor of Germany's Weimar Republic—the youngest man ever to hold the office. He was appointed by the elderly president of the republic, Field Marshal Paul von Hindenburg. The new chancellor inherited an economy in which one out of every two workers was unemployed, but Hitler refused to be discouraged. He saw Germany's abject position on the world stage as his opportunity. "Everything I have done or will do," Hitler announced, "has only one aim: to restore the nation to greatness."

PROPELLED by young leaders with radical ideas, Europe was rebuilding itself in new patterns. Meanwhile Ireland was increasingly narrow and inward-looking. The departure of so many of their British colleagues had meant new opportunities for educated Irish Catholics. Doctors, lawyers, and senior civil servants were finding their way into the upper levels of society, joining those businessmen and large farmers who had survived the revolutionary years. Fearing the very winds of change that had once blown so gloriously through the souls of Ireland's revolutionaries, they resisted anything that might upset their new and fragile sense of self.

The result was a deepening of the national conservatism. Eamon de Valera, who claimed to know the heart of the Irish people, responded with increasingly conservative policies of his own.

THIS country is going backward while the rest of the world is rushing forward," Ursula complained in a letter to Henry Mooney. "It is a pity that Germany was prevented from helping us during the Rising. One has to admire the way the Germans are struggling to overcome their difficulties. We could benefit from their example now."

Henry replied, "In 1916 the Germans did not care about helping Ireland. They simply wanted to encourage Irish rebellion in order to distract England from the war in Europe. Never make the mistake of thinking that a small, poor country like Ireland means anything to the great powers, Ursula—except as a pawn. Whatever Ireland accomplishes she will have to do for herself."

In Munich, Heidi Neckermann received a letter from Ursula seeking information about Adolf Hitler. She replied,

Several weeks ago I attended one of Herr Hitler's rallies. Physically he is an unprepossessing Bavarian with a ridiculous moustache. His voice, though sonorous, turns shrill when he is excited. But he has great dynamism and a gift for oratory that can hold an audience spell-bound.

Hitler espouses the fascist concept of a corporate state: a unified nation with a strong man at its head who is empowered to make all the decisions. He is more than a politician, however. Perhaps he is not a politician at all, but a new type of leader who has emerged when he is most needed. History has a way of throwing these up from time to time.

His rallies have a strong military element. They feature breathtaking displays of precision marching by thousands of Sturmabteilung,* many of them veterans of the Great War. Within the stormtroopers is an elite cadre called the Schutzstaffel† that serves as Hitler's personal bodyguard. The atmosphere is one of invincibility and, I must say, inevitability.

In his speeches Hitler tells his audiences they owe a debt to the Fatherland and exhorts them to patriotism with language that sets the soul afire. He says the majority of Germans belong to a white race called the Aryan, which is naturally superior by blood and heritage. I myself am Austrian, as you know, but Hitler is Austrian too. We are both members of the wonderful Aryan race. It is a breathtaking discovery. One leaves a Hitler rally walking ten feet off the ground.

Ursula tried to envision this new Germany and its new leader. To an Irish woman there was something sinister about huge military displays combined with fervent speeches about racial superiority.

"The only foreign newspapers in Dublin are English," she wrote to Heidi. "Can you please send some German papers?" When she came home from work to find a thick package waiting, she hastily tore it open and spread the contents on her bed. What she read presented a disturbing picture.

Supported mainly by the middle class, the National Socialist Party was obsessed with images of order. Hitler hated the people the middle classes hated, Communists and Jews, and blamed them for Germany's troubles. When they were brought under control all would be well.

Some, though not all, of the German people agreed. The voices of those who disagreed were silenced.

Hitler spoke in grandiose visions. His underlings tried to translate his sweeping oratory into concrete plans, but the reality sometimes fell short of

*Stormtroopers; also known as the SA.
†Protection Squad; the SS.

the dream. Beneath a veneer of strict discipline was the potential for chaos.

Under Hitler the Germans were regaining self-respect, however, and for this they adored him. In his public pronouncements Hitler frequently referred to the Holy Grail, invoking the aura of the Knights of the Round Table to ennoble his followers. Using great public spectacles, he introduced rituals that subsumed heroic Teutonic myth into modern Nazi symbols. He was restoring pride, pageantry, and mysticism to the lives of people exhausted by defeat and inflation.

After the Great War the Allies had demanded total German disarmament. France in particular had insisted that her enemy be humiliated. Now, in open defiance of the Versailles Treaty, Hitler was building a new army. Germany would never be humiliated again.

Chapter Twenty-four

THE Athlone broadcasting station enjoyed an official opening in February of 1933. Ursula went down on the train for the event. As she ate the cheese and pickle sandwiches she had brought, she gazed out the windows of the railway carriage at men and women laboring together in the fields. They waved cheerfully at the train speeding past.

From Arthur Griffith, the founder of Sinn Féin, de Valera had inherited the dream of a self-sufficient nation. The plain people of Ireland were attempting to make that dream a reality. The Fianna Fáil government was rewarding them with a shower of benefits including improved health services and free milk for schoolchildren.

Mothers blessed de Valera in their prayers.

ATHLONE was roughly halfway to Ennis, so Ursula had asked if she might take a couple of extra days and pay a visit to the farm. It would be a pleasant surprise for the Hallorans and a chance to spend time with Saoirse, who was beginning to show his age.

And perhaps, just perhaps, Ned might be there. She pictured Ned and Frank in the barn, putting together a crystal set so they could listen to Athlone on the wireless.

Ursula was not expected; there was no one to meet her at the station. She did not mind walking. The day was cold and overcast but dry, and she had wisely packed her clothing into a soft bag that could be slung across her shoulder. As she set off along the road, familiar fields spread their gracious laps on either side. Familiar trees waved to her from the hedgerows. Her imagination ran ahead to summer, when ribbon grass and cocksfoot and meadow foxtail would infuse the air with an ever-deepening fragrance.

Here, if anywhere, was home; the place where something deep and sweet settled into Ursula's soul and nestled there.

In a farmyard beside the road a man was preparing to sharpen a plowshare. Glancing up, he nodded to the young woman walking past. "No rain 'til night, please God," he said.

She smiled. "Please God." And walked on, ears waiting for a familiar sound.

At first the iron blade rang harshly against the grindstone. The farmer persevered until the screech smoothed into one musical note, then began to purr as though stone and iron were perfectly suited.

The plow was sharp.

Ursula paused to greet a magpie perched atop a stone wall in his dazzling black-and-white livery. It was bad luck not to speak to a lone magpie. *Do I ever see magpies in Dublin? Can't remember. But I know I never hear the cuckoo.*

The clouds grew thicker; the air was textured with damp. Ursula drew a breath that filled her lungs to the very bottom. *This is what home smells like.*

Almost before she knew it, she reached the foot of the farm lane. She had once commented to Norah Daly on the length of that lane. Norah had replied, "Sure and if it was any shorter it wouldn't reach the house!" Remembering, Ursula smiled. She was still smiling when the farmhouse came in sight around the last bend. The smile froze on her face.

On the front door was a large black wreath.

Ursula dropped her bag in the lane and began to run.

Norah. It must be Aunt Norah. She's old and she hasn't been well . . . surely it's Norah!

For once Ursula entered by the front door. A death in the family demanded dignity. The farmhouse was eerily quiet. The clock in the hallway was stopped and the mirror over the side table was draped in a sheet. Ursula stared at the closed parlor door. Reached out to open it; drew back her hand. Ran down the passage to the kitchen.

Lucy, blank-faced, sat at an empty table. She stared at Ursula without recognition.

"It's me, Lucy. What's happened?"

The older woman gave herself a shake. "Ursula? How did you hear about it so soon? We tried to reach you, but . . ." Her voice faded away.

"I did not know until I saw the wreath on the door. Was it easy? Did she suffer?"

"She?" Lucy looked baffled. "She who?"

Not Norah. Oh, God. Take me away from here. Put me back on the train, put me back in Dublin, let this not be happening. Ursula clutched her thumbs. "How did it happen?"

"No one really knows. He was digging rocks out of the upper field yesterday afternoon and just collapsed. We didn't go looking for him until dark, and then it was too late."

It was Ursula's turn to be baffled. "Digging rocks? Why ever would Papa do that?"

"Ned? I'm talking about Frank."

Ursula was swept with contradictory emotions: joy and grief so painfully intertwined she could not tell them apart. "Where's Aunt Norah?"

"One of the neighbors took us into town earlier to get a wreath and make the arrangements. She's upstairs resting now."

"Should I not go up to her?"

Lucy shook her head. "Leave her be. She probably heard you come in, she'll be down soon."

Norah appeared a few minutes later; a tiny old lady as fragile as a cobweb. When she saw Ursula she collapsed into her arms. "Thanks be to God you're here, girleen. Can you contact your father and tell him about Frank?"

"The only address I have for Papa is this one, that's why I send letters through you. I doubt if more than three or four people in Ireland know where he is at any given time." *And one of them would be his commanding officer, but he never told me who that is. For my safety, he said.* "If you put notices in the newspapers, Aunt Norah, perhaps he'll see them. And ... is there a telephone in the post office in Clarecastle now?"

The old woman nodded.

"I'll take Saoirse," Ursula said.

The aging gray whinnied an eager welcome when he saw her coming toward his field. Soon she was on his back and they were galloping toward the nearby village.

A telephone call to the broadcasting station in Athlone went through in minutes. By the time Ursula returned to the farm an announcement was being broadcast. "Will Edward Joseph Halloran of County Clare please contact his family immediately for an urgent message?"

Ned arrived the next day. The death of his brother stunned him. "All he ever knew was the farm," Ned said to Ursula. "It wasn't what he wanted, it was just what came to him."

"Are we so helpless we must accept whatever comes?" she challenged. "Could Frank not have made another life for himself if he really wanted one?"

Ned considered the question. "I don't think he dared to really want anything. He was of that generation."

"So are you, Papa. But you know what it is to want something and fight with all your heart and soul for it."

"Much good it's done me, all that fighting. Much good it's done any of us. Síle dead, me in bits, hundreds of good men killed, and the poor sods in the north are still being hounded from cradle to grave. Now Dev is distancing himself from the IRA. Doesn't want us given weapons, doesn't want us acknowledged at all. Political expedience," he added sourly. "If I knew how to stop wanting the Republic, I swear to God I would."

But he did not mean it. She knew he did not mean it.

Scores of people crowded into the house for the wake. Eileen came, though without her husband. They were living at Newmarket-on-Fergus and had two children now, with another on the way. Eileen entered the house as if expecting a rebuff. Lucy and Norah ignored her but did not ask her to leave. Ned briefly touched her hand in passing.

Ursula spoke to her. "I'm sorry for your trouble," she said in the time-honored way.

"Which one?" Eileen asked. Her hair was turning gray and her breath smelt sour.

DRESSED in the same dark suit he had worn to Mass for twenty years, Frank was laid out in the parlor. In death his cheeks and mouth had sunken. His false teeth protruded slightly. Norah and Lucy had washed him as best they could, but dirt was still ground into the fingers that held his rosary. He would be buried with the soil of Clare on his hands.

Friends and neighbors gathered around the corpse, drinking whiskey or poitín, smoking, talking about the economy and livestock prices and the weather. Mostly the weather. Then someone began reminiscing about seisiúns in the Hallorans' house when Frank was young.

Ursula jumped up and left the parlor. They heard her running feet on the stairs. After a few minutes she returned carrying Frank's long-neglected fiddle and bow.

An old schoolmate of Frank's reached for the instrument. Blew the dust off the strings. Tucked the fiddle under his chin and tuned it with agonizing patience. Drew the bow tentatively, eyes closed, listening. Waiting for the music to come to life.

One man produced a tin whistle, another had brought a squeezebox. Jigs and reels like "Farewell to Connacht" and "the Ballinasloe Fair" soon set feet tapping. Norah Daly requested the *"Taim im Chodhladh,"* an ancient ballad she had loved in her youth, and a selection of slow airs followed. Then Ned asked for the *Cúileann*.* "It was my brother's favorite," he recalled.

As the plaintive love song filled the room, Ursula lowered her head and wept for Frank Halloran. Wept for the life he had never had.

The funeral Mass was held the next morning, with burial in the small local cemetery afterward. That cemetery held generations of Hallorans, though not Ned's parents. They were rocked in the arms of the Atlantic. Síle Halloran was not buried there either. *Nor will Papa be, when the time comes,* Ursula vowed.

She walked beside Ned as the mourners followed the casket on its black cart from church to cemetery. Once again the day was damp and overcast. There was no conversation. A foot-beaten path wound across the fields to a painted iron gate. The gravediggers in their earth-spattered smocks stood respectfully on either side.

The mourners filed through the gate and up the hill beyond. When they reached the waiting grave the priest sprinkled the earth with holy water, then stepped back.

Mist swirled around tombstones leaning against the winds of time.

The keening began.

In most of Ireland the priests dominated the burial service as they had the funeral Mass. But this was west Clare, on the edge of the wild ocean. Here the old women still spoke directly to the dead in an eerie singsong cadence, an unearthly wail.

Standing with Ned on the far side of the grave, Ursula hugged herself to keep warm while Norah Daly keened for her dead nephew.

The sound chilled the marrow of living bones.

NED was going back to the north, though he would not say where. "If you need to reach me you can always broadcast another message," he told Ursula. "I'll get a wireless for the farm; it will be company for Norah and Lucy. The IRA has its own wireless equipment now. I've learned to operate

---

*"Fair Maiden."

it, I might even go into broadcasting myself. I can mimic most any accent, you know, even BBC posh. I could have the sort of job that pays a real salary instead of relying on donations."

"You're teasing, Papa."

He nodded. "I am teasing."

"If you want another career, what about the farm? I suppose it's yours now."

"Let Lucy have it, I'll transfer the deeds to her. Hired men can do the work. I'm no farmer and never will be, and I have no intention of being trapped here the way Frank was."

Yet Ned was devoting his life to a war that could not be won. Perhaps physical-force republicanism had become a trap too, Ursula thought.

I hope he does die in battle! That's the only proper end for a warrior.

In sudden panic Ursula tried to wipe the thought from her mind, terrified lest God hear.

Chapter Twenty-five

URSULA returned to Dublin haunted by thoughts of Frank Halloran. Finbar met her at the train station. "I come from a large family myself," he said, "and in a large family people die from time to time. But you never get used to it." On sudden impulse, he put his arms around her and gave Ursula a comforting hug.

She let herself melt against his body for a moment, then hastily pulled away. No traps accepted.

THE expansion of the news department meant more political coverage. Eamon de Valera made the most of the opportunity. Public support was vital in the economic war his administration was waging on Britain. 2RN became a major source for disseminating Fianna Fáil policy. It was not uncommon for God and de Valera to be mentioned in the same sentence.

Treatyites, who believed they held a monopoly on public morality, protested. De Valera responded by quietly removing his most outspoken critics from sensitive government posts. P.S. O'Hegarty was sent to the Board of Works. He took it with good grace, part of the price to be paid for being on the wrong side of the fence.

But when General Eoin O'Duffy, the abrasive and confrontational garda commissioner, was sacked in March of 1933, he did not go quietly.

O'Duffy had served as chief-of-staff of the Free State Army during the Civil War. He now belonged to the Army Comrades' Association, a voluntary service group founded by former Free State soldiers a week before the 1932 elections. Following the elections, politically inspired violence had continued. When Cumann na nGaedheal meetings were attacked by Fianna Fáil supporters and members of the IRA, shouting "No free speech for traitors!" the ACA had stepped in to serve as stewards and bodyguards.

Working behind the scenes, O'Duffy had developed the ACA into a highly organized, quasi-military body. A Nazi-style salute was adopted, and a uniform that included a distinctive blue shirt. Inevitably they became known as Blueshirts. Treatyites were complaining that de Valera was "soft" on IRA lawbreakers, so the Blueshirts extended their remit to civil defense with the IRA as their specific target.

THE firing of O'Duffy precipitated a crisis in public confidence. de Valera's enemies claimed the dismissal was the result of a secret pact he had made with the IRA, aimed at turning the country over to the more radical Republican element.

The general public was unaware how much the relationship between de Valera and the IRA had deteriorated. Volunteers were being arrested; the military tribunals were back.

When Cosgrave told a meeting of Cumann na nGaedheal supporters that he suspected Fianna Fáil had Communist leanings, the Blueshirts added communism to their list of enemies.

Fianna Fáil propaganda broadcasts accelerated. Ursula Halloran was kept busy at 2RN, honing the language to keep people on the side of Eamon de Valera. When he first came to power the Republicans who had supported him through all the hard years had accorded him an almost religious adulation. But as his policies took hold they saw the Ireland they had imagined vanishing before their eyes.

De Valera's economic war on Britain was beginning to have an effect— mostly on Irish farmers who no longer had an English market for their livestock and produce. Although his critics were quick to point this out, the farmers themselves continued to support Dev. Many of them had wireless sets and listened to 2RN every night. *Starve John Bull!* they painted defiantly on the sides of their barns and outhouses.

In May of 1933 Joseph Goebbels, Hitler's minister for propaganda and ethnic enlightenment, ordered the burning of all books and publications he deemed subversive to the German Reich. Among them was the just-published *The Shape of Things to Come,* a novel by H. G. Wells that predicted a terrible war enveloping Europe in 1940. A war begun by Germany.

·   ·   ·

W HEN Ursula wrote to Ned by way of the Hallorans there was no reply. He had disappeared again. Every time this happened she tried to tell herself he had not been killed, but that which was ancient and Irish and superstitious within her feared otherwise. *I'll hear from him in his own good time,* she tried to reassure herself.

I N July of 1933 Eoin O'Duffy was elected as leader of the Blueshirts.

O N the twenty-ninth of August it was officially confirmed that the Nazis were rounding up large numbers of Jews and dispersing them among a number of "concentration" camps, the largest being Dachau, outside Munich. In justification of these camps Germany cited similar camps established by the British during the Boer War. An ill-omened choice, considering that thirty thousand Boer women and children had died of neglect in the British concentration camps.

The following day a 2RN broadcast startled Irish listeners. De Valera was acting "to defend the government from two groups of armed men roaming the country, the Blueshirts and the IRA." A mass meeting of Blueshirts had been banned, an IRA camp in the Dublin mountains had been raided, and armed policemen were stationed on permanent guard outside de Valera's office.

"What's Dev playing at?" Ursula asked Helena Moloney at a Republican women's meeting. "How can he afford to alienate the IRA?"

"He's playing the political game," Helena replied, "disowning the Republicans to enhance his relations with the British. Perhaps he thinks that will help him negotiate an end to partition. It's clear de Valera thinks he doesn't need us anymore. But he's wrong," she added angrily.

Ursula walked home lost in thought. She had invested so much emotional coin in Eamon de Valera. His latest action felt like a betrayal.

T HE months passed; summer became autumn. The web of the wireless was expanding. France and tiny Luxembourg began bombarding British airwaves with advertising. Although hard-pressed for funds itself, the Irish broadcasting authority publicly decried such crass commercialism. By implication the Free State was above all that.

Radio Luxembourg had started up in the spring on an unauthorized wavelength. It was considered a pirate station, but many in Ireland listened. Ursula Halloran was not the only person hungry for word from the outside world.

In October Seán Lester wrote,

Dear Ursula,

Good news—I think. The League of Nations has invited me to be high commissioner for Danzig. At one time it was the preeminent port on the Baltic. When the Treaty of Versailles awarded Poland a corridor to the sea, Danzig was excluded and designated as a Free City.

The high commissioner will arbitrate disputes between the city and the Polish government, as well as dealing with Germany. The Germans feel they have a claim to Danzig because it has a mixed German-Polish population.

I have decided to accept the League's offer. At the least it will mean an increase in income. For lack of sufficient funds the Irish government has spoken of closing its office here in Geneva altogether. We shall be sorry to leave Geneva for we love the city, but these are uncertain times and one must seize an opportunity when it presents itself.

I shall take up my new post next January. As you can imagine, Elsie is excited at the prospect of having a new house to decorate. The high commissioner's residence is a former military command post, so will test her skills to the utmost!

Now I come to the point of this letter. Once again I am soliciting staff, and the League will be paying. Are you interested, Ursula?

She purchased a map of Europe as it had been redrawn by the Versailles Treaty and pinned it on her wall.

"Danzig," she whispered to herself, running her fingers over the map. "Poland. The Baltic Sea." The names were tempting on her tongue.

But the reasons that made her say no to Lester in the first place were still there.

In a speech in December Eoin O'Duffy referred to de Valera's Spanish father by saying: "Eamon de Valera does not understand the people of this country because he is a half-breed!"[1]

• • •

URSULA went home to Clare for Christmas, a season muted by Frank's death. Ned made a brief appearance but had very little to say. Ursula hoped he would reassure her about de Valera's policies, but he would not discuss de Valera at all. He only stayed one night. The next morning his bed was empty, his room once more unlived-in.

Ursula spent most of the holiday with Saoirse. With her horse there were no awkward misunderstandings, nothing to be explained. Only a warm flowing of emotion from one to the other; friendship and love and trust.

No betrayal.

BY the end of the year thirty-four IRA Volunteers had been convicted by military tribunal.

Although Ursula was furious about the IRA arrests, in the New Year she continued her work on behalf of Fianna Fáil. *They're what we have,* she reminded herself. *Somehow it will come right.*

Her work had become her life. "I am a career woman," she remarked to Louise one Sunday. She had been invited for dinner at number 16.

Louise made a face. "I don't know what that means, and I'm not sure you do either."

"It means," said Hector Hamilton, "that she's getting too long in the tooth to find a husband."

Strange new words, "Americanisms," began to pepper wireless broadcasts. There were references to such alien objects as *refrigerators* and *television* and *robots*. A woman's program even mentioned *slimming*, an unimaginable concept in a land still haunted by the memory of the Great Famine.

"We shall have to learn a whole new language," Ursula wrote to Henry Mooney in May of 1934. "But I suppose it is already familiar to you."

URSULA was restless and irritable and did not know why. The thread of her patience was stretched to breaking point.

Her moodiness was a source of comment in the broadcasting station. Finbar Cassidy felt it too. She lost her temper over trivial matters. Even avoiding politics was not enough to escape the lash of her scorn. "You're so provincial!" she exclaimed one evening when he made a comment about preferring mutton to beef.

"Provincial? And me only ordering supper. What's wrong with you, Ursula?"

"Nothing's wrong with me, I'm just bored to the back teeth with ... with ..." She waved her hands in the air, trying to create a shape to indicate her sense of walls closing in.

Wisely, Finbar devoted himself to his food. But when he took her back to Moore Street he lingered at the door. Without saying a word he put his arms around her and folded her tightly against his chest. He had expected resistance. Instead she went boneless in his embrace. He was surprised at how small she felt. He had imagined her as larger.

He pressed his lips against the top of her head. "Please tell me what's bothering you," he murmured into her hair. He was ready to defend this fragile creature against the world and all its troubles.

Ursula did not answer. It was not possible to answer, though she realized his question was kindly meant. But how could she explain her worries about Ned and her feeling of being stifled as a person and ... Lewis Baines. How could she possibly tell Finbar Cassidy that she was yearning to hear the voice of Lewis Baines?

Lewis, who had forgotten all about her.

Ursula closed her eyes and listened to Finbar's heart beating against her ear. Steady and strong. As if they had a will of their own, her fingers slipped inside his jacket. Slid down his body. Hooked in the waistband of his trousers.

"Come inside with me," she whispered.

"I thought your landlady had a rule about—"

"Devil take the rules. Come." She gave a tug.

Finbar followed her through the blue door.

The gaslight in the stairwell had been turned off to save money. Dusty darkness smelled of old wood and peeling paint and the soap jelly used to scrub the stairs.

Finbar fumbled for the handrail.

"We're not going upstairs," Ursula said.

"But—"

"Make love to me here."

Blood pounded in his temples. "Someone might come in."

"I know. Do it. Do it here and now or not at all."

Finbar's body was in revolt against his conscience. He had imagined making love to Ursula—imagined it too many times, resulting in too many sleepless nights and too many embarrassing sessions in the confessional—

but he had never envisioned the act taking place with the pair of them fully clothed in a dark stairwell.

A shudder ran the length of his body. "You don't want to do this," he whispered hoarsely.

"Don't tell me what I want!" She was illogically angry with him for not understanding something she did not understand herself. Her hands began moving on him, sliding under his clothes. Exploring.

Wherever she touched, he felt fire.

Jesus Mary and Joseph help me. Help me protect her.

He tried to back away but there was very little room at the bottom of the stairs. "Listen to me, Ursula," he panted. "This is all wrong and you will regret it surely."

"You don't want me," she said in a strange, flat tone.

Finbar moaned. "More than anything else in this world I want you. But not like this, *a stór,** not like this! When I . . . make you mine . . . we will be properly married and . . ."

She stiffened. "I never said I would marry you. I don't intend to marry anyone."

As if someone had pulled a plug, Finbar felt passion draining out of him. "And I don't intend to treat the girl I love like a whore."

Her hands dropped to her sides. "Is that what you think I am?"

"Is that what you want to be?" he shot back.

In the darkness he could not see her face. "You had best go," she said tightly.

"I . . . I'm sorry, Ursula, I didn't mean that, I . . ."

"Please, just go!"

The door opened, closed, and she was alone.

She leaned back against the wall. *Sin é. That's it.*

No one heard the sobs that shook her body.

On the corner of Ursula's desk at 2RN was a jam jar filled with pencils. Her first task every morning, as soon as she had taken off her hat, was to sharpen her pencils with an old penknife of Ned's. No one else was allowed to touch them and she did nothing until they were sharp.

The overnight reports waited in a stack beside the pencil jar. On the second of July Ursula finished her ritual with the pencils, then glanced at the first sheet on the stack. She drew a sharp breath and picked it up. The

*"Sweetheart."

report was taken from a German radio broadcast by Joseph Goebbels.

Ursula read with increasing horror.

According to Goebbels, the leader of the storm troopers had been plotting to overthrow Hitler. The man was seized by the SS while he was allegedly engaged in homosexual activities in a Munich hotel. Although he had been one of Hitler's closest comrades since the early days of the Nazi party, he was dragged from bed and shot. On the same night hundreds of his followers in Munich and Berlin were executed without trial. The incident was already being called the Night of the Long Knives.

Ursula shuddered. *The State committing murder with impunity. Someone has to do something about this!*

On the twenty-fifth of July, 1934, Nazis burst into the office of the Austrian chancellor in Vienna and shot him to death. No official sanction was imposed by the League of Nations.

WITHIN the Blueshirts was an intellectual elite composed of men such as Ernest Blythe and Desmond FitzGerald who admired Mussolini's ideal of the corporate state. But it was the military aspect that came to the fore. Under O'Duffy's direction the organization was reconstituted as the National Guard, a title the government did not sanction.

Eamon de Valera promptly revoked all civilian firearm certificates, including those for legally held weapons that members of government had been carrying since the O'Higgins assassination. When his action was challenged in the Dáil, de Valera accused O'Duffy of trying to set himself up as a dictator. With no apparent sense of irony, de Valera said the Irish government would not tolerate any man having a private army.

O'Duffy claimed membership in the Blueshirts was 62,000 and rising. Fianna Fáil hotly disputed that figure. But there was no doubt the Blueshirts were expanding. They viewed themselves as patriots dedicated to maintaining free speech and resisting a one-party state. Their new constitution included a women's section and stressed physical fitness. It also limited membership exclusively to Irish citizens who professed the Christian faith.[2]

"Although I approve of their enlightened attitude toward women," Ursula wrote to Fliss, "and I am not really happy with Fianna Fáil, I could never support the Blueshirts. Not only are they anti-Republican, but anti-Semitic as well. I despise any form of bigotry! In Northern Ireland we have proof of its terrible consequences.

"I think bigots secretly feel inferior, Fliss, which is why they claim a superiority effortlessly conferred upon them by race or religion. That is as bad as an inherited monarchy in which the laziest villain can become king."

"With tongue firmly fixed in cheek," Fliss replied, "I take umbrage at your remarks. I certainly am not inferior. How could I be? I am English. Yet I do admit to being anti-Semitic, which is a perfectly acceptable prejudice. Fashionable, even. The Jews are intellectuals and bankers and one always hates *them*.

"Adolf Hitler's animosity toward the Jews does seem excessive, though. He blames them entirely for Germany's defeat in the Great War. The Gestapo—that's the secret state police—are confiscating Jewish property. Often the owners simply disappear. German Jews are beginning to arrive in Britain, telling rather frightening stories that no one really believes, but one has to feel sorry for them. In some cases they have lost everything. I cannot imagine how awful it must be to arrive in a strange land with nothing but the clothes you stand up in."

That's because you're not Irish, thought Ursula.

Fliss's letter continued: "Sir Oswald says Hitler is doing wonderful things for the German economy, however, and continues to champion him. The younger members of our set use Munich as a sort of finishing school cum social springboard,[3] and Sir Oswald's wife and sister-in-law, Unity Mitford, often visit Germany. In fact Unity has become quite passionately devoted to dear Adolf, it's something of an open scandal. She has taken to whizzing around London in an MG with a swastika painted on it."

19 August 1934
HINDENBERG, GERMAN PRESIDENT, DEAD
ADOLF HITLER DECLARES HIMSELF HEAD OF STATE
Title of President Abolished. Hitler to Be Known as Fuehrer and
Reich Chancellor

Chapter Twenty-six

IN September the Blueshirts merged with Cumann na nGaedheal to form a new party called United Ireland/Fine Gael. Like its predecessor, *Fine Gael** drew its primary support from large rural landowners and the prosperous middle class.

When Eoin O'Duffy was elected president of the party, Fine Gael acquired an overtly fascist element.

As soon as 2RN received the announcement of his election, Ursula placed an urgent telephone call to the Department of External Affairs.

De Valera's removal of political opponents had not extended to the lower echelons of civil service. Finbar Cassidy was assured of retaining his job if he kept his head down and the department running smoothly.

When Ursula heard Finbar's voice on the telephone she said briskly, "Can you have lunch with me?"

"What? Today?"

"If possible."

"Why ... certainly, I can meet you for lunch. Where?"

"Flynn's? In an hour?"

Finbar was already there when Ursula arrived. When she approached his table he stood up and pulled out a chair for her. A smile set his freckled face aglow. "I'm glad you rang me," he said as she sat down. "I hope this means—"

"I'm not picking up where we left off," Ursula interrupted before the

*"The Family of the Irish."

conversation could become embarrassing. "I came to urge you to think again about your political affiliations. When we Irish dig ourselves into a hole we tend to stay there, but..."

Finbar's smile congealed on his face. "You wanted to meet me just to launch into a political harangue?"

"I'm not haranguing you, I'm concerned about you. As a friend," she hastened to add. He looked so crestfallen she reached across the table to touch his hand. "You once warned me about the fascists, remember? Now you're consorting with them."

"Hardly consorting, Ursula. I don't believe I've spoken ten words to any of the Blueshirts. But surely a political party should be flexible enough to embrace more than one point of view."

"You think the fascist point of view is worth embracing? Hitler is a fascist. Do you realize what's happening in Germany?"

"External Affairs follows international developments closely, it's our business," he said huffily.

She must make him understand. "Somewhere along the line the legal German chancellor has become the legal German dictator, Finbar—and no one's made a move to stop him. Now he's persecuting the Jews just as the English persecuted us. It's monstrous! All fascists should be locked away where they can't do any damage. Or better yet, shot."

"That's a bit extreme, isn't it?" said Finbar. "People are either saints or sinners, wonderful or rotten to the core; there's no middle ground with you."

Ursula recognized the truth in his words but did not consider it a character flaw. She was Ned Halloran's daughter, passionate and committed when others were apathetic. She leaned earnestly toward Finbar. "Please disassociate yourself from the Fine Gael party. For my sake, if no other reason."

"Why don't you disassociate yourself from Fianna Fáil for my sake?" he countered. "De Valera insists that only he knows what's right for Ireland, but what he really wants is to do all our thinking for us. And that's dangerous."

The remark was too close to the bone. "Not as dangerous as Eoin O'Duffy," Ursula said defensively. She would never admit that she was beginning to question her own loyalty to Dev.

"Listen to me, Ursula. I work in government, and I can tell you there's no perfect party and no perfect leader either."

She gave a sniff. "You're just jealous because you backed the wrong horse."

He realized there was no point in continuing the discussion; they would only quarrel again. She was, he told himself, incapable of compromise.

"We both have to go back to work soon," he reminded her. "May I buy you a sandwich first?"

Ursula cocked her head to one side, surveying the menu chalked on a slate on the wall. "A bowl of soup, I think."

"Whatever you say." His mind began to drift away. Back to his desk with its piles of folders; back to the afternoon's appointments; back to what was mundane and certain.

When they left Flynn's he went one way and she the other. After a few paces Finbar looked back, only to see Ursula striding away from him with her lovely free-swinging walk.

At the corner she stopped. Turned around. But Finbar was gone.

URSULA had too much energy and not enough outlets for it. She visited every livery stable in Dublin, hoping at least one of them would quote a price cheap enough to allow her to bring Saoirse up from the country. None did. She hired horses to ride by the hour or took long walks through the streets of the city. Nothing tired her sufficiently to turn off her mind and allow a peaceful sleep.

She worked all the hours she could, then went home to write endless letters late into the night. And read. Because she knew most of her own books by heart, she began borrowing others from the library. One evening she hurled a popular "woman's novel" across the room after reading only a few pages. *Do women really want to read this saccharine rubbish? Or is it foisted off on them to discourage them from using their minds?*

ADOLF Hitler refused to take any further part in the Geneva Disarmament Conference. He also withdrew Germany from the League of Nations, claiming the country could no longer tolerate the humiliating and dishonoring demands of the other Powers.

Meanwhile the Gestapo were encouraging Germans to denounce one another as traitors. Anyone considered a threat to the New Order was dealt with summarily. Thousands of Communists and socialists, denounced by neighbors and workmates, were sent to concentration camps.

·   ·   ·

IN November the Irish gardaí raided Blueshirt headquarters in Parnell Square. Some weapons were found, but nothing sufficient to allow the government to bring criminal charges against Cumann na nGaedheal. However de Valera did bring charges against individual members of the party. Eoin O'Duffy and two colleagues were arrested at Westport. The arrest was declared illegal by the High Court a few days later.

That same month, Séamus Clandillon left 2RN on indefinite sick leave.[1] He was clearly exhausted, but promised to return as soon as he had a little rest.

When Ursula went to Clare for Christmas, as a present for the family she bought a gramophone record of John McCormack singing "Friend of Mine."

Shortly after the New Year a man from Posts and Telegraphs was brought in to serve as acting director at 2RN.

Chapter Twenty-seven

IN February of 1935 Fliss wrote to Ursula:

The family and I are no longer on good terms and I am looking for
a flat of my own in London. What a pain! I do hope female emancipation is all it is cracked up to be.

I have Sir Oswald Mosley to thank. Last month I attended a huge
rally for him in Birmingham. Needless to say, my father refused me
permission to go. Needless to say, I went. Now I am no longer welcome in the familial nest.

Over ten thousand people were at the rally. Three thousand of them
wore black shirts and leather belts like Mussolini's followers, and gave
Sir Oswald the stiff-armed fascist salute. There is a rumour that he is
receiving funds from Mussolini. I would not be surprised.

In his speech Sir Oswald said he will ask the nation to return a
fascist majority in the next election. He quite bluntly stated his aim as
a modern dictatorship that would have sufficient power to overcome
all the problems the people want overcome.[1]

The speech was rousing and full of fire but the longer I listened,
the more uncomfortable I was, Ursula. When we were at Surval you
used to talk a lot about freedom for Ireland. You started me thinking
about freedom in the abstract, which I had never done before. One
does not give much thought to something one takes for granted.

If Sir Oswald has his way we might lose quite a bit of our freedom.
He wants to take it from us as a parent denies freedom to a child: for

its own good. But we are not children and I am no longer convinced he is a kindly paterfamilias. Ambition drips off the man like perspiration.

At the Birmingham rally Sir Oswald's Blackshirts were handing out membership applications to join the British Union of Fascists. I took one—frankly, I was too intimidated not to—but as soon as I was on the train I wadded it up and threw it under the seat.

Call me reactionary if you like, but I want no part of the "brave new world" Aldous Huxley described in his latest novel. Have you read it yet, Ursula? It sent chills up my spine.

Brave New World, with its nightmarish vision of a totalitarian society, was among the books banned by the Irish censorship board. Ursula asked Fliss to send her a copy at once.

That same month John A. Costello, a Fine Gael lawyer, declared in the Dáil that the Blueshirts would be as victorious in Ireland as Mussolini's Blackshirts in Italy, and the 'Hitlershirts' in Germany.[2]

In March of 1935 Germany announced conscription. Tanks came out in the open, rumbling ominously down city streets. Luftwaffe planes slashed across the sky in formation.

Britain was the first democracy to make a pact with the Nazis, signing a naval agreement.

In Vienna, an uprising of the Social Democrats was ruthlessly crushed by the government. The 2RN newsreader gravely reported, "There are rumours circulating that Adolf Hitler plans to annex Austria. Jews are fleeing the country in their thousands."

Meanwhile gangs of drumbeating sectarian thugs paraded nightly through Belfast, inciting anti-Catholic violence.

DURING Easter Week a bronze statue of Cúchulainn was unveiled at the GPO. At Ursula Halloran's suggestion, a special 2RN broadcast featured the surviving men who had fought there.

ONE morning Séamus Clandillon reappeared at the station.

"Welcome back!" Ursula called happily.

"I'm not back. I've just called in to pick up some personal items and to say good-bye to everyone."

"You're leaving permanently? I don't believe it."

"Neither do I, but it's true enough." He gave a rueful shake of the head, and Ursula noticed how thin his hair had become. There were dark circles under his eyes and his chest had a strange, caved-in look. "I've been here nine years and hoped to die in the traces," Clandillon told her. "My mistake was in falling ill. That gave them a chance to stick the knife in my back while I wasn't looking."

"But what will you do, Séamus?"

"Oh, they're looking after me in their fashion. I have orders to go back to my old job as an insurance inspector." He did not add, though Ursula understood full well, that the position would be a demotion and involve a cut in salary.

She was outraged. "What an appalling way to treat you! You made this station what it is today. Whom shall I protest to?"

"Don't, Ursula. It will do no good to campaign for me, the decision's already made. In a way, I'm relieved. No more responsibility for staff, no begging for funds, no sticking my head above the parapet to be shot off by every politician looking for an easy target."

"How can they ever replace you?"

"Be assured they'll find someone. They're offering nine hundred pounds per annum, which is a damned sight more than they ever paid me. There'll probably be an advert in the papers. Responsible position in broadcasting available, knowledge of Irish essential. Brass balls definitely required," he added wryly.

"Could I apply?"

"Your Irish is excellent—and you have that other qualification too. But you're a woman, my dear. Unfortunately, you are a woman."

Clandillon had a kind word for everyone before he left. "You must soldier on and you will do admirably," he assured them. "This is better for me, truly it is."

On the first of May a government news release arrived on Ursula's desk with instructions to have it read following the evening news. "The Dublin Broadcasting Station is pleased to announce that Dr. Thomas J. Kiernan, an expert on finance and economics, has been seconded from the Department of External Affairs to join our staff. Dr. Kiernan's new title will be director of broadcasting."

No named source for the news release was given. The decision makers who occupied the middle stratum of civil service comprised an anonymous army. As in every government, they had power without accountability.

The selection came as a shock to the acting director of 2RN, who had confidently expected to be named to the post. He only learned of Kiernan's appointment when he heard it on the wireless.

Kiernan was married to the popular ballad singer, Delia Murphy, whose recordings were frequently played on 2RN. "Rather more frequently now, I expect," Mairead remarked to Ursula.

John MacDonagh, a brother of Thomas MacDonagh who had been executed in 1916, was appointed as productions officer. An actor and playwright, he had produced a number of programs for 2RN over the years. For the sake of his dead brother Ursula gave MacDonagh a warm welcome to staff. She even brewed a pot of tea for him.

THE approaching summer brought warm, moisture-laden air, heavy with the scents of country fecundity even in the city. Ursula arrived at 2RN after yet another night of insomnia. The lack of sleep was spinning gray cobwebs through her brain.

Someone has to do something about this, she decided.

The black telephone on the wall was smeared with finger marks. Under Séamus Clandillon, employees had turned their hand to anything that needed doing. The station director himself had not been above rubbing candle wax on a sticking drawer, or mopping up spilled tea. But since his departure an attitude of "that isn't my responsibility" was developing.

Ursula ostentatiously wiped the telephone clean with her pocket handkerchief. She wound the crank, and when she was connected with the exchange, told the operator, "I wish to speak to London, England. The offices of the *Daily Mail.*" She did not have to give her number, which was illuminated on the switchboard at the exchange.

The call was put through within minutes. In her most businesslike voice Ursula told the newspaper's managing editor, "This is the Dublin Broadcasting Station." She did not give her name. "We are planning a program of interviews with foreign correspondents, and your Mr. Baines was suggested. Might he be available to come to Ireland in the near future?"

Silence for a moment. "Haynes? I don't . . . eh, what?" A brief conversation was held with someone else in the room. Then, "Is Lewis Baines the man you mean?"

"I believe so."

"Usually he's . . . ah, thank you. Here's Baines's home address and telephone number, you might want to contact him yourself."

Séamus Clandillon had once ordered a supply of heavy bond embossed with the station letterhead. The extravagance had been criticized by the Department of Finance, and Clandillon had put most of the stationery away unused. From the bottom drawer of the station director's desk Ursula surreptitiously took one sheet and a matching envelope. She typed a formal letter addressed to Mr. Lewis Baines suggesting the proposed interview, signed the letter in an indecipherable backhanded scrawl, and posted it to England.

She began taking the incoming mail from the porter and distributing it herself. When a letter arrived from London with *L. Baines* on the flap of the envelope, Ursula quietly slipped it into her pocket.

"Dear Sir," Lewis Baines had written. "I shall be glad to oblige by giving an interview to your station, but I cannot come to Ireland for a few weeks as I have other commitments. Please let me know if that will be satisfactory. Transportation will be no problem. I assume you will reimburse me for aeroplane fuel and tie-down costs."

Chapter Twenty-eight

2RN was preparing for the evening broadcast. As Ursula searched through a sheaf of news items, she heard a feminine gasp. "Who ever is that?" a female member of staff asked in an awed but audible whisper. Ursula followed the direction of her gaze.

In the doorway stood a strikingly handsome man who announced to the room at large, "I'm looking for the program director."

His voice resonated in Ursula's bones.

She stood up. "Lewis Baines?" She contrived to sound surprised.

"Miss Halloran? I didn't know you worked here."

"I do work here." Spoken offhandedly; the sort of response she would make to anyone. "Is there something I can do for you?"

"Someone—I couldn't quite make out his name—wrote me about giving an interview for a program on foreign correspondents."

"Really? No one mentioned it to me. Of course I'm in the news department, but . . ." Ursula raised her voice. "John, are we doing a program on foreign correspondents?"

"Not that I know of." John MacDonagh riffled through the scheduling. "There's nothing here about it."

Ursula said, "I'm sorry, Lewis. It must have been a project our Mr. Clandillon planned, but he is no longer with us. I hardly know what to tell you."

She was embarrassed and apologetic. Lewis was amused and gallant. "No problem at all, it simply gave me an excuse to return to Ireland. I've been meaning to anyway. And fancy finding you here! There are no coincidences, don't you agree?"

Ursula agreed. She smiled. He smiled.

No mention was made of reimbursing him for his travel expenses. Lewis Baines did not look like a man who needed money.

He waited while Ursula rang the Shelbourne Hotel to book a room for the night. "Four nights," Lewis corrected. "I'm taking you to dinner this evening. And you do have the weekend free, don't you?"

Thursday Friday Saturday Sunday. Lewis Baines filling every available moment. A golden circle surrounding us, shutting everyone else out.

After charming every female in the broadcasting station, Lewis sauntered off to enjoy the city. When her workday was over Ursula ran all the way home. She spread what remained of her Surval wardrobe on the bed and surveyed it with a critical eye. Styles had changed in the interim. *But not drastically, thank God. Not in Ireland.*

She dug out a paper of needles and pawed through her bedside locker until she found a spool of thread. Screwing up her mouth in concentration, Ursula mended the sagging hem of her most fashionable frock. Twice she pricked her finger with the needle, but the bloodstains were on the inside of the skirt and would not show.

Clean underthings. Fresh stockings. The shoes that had hurt her feet during the Eucharistic Congress. Face scrubbed to a glow, hair brushed to a shine. She felt a momentary regret that she had no perfume, but she never wore scent.

Fully dressed, Ursula stood in front of the looking glass. Maud Gonne in the role of Caitlín ní Houlihan gazed back at her. Proud. Regal.

That night Precious, child of the slums, swept into the Shelbourne Hotel as if she owned the place.

The elegant hotel was curiously immune to the worst effects of the depression. Since the twenties, when the "new" Ireland was perceived to be an exciting young country lacking the postwar lassitude that drugged Europe, well-to-do visitors had flocked to enjoy the Shelbourne's hospitality. By the thirties, British guests luxuriated in the belief that Britain had granted Ireland her freedom in a spirit of generosity.[1]

The Irish understandably held a different opinion.

The Shelbourne's décor was luxurious but bland. Over the years contemporary furniture had been added to antique, blending into a comfortable melange. Pale walls set off furnishings upholstered in floral cretonne to make British visitors feel at home.

Lewis and Ursula were seated at a choice table in the main dining room. A draped and carpeted hush, hardly disturbed by the clink of china and glassware, encouraged conversation.

Since they last met, Lewis told Ursula, he had done quite a bit of traveling. India, Hong Kong, Crete. Ursula wanted to ask what "other commitments" had kept him from coming to Ireland sooner, but that would mean admitting she had read his letter. "Have you been on journalistic assignments?" she asked.

"Only in India. Covering a spot of trouble with this Gandhi fellow. Aside from that I've just been wandering. It's in the blood, I suppose. My grandmother went to Africa at a time when most women went no farther than the nearest spa. We even have a photograph of her riding on an elephant."

Ursula had nothing comparable in her conversational arsenal. Her family stories were private and definitely not to be shared with an Englishman. But Lewis was intrigued by her interest in foreign affairs. Women did not usually talk to him about European politics.

When Ursula expressed concern about the rapid growth of fascism, he agreed it was a worrying trend. "People are reluctant to confront the fascists head-on, though," he said. "The Great War cured most Europeans of their tribal bellicosity."

Bellicosity. Oh Sacred Heart of Jesus. "Henry Mooney tells me the Americans are nervous of fascism too," Ursula replied. "Their response is to retreat into isolationism."

"That's not going to be good enough. One of these days the whole thing's going to erupt. There's even a strong fascist element in Spain; I saw it firsthand not so long ago."

"You've been to Spain?"

"Of course," he said as if everyone had been to Spain. Lewis Baines gave off an aroma of exotic landscapes.

"Have you ever thought of investigating the northern Irish situation?" Ursula asked. "The politicians on both sides of the border are pretending there's no sectarian violence up there because they can't deal with it. You could advance the theory that Northern Ireland is a microcosm of what's going on in Europe." *Good word, microcosm. Every bit as good as bellicosity!*

"I never thought of Ulster that way," said Lewis.

"To begin with, don't call it Ulster." *I'll show him I'm as knowledgeable as he is. At least on one subject.* "Ulster has been one of the four provinces of Ireland since ancient times. It's composed of nine counties: Derry, Antrim, Down, Armagh, Fermanagh, Tyrone, Donegal, Cavan, and Monaghan. When partition was devised the original intention was to include all nine.

"The Unionists were trying to circumvent democracy by creating an artificial statelet on the island of Ireland where Protestants would be in the majority. But in Cavan, Monaghan, and Donegal, the Catholics were in the majority. So the Unionists had to limit their 'Northern Ireland' to six counties. Therefore it isn't Ulster at all. To use that term is to stake a British territorial claim on three counties which, under the Treaty, are ours."

"Ours?" Lewis queried with amusement. "You're very nationalistic, aren't you?"

"More than that, I'm an Irish Republican. All the Hallorans are. It's in the blood."

"Ah," Lewis nodded. "In the blood. I like spirited women with minds of their own. Great Britain abounds in them."

Her blood was up now. "*Great* Britain?" Ursula retorted. "There's a fine irony in that name. Britain—in fact, the whole concept of Britishness—was a mythical identity invented by England to encourage the Scots and the Welsh to join the English army and fight for the English king. Ireland was never considered 'British.' That's why the official title was the United Kingdom of Great Britain and Ireland."

"Migod," said Lewis Baines. "You really are a spitfire, aren't you?"

She smiled sweetly. "I'm an educated woman," she replied.

He ordered dessert and tea for both of them, but the tea grew cold in their cups. Conversation dwindled away while he smoked a Turkish cigarette and held her with his eyes, smiling a slow, lazy smile.

The silences were better than the conversation. Between them was developing a powerful erotic chemistry that contradicted everything Ursula thought she knew about herself.

When Lewis took her back to Moore Street he kissed her again. More deeply than before. She longed to invite him in but dare not.

On Friday night he had tickets to the Abbey Theatre. Ursula sat through the play achingly aware of the man in the seat beside her. Afterwards she could not have told the plot of the play.

At her door Lewis kissed her with such passion she thought he might try to force himself upon her, but he did not. Breathing hard, he gave her a last hug and bade her good night.

That night in his hotel bedroom Lewis recalled the ever-shifting shadows in her blue-gray eyes. Like the play of clouds and light on water.

On Saturday he took her to Baldonnel Aerodrome for a ride in his aeroplane. Ursula dressed for the occasion in her only pair of jodhpurs, a cream-colored blouse and a woolly jumper. When Lewis called for her he was wearing plus fours and a leather aviator's jacket. She bit her lip to keep from laughing. No one she knew wore plus fours! But she had to admit they suited him.

Baldonnel was thriving. A brisk traffic in air taxis had begun. One could fly Baldonnel to Liverpool and return for five guineas, via the Midland & Scottish airline.[2] The days of being restricted to sea travel were well and truly over, Ursula thought with relief.

She had never seen an aeroplane up close. Lewis's biplane had a fabric fuselage and two pairs of wings stiffened by sizing. Intellectually she knew the machine could fly; rationally it seemed impossible.

"She's a beauty, isn't she?" Lewis said. "She's my second Moth; I ground-looped the first one. Nasty crosswind. Half a mo." He stepped away to give instructions to one of several men in greasy coveralls who had gathered around the plane.

Ursula eyed the Moth with trepidation. *There'll be nothing between me and thin air but a shell of stiffened cloth.*

And what is "ground-looping?"

"That sweater of yours won't be warm enough once we're up there," Lewis told her. "Here, take my jacket."

"What about you?"

"Oh, I always keep a spare in the cockpit. You aren't the first young lady I've taken closer to heaven."

When she put on his jacket, it still held his body heat.

"Put your foot there, Ursula, where I'm showing you, and step up. Mind the struts. And be careful you don't step anywhere else or you'll break through the wing."

Break through the wing? With my foot?

Wedged into the tiny front cockpit of the plane, Ursula was slanted backward at an angle. She could see only the tip of the propeller beyond the cowling.

Lewis nimbly slid into the rear cockpit. "You'll find a helmet and goggles wedged down there beside you," he instructed. "Put them on while we warm up. I promise not to keep you waiting long."

With fingers gone strangely numb, Ursula donned the snug leather helmet and adjusted the goggles. *All I need now is the silk scarf.*

Lewis shouted something. A man on the ground spun the propeller. The engine coughed several times, then roared into life. Ursula gripped the rim of the cockpit with both hands as the slipstream roiled past. The aeroplane vibrated like an eager animal.

The engine settled into a rhythm that eventually became one long musical note, purring as if the elements involved were perfectly suited. Time stood still. When she could stand it no longer, Ursula twisted around in her seat to look back at Lewis. She could not see his eyes behind his goggles, but she saw him give the thumbs-up signal.

The crewmen who had been leaning against the wings and tail stepped back. Other men pulled the wedges from under the wheels. The speed of the whirring propeller increased. The plane's tail lifted, bringing the seats in the cockpits level. The vibrations became an intermittent thunder as they sped forward. The ground on either side of the plane blurred. Then suddenly . . . a relative silence. A silence like none other.

They were flying.

Flying!!!

Literally riding on the air. Up, up, up toward the blue portal of an endless sky.

And I'm not the least bit airsick! How could I be when I'm flying like the angels?

Showing off for Ursula, Lewis Baines put the plane through its paces. With great banking sideslips he drew patterns on the air. He set the Moth spinning spinning spinning, squeezing the stomach out of her and the laughter too. At the bottom of a long dive, when they pulled up just as the earth was rushing at them with terrifying speed, she screamed. But she loved it. The feeling was like nothing she had ever experienced.

As they soared over Kildare she looked down at the green lap of the Curragh, sheep-cropped to the smoothness of a croquet lawn. From such a height one could not see the mud and the sheep droppings. Or the problems people created with artificial borders and hypocritical morality.

There was nothing narrow-minded about the sky.

Looking at Ursula, Lewis Baines decided he had been wrong in his original appraisal. When they first met he had thought the Irish girl not pretty, but interesting-looking. Now he saw that she was beautiful. The flight had set her cheeks aflame and filled her eyes with stars.

When they returned to the city Lewis bought Ursula an armload of roses at Jameson's Flower Shop in Nassau Street. "Roses for an Irish rose," he said. "Are you hungry?"

Madame had insisted ladies must never admit to having an appetite. "Starved," Ursula replied.

"There's a hotel just around the corner, shall we see what they have on offer?"

The doorkeeper of the hotel dining room raised his eyebrows at Ursula's masculine attire. Young women these days were behaving scandalously, his expression said. But business was business and the dining room was almost empty anyway. He ushered them inside.

"I don't think he approved of your jodhpurs," Lewis remarked *sotto voce*. "At home no one would turn a hair. Women can go anywhere in riding clothes."

"Even to balls?" Ursula asked with wide-eyed innocence.

"Especially to balls," he assured her. "They wear jodhpurs underneath their gowns, so if they get bored they can sneak off to the stables and have a canter in the moonlight."

"Fliss never told me she could dance in riding boots."

He waved a hand in the air. "They can all do it. It's a required study for Saxons."

In response to his gesture, a waiter appeared at their table with a menu. "Would you like a glass of wine before we order?" Lewis asked Ursula.

"I think not, thank you. But I could do damage to a pint of stout."

"Do you mean that?"

"I do mean it."

The dining room did not serve pints, the waiter informed them. Particularly not to ladies, his tight-lipped manner added. He directed them to the hotel bar next door.

The darkly paneled retreat was textured with pipe smoke. When Ursula described the late-afternoon clientele as "a bulge of bankers and a slither of solicitors," Lewis bit the inside of his lip to keep from laughing out loud.

Stepping up to the highly polished mahogany bar, he ordered two pints of Guinness. The exclusively male drinkers ranged along the bar turned to stare at the young woman in jodhpurs who stood beside him, carrying a bunch of roses. But no one challenged her right to be there. Her companion was too well dressed; his accent too clearly identified him as a member of the British upper class.

The Irish might be struggling out from under the yoke of colonialism but the feelings of inferiority were still there. The drinkers went back to their drink.

Lewis took one taste of Guinness, grimaced, and pushed the glass aside. "Gin and bitters," he told the bartender.

"You don't want your Guinness, sir?"

"Don't worry," Ursula said brightly, "it won't go to waste. I'll drink his when I finish mine."

The stout sang in her blood like wind through the struts of the Moth.

Chapter Twenty-nine

LEWIS Baines's room at the Shelbourne was actually a small suite. The sitting room was a snug, low-ceilinged chamber on the mezzanine floor, with windows looking out on Kildare Street. Traffic sounds were magnified by the canyon-like acoustics of the street until Lewis drew the heavy curtains, shutting out the twilight. "There, is that better?"

"Much." Ursula smiled up at him.

"Since we never got around to eating in that other hotel, shall I order a meal sent up?"

She shook her head. "I'm not hungry right now. I just want to sit here and—"

"And?"

"Enjoy it, I suppose. I've never been in one of the private rooms before."

"I'm sorry now that I didn't ask for the best suite."

"You should always have the best," Ursula replied dreamily.

"That is the sort of thing I should be saying to you." Lewis sat down beside her on the couch and took her hand. "You really are the most smashing girl, you know."

"Am I?" That same dreamy voice. *He is going to try to seduce me.*

And I am going to let him.

They kissed. Tentatively at first, then as deeply as before. Body pressed against body. Low, wordless syllables of pleasure. Hands beginning to search and seek.

Lewis stood up. Keeping his back to her, he crossed the room to the bed and turned down the covers, then brought a towel from the adjacent bathroom to spread over the sheet. Ursula was surprised. *Are men in the throes of passion always so fastidious?*

He looked at her over his shoulder. "Take off your shoes, you look as if you might bolt for the door at any minute. Are you frightened of me?"

She raised her chin. "Of course not."

"Then come sit here beside me." He patted the bed.

When he began to undress her, she clutched her thumbs. She had never been seen naked by anyone else. *I have good bones,* she reminded herself fiercely behind closed eyes.

Lewis praised the grace of her shoulders as he uncovered them, coping easily with the tiny buttons of her blouse. She wore her best chemise beneath. "Your breasts are whiter than the linen," he said. Lowering his blond head, he kissed each one gently just where the swell began.

"Lie back now."

She kept her eyes closed while he removed her jodhpurs. As the fabric slid down her body he flattered her waist, her hips, her thighs with poetic phrases.

Too poetic, said an acerbic voice in Ursula's mind. *He's plundering Lord Byron and George Meredith and he thinks I won't know.* But she had gone this far out of a mixture of repressed desire and long-standing curiosity; she would go the rest of the way.

Opening her eyes, she reached toward him. "Let me help you with your shirt buttons."

Lewis gently pushed her hand away. He removed his clothes by himself and folded them neatly on a chair. Placed his shoes side by side underneath. Rolled up his socks and thrust them into the shoes. When he rejoined Ursula on the bed he plumped the pillows before gathering her into his arms.

How dare he roll up his socks!

"Pretty girl," Lewis said softly. "Pretty rose. You're very tense. Relax for me, my Irish rose."

His fingers sought out the tenderest parts of her body. Patiently, expertly, until at last she felt her breath catch in her throat. Her entire being focused on what was about to happen. The most intimate of mysteries to be solved, the miracle of flesh on flesh to be experienced at last.

With consummate skill Lewis brought her nerves singing to the surface.

A great shudder ran through her body. *Electricity. Magic!*

Smooth hands, silky sheets. The fragrance of expensive soap and shaving cream. Intimate caresses. Thought fading away. The potential for bliss lay sweetly heavy at the core of her being, waiting for a very special man . . . this man . . .

Lewis began whispering obscenities.

Like filth pouring out of a golden goblet, his beautiful voice applied the terminology of the gutter to her private parts.

Ursula went cold.

His hot breath with its freight of forbidden words continued to wash over her, but she did not feel it. She had mentally withdrawn from her body. His vulgarity could not touch her. It demeaned only him.

Absorbed in his own sensations, Lewis did not notice that she had become a detached observer.

She had expected pain. When it came, it was short, sharp, and over. Lewis supported his upper body on his elbows so Ursula did not bear his full weight. His rhythm had the smooth acceleration of an aeroplane engine. She was aware of him moving inside her, but there was none of the excitement she had felt while flying. Her heart did not race. Her body did not thrill.

The observer inside her head asked, *Is this all there is?*

WHEN it was over he inquired solicitously, "Did I hurt you?" as if he had stepped on her toes while dancing. The incongruity, compared with his recent vocabulary, made her burst into laughter.

He thought she was laughing for joy and took it as a compliment.

"You're very sweet," he said.

Lewis lay for a time with one arm flung over his eyes. Then he kissed her forehead, slipped from the bed and went into the bathroom. When Ursula heard the water running she got up. Her genitals were excruciatingly sore. There was blood on the towel. She rolled it into a ball and stuffed it under the bed.

When they had both washed and dressed Lewis suggested they go down to the Georgian Bar off the lobby for a nightcap. She said she was very tired and would prefer to go home instead. He took her to Moore Street in a taxicab. Kissed her at the door. Promised to collect her in the morning after early Mass and take her to breakfast. Went back to the waiting taxi, whistling.

Ursula closed the door and stood white-lipped with anger.

TRUE to his promise, Lewis appeared at her door the next morning. She accompanied him to the Gresham, where they were served a leisurely Sunday breakfast. He asked how she had slept. She assured him she slept very well, thank you. And you? Topping. Absolutely topping.

He remarked on the appointments of his suite and the comfort of his mattress. He did not mention finding a bloodstained towel. He made no allusion to her virginity. *The supposedly precious gift of my virtue,* Ursula thought. *And he didn't even notice.*

Chapter Thirty

LEWIS Baines had made love to his first woman when he was fifteen years old. Until then his sexual experience had been limited to masturbation or the encounters common among boys in British public schools. Females had come as a revelation to him.

He loved the texture of their skin. He loved the way they smelled, the way they walked, and most of all the way they adored him. He loved women in general and in the particular. Pursuing them provided the greatest excitement in his life. Like a hunter on safari, Lewis Baines was always on the lookout for the next trophy.

His romances were real while they lasted. He was simply too fond of the whole sex to limit himself to one individual forever. But while he was with a woman he treated her with the greatest respect—except in those dark and private moments when whatever was darkest and most private in a man rose up in him and demanded its turn.

Ursula Halloran was something outside his experience. Lewis had expected an Irish girl—Catholic, and therefore fanatically virtuous—would be the most challenging of trophies. This one had practically fallen into his arms, but he was not disappointed. Although he had enjoyed her body he had not captured her. Not yet. There was an elusive quality about Ursula that intrigued him.

He had awakened thinking about her. While he shaved, he planned the next step in the courtship. Much would depend upon her, of course. Lewis had learned to follow a woman's lead after the first sexual encounter, allowing her to set the tone for the next. That way one could be certain there would be a next.

Would Ursula be shy when they met? Would there be tears bravely fought back? Or would she be a step ahead of him in the game, tantalizing him with knowing smiles? He was electric with anticipation.

The reality was not quite what he expected.

As they sat together at breakfast, Ursula chatted about aeroplanes, the weather, and her Aunt Norah's cooking. Her conversation was animated but impersonal. Not once did she refer, even obliquely, to their recent intimacy.

Lewis was perplexed. Another girl would have sought some pledge of affection. Ursula did not even ask when he was leaving. At last he had to bring up the subject up himself. "I'd planned to fly back to London in the morning but—"

"I'm sure you have important business waiting for you," she interrupted sunnily. "We mustn't keep you."

There was no urgent reason to return to London, but now he could not admit it. "We can spend today together, Ursula, and have dinner."

"That would be nice," she replied, gazing past him at something she obviously found of more interest, "but I don't have the time. I must go in to the broadcasting station for several hours."

This was not strictly true either, but he was not to know.

"Supper then, afterwards?" he said, feeling slightly desperate.

She kept gazing past him. "I suppose," she replied indifferently.

INSTEAD of allowing Lewis to take her back to the Shelbourne that evening, Ursula suggested Mitchell's in Grafton Street, which served wholesome but unremarkable Irish food. The sort of place one might take a casual acquaintance.

Halfway through the meal she stifled a yawn. "I suspect I need an early night," she said, laughing.

A baffled Lewis Baines delivered her to Moore Street by ten o'clock, then returned to the Shelbourne alone.

Next morning he was winging his way east. When he looked down at the Irish Sea, it was the color of Ursula Halloran's eyes.

When Ursula arrived at 2RN on Monday morning John MacDonagh was waiting for her. "About that program of interviews with foreign correspondents," he began. "It was a good idea and I think we should go through with it."

Ursula stared at him. *But it was only a ruse, a way to . . .*

MacDonagh said, "Is that fellow Baines still around?"

"I believe he's gone back to England." *Please God he's gone back to England.*

"Pity about that. He had a wonderful voice, did he not? Do you have an address for him? Let's see if he can come back sometime soon."

Ursula could only nod.

"You know more about the international scene than anyone else here," MacDonagh went on. "You could present the program."

"On air, you mean?"

"Of course on air." MacDonagh smiled at her dumbfounded expression. "It's a wonder someone hasn't thought of it before, Ursula."

"Dear Papa," Ursula confided to her journal that night. "I have been put in an invidious position—and by John MacDonagh of all people. How can I refuse anything to Thomas MacDonagh's brother? And how can I refuse the only chance I may ever have to achieve something I've always wanted to do? Why is life so perverse!"

The next morning she typed a polite, businesslike letter to Lewis Baines, inviting him to return for an interview on the wireless. The letter was signed *Miss U. Halloran,* and went out in the first post.

That afternoon MacDonagh gave her a list of other foreign correspondents to contact. He was envisioning a program an hour long, with fourteen minutes allotted to each man to discuss his views of the international situation, and the remainder of the time used for introductions and a summation.

By Miss Ursula Halloran.

"It will make great radio," MacDonagh predicted. "Don't wait for the mails. Find out how many of them are on the telephone and ring them today, will you?"

When Ursula rang the London number she had been given for Lewis Baines, a woman answered. Her voice sounded young.

Ursula steeled herself to ask, "Is this Mrs. Baines?"

"Did you wish to speak to Lewis?"

"Is he there?"

"He's in France at the moment, but we expect him back in a few days. May I take a message?"

We expect him back. We who? Ursula hung up the receiver without replying.

Why did I do that? What dreadful manners; Madame would kill me.

It was an omen. She was not meant to make contact with Lewis, much less see him again. He probably had a wife and a houseful of children anyway.

Perfidious Albion, she thought angrily. *The British didn't tell Michael Collins the truth; why should I expect an English man to be honest with me?*

A personal letter for Ursula was waiting when she got home that night. The sight of the American postage stamp lifted her spirits. Henry Mooney wrote, "This country is still deep in the throes of the Depression, but President Roosevelt is making every effort to turn things around. In a modest way I have done the same thing. At least I have been able to rehire two of my former employees. We are all trying to help one another. It reminds me of home."

Ursula read those words with a pang. *Home. Ireland will always be home.*

"Since Kathleen Campbell's husband died I have been corresponding with her," Henry's letter went on.

Although we have yet to meet in person, Ned's sister and I have become good friends. Kathleen rents a house every summer in Saratoga Springs to escape the heat of New York City, and this year she invited Ella and the girls to visit her.

I insisted they go. New York City may be hot, but Texas in the summer is Hell's front lobby. In addition, much of Texas and Oklahoma has been devastated by prolonged drought. Poor farming practice has resulted in the destruction of the topsoil, and the result is massive dust storms that turn the day as dark as the night. The entire region is being called the Dust Bowl. Tenant farmers, known as sharecroppers here, are abandoning their land and streaming west with everything they own piled atop jalopies—dilapidated old motor cars. It puts me in mind of Cromwell sending the Irish "to hell or Connacht." In this case it means stay in hell or flee west to California.

Although I am lonely without my ladies, I am thankful they have spent the summer in a cool green place. They will return soon so the girls can go to school. It is hard to believe, but do you realise our Bella is almost twelve years old? Hank, as I call Henrietta, will be nine in November. You will be amused to know that she has a penchant for nicknames too, it must be in the blood. She calls Ella "Muddie," which my dear wife does not like very much, and calls me "Pop-Pop." Bella eschews the former but delights in using the latter.

There is not much I can do to repay Kathleen for her kindness to my family, but I know she would appreciate any news you have of Ned. I gather he does not write to his sister very often.

He doesn't write to anyone, Ursula thought resignedly.

Lewis Baines, however, did write. "I shall be happy to do that programme for you, Miss Halloran. When did you have in mind?"

Eschewing the telephone, Ursula sent him another businesslike letter. She explained that there were others whose schedules must be coordinated, so the program was planned for late September.

Meanwhile there were other stories to cover. In July Belfast experienced violence on scale unknown since the partition years. An Orange Order march through the city set off a riot that expanded to leave eight dead, hundreds wounded, and 384 Catholic families driven from their homes.[1]

August saw more changes at 2RN. Frank Gallagher was appointed deputy director, and Mairead ní Ghráda left the broadcasting station.

Gallagher, a cofounder of the *Irish Bulletin,* had once worked with Henry Mooney. Ursula gave him the same warm welcome she had given to John MacDonagh.

Mairead's departure upset her. "Must you leave?" she demanded to know.

"I'm afraid so. Thanks to Ernest Blythe's influence they've kept me on here in spite of my being a married woman. I needed the work because my husband was dismissed from the civil service for political reasons when the treatyites came in. But now Fianna Fáil is reinstating him, so it's out of the question for me to remain on the government payroll as well. The law, you know. No jobs for married women."

"But that isn't fair!"

Mairead sighed. "No, it isn't fair."

After she left, the first of a succession of part-timers was hired to fill the position of announcer. He was a well-spoken young law student who immediately took a fancy to Ursula. She was polite, but made it plain that she was not available for anything more than a business relationship.

There's no place for a man in my life, she reminded herself sternly. *A man only causes complications.*

Whenever she found herself thinking of Lewis Baines, she recalled his voice whispering to her in the dark. Whispering words of degradation fit only for whores.

That memory slammed the door on her emotions.

She devoted herself to preparing the program. Each of the four men would discuss a different aspect of the international situation in order to build up a rounded picture. She would have Lewis speak next to last, neither opening the program nor closing it. No preferential treatment.

Chapter Thirty-one

HENRY Mooney had missed his ladies very much while they were in New York State with Kathleen Halloran Campbell. When he met them at Union Station in Dallas he was amazed by how much the girls had grown over the summer.

There had been other changes as well. Saratoga Springs, where members of New York society spent the summer entertaining one another in high style, had made a powerful impression on Bella Mooney. She was no sooner off the train than she demanded to be addressed by her full name in all its grandeur. "I am *Isabella*. I wish you would all *remember* that!"

Henry drove his family home in a Chevrolet coupe he had bought secondhand while they were away. He was proud of the car and Ella seemed pleased. But with the suitcases taking up the rumble seat, everyone had to cram into the front. Hank sat on her mother's lap while Bella claimed the window.

The windows were down in the heat and the girl thoughtlessly rested her arm on the top of the door. In the first week of September the metal was red-hot from the Texas sun. With a gasp, Bella snatched her arm away. "This is an appalling place, simply *appalling*. I don't know how *decent* people are expected to *survive*."

"We manage," Henry remarked dryly.

"Mrs. Halloran has a much *larger* car than this," his daughter continued, "and a *chauffeur*."

Henry was trying to keep his eyes on the road. "Mmm. Does she now."

Ella volunteered, "Kathleen's involved with a number of Irish-American organizations in New York. Through one of them she met a man—from Wexford I think—who had brought his whole family over here after the Civil War. Rather like us. He was desperate for work, so Kathleen hired him as a handyman and driver."

"Chauffeur," Bella corrected pointedly. "Really, Mother!"

HENRY was not surprised to learn of Kathleen's chauffeur. After the Irish Civil War a number of embittered anti-treatyites had emigrated to America to help found an IRA-sympathetic political movement. It was exactly the sort of thing that would have appealed to Ned Halloran's sister.

THAT night as they were getting ready for bed, Ella told Henry, "I don't know what's come over Bella. In Saratoga Springs she began giving herself the most frightful airs."

"She's still a child, Cap'n, and children love make-believe. Today Bella's a princess, tomorrow she may be Florence Nightingale. And a schoolteacher the day after."

"I hope so. I was thankful we left Tilly here to keep house for you, because otherwise Bella would have been bossing the poor woman around. As it was, she kept referring to 'my maid Tilly,' as if she had a personal servant at home."

"She must get it from your side of the family," Henry teased.

Ella's golden-brown eyes blazed. "That is not funny. My people aren't snobs."

He laughed. She had the grace to blush. "Well, they aren't *all* snobs."

When they were snuggled comfortably in bed, and after Henry had welcomed his wife home very, very thoroughly, Ella remarked, "I'm not so certain it was a good idea to take the girls to visit Kathleen at all."

"Why? Did the two of you not get along?"

"Nothing like that, I like her very much. But our girls are at an impressionable age and . . ."

"And what?"

"Kathleen has a male friend who often dined with us. And stayed overnight. Saratoga Springs is very social, everyone has houseguests and plenty of guest rooms, but . . . when she and this man looked at one another there was something in their eyes. When they spoke there was something in their voices. He and Kathleen are lovers, Henry. I'm certain of it. And they're middle-aged!"

Henry ran one hand along the curve of his wife's hip. "Don't sound so shocked, Cap'n. We're middle-aged. And we're lovers."

"We're husband and wife." She shifted slightly to accommodate his hand.

"We're lovers," he replied, his voice dropping deeper. "Without a doubt. If the widow Campbell has found something half as good as we have, she's a lucky woman."

"I don't think you fully understand the seriousness of . . ."

"Don't tell me you're turning into a prude after all this time. I remember when . . ."

"I remember too," Ella interrupted hastily. "And I'm not prudish, as you have good reason to know. But the man is . . . was . . ."

"Was?"

"A priest. A defrocked priest called Paul O'Shaughnessy."

"I know him," said Henry.

"You're not serious!"

"I am serious, Cap'n; I met him in Ireland."

"Are you sure it's the same person?"

"Has to be," Henry replied. "Father Paul O'Shaughnessy had been the priest at Saint Xavier's in Manhattan, which was Kathleen's parish. He was sent to Ireland on a sabbatical and while he was there he looked up her brother. That's how he came to marry Ned and Síle in my cousin Louise's parlor. I was Ned's best man."

"Why on earth did he leave the priesthood? Was it because of Kathleen?"

Henry said teasingly, "If she wanted you to know, I'm sure she would have told you."

"She never discussed her personal life with me."

"She's like her brother in that respect, then," said Henry. "They're close-mouthed about private matters, the Hallorans. It's the Irish in them."

"Sweetheart, you can't leave it there! You know the story, I'm sure you do. Tell me or I'll burst with curiosity!"

Henry chuckled. "Sure and a burst wife would be no good to me at all. I only know the bare bones, mind; the little that Ned told me. Apparently Kathleen's American husband abused her and she turned to her priest for comfort, as many a woman had done before her. But then she and Paul fell in love. That's why his bishop sent him out of the country. It broke his heart, leaving her. When Ned, bless his romantic soul, learned the story, he urged Paul to go back to America and fight for her. Ned always was one for the fighting. From what you tell me, it sounds as if Paul took his advice."

"Do you suppose they were . . . I mean, while Kathleen's husband was still alive . . ."

"I wouldn't begin to speculate," Henry replied. "Nor should you."

"You don't sound like you disapprove, though," Ella remarked.

Henry Mooney chuckled. "Let's just say I love a happy ending."

THE flight across the Irish Sea was a difficult one. A strong headwind buffeted the Moth all the way, and Lewis Baines was tired by the time he checked into the Shelbourne. According to his instructions, he and the other foreign correspondents were to meet the following morning at 2RN and go over the program before the actual transmission that evening.

Lewis had a light supper in the hotel restaurant and then several whiskies in the bar. Perhaps too many whiskies. The next morning, he overslept. When he arrived at the broadcasting station he expected an angry Ursula to be waiting for him. Instead a thin, rabbity woman with a reddened nose met him at the door. "Are you here for the interview with Miss Halloran?

"I am. Is she . . ."

"You're late, I'm afraid. You'd better come with me." Sniffling audibly, the woman showed him into a small room furnished with a table and four chairs, and closed the door behind him. There were two men in the room. He knew one of them, a large-framed, balding individual who carried himself like a former prizefighter.

"Hullo, Bob. I didn't know you'd be taking part in this. I heard that you were retiring from Reuters."

Robert Averitt shrugged. "Rumors, Lewis, merely rumors. I decided to stay with the agency for a while longer because my wife couldn't bear the thought of having me underfoot all day. I just came back from Italy, you know. Lots going on over there. Miss Halloran was very interested in hearing about it."

"You've spoken to her already?"

"Oh, yes. Charming young woman. Got right to the point, no dithering. I like that."

Lewis felt a surge of jealousy. "Where is she now?"

In a voice rasped raw by too many cigarettes, the second man said, "She's in the other room, talking with Malcolm Weed about his segment. Said she'd be back in half an hour or so."

Lewis sat down on a straight-backed chair and waited for what felt like much longer than thirty minutes. He chatted desultorily with the other men, feigned interest in yesterday's edition of the *Irish Times*, and examined his lapels for lint.

There was none.

He took out his pocket handkerchief and carefully refolded it. Twice.

At last the door opened. And there she was.

Glossy brown hair worn close to the head like an aviator's helmet. Slim, fine-boned body. Smoky crystal eyes that looked at him, looked through him, looked beyond him as if the fact of his presence did not register. Smoky crystal eyes summarily dismissing him for some transgression he did not even recall.

He jumped to his feet. "Ursula!"

Her gaze swung back to him. "Oh, Mr. Baines. Thank you for coming." A flickering, impersonal smile, as cool as rainwater. "I'll be with you soon. In the meantime I'm ready for you, Mr. Bletherington. Would you like to come with me so we can run through your segment?"

Before Lewis could respond she was gone.

URSULA had approached this day in a state of nervous anticipation. She tried to tell herself it had nothing to do with seeing Lewis Baines again. When the other three interviewees arrived on time but there was no sign of him, she was relieved. *How typical. How arrogant. He probably won't even come and that's all to the good.*

Then she entered the room and there he was.

Chapter Thirty-two

THE program went smoothly. John MacDonagh was waiting for Ursula when she came out of the sound studio.

"You have a fine sense of dramatic structure," MacDonagh said. "Averitt's analysis of the crisis between Italy and Abyssinia was an ideal opener. Many of our listeners may not have known that Mussolini's been threatening to invade Africa. Then by having Malcolm Weed explain the League of Nation's proposed peace plan you reassured the audience. Lulled them into a false confidence.

"Your closing interview was positively inspired. Bletherington's raspy voice describing the massive German rearmament program sounded sinister enough to jolt our listeners right out of their chairs. In fact, the only part of the program I felt was weak was Baines's segment. Who cares if some American millionaire called Howard Hughes has set a new air-speed record?"

"That bit underscored the rapid developments in air power," Ursula explained. "You'll recall that Mr. Baines also said the Royal Air Force is expected to treble in size over the next two years, so when Mr. Bletherington spoke of Hitler building fifteen hundred aeroplanes . . . well, the conclusion is obvious. Europe's preparing for another war."

Three vertical lines furrowed MacDonagh's high forehead. "There's not much we in Ireland can do except try to keep out of it. God knows, we've suffered enough from our own wars. But keep an ear to the ground, will you? You seem to be our foreign affairs expert."

. . .

FINBAR Cassidy had listened with inordinate pride to Ursula's program. When it was over he tried to think of a graceful way to congratulate her without looking as if he was pushing himself forward again.

URSULA invited all four interviewees to join her for dinner at Wynn's Hotel. She knew better than to ask the broadcasting station to pay for it. The envelope beneath her mattress would be plundered instead.

Malcolm Weed was a sunburnt man with faded eyes. E.G. Bletherington insisted he had no Christian name, only initials, "Because I am not a Christian, my dear." As for Robert Averitt, Ursula had liked him the moment they met. He treated her as a fellow professional.

When they entered the hotel restaurant, Lewis Baines strode forward and requested a table for five.

Ursula cleared her throat. "I've already booked a table."

The headwaiter noticed the sudden, resentful set of her jaw. "Indeed you have booked a table, Miss Halloran. The best in the house, the one we always give you," he added with a straight face, although he had never assigned her to "the best table" before. But Ursula had been a customer for years, and he did not like aggressive Englishmen.

"Right this way, please." The headwaiter seated Ursula first. The Englishman was placed as far from her as possible.

As she unfolded her napkin she turned to Robert Averitt. "Would you care to choose the wine?"

Lewis frowned. Ursula knew he was knowledgeable about wines, yet she was deliberately deferring to someone else.

Throughout the meal he tried to engage her in conversation, but she always managed to speak to someone else first, or change whatever subject he introduced. She was bright and gay and full of laughter; she turned the full force of her personality on every man in turn, dazzling him. Every man except Lewis.

He was mystified. It never occurred to him to examine his recent performance in case he had done something to upset her. Secure with ten centuries of breeding and the Magna Carta behind him, he had the typical British distaste for introspection.

Meanwhile Ursula sat in her body—her treasonous body that had a will of its own, and was irrationally, inexplicably yearning for him in spite of everything, as a plant reaches for the light—and tried not to look at the handsome Englishman glowering at her across the table.

As they were leaving the hotel Lewis took her elbow. "What's wrong, Ursula?" he asked in an undertone.

"I thought everything went perfectly. Did you not enjoy your dinner?"

"That's not what I mean and you know it. I'm flummoxed; I can't think of what I've done to turn you against me."

"Why, nothing. It was an excellent interview."

"That's not what I'm talking about!"

A large hand descended on Lewis's shoulder. "Steady on, old fellow," said Robert Averitt. "You can't have all the women, you know. Clearly this girl isn't interested."

"You don't know anything about it."

"I know what I see," Averitt said evenly, "and I won't have you annoying Miss Halloran."

Turning to Averitt, Ursula linked her arm with his. "You're very kind and I appreciate it," she murmured, "but there's no problem."

The big man patted her hand like an avuncular uncle. "Not while I'm around, m'dear," he assured her. "Please allow me to get a taxicab to take you home."

The distance from Wynn's to Moore Street was only a few hundred yards, but Ursula accepted the offer. As she was driven away she sneaked one quick glimpse out the window.

Lewis Baines was standing on the curb, looking disconcerted.

19 September 1935
HUGE NAZI RALLY AT NUREMBURG
Hitler Issues Decree Depriving Jews of German Citizenship

3 October 1935
MUSSOLINI'S FASCIST TROOPS MARCH INTO ABYSSINIA
League of Nations Threatens to Impose Economic Sanctions

Chapter Thirty-three

B<small>Y</small> being officially unavailable, Ursula had managed to avoid seeing Lewis Baines before he returned to England. Although he left several messages for her at 2RN and even sent flowers, she did not respond.

"You're daft," the other women in the station told her.

"He's not for me," was all she said.

When she was certain Lewis had left the country—she rang the Shelbourne to be sure—she was glad. Part of her was glad. As long as he was in Ireland there was always the chance her determination might falter.

Using coarse language in bed was such a small thing; hardly enough reason to reject a man. So said her rational mind, and she agreed. Even having a wife in England was not the reason.

The explanation went deeper than that. Much, much deeper.

Thankfully she had something else to think about. The Irish public paid little attention to the Nuremberg rally, which was seen as the internal business of another nation, but Mussolini's invasion of Abyssinia made headlines in all the Dublin newspapers. *Invasion* was a word the Irish understood. Men who had never thought of discussing international affairs with a woman began asking Ursula for her opinions.

When she proposed doing a documentary on the fascist regimes gaining strength around the world, the idea was accepted at once. Ursula Halloran would be the presenter. No one said her voice lacked sufficient gravitas.

•   •   •

TRUE to Ursula's prediction, Eoin O'Duffy's leadership of Fine Gael had proved disastrous. A demagogue in an age of more gifted demagogues, he overestimated his own importance and alienated his constituency. Leaving Fine Gael deeply in debt, he had formed a new, more radical party with a handful of his most loyal Blueshirts. Without his influence Fine Gael returned to the ideals of the earlier Cumann na nGaedheal.

Ursula wondered if Finbar Cassidy was pleased.

From time to time she glimpsed him in the street; Dublin was a small city. They smiled and nodded and went their separate ways.

AT the start of 1936 one item above all others dominated the news. King George V of England died at Sandringham on the twentieth of January. The king had been in poor health for years, but nevertheless his death came as a shock to his people.

Many in Ireland still considered themselves his people.

The following Sunday Ursula had dinner with Louise and Hector Hamilton. The late king was the sole topic of conversation. The wireless had made him the best-known monarch in history.

"How many times have we heard that dear, gruff voice," Hector rhapsodized. "It brought him right into our parlor and made him almost one of us. With our own ears we heard him say, 'I don't like abroad, I've been there.' "[1]

Ursula laughed. "King George will be remembered for that one quote more than any other because it was such a narrow-minded remark."

Hector glared at her. "Are you insulting our king?"

The laugh curdled in her throat. "Not my king. George Windsor was never my king."

BBC coverage of the splendid state funeral of George V was broadcast in Ireland, but could not match, for poignancy, an earlier and more private event. "After His Majesty's death at Sandringham," an announcer related in somber tones, "the coffin was placed on a farm trolley and taken, at dusk, across the fields to the local church, while a lone piper played 'the Skye Boat Song.' The king's body was followed by a dozen friends and estate workers, and his beloved gray horse, Jock, with an empty saddle."

Ursula had not expected the death of the king of England would make her cry.

．　　．　　．

KING Edward VIII succeeded his late father on the throne of England. To focus attention back on Ireland, Ursula helped present a radio dramatization of Eamon de Valera's escape from Lincoln Jail in 1919[2]—an escape in which Ned Halloran had played a small part.

ELECTIONS in February in the Spanish Republic brought the leftist Popular Front to power. They were unable to prevent the increasing disintegration of the social and economic structure. Although in a wireless broadcast to the people Premier Azana promised "liberty, prosperity, and justice,"[3] martial law was enforced in four provinces.

The right-wing National Bloc, led by General Francisco Franco, began conspiring against the new government. As army chief-of-staff, Franco had the support of the military. The possibility of a Spanish civil war added to the tensions building throughout Europe.

ON the afternoon of March seventh Finbar Cassidy telephoned 2RN and asked to speak to Miss Halloran. When she came on the line he said, "The Nazis have invaded the Rhineland, Ursula. Unopposed, as far as we know. They began marching across the border before dawn. I thought you'd want to have the story without waiting to get it from the BBC."

Ursula was so surprised to hear from him she needed a moment to regain her composure. "That was thoughtful of you, Finbar. Are you certain it's true?"

"We're certain. External Affairs looks on it as a significant development. Hitler's openly defying the Versailles Treaty that awarded the Rhineland to France. He may justify his actions by saying the territory was part of Germany originally, but who knows what he'll do next? For years he's been claiming the German people need more land. A lot more land."

"I'll write a news bulletin immediately. Can I say the information came from a highly placed government source?"

"You can."

"I appreciate this, Finbar."

"It was nothing," he replied before ringing off.

Ursula had her scoop on the air before the first news came through from the BBC.

While Eamon de Valera was giving his annual Saint Patrick's Day broadcast over 2RN, the transmission from the studio was suddenly interrupted by a clear, unaccented male voice saying, "Hello, everybody. This is the IRA!"[4]

Ursula laughed out loud with surprise, then clapped her hand over her mouth as her colleagues exchanged shocked glances.

Government agents began scouring the countryside for hidden transmitters that could have been used in the sabotage. Throughout the day, Ursula smiled to herself from time to time as she went about her work.

Seven days later a grimmer news item was carried on the wireless. With a heavy heart Ursula prepared the announcement. "We regret to announce that Vice Admiral Henry Boyle, late of the British navy, has been shot dead at his home in County Cork by members of the Irish Republican Army."

Once Ursula would have cheered when any member of the British military was slain. But that time had passed. There was something callous and brutal about shooting down a retired old man whose war was long behind him.

I hope it wasn't you, Papa. Please God, don't let it be Ned who pulled the trigger.

On May 27 the 2RN newsreader announced, "Today marks the inaugural flight of Aer Lingus, the new commercial Irish airline service. The first flight will be from Baldonnel Military Aerodrome to Bristol in the United Kingdom, using a five-seater de Haviland Dragon called *Iolar*."*

A de Haviland, like Lewis Baines's Moth.

Damn him damn him damn him.

On the twenty-fourth of June, Eamon de Valera officially declared the Irish Republican Army to be an illegal organization.

When she returned to her room that night Ursula went through the newspaper clippings she was saving and threw away every one referring to de Valera.

Damn him damn him damn him.

But she kept on working for his government. Forcing her rebel soul to embrace the contradictions.

·   ·   ·

*Eagle

LLOYD George, the former British prime minister, visited Adolf Hitler in his mountaintop retreat in Bavaria and was deeply impressed with the man. When he returned to England Lloyd George wrote glowingly in the *Daily Express,* heaping praise upon the Fuehrer for his transformation of Germany. "The Germans are the happiest people in Europe," Lloyd George stated.

Hitler continued to flex his muscles. Two years earlier he had sent Heinrich Himmler to Danzig to stage a Nazi parade with twelve thousand uniformed men, obviously intended to intimidate the new high commissioner, Seán Lester. As time passed Berlin had increased pressure on the Free City. By the summer of 1936 headlines such as NAZI COUP FEARED IN DANZIG and HIGH COMMISSIONER DASHES TO GENEVA TO CONFER WITH LEAGUE OF NATIONS were appearing in the world press.

IN Dublin a special abattoir for Jewish meats was opened. A rabbi told newspapers covering the event that Jewish communities all around the world looked to Ireland as a haven of tolerance.

AUGUST 1936 is a banner month for news," Ursula wrote in her journal, "and the communications industry is at the heart of the excitement. The British Broadcasting Company has begun transmitting talking pictures on television! They are not available here, of course, but Fliss writes that the pictures look something like rice pudding with raisins. The Radio Corporation of America has been experimenting with television technology for several years. Scientists predict that television will replace the wireless but not many people believe them. Except me. I think the nature of magic is to evolve."

THAT month the Olympic Games opened in Berlin to record crowds. Within three years of taking power, Hitler and National Socialism had transformed Germany. Visitors to the Games were awed by the grandeur of the facilities and the enthusiasm of the people. When German athletes won thirty-three gold medals, Hitler proclaimed it a triumph for Aryan superiority. But the undisputed star of the Games was non-Aryan and very black. American Jesse Owens won an astonishing four gold medals. As the vast crowd rose to salute Owens after his victory in the 200-meter sprint, Adolf Hitler pointedly left the stadium.

Also in August, the Irish government designated Aer Lingus as the national airline. Planes were based at Collinstown Airfield north of Dublin, a facility previously used by both the Royal Flying Corps and the Royal Air Force. Irish wits promptly dubbed the national airline "Air Fungus." Those with a bawdier turn of mind, the wild pagan past still existing under the sanctimonious surface, sniggeringly referred to "Cunni Lingus." But not in public. Not where a priest might hear.

The new national airline attracted little public interest, for by that time General Franco had broadcast a rebellion manifesto and Spain was engaged in civil war. Franco's Nationalists against the government's Republicans. Photographs of burnt-out buildings began appearing in the world press. Churches and convents were reported under attack. The *Irish Independent* informed readers that the bodies of murdered Catholic nuns were lying on the sidewalks in Barcelona.[5]

Catholic Ireland was outraged.

SOMETIMES it seemed that the fighting had become more important than the winning. A way of life, an end in itself. Against the horrific background of kill or be killed there were occasional moments of sensual and intellectual clarity that Ned Halloran never experienced in any other way. They acted upon him like a drug. He suspected other men had the same experience. "We fight, therefore we are," he scribbled on the flyleaf of the notebook he always carried with him.

"I'm writing a novel," he explained if anyone asked, though very little actual writing took place. His energy was either used up in skirmishes or, more commonly, sapped by boredom. On March seventeenth he had spent an exhilarating day in the Free State on special assignment, but that was the exception. He had been ordered to come straight back to the north... and wait. Wait for weapons, wait for instructions, just wait.

Young lads who thought joining the IRA was a guarantee of excitement were sadly mistaken, he told new recruits.

Months could pass without Ned consciously thinking of "the Irish Republic" at all. When one of the new recruits in his unit, a boy called Séamus Burke, asked Ned how long he had been in the IRA, he had to stop and count back. "I joined in 1914, I was one of the early ones. And this is what—'36? So I've spent twenty-two years in the army."

They were sheltering in a ramshackle lean-to behind a row of tenements in the nationalist area of Belfast. Rain beat on the roof with an insistent rhythm, like the fists of the enemy demanding admittance. The floor of the shed was littered with pellets of goat's dung. To Ned they looked like lead shot.

The day's rations consisted of a quarter loaf of bread smuggled out to them by the woman of the house, with many a fearful glance over her shoulder. "I'm that grateful to you lads," she had said. "But would you be off in the morning? Otherwise it will go hard with us and I've a sick husband in the bed and five babbies to think about."

"Twenty-two years in the army. That's longer than I've been alive," Burke told Ned as they divided the bread between them. "Has it been worth it, would you say?"

Ned shrugged. It was a question he no longer knew how to answer. 1921 had been victory. Everything that came after had been a slow slide downward. If he let himself think about it, it would break his heart.

The persecution of Catholics in Northern Ireland went on; a random, unthinking violence so ingrained in the culture that Ned could not imagine the Six Counties without their sectarian undertone. Sometimes rifles and other weapons came north, via various circuitous routes, from supporters in the Free State. More often than not the IRA found itself defending northern Catholics with fists and clubs. Deaths on both sides mounted up. Nothing got better. Incised in blood, the hatred grew deeper.

People on either side claimed they could tell a person's religion simply by their appearance.

"He has a Prod face on him, so he does."

"She's a Papist, I'd know that mouth among hundreds."

Amazingly, more often than not they were right. Ned was confident he could recognize a Volunteer anywhere by the look in his eyes.

The sense of comradeship in the IRA was intense. Even more than the Republican philosophy, their shared experience of war instilled the Volunteers with a deep, unspoken love for one another. Trust was the cement that bound them together.

Any who betrayed that trust were dealt with severely.

"If peace broke out tomorrow," Séamus wondered aloud as he dug in one of his pockets and produced a sodden half-cigarette to conclude their meal, "what would you do?"

Ned shook his head at the cigarette. "Never got the habit," he said. "You mean what would I do if they dissolved the border and everything was sweetness and light?"

The boy grinned. "Something like that."

Ned stared off into space. "I honestly don't know. I don't even know who I would be, in a situation like that. I'd lose myself."

On the thirtieth of September Seán Lester was appointed to be deputy secretary-general of the League of Nations. Finbar Cassidy telephoned Ursula with the news, and she sent a personal letter of congratulations to Lester.

He responded, "As a result of my determined resistance to anti-Semitism in Danzig, some say I am now the most hated man in the Reich. I consider that a compliment. The Nazis have been eager to get me out of Danzig, and are crowing about my new appointment as if it were a defeat for me and a victory for them.

"I must confess that Elsie and I were looking forward to returning to Dublin when my Danzig posting was over. But that is not to be, not yet. I shall continue to do my best here until I take up my new post in Geneva next February. Elsie joins me in inviting you to visit us there once we're settled in again."

In October the Nationalist forces of Francisco Franco attempted to surround Madrid. Although the Republican government had already moved to Valencia, Franco ordered air strikes on Madrid.

The bombers belonged to the German air force. They were sent to Franco by Adolf Hitler.

On the twentieth of November Eoin O'Duffy led several hundred men—the majority of them Blueshirts—to Spain to support Franco in his right-wing rebellion.

The news was broadcast on 2RN but Ned Halloran did not hear it. Together with a score of others, he had set up operations in a wooded area near Derry—or Londonderry as the British persisted in calling the ancient Irish town. Séamus Burke had been captured by the RUC and reportedly beaten to death during "interrogation" in Derry Jail. Ned and his companions were lying in wait for the killers.

Chapter Thirty-four

FRANKLIN Delano Roosevelt was reelected as president of the United States by a landslide, and Mussolini and Hitler proclaimed a Rome-Berlin Axis. As 1936 wound down, Finbar Cassidy was kept busy in the Department of External Affairs. Although Ireland was playing no role on the world stage, protocol demanded that such events be acknowledged.

From time to time Finbar paused in his work and swiveled around in his chair to gaze out the window. Daydreaming.

Aside from telephone calls with news items, his contact with Ursula remained limited to an occasional glimpse in the street. Or in dreams.

Dreams which sent him, red-faced and embarrassed, into the confessional box every Friday. Finbar was a devout Catholic thoroughly indoctrinated with the tenet of chastity until marriage. But oh, the years were passing and the little sum of money he was able to put aside never seemed to grow the way it ought! Ailing family members at home, unexpected expenses . . . he began to fear he might spend his life unmarried.

The prospect of permanent celibacy depressed him. Yet so strong was the influence of the Church, he would accept it if he must. "That is your cross to bear," his late mother would have said.

So why must his body insist upon rebelling in his dreams?

And why must his heart leap when he glimpsed Ursula walking down the quays with her long free stride and her head held high?

Every day he scanned the dispatches that crossed his desk, watching for choice nuggets of information he could pass to her like a gift.

.   .   .

On the tenth of December King Edward VIII of England abdicated to marry the woman he loved.

Eamon de Valera summoned the Dáil for the next day. At his direction the government introduced an amending act removing all references to the king and his appointed governor-general from the Free State constitution. The bill passed at once.

As usual, Ursula went to Clare for Christmas. At the farm a letter was waiting for her. "I haven't opened it," Lucy was quick to point out. As she grew older Lucy imagined herself the subject of endless criticism, all of it undeserved. Her lips were permanently pursed as though she tasted something sour.

The envelope was addressed in the exquisite copperplate handwriting Ned Halloran had mastered at St. Enda's. Ursula felt her heart lurch. *Something must be wrong, or he would not have written.* She ran an impatient thumb under the flap, tearing the envelope.

> Dear Ursula,
> Frank Ryan is recruiting Volunteers to go to Spain with the International Brigades. De Valera's government has all but emasculated the IRA here, so some of us are going to fight Franco and save the Spanish Republic.
> By the time you read this I shall be on my way. Say a prayer for me, Precious.

The postmark was dated the fifteenth of December.
He could be anywhere by now.
"Well?" Lucy said sharply. "Is he coming home for Christmas or not?"
"Not," said Ursula.
Lucy curled her lip. "If that isn't just like the man. Putting the army ahead of his own family."
Norah Daly whispered, "Leave it be, child." Norah was very frail. Her bones showed through skin worn translucent by the years. The house had an unpleasant odor Ursula had never noticed before: chill, dusty, with a bitter undertone like the smell of moldy leaves at the bottom of a pile. The smell of old women.

As soon as she could, Ursula fled to the barn and Saoirse.

The deep hollows over the gray horse's eyes reminded her that he too was old. He had been foaled in the spring of 1917, long before independence. She had named him Freedom.

"You're a good age for a horse," Ursula whispered to him, stroking the soft nose that insistently nudged her arm, "but please God there are years left to you yet. I need you to be here for me." Throwing her arms around his neck, she buried her face in his mane.

King George's gray horse following the coffin. . . .

CHRISTMAS was a muted affair. After the three women attended Mass Lucy cooked an indifferent dinner. Then they sat in the parlor struggling to make conversation. Ursula had so little in common with the other two anymore that she found it almost impossible.

At last she inquired, "Have you heard from Kathleen in America?"

Lucy's pursed lips drew tighter.

"Kathleen wrote us a while back," said Norah in a voice as faded as the parlor wallpaper. "She's thinking of remarrying."

"So we're all that's left," Lucy added. "The Halloran dynasty. End of the line."

Ursula cleared her throat. "You can't forget Ned."

"Can I not? He forgets us easy enough!"

"I have to go out and feed Saoirse," Ursula said abruptly. She jumped to her feet and fled again.

In the barn the shadows were soft as velvet and the air was fragrant with hay. Saoirse, chomping his oats, provided a rhythmic counterpoint to her troubled thoughts.

How could Papa leave Ireland to fight for a different republic? If the IRA's suppressed, could he not just come home? Surely he's earned a little peace.

Saoirse raised his head and glanced over at her, then gave a contented sigh and returned to his oats. "Food, shelter, and companionship. That's all your nature requires, isn't it?" Ursula remarked fondly.

All your nature requires.

Perhaps that was the answer.

Perhaps it was not the fight for a republic that drew Ned to war. He was a man in conflict with the two sides of his own nature, the tender and the brutal, and he sought to ease his pain by fighting in the physical world. The war in Spain looked more capable of resolution than the one in Ireland. So, worn and weary, Ned had set off in hopes of winning at last.

Ursula felt a wrenching pity for him.

Long ago Precious had observed to Henry Mooney, "I'm lots of different people and so are you. You're a little boy who used to ride in a pony cart, and a grown-up who talks to me like a grown-up too, and my papa's best friend who laughs a lot, and a lonely man who looks sad sometimes when he thinks no one is watching."

"Be thankful you're a horse," Ursula said aloud to Saoirse. "At least you know for certain who you are."

He flicked an ear in her direction and went on eating.

THE day after Christmas was St. Stephen's Day. The Wren Boys would be out. Following an ancient tradition still observed in many parts of Ireland, local boys would scour every hedgerow until they captured and killed a wren. They would tie the tiny body to a bush and carry it in triumph from house to house while they chanted, "The wran, the wran, the king of all birds, on Saint Stephen's day was caught in the furze." Every household they visited was expected to pay them a sum of money in tribute.

Ursula hated the custom. But it was tradition and in Ireland one did not speak out against tradition. That would be heresy second only to denying Christ.

Norah did not come down for breakfast on St. Stephen's morning. "Christmas probably tired her out," Lucy said without any show of concern. "Go up and ask her if she has some pennies put aside for the Wren Boys when they come."

Ursula knocked once, twice, on Norah's bedroom door. There was no answer. She eased the door open. It took her eyes a moment to adjust to the dim light in the room, for the curtains were still closed.

The old woman lay on her back in bed with the covers pulled up under her whiskery chin. Her eyes were open. Staring past Here and Now. When Ursula pressed her fingers against Norah's throat, she already knew there would be no pulse.

She dropped to her knees beside the bed and said a long, heartfelt prayer, then went to the head of the stairs and called down to Lucy.

URSULA rode Saoirse to Clarecastle to use the telephone at the post office. Although the journey was short the old horse stumbled several times, he who had been so surefooted in his youth. *I should have spent whatever it took—even borrowed the money; Geraldine Dillon would have loaned it to me— in order to bring him up to Dublin. But it's too late for that now.*

With a heavy heart, Ursula admitted to herself that the two of them were sharing their last ride. Saoirse was slowly failing. To subject him to a jolting train ride or lorry journey at his age would kill him.

When her telephone call to John MacDonagh was put through, she told him, "My great-aunt has died and I'll be needed here until after the funeral."

"Stay as long as you must, we'll manage," he assured her.

To Lucy and Ursula fell the task of sorting Norah's things. It had never occurred to the old woman to write a will, nor was there any need for one. She had possessed so little of her own. However to Ursula it seemed that each apron, every handkerchief, embodied some fragment of Norah Daly that had escaped the grave.

"Isn't it strange," she remarked to Lucy as the two women sat in the kitchen going through them, "the way things outlive people? And have the power to hurt us for that reason?"

Lucy gave her an uncomprehending look. "I'm glad things do last. I'm after needing more handkerchiefs."

The paper records of Norah's life consisted of her baptismal and confirmation certificates and a thin bundle of letters tied with the same twine Frank had used to bind up raspberry canes. Glancing at them without bothering to read, Lucy said, "We can just toss these in the fire."

"Wait a minute." Ursula reached out and selected one letter at random. When she unfolded the paper it was soft with age. *Like Norah's cheek,* she thought. The ink was very faded. The handwriting was Norah's, though not the crabbed hand of an old woman. The letter had been written at some time in Norah's youth and apparently never sent—or retrieved afterward and secreted away.

My darling Patrick,

Tomorrow you will be married to my own dear sister. I truly wish you and Theresa every happiness. She loves you as much as I do, and you have told me that you love her, so I accept your decision.

We should not have met last night. One last time, you said. Did you know how much it hurt when you took me in your arms? I should not have let you, but I was greedy for a final embrace before you were lost to me forever. I hope it has not cost me my immortal soul.

God go with us all.

I remain yours, only yours,

Norah

Ursula swallowed. Hard. "Do you know what this says?" she asked Lucy.

"How can I? You're the one reading it."

"Norah—Aunt Norah—was in love with Patrick Halloran. Your father. All these years, since before your parents were married."

Lucy snatched at the letter. "I don't believe it!"

"It's true all right. And she . . ." Ursula struggled to comprehend. ". . . she must have agreed to live with them and help her sister look after the children as they came. His children."

Lucy was staring at the letter in disbelief. "None of us knew. She never gave any sign. Our parents were devoted to one another and she was always just Aunt Norah. Cooking, cleaning, mending his clothes." Lucy raised her eyes to Ursula's. "Mending his clothes."

ON the train going back to Dublin Ursula sat hugging herself. The train carriage was warm enough because it was packed with people returning to the city after Christmas, but a chill had entered Ursula's bones.

When she returned to work a stack of news reports was waiting for her. Hitler had agreed to support a nonintervention pact on Spain if the other great powers would do the same. Mussolini's government had banned interracial marriages in its colonies in Africa. And Franklin Roosevelt, in his inaugural speech in America, had spoken of his nation as being ill-housed, ill-clad, and ill-nourished.[1]

"Things have to get better," Ursula remarked out loud, "because there's no way they can get worse."

"I couldn't agree more," said an English voice.

She looked up in astonishment.

Lewis had entered the studio without her noticing, so intense was her concentration. Now he stood smiling down at her. "I couldn't leave things as they were. Whatever I've done that upset you, I want to apologize and make it up to you if I can."

A seismic shift rattled her emotions like windows during an earthquake. "Hello, Lewis," she said, rather more warmly than she had intended.

"I wasn't certain you'd be glad to see me."

"Why?"

"Please have dinner with me later," he urged, "so we can talk."

She meant to say no. She said yes.

When he left the broadcasting station, the eyes of the other women followed him while Ursula pretended to concentrate on her work.

In actuality she was giving herself a stern lecture on how to behave when he called for her that evening. She would show him, once and for all, just what sort of woman she was.

L EWIS brought roses for her—out of season and prohibitively expensive—and took her to Jamets. The Ursula Halloran who sat across the table from him, ramrod straight and coolly polite, was as dignified as a duchess.

Yet Lewis had a vivid memory of her shrieking with joy while he did stunts with his aeroplane. Poking fun at the stuffed shirts in the hotel bar. Which was the real Ursula?

He allowed her to keep their conversation on an impersonal level during dinner, but while they were waiting for dessert he finally asked outright what he had done to displease her.

She gave him an opaque look. "I don't know what you mean, Lewis."

"We were such good friends, at least I thought we were. Then all of a sudden you just went away."

"Did I?" Coolly. "I thought you were the one who went away. You returned to England, did you not?" She waited a moment, then added, "To your family."

"My family?"

"Your wife and children."

To her surprise, Lewis laughed. "Oh, lord, is that what you think? I don't have any wife, Ursula, and as far as I know I have no children either."

"I was asked to ring you and a young woman answered the telephone. She spoke as if—"

"That must have been my sister. Muriel lives with me when she's not gadding around the world. Since we both have itchy feet, often there's only one of us there. Plus the housekeeper, of course, but she's an old dragon with voice to match. Is that what's wrong? You thought I was married?"

Ursula shrugged one shoulder. "It doesn't matter to me one way or the other."

He thought he understood everything. "You silly goose, you shouldn't make assumptions about people. I promise you I'm not married, I'm not engaged, I'm as free as the wind. Or was until I met you. Now I don't seem to be able to get you out of my mind."

"I'm no threat to your freedom," Ursula said crisply. "I don't intend to marry, ever. I couldn't keep my job if I was married."

Just then the waiter brought their dessert, an apple tart with custard. As he placed Ursula's portion in front of her she was thinking, *You shouldn't make assumptions about people. Where have I heard that before?*

As her fork cut through the pastry she wondered, *Should I give Lewis the benefit of the doubt?* The apples were tart on her tongue but the custard was rich and sweet. *The girls at Surval used to claim the English lack passion. Perhaps the words Lewis used with me were just his way of exciting himself, like a naughty schoolboy writing bad language on a fence.*

She let herself thaw toward him, just a fraction. Like the first faint hint of warmth at the end of winter, it was not enough to melt the ice. But it contained the possibility of spring.

Chapter Thirty-five

ON the eighteenth of February, 1937, Seán Lester officially took up his new position in Geneva. In the same bulletin, the 2RN newsreader announced, "One hundred men are preparing a site near Limerick to be used for transatlantic flights. Commercial passenger planes capable of crossing the ocean are not yet available but it is anticipated they soon will be. Éire hopes to become the first port for air traffic between Europe and North America."

LEWIS Baines and his little plane were making fairly frequent trips across the Irish Sea. He did not attempt to resume a sexual relationship with Ursula. He took her to dinner, he took her to the theater, he took her for long walks during which they talked about everything on earth. He enjoyed her intelligence, a quality he had never sought in a woman before.

As he ate eggs and kippers in the Shelbourne dining room one morning, an odd thought occurred to him. Should a man not marry an intelligent woman if he hoped to have intelligent children?

Lewis dismissed the thought as quickly as it came. Marriage was for some time in the distant future when the juice had been wrung out of life and there was nothing left but to settle down with the pipe and slippers. In the meantime he enjoyed many women for many different reasons, though none intrigued him quite as much as Ursula Halloran.

She was like a leaping salmon that must be played skillfully. He enjoyed the game, of which patience was an integral part.

When the exactly right moment presented itself he would reel her in.

His sister Muriel—whom Lewis had called Moo for as long as he could remember, for no reason that either of them remembered—teased him about the frequency of his flights to Dublin. "You must have a girl over there, Lew."

"I have girls every place."

"You reprobate. I mean a serious girl."

"Sometimes she's serious."

"I suppose next you'll be telling me she's Irish. You know perfectly well you can't get involved with an Irish girl, it would be quite unsuitable. Besides, I thought you and Fliss were—"

"That was years ago. You're 'way behind in your gossip."

A tall, fair woman who looked remarkably like her brother, Muriel Baines thought of herself as having all of the virtues and none of the vices of her race. "I don't gossip," she said icily.

But she kept on asking questions.

If she had not done so, Lewis might never have thought of Ursula as a prospective wife. He was perfectly aware that she was unsuitable. She was not even one of the Ascendancy, though with her poise and diction she could pass for one.

Lewis rather liked the idea of shocking his friends by making an unsuitable marriage.

URSULA held her emotions in tight check. While she could not deny the almost galvanic attraction she felt for Lewis, she was determined not to surrender to it again. Surrender made one vulnerable.

But she was glad to see him whenever he arrived in Dublin, and when he left she counted the weeks until his next visit.

ON the tenth of March the draft of a new Irish constitution largely written by Eamon de Valera was introduced in the Dáil. Under its provisions the Free State was to be called by the Gaelic name of Éire. This was partially out of deference to the sensibilities of northern Unionists, who resented any implication that Northern Ireland was unfree.

The preamble began, "We, the people of Éire, humbly acknowledge all our obligations to our Divine Lord, Jesus Christ, Who sustained our fathers through centuries of trial."

Ignoring the forthcoming constitution, the obscure Gaelic Monarchist

Party announced their support for the O'Conor Don as potential king of Ireland.[1] Ursula invited their spokesman to put his case on the air, but he declined, saying it was beneath royal dignity.

Quick to spot a controversy that could sell newspapers, the *Cork Examiner* argued that Donough O'Brien, the 16th Lord Inchiquin, was a more suitable candidate. "He is in direct descent from Brian Bóru who, if he had survived Clontarf, would have established the O'Brien dynasty so firmly that the present O'Brien would be King of All Ireland and there would be no Irish problem to be solved."

A<small>T</small> the end of April Henry Mooney wrote to Ursula, "In your last letter you mentioned your interest in aeroplanes—which we call airplanes over here—so I thought you might like to hear about the latest. A new Boeing bomber called the Flying Fortress has just been unveiled, supposedly putting America well ahead of other nations when it comes to military air power.

"Ella has drawn a sketch of the Flying Fortress for you; I am including it with this letter. I am not happy about our perceived need for such a plane, however. Here's a question for you to ponder, Little Business: Does war fuel the armaments industry, or does the armaments industry fuel war?

"Here's another question: why did you develop this sudden interest in aviation?"

When Ursula answered Henry's letter she did not answer his questions.

She was not telling anyone about Lewis Baines. How could a dedicated Irish Republican justify an interest in a member of the British ruling class? It was embarrassing.

And perversely exciting.

She did not even mention him in her letters to Fliss. Instinct warned her that Fliss might have more than a casual interest in Lewis herself, and she did not want to jeopardize their friendship.

T<small>HE</small> new Irish constitution was overwhelmingly approved by the Dáil. When it was published there was little public debate, though men argued some of the issues in pubs while women discussed them over back fences. "It's the Civil War being fought all over again with documents instead of guns," some people claimed.

"Rubbish! De Valera's redefined the Treaty but he certainly hasn't destroyed it."

As concerned Northern Ireland, this was true. Articles 2 and 3 of the new constitution claimed the right of the Dublin government to exercise jurisdiction over the whole of Ireland while in practice confining the exercise to twenty-six counties, "pending the reintegration of the national territory."

Strangely, the constitution did not take the additional step many expected and proclaim Ireland a republic. Frequent references were made to the Nation without any attempt to define its identity, which was still a thorny question in a land so divided.

The new constitution created a new office, that of president of Ireland. This forcibly underscored the fact that the British king was no longer head of the Irish state. Not everyone was happy with the new arrangement; it caused more controversy than any other part of the document. "De Valera wants the Irish presidency for himself," adherents of Fine Gael muttered darkly. "You have to be watching him all the time. Didn't the British say dealing with him was like eating mercury with a fork?"

But de Valera preferred to be *An Taoiseach,** the Irish equivalent of prime minister. The taoiseach would wield the most power in the Dáil and the Dáil would run the country. The presidency would be little more than a ceremonial position.

The role of the Catholic Church was greatly strengthened in the new constitution. Article 44 recognized "the special position of the Holy Catholic and Roman Church as the guardian of the Faith professed by the majority of the citizens." However, in deference to the Republican ideal of religious tolerance, the same article took care to acknowledge both the various Protestant denominations and Ireland's Jewish congregation. Given what was happening in Europe, the Jews in particular appreciated the gesture.

Women saw the new constitution as retrograde and paternalistic. The equality they had enjoyed during the revolutionary period was swept away. Life "within the home" was to be a woman's rightful place and highest ambition. Mothers were actively discouraged from working elsewhere no matter what their economic condition. "We all believe that woman's place is in the home," Helena Moloney commented sarcastically, "provided she has a home."

A group including Kathleen Clark and Hanna Sheehy-Skeffington met to organize a protest. Ursula joined them in sending a barrage of letters to the major newspapers. "True republicanism is about fairness and equality, about inclusion and solidarity," she wrote. "Mr. de Valera's constitution denies women these basic rights."

*"The Chief."

Knowing he might read the printed letter, she signed her name with a defiant flourish.

The following Saturday she had afternoon tea with Geraldine Dillon. After years of debate with herself, Geraldine had finally cut her graying locks to a fashionable length. Her hair was now dressed in marcelled waves that rolled across her pink scalp like a lacquered sea. She waited expectantly for Ursula to notice.

But Ursula's mind was on other things. "Eamon de Valera is the worst mistake this country ever made," she fumed as she peeled back the top of a dainty sandwich to examine the filling.

"I thought you were such a great admirer of his."

"I was. But now that I've seen Dev's true colors I'm not sedimental about him."

Geraldine raised her eyebrows. "Sedimental? Don't you mean *sentimental?*"

"I mean the dregs of emotion," Ursula replied, "which is all I have left for de Valera. Something bitter at the bottom of the cup. Do you want this? I don't care for egg salad."

Trying to steer the conversation around to her chosen topic, Geraldine said, "I've been using an egg shampoo on my hair. Do you think it has more shine?"

Ursula did not even glance up. "I hate eggs."

SEÁN Lester wrote to Ursula, "I understand that Dev has spoken in the Dáil about the possibility of the Free State pulling out of the League of Nations if it does not become 'universal'—meaning if America continues to refuse to join, I suppose. But where the blazes would Ireland be if she left the League? We withdrew from the British Commonwealth; surely the necessary corollary is that we hold with might and main to our only place in the world! Otherwise we will become more than ever an 'Island beyond an Island.' "[2]

ON the twelfth of May King George VI, a man who had never expected to be monarch, was crowned in Westminster Abbey. In order to cover the coronation procession the BBC made its first outside television broadcast.

The next month the former king, now Duke of Windsor, married American divorcée Wallis Simpson in a chateau in France. One of the witnesses was the mayor of Monts. He said he represented a nation "which has always been sensitive to the charm of chivalrous unselfishness and bold gestures prompted by the dictates of the heart."

FINBAR Cassidy loved children. He could not pass a pram without pausing to bend down and admire the tiny occupant. Toddlers adored him because he talked to them as if they were grown-ups. Many Irish men retained a stern paternalistic distance from their children, but Finbar daydreamed about playing with his sons and daughters.

If he ever had sons and daughters. If he ever got married at all.

He finally had almost enough money put by to allow him to marry, but there was no woman he wanted to marry except Ursula Halloran. Who seemed hopelessly involved with someone else.

Several times he saw them together in Dublin, strolling along the quays or entering a restaurant. The sort of restaurant he could not afford.

On these occasions Ursula never noticed Finbar. She had eyes only for the tall man at her side.

Tall blond blue-eyed man with an air of insufferable arrogance about him. "Damned *sasanach*,"* Finbar muttered under his breath.

7 July 1937
BRITISH GOVERNMENT TO PARTITION PALESTINE
Described as Only Solution to Conflict Between Jews and Arabs

---

*Englishman.

Chapter Thirty-six

THE Irish general election in July included a referendum on the new constitution. Fianna Fáil won both, handily, causing gloom in the Fine Gael party. Its political future looked bleak.

Finbar began to feel that everything he touched turned to ashes. Even his work. External Affairs was increasingly absorbed with internal affairs. He could imagine what Ursula, with her internationalist outlook, would say about it.

He wished he could sit down with her and talk about it. He wished he could sit down with her and talk about almost anything.

How did it go wrong? Had he lost her before that damned Englishman showed up?

But surely not. The Eucharistic Congress . . . she was his then, most assuredly. She let him hold her and touch her and . . .

He tried not to let his thoughts follow that dangerous path to its conclusion, but sometimes he could not help it.

Ursula Halloran was a knot of agony in his mind.

ON the twenty-eighth of September Hitler and Mussolini staged a massive floodlit demonstration in Berlin to announce that they believed in peace. However Hitler also reiterated Germany's pressing need for more living space to feed and support her people.

In October the Duke and Duchess of Windsor announced they would visit Germany to study conditions under the National Socialist Party. When they arrived in Berlin they were warmly greeted by Adolf Hitler, and lavishly entertained as his guests.

For once Finbar did not go home to Donegal for Christmas. He bought a Pilot 5 shortwave radio that guaranteed American reception, and remained in Dublin, hoping against hope he would run into Ursula.

Ursula was in Clare for Christmas. Hoping against hope that a letter had arrived from Ned. There was none. Lucy would not even discuss her brother. Her talk centered on the dreadful burden of her own life. She was sure she had tuberculosis, the hired men were stealing her blind, the farmyard gate was rotten and gone to splinters but she could not afford a new one. . . .

Ursula lost her temper. "You don't know how lucky you are! You own land and have a decent roof over your head. You can afford to pay other people to do the hard work for you. Nine-tenths of Ireland is worse off than you. You should be down on your supposedly rheumatic knees thanking God for your blessings."

"It's easy for you to talk," Lucy retorted. "You with a good job in the city and a lot of fancy frocks. Meanwhile the years are passing me by. I haven't even had a new dress in ages."

"We're all getting older," Ursula observed dryly, "and my frocks are far from fancy anymore. Besides, you could afford to buy a new dress if you really wanted to."

Lucy bridled. "And who would I wear it for?"

"You could come with me to pay a call on Eileen," Ursula suggested. "We haven't seen her since Frank's funeral."

Lucy pretended not to hear.

The following day Ursula went alone to Newmarket-on-Fergus. The shopkeepers from whom she bought presents for Eileen's children could not tell her where to find the Mulvaneys. Only the coal merchant was able to give directions. Lucas owed him money. "If it weren't for the babbies I'd let them freeze this winter," he growled.

Ursula gave the man the few shillings she had left.

Ned's youngest sister was living several miles east of the village in the most recent of a long series of rented hovels. The family moved almost as often as the rent came due, because Lucas Mulvaney drank most of what he earned. His work record was like his rental record: a long series of odd jobs from which he invariably was fired.

Ursula was dismayed by Eileen's appearance. The flirtatious charmer had transmogrified into a slatternly, middle-aged harridan with bleary eyes.

"I'm Precious," Ursula said when Eileen did not seem to recognize her. "Ned's daughter."

"Oh. Well, you'd best come in, then." With a weary sigh, Eileen stepped back and let Ursula enter the house.

W HEN she left the shack an hour later Ursula was crying. Saoirse's money, which she had been sending to Lucy since Norah's death, would have to be divided and a portion sent to Eileen with strict instructions never to tell Lucas.

Knowing Lucy would not approve, Ursula did not tell her.

O N the twenty-ninth of December, 1937, the Constitution of Éire came into force. At the instigation of the Republican women, a black flag was flown from Sinn Féin headquarters in Dublin.

The first week of the new year brought Ursula a late Christmas present from Henry and Ella, and an angry letter from Lucy.

The present was a new novel by an American writer, John Steinbeck. "*Of Mice And Men* was recently published here to wide acclaim," Henry explained in an accompanying note. "It is the ultimate novel about friendship, and all the more powerful because the friendship leads to shocking violence. As I read it I could not help thinking of Ned and the quarrel between us. I wish we could heal those wounds before it's too late. Perhaps someday we can."

Lucy wrote, "Why are you sending less money to buy feed for your horse? Do you expect me to make up the difference? I will not waste good money on an animal that does not earn its keep. Just last week a young man came around selling iron gates made of heavy pipe. If I had any money to spare I would buy one for the farmyard."

Reluctantly, Ursula approached Thomas Kiernan to ask for a rise in wages.

He refused. "My dear girl, you are already being paid over half as much as a man, though you have no wife and children to support. What would you spend more money on? Cinema tickets and fripperies, I suppose. Well, a rise is out of the question. Even if the station could afford to give you one, which it can't."

She would not, could not, tell him her private business. If she said, "I have an old horse to support and an impoverished aunt who isn't really my aunt but needs help," what would Kiernan say? He would laugh at her. She would have confirmed his belief that young women were frivolous.

Her small list of personal indulgences was already pared to the bone. Now she eliminated it altogether. She would give up the occasional pint of Guinness after work. She would not buy any more books, even secondhand. There would be no replacements for clothes that wore out and no professional services for them either. Instead of taking her clothes to Louise for washing, as she might have done, Ursula would buy a box of Rinso at the corner shop and wash them herself.

Pride would not allow her to admit her problems to Louise Hamilton. Louise would tell Hector and he would gloat.

On the seventeenth of January Eamon de Valera visited London for talks with Neville Chamberlain. "Government sources predict," said the 2RN newsreader, "that there will be a positive resolution of the economic war."

A few days later Ursula sent the usual sum to Clare to buy feed for Saoirse, and an equal amount to Eileen for herself and the children.

The next month, charging that Prime Minister Chamberlain was too anxious to please Hitler and Mussolini, Anthony Eden of the Foreign Office resigned from the British cabinet. It was true that Chamberlain's inclination was to placate the fascists. Like most of Europe he was terrified at the prospect of another war only twenty years after the last.

"Appeasement is a dreadful mistake," Ursula remarked to Helena Moloney. "For centuries Ireland tried to appease England and look where it got us."

In March Adolf Hitler annexed Austria. Ursula prepared the news announcement herself, frowning as she typed: "The German Fuehrer drove through Vienna today in a triumphant cavalcade, wearing the brown Storm Trooper uniform and giving the fascist salute to wildly cheering crowds. In reclaiming his native land, Hitler has become the absolute ruler of an empire of seventy-four million people."

None of the great powers protested the annexation of Austria.

A plebiscite put to the Austrian people overwhelmingly approved the arrangement. As Heidi Neckermann wrote to Ursula, "It would take a courageous individual to vote 'no' in a room draped with Nazi flags and filled with storm troopers. Jews, of course, were forbidden to vote."

She no longer sounded as enthusiastic about Hitler as she had been.

AFTER months of complex negotiations, in April Eamon de Valera and Neville Chamberlain signed a new Anglo-Irish Agreement ending the economic war.

The *Irish Times* wrote: "On April 25, 1916, Eamon de Valera was in command of Boland's Mill, in armed rebellion against the British Crown. On April 25, 1938, the Prime Minister of England, with a gracious gesture, handed back to the prime minister of Éire a pair of field glasses that had been taken from him by the British officer who arrested him twenty-two years ago.[1]

De Valera had won large concessions. Under the new agreement Éire was granted the so-called "Treaty Ports"—fortified naval bases at Cobh in Cork, Berehaven in Kerry, and Lough Swilly in Donegal—which Britain had denied to the Free State in 1921. De Valera stressed that the Irish people were only recovering what had been wrongfully taken away from them.

There would be no Royal Navy access to these ports in time of war unless the Irish agreed. Henceforth Éire would be responsible for her own coastal defense.

New trade arrangements favorable to Irish farmers caused widespread rejoicing. The British government also relinquished its claims for all unpaid land annuities in return for the comparatively small sum of ten million pounds.

Partition would remain; apparently there had been no serious effort to remove it. But the agreement was seen as a triumph for de Valera.

It was not enough to change Ursula's feelings about him.

LEWIS Baines paid a visit to Dublin in May. He had been absent for several months, an absence Ursula did not comment on. She did not want him to think she was pining for him.

In fact, he had wanted to come but decided against it. Best to let the affair cool off a bit, he told himself. Make her anxious. That was part of the game.

They went to the races at Fairyhouse and sat in a box, the first time Ursula had done either. But she had a knowing eye when it came to horses. Betting on the ones she picked, Lewis won seventy pounds. When he tried to give her half, she declined.

He was aware, though he was too much of a gentleman to say so, that her clothes were beginning to look a little shabby. He could not understand why she refused to take money she obviously needed. His repeated insistence on sharing the winnings almost provoked a quarrel. Ursula threw the pound notes onto the ground between them. "I never take money from men."

ON the twenty-fifth of June, Douglas Hyde, the modest and unassuming founder of the Gaelic League, was inaugurated as the first president of Éire. There had been rumors that the office might be offered to Seán Lester, but nothing came of them.[2] Within a matter of days, President Hyde took up residence in the former Viceregal Lodge, officially re-renamed *Aras an Uachtarain*.* On his way to the Phoenix Park the president paused at the GPO out of respect for those who had fought there in 1916.

The gesture touched Ursula's heart. In his honor—and at her suggestion—2RN presented a program in which the surviving members of the first Dáil reconstructed the session during which the Irish Declaration of Independence was drafted.

Eamon de Valera had been president of that Dáil. The Republican Dáil.

When he entered the broadcasting studio Ursula contrived to be busy elsewhere.

"I won't be a hypocrite," she told Helena Moloney afterward. "I respect Dev for what he did in the past, but as far as I'm concerned he's betrayed the Republican cause since he came to power."

She did not discuss these feelings inside the broadcasting station. Like many people in the years following the Civil War, Ursula Halloran had become expert at dissembling.

WHEN the map of Europe had been redrawn at the end of the Great War, the Republic of Czechoslovakia was created by the union of Bohemia, Moravia, and Slovakia. A parliamentary democracy closely allied to Britain

*The House of the President.

and France, Czechoslovakia became the most industrially advanced country in Eastern Europe. Eventually it was ripe for the picking. Both Poland and Hungary pressed territorial claims.

Czechoslovakia included the Sudetenland, a mountainous region in northern Bohemia with a predominantly German population. Adolf Hitler began inciting the Germans of the Sudetenland to demand union with the Third Reich. By March of 1938, officers wearing German uniforms had been seen in the streets of Prague.

The Czechoslovakian government was willing to fight rather than surrender the Sudetenland. Everyone expected Britain and France would use their diplomatic clout on behalf of their ally, and keep the situation under control.

Ursula wrote to Henry, "It would be nice to believe all quarrels can be resolved by diplomacy, but I am not convinced. In Ireland we have learned the hard way that bullies will not back down just because someone talks reason to them."

THE summer that had begun with warmth and sunshine turned cold and wet. By July the weather was almost the sole topic of conversation. A bomb blast in Palestine and growing tensions in Europe did not compel half as much attention. They were far away. Weather was here and now, in your face, down your neck, squelching in your shoes.

As Finbar Cassidy was crossing Dame Street on the last day of August he saw Ursula emerging, white-faced, from a public telephone kiosk. Her eyes met his. Her face crumpled into tears and she ran toward him.

Finbar barely had time to open his arms before she collapsed into them. "What's wrong?" he kept asking. She was weeping too hard to answer. Her whole body began to shake.

Finbar scooped her up and ran toward the open gates of Trinity College. Trinity had been founded by Queen Elizabeth in 1591 for Protestant students only. Although Catholics were now admitted, many Dubliners still considered Trinity as alien ground, a bastion of hated colonialism.

But it was the nearest refuge Finbar could think of.

Ursula weighed less than he expected, as if her bones were hollow. He dropped onto a bench just inside the front gates, cradling Ursula against his chest while he gazed around frantically for help.

Within moments several members of staff arrived. They helped him take Ursula to the infirmary and make her as comfortable as possible on a narrow bed. No one asked if she belonged at Trinity. She was in need and this was Ireland; nothing more was required.

The nurse on duty brought a light sedative, which Finbar persuaded Ursula to drink. Her painful sobs began to subside. She gazed up at Finbar through swollen eyes.

"What's wrong?" he asked again, as gently as he knew how.

She murmured something he thought he had misunderstood. Bending lower, he put his ear almost against her lips. "What's that? I thought you said freedom was dead."

"Saoirse!" Ursula wailed, beginning to cry all over again. "Saoirse's dead."

Getting a coherent account from her took a long time. When she spoke her voice was hoarse from weeping, the narrative interrupted by hiccups.

Lucy Halloran had rung 2RN from Clare when Ursula was away from her desk. Lucy had left a telephone number and asked that Ursula ring back. Recently there had been some unpleasantness about people using the 2RN telephones for personal business, so since Ursula was planning to meet Helena Moloney for lunch at a café in Dame Street, she had waited to use a public telephone on the way.

The conversation had left her shattered. "Saoirse died three days ago and Lucy didn't think it was important enough to tell me!"

Finbar was still mystified. "Saoirse?"

"My horse! The horse who's been mine all his life, almost. He was found dead in his field. He went to sleep and didn't wake up." Ursula fought to keep talking through her sobs. "The only reason Lucy finally rang me was because the knacker had failed to come and she wanted to know what to do with the body. I told her to have the hired men bury Saoirse in his field. I even said I'd buy the field from her to guarantee no one would plow over him. But I can't. I can't afford it!"

She began to cry again. Bitterly, despairingly. The skies were not weeping half as hard.

Saoirse was one loss too many. Into her mourning for him Ursula poured all the grief she had been storing up for years.

FINBAR paid a small boy to carry a hastily scribbled note of apology to the café where Helena Moloney was waiting, then took Ursula home to Moore Street. Along the way he bought a small bottle of brandy.

He carried her up the stairs and sat her, fully dressed, on her bed. There was no mention of men not being allowed upstairs. An army with rifles could not have driven him away.

Finbar found Ursula's tooth glass and carefully poured one finger of brandy at a time, until she lost patience and snatched the bottle out of his hand. He watched aghast as she tossed off the contents like a man. "You'll make yourself sick."

When the bottle was empty she handed it back to him. "I won't be sick. I'm used to drink, I drink Guinness all the time."

She did not feel the effects of the brandy at all, she thought.

Chimes sounded far off. *Fairy bells ringing?* Or maybe it was the buzzing in her ears. The sound came closer, receded, came back again. How easy it was to sink into that music. Sink down; spin around . . .

She reached for Finbar to steady herself. He was warm and alive and she needed someone with her because her heart was broken. Broken by all of them. By all who had left her. *Síle and Henry and Ned and Saoirse* . . .

She knew what she was doing yet she did not know. The brandy transformed itself into a permeable barrier that allowed no more awareness than she was willing to accept.

F INBAR had an abhorrence of women who drank. But this was Ursula. He could not walk out and leave her.

He firmly resolved that nothing would happen. He would take her in his arms and hold her until she fell asleep, then tuck her properly into her bed and go home. Yes. That was what any decent man would do and he was a decent man.

He was also a man in love and this was the third time she had tempted him. Where were the saints when one needed them most? Where were the priests to guard her chastity?

Not here, he thought with a groan as her arms folded around his neck. Her breath was saturated with brandy. Her kiss intoxicated him.

Finbar made one more attempt to live up to his own expectations for himself. "We mustn't do this," he said hoarsely, trying to pry her arms away from his neck. "I won't let you do this."

She pulled her face a few inches back from his and gazed at him with unfocused eyes. "Are you going to leave me too?"

"I'm not going to leave you, but . . ."

"You won't leave me ever? You'll always be here when I need you?"

"I'll always be here," he assured her.

"Ah." She increased her grip on his neck, pulling him down against her body. "Ah." Her small breasts pressed against his pounding heart. "That's so good," she murmured. "But hold me tighter. Oh, please hold me tighter. Open your skin and let me in."

With another groan, Finbar gave up the unequal struggle.

Chapter Thirty-seven

A T first she did not feel anything except pressure and a sense of movement. A man—was it Lewis? It must be Lewis—she could not make out his face, everything was blurred—was clasping her in his arms while the world spun dizzyingly around them. If he turned loose she would fall. "Don't let me fall!" she tried to say, but her traitor lips were numb. They would not shape the words.

The buzzing in her ears grew louder. From deep inside, a blind, primordial ache swelled to fill her whole being.

If you don't know what you're doing, Ursula thought giddily, *it doesn't count.*

A good Catholic all his life, Finbar had remained chaste in a society where male virginity was not uncommon. Behind the dam of abstinence a mighty reservoir had filled to overflowing. Now nature reclaimed her own.

Tentatively at first, but with increasing confidence, his body took charge. The first touch of naked womanflesh against his penis was maddening. It took all the willpower he had accumulated in decades of rigorous self-denial to keep from climaxing. Panting, he had to stop for a moment.

Ursula's thighs parted beneath him. He sank into warmth and wetness and then there was no stopping.

She was very small and he was very large. He was afraid of hurting her. Yet with astonishing strength, the pelvic muscles she had developed through years of horse riding pulled him deeper inside. Her body responded to his with an identical rhythm, so that what they did was not the act of two, but of one. One flesh and blood and bone, giving and taking.

His long agony pouring out of him.

Her long hunger assuaged.

Something deep and sweet settled into Ursula's soul and nestled there.

Before she could give it a name, she was asleep.

Finbar raised himself on one elbow and bent over her. "I'll take care of you, *a stórín*,"* he promised, though she did not hear him. "I'll take care of you always."

Sitting on the only chair in the room, Finbar never took his eyes from the woman on the bed. He had been dressed since before dawn. Thoughts roiled in his head like stones in the shallows of a turbulent sea.

Ursula was his now. He had possessed her. They must marry, preferably at once. Of that there was no question.

He mentally ran the sums. Augmented by his savings, his wages would just about pay for a small terraced house in a less than fashionable neighborhood. He resolved that someday he would give her a palace. At this moment he felt as if he could do anything. The amazing relief of sex had left him drained but exultant. Oh, yes, exultant! He wanted to open the window and shout down into the street, "I just made love with Ursula Halloran!"

He could not do that, of course. He could never ever say those words out loud, even after they were married. She must be treated with total respect.

He must forget the circumstances under which they had first made love. Made love. Gazing at the sleeping form on the bed, suddenly he was beside her again, lost in her flesh, drowned in the fragrance of her hair, burrowed between her thighs . . .

He tore his eyes away from her and fumbled in his waistcoat pocket for a cigarette.

He had none.

His body was thundering its demands, but not for cigarettes.

"Ursula," he whispered.

No response.

He had taken her when she was drunk, a terrible sin surely. He must not compound it by taking her again while she was asleep and unaware.

*"Little darling."

"Ursula." He raised his voice just enough to seep into her consciousness and waken her gently.

BRANDY, Ursula told herself through a fog of pain, *is not the same as Guinness.*

She kept her eyes tightly shut and waited for the pain to recede. It did not. When she tried to remember the events of the preceding night they eluded her like eels flashing through a weir. A momentary glimpse, a sparkle and a slither . . . then nothing.

What happened?

Memory returned in jagged flashes. Being carried through the gates of Trinity. Someone comforting her as she wept. Wept for . . .

When she opened her eyes, the first thing she saw was the bridle hanging on the wall like a silent reproach. *"Saoirse!"*

Finbar jumped up and hurried over to her. She gazed up at him with bloodshot eyes. "Saoirse," she repeated in a voice breaking with agony.

"Finbar," he corrected.

"What are you doing here?"

"I spent the night. Don't you remember?"

If you don't know what you're doing, it doesn't count. "I must ask you to leave." Her mouth was dry; her stomach heaved. In a moment she would be sick. She could not bear to let anyone see her vomiting.

"I can't leave you," said Finbar, "not after what happened. I have to take care of you. What sort of man do you think I am?"

"If you're any sort of man at all you'll go right now," Ursula told him through gritted teeth. She sprang from the bed with her hands over her mouth, brushing Finbar aside as she ran from the room. The door of the toilet on the landing banged shut. Unmistakable sounds came from within.

Embarrassed, Finbar could not decide whether it was best to wait, or to leave and come back later. He stood in the door of her room with his hands thrust deep into his pockets. My poor girl, he thought. *My* poor girl.

URSULA hunched over the water closet while the sour contents of her stomach scalded her throat and backed up into her nasal passages. She was choking, she was suffocating!

Vomit exploded into the bowl.

She was being turned inside out. *Never again. Oh sweet Jesus never again.* Gripping the edge of the bowl, she retched repeatedly.

The piece of lino around the base of the water closet was filthy. She found herself staring at it with disgust. Or perhaps the disgust was at herself.

With the emptying of her stomach, her brain began to clear. She could remember almost everything. Including intense, totally unexpected pleasure.

Oh sweet Jesus!

I thought it was Lewis. It wasn't.

It was him. Finbar.

Ordinary, oh-so-familiar Finbar. How could he make me feel those things?

Because I thought he was Lewis.

Or pretended he was Lewis, she added in a moment of painful self-knowledge.

Please God when I come out of here, let him be gone!

WHEN the sounds from the toilet ceased, Finbar pasted a smile on his face. She would be coming out any minute now. He would be loving and tender and concerned. She would apologize for her outburst and he would be infinitely understanding.

Ursula emerged looking very pale. Before Finbar could speak she said, "I apologize, that was disgraceful."

"You drank too much brandy, that's all. It could happen to a bishop as they say. Come here to me." Finbar attempted to put his arms around her, but when he smelt her breath he flinched inadvertently.

Ursula was mortified. *How did I get myself into this?* Her head was pounding like the roll of drums. "Please go now," she whispered, moving farther away from him.

"I have to take care of you."

"I can take care of myself, Finbar. I just want you to go."

"May I see you tomorrow?"

She gave her head the tiniest shake and instantly regretted it. Every movement hurt.

"The day after, then?"

"Can't you understand? I don't want to see you."

"Is there someone else?"

Ursula would not meet his eyes.

"The Englishman," Finbar said in a tight voice. "He's not good enough for you."

"I don't want to talk about him, I don't want to talk about anything. How many times do I have to tell you? If you don't leave this minute I shall never ever speak to you again!"

Finbar left with as much dignity as he could muster.

But the retreat was not a surrender. Ursula was his now, Englishman or no. He need only find a way to convince her.

URSULA arrived at work late and with a dreadful hangover. At lunchtime she pleaded a splitting headache and went home to bed. "I'll be back on form tomorrow," she promised.

In the dismal hours before dawn she woke herself up, crying.

FINBAR'S plans for winning Ursula included handwritten notes to himself and long columns of figures. Eamon de Valera, former mathematics teacher, wanted every department of government to support its actions with figures. The habit had become ingrained in Finbar Cassidy.

First he drew up a column listing his assets and liabilities. On the liability side were his wages. Lower-echelon civil servants could never hope to make much money. On the asset side he had some savings, excellent health, and he was Irish. If not a Republican, at least Irish. Perhaps he could convert to republicanism. It would not be such a long leap, not like changing one's religion, for example.

He could do it for Ursula.

Over the weekend Finbar scoured the city looking for houses he could afford. He prepared a painstaking analysis of each prospect, comparing its condition and square footage with every other house under consideration. Sums were allocated for painting and replastering. Most of the eligible structures were suffering from the curse of the Irish climate, rising damp, so additional expenditure would be necessary to protect floors and skirting boards from rot.

Somewhere along the way Finbar Cassidy realized that he enjoyed looking at houses and making plans to improve them.

With the departure of the British ruling class, residential architecture in Ireland had fallen into serious decline. The elegant Georgian houses that had graced Dublin in the nineteenth century were now, many of them, tenements. During the War of Independence the IRA had destroyed a number of magnificent "big houses," the country homes of the hated ruling class.

In his inmost heart, Finbar longed to offer Ursula a palace. But nowhere in Ireland was there a palace that a working man could afford to buy.

Chapter Thirty-eight

THE following Monday, Ursula urged 2RN to do a program analyzing the European situation. John MacDonagh readily agreed.

"An interview from the British perspective would give it depth," Ursula suggested. "Shall I invite Lewis Baines to take part? He really does have a fine voice for broadcasting."

She needed to see Lewis, to interpose his image between herself and Finbar. She had lost control and allowed something to happen that she never intended. Being with Lewis again was the only way to blot out those troubling memories.

She telephoned him on Tuesday morning. "I can't leave today," he told her, "But meet me at Baldonnel tomorrow afternoon. I should be there by three."

Instead of having lunch on Wednesday, Ursula went home to change her clothes before meeting Lewis. Her only pair of good stockings had a hole in them. She had darned it as best she could. But as she walked to the Gresham Hotel to engage a taxicab to collect Lewis at the aerodrome, a coarse ridge of thread rubbed against the ball of her foot.

Baldonnel had lost its earlier informality. The gathering storm clouds in Europe had precipitated a long overdue move on the part of the government to strengthen the Irish Air Corps in the interest of national defense. There was now a soldier at the gate who asked Ursula to identify herself before passing her through.

Lewis's Moth had already set down on the runway. Plans were underway for a large three-bay hangar to accommodate Air Corps planes, but construction had not yet begun. In the meantime military planes, like civilian aircraft, must be tied down in the open.

Ursula called to Lewis and waved. He waved back, but was busy removing something from the plane. By the time she got to him his arms were full of shiny boxes. "I brought you a little present," he said.

"A little present? Not all of that, surely."

He laughed. "It is, in fact. I hope you don't mind. Here, watch these while I finish making arrangements for the plane." He set his burden down on the concrete and walked toward the aerodrome office.

Ursula eyed the boxes with trepidation. When she nudged them with her foot one slid off another, revealing the label of a famous London clothiers.

With an effort of will she asked no questions as the taxi drove them toward the city. From time to time Lewis glanced at her out of the corner of his eye. As the taxi pulled up in front of the hotel he finally asked, "Don't you want to see what I brought you?"

"I expect you'll show me when you're ready."

Lewis smiled the smile of a man who had done something wonderful and was anticipating praise.

Snapping his fingers, he summoned a porter to deliver the luggage and the stack of boxes to his rooms. It had become a tradition with Lewis to engage the same small suite at the Shelbourne. On several previous occasions he had invited Ursula into the sitting room, but had made no attempt to maneuver her into the bedroom.

"Now," he said when the door closed behind the porter. "Open your presents."

He watched as she lifted the lids and threw back layers of rustling white tissue paper. The first garment, a dress of pleated chiffon the color of sea foam, brought a gasp from Ursula. Nestled beside it in the box was a pair of matching fabric-covered slippers.

"You can wear those when we go dancing," Lewis said. "We are going to go dancing, you know. Often."

"How did you know my size?"

"Trust me," said Lewis Baines.

More boxes. Beautifully tailored skirts, stylish shirtwaists. Cashmere sweaters. Even . . . *Oh my God, silk stockings!* As she let them slide through her fingers, Ursula was all too aware of the ridge of knotted thread cutting into the tender flesh of her foot.

"This is far too much," she told Lewis. "And stockings are far too intimate a gift."

"Don't be so Irish. I want you to have them and you can't tell me you don't need them."

Her eyes flashed. "What makes you think I can't buy my own clothes?"

He shook his head. "My dear girl."

She stiffened her Republican spine, willing herself to resist the seduction of the clothes. But they felt so wonderful to the touch!

LEWIS took her out to dinner and then back to his suite in the Shelbourne. They both knew what was going to happen next.

She was prepared for his fastidiousness. She was prepared for everything, even the words he whispered at the height of passion. She steeled herself to ignore them as she had learned to ignore the crackle of static on the wireless.

This time the sex was better. Ursula did not experience the rapture she had felt with Finbar, but, as she told herself sternly, she was not drunk, either. She had taken only water with dinner in order to keep her head clear.

While Lewis made love to her she concentrated on her body's responses. Pleasure in the feel of his hands on her skin; pleasure in his skill. And afterwards, as she lay beside him in the dark, there was the wonderful sense of not being alone.

LEWIS kept her with him all night. They had crossed an invisible border in his mind.

In the morning he selected and ordered a breakfast for two to be brought to his suite. They chatted over *oeufs en gelée*—which she pronounced correctly and he did not—like an old married couple. Ursula did not mention that she hated eggs. She ate every scrap of hers and said they were delicious.

In the morning light Lewis thought she looked like a young girl. Hers would be a delightful face to find on his pillow every morning.

As he shaved he contemplated the problems they would face in England. Gaining acceptance for Ursula would be difficult, but she must be accepted before things went any farther. Muriel would be upset at first. His friends would cloak their disdain in a thin patina of good manners that would not fool anyone. He could just imagine the barbs they would hurl, thinking Ursula too stupid to understand.

But her intelligence could not be long denied, and in time her knowledge of the social graces would make people overlook her Irish origins. With a decent wardrobe and a proper hairdresser, she could hold her own in any company.

Ursula luxuriated for half an hour in the suite's big white bathtub, then dressed in one of the outfits Lewis had given her. It fitted perfectly, as he had known it would.

Lewis was familiar with the bodies of women.

Ursula took the rest of her new clothes back to Moore Street and left Lewis waiting below while she put them away. He had never seen her room and she did not want him to.

They spent Saturday afternoon enjoying the delights of Dublin, returning to the Shelbourne for dinner. At Lewis's insistence, this time Ursula had wine.

She rarely took her eyes from his face. Her surrender was total and she was glad. She wanted to stay in this bubble of time forever.

"My little rebel," said Lewis as they lay together in his bed. He drew Ursula closer, fitting her against his body. Skin on skin.

Bliss. Wine and love flowed through her veins together. Knots that she had never known existed loosened in her soul. Her eyes drifted shut.

"My little rebel," he said again, his voice deep in his chest. "Like your parents. Isn't there an Irish saying: 'What's bred in the bone comes out in the blood?'"

"I have no idea what's bred in my bones," she murmured drowsily. Her guard was very far down.

"Why not?"

"The Hallorans weren't my parents."

In his body she felt no change, in his voice she heard nothing but concern. "Did your real parents die?"

"I don't know. I was a foundling."

He continued to hold her as tenderly as before. "You're joking."

"I'm perfectly serious. Ned Halloran found me abandoned in a Dublin street when I was only a toddler. He and Síle married soon after, and raised me as their own." How liberating to tell the truth at last!

"You mean they adopted you?"

"No."

"Why not?"

Ursula hesitated. His questions were probing defenses she had constructed with care over many years. "It's complicated, Lewis. When I was little I accepted without question the story of the way Ned found me. He was—is—a wonderful man, and Síle was the bravest woman on earth. Ned was a bit too young to be my real father but Síle was a couple of years older than he was. As I grew up I began to wonder if she might be . . . my real mother."

"A natural enough fantasy under the circumstances," Lewis said.

"That's just it; I didn't want her to be my real mother. Let me explain about Síle. I loved her dearly, but she . . . she was . . . always *touching* Ned. She couldn't keep her hands off him. Síle was 'a man's woman' through and through. Do you understand what I'm saying?"

"I'm not sure I do."

"Síle didn't belong to herself. She *never* belonged to herself! Something inside her made her a slave to a man, and she was awfully lucky that Ned adored her and treated her well. I didn't want to be another Síle Halloran. I willed myself to be a different person entirely, a woman who wouldn't let any man have power over her.

"Until I met you, Lewis. Suddenly my precious independence didn't seem so important anymore. I just wanted to touch you and have you touch me. I felt like that right up until the first time we went to bed together.

"But the way you spoke to me that night . . . how can I explain the effect your words had on me? Your language was vile, Lewis. I hated those words and hated you for saying them. It was as if you had recognized Síle . . . in me."

"You poor girl, why didn't you say something? I never realized I was offending you. I'm not even aware what I say when I make love."

"It's all right, really." She nestled more closely against him. "We're together again and everything's sorted out."

"Except you still haven't explained why the Hallorans didn't adopt you."

Ursula was too far committed now. Willing Lewis to understand that she was giving him the incomparable gift of trust, she said, "Because before she married Ned, Síle Duffy was a prostitute."

The arms holding Ursula turned wooden. There was a change in the very atmosphere of the room, as if all the warmth had drained away. They were not lovers lying joined in a bed. They were two separate people.

In sudden desperation, Ursula threw words like bridges across the void between them. "They never wanted me to know, but from what I heard over the years I put things together. Ned and Síle let people think I was their natural child because if they applied to adopt me and the authorities found out about her past, I would have been taken away from them.

"So now you know everything. And it's all right, isn't it?" She waited. Feeling knots re-form in her soul. "Isn't it?"

Lewis rolled away from her to light one of his Turkish cigarettes. He began blowing smoke rings into space, watching them with total absorption.

Chapter Thirty-nine

NEVER *again,* Ursula promised herself. *Never again.*

She was tortured by humiliating memories of her final minutes with Lewis. Her awkward attempts to repair the damage. His chilling indifference. While she struggled into her clothes he had stood smoking, not even watching her. She had slammed out of the room and run through the lobby of the Shelbourne with her pride in tatters; too angry to cry, too hurt not to. Afraid he would follow and furious when he did not.

SHE was thankful for the distraction of her work.

On the thirteenth of September she prepared a momentous newscast: "Yesterday Eamon de Valera was elected president, for one term, of the Assembly of the League of Nations. Meanwhile the Czechoslovakian premier has appealed for calm as the situation in his country worsens. Chamberlain of Britain and Daladier of France are to meet with Hitler and Mussolini in Munich to discuss the crisis."

The resulting Munich Pact at the end of the month allowed for the peaceful evacuation of the Sudetenland by the tenth of October. Military confrontation would be avoided.

Neville Chamberlain returned from Munich to announce triumphantly to the British press, and the world, that he had successfully negotiated "peace in our time!"

·   ·   ·

FINBAR went to the broadcasting station, hoping to meet Ursula when her workday was over.

"Miss Halloran left already," the door porter told him.

"Did she go home?"

The man narrowed his eyes. "Why do you need to know?"

He was only being protective, but it irritated Finbar. Protecting Ursula would be his obligation from now on; his obligation and his privilege.

"I'm a friend of hers, you've seen me here before."

The man gazed at him impassively.

Finbar threw discretion to the winds. "A close friend," he stressed.

"She said something about going to a women's meeting in the Rotunda. Maybe she went home first, though. If you're a close friend of hers you'd know where she lives."

Finbar almost ran around the corner to Moore Street. When he arrived at the blue door, it was firmly closed. He banged the rusty iron knocker for a while but no one came down to let him in.

The greengrocer popped his head out of his shop. "Who're ye lookin' fer?"

"Miss Halloran."

"She'll be along. Here, would ye give her this when she comes? The postman dropped it in here for 'er."

Finbar started to put the letter in his pocket, but the quality of the cream-colored envelope made him take a closer look.

On the flap a firm hand had written *L. Baines.*

Finbar wrestled with his conscience. He looked up and down the street. He did not see Ursula coming from either direction. Thrusting the offending letter into his pocket, he set off at a brisk walk and did not stop until he reached the foot of O'Connell Bridge. The ornate wrought-iron street lamps were on, providing enough light for him to read by.

My Irish rose, the letter began.

My Irish rose! Finbar knotted his brows in fury. How dare that man call Ursula his!

> I should have written sooner, but what you told me was something of a shock. I had to have time to come to terms with my feelings. I regret now that I was not more understanding. I behaved like a cad and do not blame you for walking out on me. Any woman with a shred of pride would have done the same.
>
> On reflection, and knowing you as I do, I am convinced that you were mistaken in your conjecture. It does not matter anyway because I love you. I should have said that before, but we are inclined to be

reticent about such things. I'm telling you now and I mean it with all my heart.

I love you for who you are, for the unique person who is Ursula. None of the other girls I know can hold a candle to you. When I am with them I keep thinking of you. If you are not in my life it will have no flavor.

There's nothing for it, dearest girl, but to ask you to forgive me and agree to be my wife. You will, won't you? Tell me so and I shall be on my way to you at once.

> In love and hope,
> Lewis

Finbar wished Lewis Baines was in front of him at that moment so he could punch him in the face. Obviously Baines had hurt Ursula, yet every other word was about himself. Coldhearted self-centred bastard.

Finbar's arms ached with the desire to lift Baines over his head and hurl him into the river.

He did the next best thing.

Slowly, methodically, he tore the letter into tiny pieces. Then he leaned over the bridge rail and dropped them into the Liffey.

Fragments of a life never-to-be swirled away on the dark water.

On the fifth of October the German army invaded Czechoslovakia.

In Eger, capital of the Sudetenland, Adolf Hitler announced, "I bear you the greetings of the whole German people. Over the great German Reich lie as protection the German shield and the German sword. You are part of this protection now. Never again shall this land be torn from the Reich. Thus we begin our march into the great German future."[1]

Ursula tumbled into bed each night exhausted. In the press of events, her extraordinary energy was deserting her. She had heard nothing from Lewis Baines, nor did she expect to.

However Seán Lester did send a brief note in response to one from her. He commented, "France and Britain have retired behind their Chinese Wall in Europe—the Maginot Line—and abandoned the rest of the Continent to Germany." Ursula saw that he was quoted on that night's news.

Thursday morning, November tenth, dawned clear and bright but bitterly cold. As Ursula walked to work she noticed ice glittering in the gutters.

She had just reached her desk and taken off her hat when Finbar Cassidy entered the office. He was flushed and breathless, as if he had been running. "Overnight we had an urgent cable from Berlin. I think you'll want to issue a news bulletin." He handed her an envelope containing a folded sheet of yellow paper. "It seemed best to bring this over rather than telephone."

Ursula read rapidly, her eyes widening. "I appreciate this, Finbar. Wait while I compose the bulletin, then you can take the cable back to External Affairs."

Her fingers flew over the typewriter keys. "Germany's Jewish community has been subjected to a reign of terror unprecedented in modern times. Last night a series of simultaneous attacks erupted throughout the country. An unknown number of Jews were killed and thousands more injured. Storm troopers were joined in acts of violence by ordinary, middle-class citizens. In Berlin, laughing women held up their children to watch Jews being beaten senseless by youths with lead pipes. Hundreds of synagogues were put to the torch. Over seven thousand Jewish shops were looted and vandalized. The broken glass alone will account for millions in damage. Already the event is being called *Kristallnacht,* meaning Crystal Night."

When Ursula finished typing she murmured, "God help them." A wave of nausea washed over her.

Finbar said, "Could you meet me later for lunch?"

"I'm not very hungry, not after reading this."

"Tea, then. After work. I really need to talk to you, it's important."

By the time she got off work she only wanted to go home and to bed. But she owed Finbar something for the effort he had made. He was waiting for her at the Henry Street entrance, with his hat in his hands and an eager expression on his face.

"We can go wherever you like, Ursula."

"Wynn's, then."

They settled into a quiet corner of the hotel dining room. Ursula wanted only tea and toast, but Finbar insisted on ordering a full meal for both of them.

"Wonderful news," he told her while they waited to be served. "At least, I hope you'll think it's wonderful. I've bought a house."

"I'm happy for you."

"In the North Strand. A terraced redbrick house with a bit of back garden. Rather ordinary at the moment, but I have plans to make it something special."

"That's grand." Ursula smiled up at the waiter as he set the teapot in front of her.

"I'm not going to make any changes until you see the place, though," said Finbar.

"Why do I need to see it first?" She took the lid off the pot and peered in. *Still too weak. In Clare they say tea should be strong enough for a mouse to trot across.*

"Because you'll be living there with me. I'm asking you to marry me, Ursula."

Ursula dropped the spoon.

"We've already . . . been together," Finbar said. His ears reddened with embarrassment. "So in the eyes of God we are man and wife now. I simply want to . . ."

"Well, I don't."

"You have to!" Finbar had been raised to believe that a proposal of marriage was the ultimate compliment a man could offer a woman. A refusal was unthinkable.

"I don't have to do anything!" Ursula shot back.

He looked so stricken she tried to defuse the situation by making light of it. "Well, you're certainly not backward about coming forward," she said with a light laugh. "But you're joking, of course."

"For once I'm serious. I want you to be my wife."

The proposal had come when she was least prepared. Rummaging through her memory, she recalled the correct Surval response. "I'm flattered by your proposal, Finbar, but marriage is out of the question. I'm very fond of you, but only as a friend. It would be cruel to let you think there could ever be more than that between us."

She must make him understand. "I have no intention of getting married to anybody. Ever. Full stop. Now pass me your cup."

Somehow they got through the meal. The food stuck in Ursula's throat; she left most of it on her plate. Finbar ate automatically, cutting his meat into neat portions and taking a morsel of potato with each bite. He made polite conversation but he did not know what he was saying.

Afterward he walked Ursula back to Moore Street. At the blue door they shook hands.

When she reached her room Ursula shrugged out of her coat and hung it behind the curtain. Slumping onto the bed, she stared at Saoirse's bridle. *Gone. Everyone and everything.* She felt strangely cleansed, even of regret. Regret would not change anything anyway.

After a long time she stood up and squared her shoulders. *Best get on with it,* she told herself as she began undressing for the night.

There was a certain strength to be drawn from being totally alone.

Chapter Forty

FOREIGN newspapers were difficult to obtain behind the lines, Irish papers impossible. As the civil war in Spain wound down to its inevitable conclusion, Ned longed for news from home.

He could not recall the last time he had written to Ursula. Or anyone else. There were holes in his memory. Great gaping holes that swallowed whole months at a time, taking the bad memories with the good. Sometimes that was an advantage.

One morning as they were breaking camp he noticed an unfamiliar officer giving orders. Out of the side of his mouth, Ned asked a peach-fuzz corporal, "Who's that fellow?"

"You know him, it's Tom Murphy."

"Och sure, I know Murphy," Ned said without conviction. "But where's Frank Ryan?"

"Don't you remember? The bloody Nationalists captured him over a year ago and charged him with being a saboteur. He was sentenced to death but Franco's never signed the execution order. De Valera claimed that executing Ryan would prevent Éire from recognizing any government headed by Franco."[1]

Ned looked puzzled. "De Valera's the commandant at Boland's Mill."

The young corporal grinned. "He was, old-timer. In 1916. This is the hind leg of 1938 and Dev's the taoiseach now."

"The Chief?" Ned struggled to remember. "Does he know we're here?"

"I'm sure he does. Didn't he pass a law forbidding Irishmen to fight in this bloody war? After we were already in Spain, of course," the other added.

"That Dev's a cute hoor," Ned cackled. "He's the only man I know who can chew a meal and whistle at the same time. Did you know he wore bright red socks with his Volunteer's uniform, all Easter week?" He cackled again, a strange, cracked laugh.

Halloran should have been sent home long ago, thought the corporal. The man was as mad as a brush. Other soldiers regarded him with superstitious awe because he could walk untouched through a hail of gunfire. Knowing life was only a waking dream, he was indifferent to death. Knowing this as his truth, the bullets ignored him.

But when the fog lifted from his mazed mind and his eyes turned to cold green glass, Halloran could shoot better than any man in the International Brigades. An officer could point to some Nationalist bastard who was just a flyspeck on the horizon and say, "Take him down," and Halloran would. Every damned time.

The young corporal hawked, spat into the yellow dust, and ambled off to relieve himself. His liver had been ruined by copious quantities of cheap wine. Occasionally he was terrified but most of the time he was bored. He wanted to go home.

Everyone wanted to go home.

THIS war can't last much longer, Ned told himself. I should write to Ursula and tell her I'll be coming home soon.

Coming home. As if they were a magic incantation, the words cleared his brain. Ireland spread out before him in his imagination. Coolness and wetness and greenness to soothe his burning eyes.

The Spanish sun was a giant yellow balloon filled with savage birds. When the balloon burst, jagged black forms came swooping down out of the sky. Piercing and stabbing, they drove cruel beaks and sharp claws straight through Ned's eyes into his brain. The pain was intense.

Sometimes he could fight them off with an effort of will. Not always.

Not today.

By evening he was too exhausted to compose a letter. Any strength he had left must be hoarded for his book.

The book was amorphous and ever-changing. Sometimes it was about Pádraic Pearse; sometimes it was about Michael Collins. When the words came strong and true, when Ned knew what he wanted to say and how he wanted to say it, the book was about Síle. He would lie on his back at night with his fingers laced at the nape of his neck, and bring her to life on the blank pages of his mind.

But on this particular night he wanted to capture his own thoughts. For the book. The real book he was really going to write. Someday. Tomorrow.

When he got home.

Shrugging out of his Sam Browne belt, Ned pulled a notebook from his grimy pack. He had only a stub of a pencil but it would have to do. He chewed on it for a time, drawing strength from the elements of lead and wood. Then he began to write.

"In Spain we Irish are fighting a version of our own civil war, except this time we changed sides. O'Duffy and his Free State followers joined Franco's revolutionaries. We Republicans support the elected government. Am I the only person who sees how ironic this is? Our history has developed irony to an art form."

The light faded but Ned kept on writing. He sometimes experienced brief periods of darkness even at high noon—damage done by the black birds, perhaps—and had taught himself to do essential tasks by feel. Fortunately the spells had not yet occurred during combat. At other times he could cope.

"As with all wars," he wrote, "both sides claim to be fighting for freedom and truth. Franco's Nationalists want to return to a static, feudal Spain governed by strict religious principles and an aristocratic hierarchy. The Republicans hope for a society where the interests of the common man are paramount, religion no longer exercises a stranglehold, and the many political divisions can reconcile their interests.

"Which side will win? Hitler and Mussolini have thrown their support behind Franco. It is only a matter of days now, weeks at the most."

Ned put down the pencil and rubbed the bridge of his nose. One of his terrible headaches was building. Sometimes he prayed a bullet would drill into his skull and release the pressure.

ASIDE from dealing once a month with its more distasteful aspects, Ursula gave little thought to her menstrual cycle until she realized, with a shock, that her last period had been in August.

An examination of her naked body in the looking glass confirmed her fears. Frequent nausea had ruined her appetite, yet her waist was definitely thicker.

I'm infanticipating. That's a nice way of saying pregnant. *Pregnant and un-married in Catholic Ireland.*

Others would say disgraced, ruined. Ostracized and outcast. Battered by society's judgment, countless Irish girls committed suicide every year.

Ursula met her own eyes in the glass. *Life's too interesting and death's too permanent. What are my other options?*

Finbar Cassidy had proposed marriage.

I will not bind a man for life to a woman who does not love him, who would only be marrying him to give her child a name. I hope to God I have more integrity than that.

Besides, marrying Finbar would mean spending the rest of my life in domestic servitude. That's all our government wants from women now.

Thank you, Eamon de Valera.

Ned was in Spain, perhaps dead for all she knew. Henry Mooney in America seemed a million miles away. She could go back to the farm in Clare, but Lucy was a spiteful woman—look how she had treated Eileen. Ursula had a dark suspicion that Lucy had kept Saoirse's money for herself and allowed him to die. That alone was reason to shun her forever.

Louise Hamilton loved children and had none of her own. She would be sympathetic. But Hector would not; he would never allow his wife to take in a fallen woman. So there was no sanctuary in Gardiner Street.

If Ursula turned to the Church she could expect to be sent to the infamous Magdalen Laundry. Sisters of the Holy Saints Magdalen Home for Wayward Girls and Fallen Women, where the nuns had enormous power and were accountable to no one. Most of them showed no mercy to their hapless charges. Inside high stone walls from which few pregnant women could hope to escape, the nuns worked their Magdalens to exhaustion in a steamy sweatshop for the good of their souls. When a baby was born the nuns took it away before the mother ever saw it, and put the infant in an orphanage.

Ursula had a horror of orphanages.

Some Irish girls who found themselves in her predicament secretly gave birth in country ditches or abandoned outbuildings—or even graveyards. If they survived the ordeal, they abandoned their infant to its fate rather than face the opprobrium of Church and neighbor.

According to back-fence gossip, other women used wire coat hangers to abort themselves. But with the knowledge that life was growing within her came the certainty that life was sacred. She could not kill; it was as simple as that. The discovery surprised her almost more than the pregnancy. She had always believed that if she had the man who shot Síle within her gunsights, she could blow his head off.

The girls at Surval, though young and supposedly virginal, had represented a wide range of experience. When no chaperone was within earshot they had exchanged confidences that would have shocked their elders. The Turkish girl had described exotic forms of contraception secretly practiced by women in her country. Because the topic was, from the Catholic point of view, forbidden, Ursula had listened with fascination. Yet she never thought it might someday apply to her.

Now it was too late.

Mea culpa, mea culpa. And I alone to face the consequences.

There was a certain strength to be drawn from being totally alone. The answer, when it came, must come from within herself.

And it did.

Overriding her independent nature, she sent a telegram asking for a favor. She did not explain the reason for her request. *One step at a time. First I must have somewhere to go.*

Seán Lester replied immediately. "Delighted to have you on my staff. Your knowledge of German more useful than ever. Will make all arrangements. Come as soon as possible."

W HEN he did not receive any reply from Ursula, Lewis Baines convinced himself of two things: he was in love with her, and she had jilted him. For months afterward he was obsessed by thoughts of her, enjoying a romantic melancholy as pleasurable as it was painful. It made him more attractive than ever to other women, many of whom were happy to help him forget. In time the pain faded.

Yet for the rest of his life, whenever he heard some Yank sing the sentimental American ballad, "My Wild Irish Rose," Lewis would remember Ursula's eyes. And wish that men could weep.

U RSULA handed in her notice to 2RN's newly appointed staff administration officer, who protested strenuously against losing her. Everyone at the station protested. But she was adamant. That same day she gave up her room in Moore Street. The few things she could not take with her, including her saddle, would have to be stored in the attics of number 16 again.

"I've accepted a job in Geneva with the League of Nations," she explained to Louise. "I don't know how long I'll be there, but I'd be a fool not to go. The pay is better than I'll ever make at 2RN."

"I thought you loved broadcasting too much to do anything else."

"People change," said Ursula.

She spent Christmas with the Hamiltons. A cold, damp Christmas; the atmosphere heavy with the smells of cooking. Louise had a bad cold and Hector was suffering from dyspepsia. On Christmas Eve he went to bed early, leaving the two women alone to listen to Midnight Mass on the wireless.

Afterward, as Ursula was starting upstairs to bed, Louise caught her and gave her an impetuous hug. "Come back to us, Precious."

"I shall of course. I always do."

Next day she departed for Switzerland.

Chapter Forty-one

THE taxi driver grunted as he hoisted Ursula's bulging suitcase and two heavy boxes into the car. As well as her clothes and toilet articles she was bringing her favorite books—the ones she could not bear to leave behind, including Ned's old schoolbooks—and Saoirse's bridle. Plus all the new things Lewis had given her.

I suppose I should pack them up and send them back to him. But I'm not such a fool as that.

Aer Lingus did not yet have a direct flight to London. In order to use the Irish airline Ursula was obliged to take an Aer Lingus monoplane to Liverpool, then travel by train to London to catch the Geneva flight. The League, through Seán Lester's office, was paying for her transportation.

At first she was afraid she might be airsick, but fortunately that phase of her pregnancy had passed. As the small plane winged its way across the Irish Sea she tried not to think of Lewis flying across the same sea to visit her.

Never again.

In Liverpool train station Ursula heard as many Irish accents as English ones. Since the onset of the depression Irish emigration had returned with a vengeance, sending thousands of migrants not west to America but east to England, seeking work. "Welcome to Dublin east," the ticket agent joked in a Wexford accent.

During the train ride to London, Ursula stared out the window at England. England, the ancient enemy. Perfidious Albion. Although brittle with winter, the countryside strangely resembled Ireland. Except the fields were larger and not embraced by stone.

I'm here. I'm actually here.

At Heathrow she had to wait almost two hours for the flight to Switzerland. She thought about placing a telephone call to Fliss but decided against it. Fliss might rush out to the airport for a quick visit and she did not want that. Did not want to take a chance that Fliss might recognize her condition. Did not want to have to make conversation, either.

The DC3 bound for Geneva was three-quarters full. Most of the passengers appeared to be businessmen; only two were women. Ursula was given a window seat and was thankful when the seat beside her remained unoccupied. She was not in the mood to talk.

The plane roared down the runway with a thrilling surge of power and lifted into the sky. The sensation was less like flying than in a small aircraft, but as Ursula gazed through the tiny window the earth fell away at startling speed. Up and up they went, storming heaven, climbing to a height that would have been unimaginable a few short years before. The plane banked sharply, then they were threading their way among peaks of cloud, as if mountains had climbed into the sky by magic. Inured to the wonder, the businessmen began talking or reading newspapers.

Ursula put her hands over her belly where the real magic was.

After a while she moved to the empty seat to facilitate earwigging. "I was at a sales conference in Geneva when the Czech crisis erupted," the man across the aisle was telling his seatmate. "Rumors were running wild. Every country in Europe began issuing mobilization orders. The Swiss government stationed soldiers on the bridges, then plunged the city into a most inconvenient blackout.

"We went to the Palais des Nations to see the League in action. I tell you, it was bizarre. Journalists from fifty countries were swarming in the lobby, fighting for telephones and asking one another what the hell was happening. It was no good asking the delegates, they didn't know either."

The seat in front of Ursula was occupied by a man whose white knuckles gripped the armrest for the entire flight. Ursula overheard him ask the air hostess for a drink of water. "I am very nervous," he said apologetically. "I just took my children to England and I may never see them again."

"Of course you shall," the hostess consoled.

"We are Jewish."

The hostess hesitated. "Could you not . . . ah . . . stay in England with your children?"

The man made a small, hopeless sound. "My wife, her parents, my business . . . all in Freiberg. We are Germans too, you understand. I have to go back."

THE plane dropped out of the sky onto the runway of Cointrin Airport. Geneva, birthplace of Calvinism and the International Red Cross and home of the League of Nations, was Switzerland's most cosmopolitan city. Under other circumstances Ursula would have been delighted to find herself in Geneva again. As a schoolgirl she had toured historic Old Town, duly impressed by the Cathedral of St. Peter and the numerous art galleries. As an adult she would have enjoyed dining in the many chic French bistros and rustic Italian *grotti*, or exploring the haute couture shops along the left bank of the Rhone. Under other circumstances . . .

As she emerged from the door of the aeroplane a cold, dry wind hit her in the face, taking her breath away. She heard someone call her name. Beside a gleaming Daimler saloon ostentatiously parked on the apron stood Seán Lester in topcoat and muffler.

"The steps are icy," warned the air hostess.

Ursula tucked her handbag under her arm and gripped the safety rail with both gloved hands. Once she would have bounded down. Today she descended one careful step at a time.

Lester met her at the foot of the steps. "It's good to see you again, Ursula. We're right over there." He put a hand under her elbow. "That car's an embarrassment, isn't it? But that's the League for you. My driver will collect your luggage and Elsie's waiting at home to welcome you. She has more faith than I do, I wasn't even sure you'd come."

Ursula laughed. "I'm not that easily frightened."

"I'm glad to hear it. I must warn you, I've made Elsie promise that if war should break out, she'll take the children and go back to Ireland."

The Jewish man passed them, trudging across the apron toward the terminal. His was a curiously shrunken figure inside an overcoat that appeared too large for him. He had turned his collar up, but they could hear him coughing. "Could we offer that man a ride as far as the train station?" Ursula asked Lester. "I overheard him saying he's going to Basel."

"Why doesn't he fly? The Swiss have excellent air taxis."

"He plans to cross the border at Basel, but the airport there is watched by German agents and he's afraid of being picked up. He's Jewish."

"Oh."

Strange, Ursula thought, *how that one word seems to explain so much.*

"I'd be happy to offer him a ride to the train station," Lester said. "I made myself unwelcome in Danzig by trying to help the Jews; there's no point in breaking the habit now."

The airport was five kilometers northwest of downtown Geneva. During the short ride into the city the Jewish man, after profusely thanking both Lester and Ursula for their kindness, said nothing. Lost in thoughts Ursula could only imagine, he gazed morosely out the window.

Lester ordered his driver to the Gare Cornavin, Geneva's main train station. From the warm car they watched as the Jew stepped out into a bitter winter wind, passed through the bronze station doors, and disappeared.

"What will happen to him?" Ursula wondered.

"God only knows." Lester stared after the vanished figure, then gave himself a little shake. He turned back to Ursula. "Your plane was a few minutes early, so Elsie won't be expecting us yet. Would you like to have a quick look at League headquarters?"

"Please!"

The big Daimler turned north again, purring along a network of immaculate streets and avenues until it entered Place de Nations. The car swung right to an imposing set of gates. A uniformed guard in the sentry box recognized Lester's car and waved them through.

Built in 1926, the monumental Palais des Nations was a blend of art deco and stylized classicism. Ursula's immediate impression was of a fortress, a safe haven. *I made the right decision, coming here.*

A moment later Lester unexpectedly remarked, "Hitler and Mussolini are great admirers of this style. We call it fascist architecture."

At the main entrance more guards saluted as the Daimler drove up. Lester replied with a slight nod, then told the driver to continue on. "We won't stop now. You'll get to explore this place soon enough, Ursula. Just don't be too impressed by the trappings."

"It's hard not to, when I think of what the League was created for."

"Don't mistake aspirations for achievements," Seán Lester advised.

His wife and three daughters gave Ursula a warm welcome. Elsie Lester was a trim, stylish woman, with fine features and a sparkling personality. The girls, Dorothy Mary, Patricia, and Ann, were lively teenagers. Clamoring for news of Ireland, they clustered around Ursula. "Let the poor woman catch her breath!" their mother chided. "Dorothy, prepare the tea tray, please. Then we have a room waiting for you, Ursula, so you can unpack and have a bit of a rest before dinner."

Elsie Lester had created a home as charming and welcoming as she was. Her sitting room featured deep, inviting chairs with reading lamps conveniently placed, fine wool rugs, and a selection of serene landscapes and family portraits. "I want to find a flat of my own as soon as possible," Ursula told her hostess. "But nothing could be as lovely as this."

Lester caught his wife's eye. "We have the makings of a diplomat here, Elsie."

Ursula laughed. "I'm not known for my diplomacy, I assure you."

"We have plenty of those around anyway," he replied, "and much good it does us. I'd rather have one intelligent young woman with good German than a score of so-called diplomats full of hot air."

"Take Ursula's coat, dear?" his wife suggested.

For a moment Ursula panicked; her coat hid a figure beginning to ripen with pregnancy. Then she realized that Seán Lester had not seen her in years and Elsie had never seen her before. They would merely assume she was slightly plump.

The truth could not be concealed for long.

Dinner was relaxed and informal. The Lesters thoughtfully had invited no one else to join them, though Ursula would learn they entertained six nights out of seven; it came with the job.

When the girls continued to ply her with questions about Ireland she asked Dorothy, "Are you homesick?"

"Father wants Mother to take us back to Ireland in case there's a war, but we've discussed the situation among ourselves and decided we won't leave him."

Ann piped up, "We'll launch a stay-in strike if they try to ship us off."[1]

Patricia added, "Some English children recently arrived here from London. Their parents sent them to Switzerland to escape the possibility of air raids." She turned to her father. "How could you even think of sending us through London if there is such danger?"

The threat of war polluted the air.

Over dinner Lester gave Ursula a thumbnail sketch of the League's rather stormy history.

"When the Great War ended," he said, "Woodrow Wilson's dream was to develop an international organization to promote collective security and keep something like that from ever happening again. But the U.S. Congress refused to ratify the Versailles Treaty, which contained the League covenant.

So America didn't join with the rest of us. Isolated between two oceans, I don't think the Americans realize how small the world really is.

"Added to that, the current secretary-general is a Frenchman, Joseph Avenol, who makes no secret of his hatred for all things Anglo-Saxon. That includes Britain and by extension, America as well. He wants the League to be limited to Europe with him in charge, like a sort of feudal superstate." Lester sighed in spite of himself.

"You sound disillusioned, Seán."

"Not disillusioned; disappointed. The League could have been so much more."

"What about the Sudetenland?"

"The Czechs didn't even present their case to the General Assembly," Lester replied. "They seemed to feel their position was too clear to need explaining. They had no idea their allies would desert them. But almost from the beginning, Britain and France have given the League their support only when it suits their own national policies. Between them they've practically paralyzed the organization. Now they've sold out Czechoslovakia in order to save their own skins from Herr Hitler."

THAT night Ursula put her head on a goose-down pillow and dreamt... of Ireland.

NEXT morning she wrote to Henry Mooney, giving him her new address and selected details about her change of employment. "I've embarked on a new life!" she enthused. She also sent a note to the Hamiltons, informing them that she had arrived safely and asking Louise to forward her mail. But she did not write to Lucy. She had nothing to say to Lucy.

The afternoon was spent with Elsie Lester, looking at flats. Eventually Ursula found one not far from League headquarters. In good weather she could walk to work; otherwise a taxi ride would not be expensive.

Ursula's new flat had high ceilings, polished wooden floors, snugly shuttered windows. The furniture, though sparse, reflected a European mix of styles. Heat was provided by a porcelain stove decorated with blue flowers and love knots. A large French armoire held all her clothes with room to spare. The narrow iron bed hid a hard German mattress beneath a plump Swiss duvet.

Ursula did not disfigure the painted walls by driving a nail into them. Instead she hung Saoirse's bridle from the picture rail, next to a cheaply framed print of Arnold Böcklin's famous painting, *The Island of the Dead.*

The Swiss artist's vision depicted a boat gliding over the lightless waters of the Styx toward heavy cliffs resembling giant wings, waiting to enfold new arrivals. Wrapped in a shroud and silhouetted against funereal cypresses on the shore, the supernatural figure of Charon stood ghostlike in the prow.

THE deputy secretary-general was greatly admired in Geneva for his good humor and dignified reserve, but most of all for his untiring industry. His large staff worked as hard as he did. Ursula's duties would include translating some of the many German letters and communiqués that daily arrived in the secretariat. A few were urgent, a number were important, the vast majority were trivial. But someone had thought they were important, so they must be read.

Lester arranged a tour of the entire complex of League buildings so Ursula would be able to find her way around on her own. "De Valera's president of the General Assembly this term," he reminded her, "so he's here at the moment. Do you want to meet him?"

"I've met him," she replied shortly.

"From your tone, I assume you're not one of his devoted admirers?"

She raised her chin to a belligerent angle. "In my opinion, Mr. de Valera's leadership constitutes a major disimprovement for Ireland."

"I wouldn't say that here, if I were you."

Ursula relaxed and smiled. "Don't worry, Seán, I won't."

"In fact, you should say very little in public until you get your feet under the table and understand what's going on in Europe right now."

EVERY morning before she began work Ursula bought the latest Swiss newspapers, including the internationally oriented *Neue Zürcher Zeitung.* Over a cup of tea in the staff canteen she read the papers front to back. For information about Ireland she relied on the *Irish Times*, delivered to Seán Lester's office two days late.

ON the twelfth of January the IRA issued an ultimatum to the British government. If British troops were not withdrawn from Northern Ireland within four days, there would be reprisals.

In the Place du Bourg-de-Four, Ursula purchased a box of silky, white-chocolate truffles and sent them to England with a note: "Dear Fliss, You will be surprised to learn that I've returned to Switzerland. Not Surval, but close. I'm in Geneva, working for the League of Nations."

Should Fliss mention this to Lewis Baines, Ursula thought with satisfaction, he would realize that she was valued by important people. People entrusted with the future of mankind.

But Ursula soon learned that the social structures of the world were not being shaped by the League of Nations. Rather they were contingent upon an infinite assortment of possibilities, any of which might unexpectedly alter the balance. The League had become a bystander, a leaf swirling on the flood tide of events.

A balding, bespectacled little Frenchman who worked in the office of Secretary-General Avenol often had lunch at Ursula's table in the canteen. One day he remarked, "We are standing on the tracks watching the locomotive rush down upon us."

Ursula nodded agreement and took another bite of onion-and-mushroom quiche.

When she first arrived in Geneva nothing had tasted good. Then suddenly everything tasted good. Even eggs. Quiche was her current favorite. For lunch she took two helpings and had to restrain herself from asking for a third.

The Frenchman said admiringly, "I do not know where you put all that food, a little sparrow like you."

FAR away in Texas, Henry Mooney read Ursula's latest letter aloud to his wife and daughters. Henrietta, who was interested in everyone and everything, gave him her rapt attention. Isabella's mind was elsewhere.

"Bella, stop mooning," her mother ordered, "and listen to your father."

"I hear him. It's good enough for some, going to Switzerland. I never get to go anyplace."

"You go to Saratoga Springs every summer," Ella reminded her, "even when we can't afford it."

"If I didn't I would simply *die!* We can afford it this summer, can't we? Papa?"

"Come June, I think we can buy you a train ticket. How about you, Hank? Do you want to go too?"

Although she was not yet sixteen, Bella Mooney was a brunette beauty who looked and dressed like a girl of eighteen years. By contrast, her little sister was a tomboy whose favorite clothing—to her mother's horror—was a one-piece garment called overalls. "I don't want to go to New York, Pop-Pop," she told her father. "I want to stay here again and help you with the garden. You said we'd plant more vegetables this year, remember?"

"We may not have to. Roosevelt's almost got the depression licked, I think. We could put in more roses. You'd like that, Bella."

"I won't see them, I'll be in Saratoga."

Her little sister chanted, "Bella's got a boyfriend, Bella's got a . . ."

Under the table Bella gave Hank's arm a cruel pinch. "Liar!" she hissed.

Eyes welling with tears, Hank rubbed the injured arm. "I'm not a liar. I never lie. Much."

"Good girl," said Henry. "Bella, apologize to your sister. Now, where was I?"

"You were reading about Ursula's new job with the League of Nations," Ella prompted. "Do you think she's in any danger? The newspapers are predicting war in Europe."

"Ursula's quite able to look after herself, Cap'n. Besides, Switzerland's a federal republic with a long history of neutrality. They've avoided getting involved in other people's wars for nigh on three hundred years."

Hank interjected, "Does she say anything about her father?"

Suddenly Bella was paying attention. She was fascinated by the tales Henry told of dashing, romantic Ned Halloran.

" 'Fraid not, Hank. Ursula hasn't mentioned Ned in a long time and I'm almost scared to ask."

Ella laid her hand on her husband's arm. "I'm sure he's all right."

"God's eyelashes, woman, he's fighting a war in Spain! How can we be certain of anything? Talk about danger—Ned runs to it like metal filings run to a magnet. I'll tell you something for nothing. If he gets back to Ireland at all, as soon as I can scrape up the money I'm going home long enough to patch things up between us."

"You didn't go back for your mother's funeral," Ella reminded him, "nor when your sister Pauline died of tuberculosis."

"I did not," Henry agreed. "But they were the family I was stuck with. Ned's the family I chose for myself."

As time allowed Ursula wrote to her other friends. Their replies came trickling back to her. Letters from those elsewhere in Europe carried a new tension, a growing reluctance to be open about one's thoughts.

DEAR Ursula," Fliss wrote. "Thank you for the chocolates, which are delicious. Thank you also for the bomb your IRA detonated in London on the sixteenth of January. Is Adolf Hitler not bad enough?' "

She made no mention of her former enthusiasm for Oswald Mosley and fascism.

Ursula spent several hours crafting a letter that would placate her friend without actually apologizing for the Irish Republican Army. It was much more difficult than she expected.

Chapter Forty-two

ON the twenty-sixth of January Franco's victorious forces entered Barcelona. At the League of Nations there were heated discussions about Spain's future, but no action was suggested.

Plainly disgusted, Seán Lester told Ursula, "We've learned from reliable sources that when Hitler entered the Rhineland, his forces were prepared for a hasty retreat if the French showed any sign of fight. But they didn't. Will this be remembered as the century when civilization was handed over to the bullies?"

THE refurbishment of the house in the North Strand took longer than Finbar expected. His friends chided him for going to the effort and expense when he had no wife. Undeterred, he continued the work, doing much of it himself at night. He consulted the girls he knew about the fitting-out of the kitchen to be certain it was convenient and modern. Each of them harbored the dream of using that kitchen herself. One offered a window box to be planted with geraniums. Another hemmed an armload of flour-sack dish towels. Finbar was suitably appreciative, but when the house was ready, he would occupy it alone.

Sometimes Ursula went to the visitor's gallery of the General Assembly to listen to debates on the floor. Her favorite location was the front row of the second tier. From there she had a clear view of the delegates seated at the rows of desks below.

One afternoon she found herself next to a handsome, well-dressed youth who could not have been more than seventeen. "I admire Adolf Hitler very much," he told her frankly. "He has come to power like a knight to the rescue.

"My family is German by ancestry but we live in the South Tyrol, which is governed by Italy. The Italian government demands crippling taxes from my father, they take everything he has worked so hard to build up. Under Mussolini we have no rights except the right to be exploited.

"The older I grow, and the stronger Germany becomes, the more I am drawn to the Fuehrer. I want to be free, I want to be a German among Germans!

"I accompanied my father to Geneva on business as a sort of farewell time with him. When we leave here I am going to enlist in the Brandenburg Division.* I will fight for the Fatherland, I will be part of her glory. What a proud moment that will be!"

His cheeks were flushed, his eyes shone. He was the very image of a young man setting off on a heroic quest. *You can almost hear the trumpets in his voice*, Ursula thought.

The Versailles Treaty had stranded tens of thousands of ethnic Germans who must be hearing the same clarion call.

THE Lesters often invited members of the staff from the secretariat for luncheon at the weekend. Ursula was always included. One Saturday afternoon Elsie took her aside. "I'm a bit worried about you," she said.

"There's no need, Elsie. I'm in good form."

"I've never seen anyone with a healthier appetite. But then, you may have a reason. Am I right?"

"I don't know what you're talking about."

"Oh, I think you do. I've had three children, remember? I know the signs. Unless I'm very much mistaken, the weight you're gaining isn't fat."

Ursula wanted to lie. But she would not kill this child and she would not deny it, either. "Does anyone else know?"

"Not yet." Elsie gave her a sympathetic smile. "How far along are you?"

"About five months."

"You should be showing more."

"I've always been too thin. Now I'm just normal, except for the bump. Up to now my clothes have pretty well hidden it, though."

"Not from a woman's eyes," Elsie told her. "Does the father know?"

*Originally composed of Germans from outside the Reich.

"He does not."

"Do you want him to?"

"I do not."

"So there is not much likelihood of marriage."

"None. My choice," Ursula added emphatically.

Elsie's pretty face was creased with concern. "Have you given any thought to . . ."

"I have, of course. You know what would happen if I had an illegitimate baby in Ireland. So I'm going to give birth in Switzerland, where people have a more enlightened attitude. I'll apologize to your husband for using him to get here, but I mean to do the best possible job for him as long as he'll have me."

Elsie was looking at her in astonishment. "You're an amazing young woman. Have you thought about what you'll do after the baby's born?"

"I'm going to keep it."

"And stay in Europe?"

Ursula shook her head. "Not forever. But by the time we go back, my child will have been mine for so long that no one would even think of taking it away from me."

"What will you tell people in Ireland? That you married here, but your husband died?"

That was the most difficult question.

Ursula would always be grateful to Elsie Lester for her kindness. It was she who quietly, tactfully, explained the situation to her husband. If Seán Lester was shocked, his reaction never filtered down to Ursula. He was sympathetic and serious but not judgemental.

"You can continue to work as long as you feel like it," he assured her. "When is the . . . ah . . ."

Ursula smiled at his embarrassment. "May, I believe."

"I expect you'll want to stop a few weeks beforehand. I'll see that you remain on the payroll, and you can come back to your job whenever you're ready. If there's a job to come back to," he added ruefully. "Sometimes I wonder how long the League's going to last."

Elsie Lester gave a dinner party to which she invited both Ursula and the foremost obstetrician in Switzerland. By the end of the evening Magnus Leffler, a big man with a wide mouth like a frog and thick fingers capable of remarkable gentleness, had accepted Ursula as his patient.

That night she wrote in her journal, "I have thrown myself on the mercy of strangers and not been disappointed. My child will be born a citizen of the world."

Early in the morning of February 10, Pope Pius XI died at the age of eighty-one. The League of Nations was immediately informed; the secretariat announced that formal mourning would be observed for three days. Ursula bought a loosely-cut black dress with no belt, and several colorful scarves to vary her costume afterward.

Coincidentally she was wearing a scarf of emerald green nine days later, when Eamon de Valera announced that Éire would be neutral in any imminent war.

Even in the black dress it was growing impossible to conceal her belly any longer. In Ireland no decent woman would have gone out on the street at this stage, but Europe was different. Women smiled at Ursula in the shops and men tipped their hats respectfully.

True to his word, Lester allowed her to continue working as long as she wanted.

On the twenty-eighth of February the British government's recognition of General Franco caused furious scenes in the House of Commons. Several MPs cried, "Shame!"

According to the newspapers, Prime Minister Chamberlain justified his action on the grounds that Franco had gained possession of most of Spain and no one knew how much of the Republican government remained, nor even where it was hiding.

Clement Attlee, leader of the Labour Party, retorted furiously that Chamberlain would always recognize a government that outraged every law, human and divine, but any government that obeyed the rules of civilization was "bound to be done down by the prime minister."[1]

The British delegation at the League of Nations had no official comment.

On March 14 the German army seized Prague. The last democracy in central Europe was extinguished.

The knowledge was as ashes in the mouth. People passed one another in the corridors of the Palais des Nations with averted eyes.

Dead dreams and failure.

Ursula cleaned her desk and left to await the birth of her child.

ALMOST unnoticed in the midst of other events, Madrid quietly crumbled into Franco's hands after a thirty-month siege.

On the first of April, 1939, the Nationalists triumphantly declared the Spanish Civil War over.

THE next day was Sunday. Ursula was invited to dine with the Lesters, and found Seán uncharacteristically bitter. "Chamberlain's announced a Franco-British guarantee for Poland," he said. "But for what, the weekend? If Hitler makes a move on Poland, France and Britain will back down just as they did with Czechoslovakia. The man who replaced me as high commissioner in Danzig is a charming fellow and a great raconteur, but that's all. The League's never given itself the power to do anything *but* talk.

"It breaks my heart, Ursula. Poland's history is so like our own. No Irishman can have other than sympathy and admiration for the Poles."[2]

The fifth of April dawned cold and crisp. Ursula was too restless to stay in the flat. She went for a long walk, gazing wistfully into shop windows where ski clothes were still displayed. Carefully balancing her heavy belly as she stepped over ridges of snow frozen to the pavement. After eating an early supper in a café around the corner from her flat, she spent the evening reading. By ten o'clock she had turned out the light.

She struggled awake bathed in sweat. As she threw back the duvet, a savage spasm gripped her.

Jesus Mary and Joseph!

Perhaps it was only a stomachache. Too much cheese fondue. . . .

The cramp seized her again, stronger this time.

When she switched on the electric lamp by her bed the first thing she saw was Böcklin's painting. Somehow she found the strength to struggle out of bed and tear the thing from the wall.

THE hospital was white. Everything. Walls, sheets, nurses, even the light. A glaring, pitiless light beneath which she felt like a butterfly pinned to a board. A butterfly . . . no, a chrysalis being split open . . .

"Take a deep breath now," said Herr Doktor Leffler. He bent over her, smiling with his frog's mouth, kneading her belly with his sausage fingers.

Pain ripped and tore. Someone was breaking her spine from the inside.

The obstetrician stepped back to be replaced by a nurse in a white mask. She clapped a rubber cone over Ursula's nose and mouth. The world went spinning away...came back screaming...went away again...in her dreams she thought she heard the sound of gunfire. In her dreams she was Síle Duffy, running along the quays of Dublin while British artillery tore the city apart. In her dreams...

So you're awake at last," said a cheerful voice.

Elsie Lester was standing beside the bed. Sunlight was streaming through the window. Elsie offered Ursula a glass of water with a bent straw and she drank gratefully. "Is it over? I feel like a building fell on me."

"You did very well."

"How's my baby?"

Elsie hesitated.

Ursula almost shouted, "How's my baby?"

"*Ssshhh*, it's all right," Elsie soothed. "He was very premature, Ursula. He's in an incubator and I've requested à priest to baptize him as a precaution. I thought you'd want...don't look like that, nothing's wrong with him! Ten fingers, ten toes, everything; he's just a tiny little fellow, that's all. But he's breathing on his own and putting up a strong fight for life. You'll be able to visit him soon and see for yourself."

He. My son.

"The priest will want a name for the baptism," Elsie went on. "And the hospital needs one for the birth certificate."

Ursula closed her eyes and lay back against the pillows. "Finbar Lewis Halloran," she said in a steady voice. "But I'm going to call him Barry."

Chapter Forty-three

BARRY was too small to leave the hospital. They wanted to keep him for at least six weeks. His mother was so thin she had very little milk, so he would be fed on a specially prepared formula. While Ursula waited, Seán suggested she come back to work—partly to give her something to keep her busy, and partly because she was genuinely needed.

Seán Lester had been put in charge of the "Ax" committee, which meant he was responsible for reorganizing and reducing the League. There already had been a number of defections, and half the secretariat's staff of six hundred must be cut by the end of the year.

Berlin no longer believed the League had a role to play on the world stage. The number of German communications reaching the deputy secretary-general's office was greatly diminished, so Ursula began helping with correspondence from Ireland as well. "At 2RN I learned to do half-a-dozen jobs at once," she assured Lester.

Although remaining resolutely neutral, Eamon de Valera was quietly trying to distance Ireland from Germany. In a letter to Seán Lester he explained that he was recalling the Irish representative in Berlin because the man had gone a bit too far in his admiration for Hitler.

Barry was released from hospital at the end of May. Lester asked Ursula if she wanted to give up her job and stay home with her baby.

"I certainly do not! I can bring Barry with me. There are plenty of empty offices now, so I can fix one up as a nursery and do my work there."

Lester tried to protest, but Ursula had answers for all his arguments. "It was easier just to give in," he told his wife later. "I feel rather like Neville Chamberlain when it comes to that girl."

ALTHOUGH she was now well paid by Irish standards, Ursula had not lost the old habit of thrift. With a sense of relief she finally paid off the last of the money she owed Ella and began putting savings in an envelope under the mattress. She looked with longing at the smart outfits she saw other women wearing in Geneva, but bought almost nothing for herself.

She did buy things for Barry, though. Beautifully made baby gowns in rainbow pastels. Crocheted matinée jackets and matching caps. Tiny sailor suits with embroidered anchors on the collar. Miniscule leather boots, soft as butter. Socks of fine Egyptian cotton that would not chafe an infant's tender skin. And stacks and stacks of bird's-eye nappies.

At night in her room she gloated over them as if they were ball gowns.

In June, central London was rocked by more IRA bombs. No casualties were reported.

Three days later Kathleen Clarke was named as lord mayor of Dublin. The widow of a Fenian bomber was the first woman to hold such an office in Ireland.

In England conscription began.

King George and Queen Elizabeth arrived in the United States for the first visit to that country by a reigning British monarch. Ships in New York harbor welcomed them with whistles. Flying Fortresses overhead dipped their wings in salute.

"It may look like a big tea party, but they're over there for good reason: to bring the Americans on side in case of war," Lester told Ursula.

"My Uncle Henry says America has no interest in getting involved in another European war."

"This may not be limited to Europe. Keep your eye on Asia. The whole world's infected with greed. Greed for land, greed for power, greed for what they perceive as glory."

"You think it's going to be very bad, don't you?"

Instead of answering directly, he said, "I'm going to take Elsie and the girls back to Ireland for a summer holiday—and leave them there. You and Barry can go with them. I'll arrange to have his name added to your passport and get the necessary exit visas."

"Barry's not strong enough to travel yet." *And unwed mothers with infants have a hard time finding employment in Ireland. And I have no family to take us in.*

Lester read her unspoken thoughts. "You'd be welcome to stay with Elsie and the girls. They'd love to have you."

And Ireland is stifling and provincial and this is where everything's happening. "I can't, Seán. It would be taking advantage when your family's been far too good to me already."

"Nonsense. I mean it."

"I know you do, and I'm grateful. But thank you, no."

URSULA bade the Lesters farewell at the airport, then went back to work. The staff at the secretariat was still shrinking and she was busier than ever. She enjoyed the feeling of being essential.

Her tiny son was always within her sight, always within her reach. Their day began very early and often finished very late, but Barry was thriving. Sometimes she read him communiqués instead of nursery rhymes.

Those from the high commissioner in Danzig were the most troubling. The Germans were stressing the need for more food-growing space to feed their increasing population. Hitler's scientists claimed they could make German soil more productive by employing a powerful cocktail of chemical fertilizers, but this eventually would render the soil sterile, unable to produce anything. Hitler had decided the future of the German people depended upon acquiring the rich acres of Poland.

Danzig was nervous.

WHEN Seán Lester returned to Geneva on the twenty-eighth of August, Ursula met him at the airport. One look at her face told him all he needed to know.

"You should have gone back to Ireland with us, Ursula," he said.

"What's going to happen next?"

"I don't know for certain, but I can make an educated guess. You'd best come with me this afternoon and help me restock the household supplies. If I remember correctly, I'm low on Irish cigarettes and there's not much wine left in the cellar."

By the end of the month European mobilization for war was almost complete. Polish reservists and retired veterans were requested to join all men of call-up age and report to barracks. France was also summoning its reservists to arms, and the railways had been requisitioned. Belgium announced that it was closing its frontier and manning antiaircraft defenses. Switzerland moved to fully-alert status.

At the Palais people tried to reassure one another. "The Germans will back down because they don't want a repeat of 1918."

No one really believed it.

URSULA held Barry in her arms and pressed her lips to the downy top of his head. He smelt of milk and soap, a fragrance as sweet as a clover meadow. "It's you and me, little man," she murmured. "Whatever happens, I'll take care of you."

1 September 1939
NAZIS INVADE POLAND

Chapter Forty-four

THE German battleship *Schleswig-Holstein* had opened fire on the Free City of Danzig before dawn. Within hours German troops occupied the city. They seized Polish shipyards for building German warships and Polish civilians to serve as forced labor.

The war everyone had feared, and no one had prevented, was under way.

THE Nazis have to be beaten," Seán Lester stated emphatically. "Otherwise civilization doesn't stand a chance. During the Great War we Irish nationalists didn't exactly want Britain to be defeated, but we certainly weren't her unqualified supporters. We weren't pro-German, but Ireland was in captivity and Britain was the captor.

"This time it's different. Our national interest will lie with those who ally against Hitler, and please God that will include Britain. She's promised to defend Poland. Now's the time to redeem that pledge."

He was emotionally shattered; he found it difficult even to write. Ursula understood. The League existed in a vacuum, swept with rumors and despair. Helpless before the whirlwind.

The September 4 edition of the *Irish Times* announced, "Yesterday morning His Majesty's ambassador in Berlin presented the German government with an ultimatum, giving it a space of two hours in which to reply to Great Britain's demand regarding the evacuation of Poland. When the fateful hour struck, no reply was forthcoming. At eleven o'clock yesterday morning a state of war was declared between Germany and the British Empire."

.   •   •

Speaking in Dáil Éireann, Eamon de Valera said, "Back in February last I stated in a very definite way that it was the aim of government policy, in case of a European war, to keep this country out of it.

"We, of all nations, know what force used by a stronger nation against a weaker one means. We have known what invasion and partition mean; we are not forgetful of our own history and, as long as our own country, or any part of it, is subject to the application of force by a stronger nation, it is only natural that our people, whatever sympathies they may have in the conflict, should look at their own country first, and consider what its interests should be and what its interests are."[1]

In reaffirming Irish neutrality, the taoiseach was walking a very delicate tightrope. Éire was a small new nation, practically unarmed, pathetically vulnerable. It was by no means certain what the outcome of the war would be. Hitler might win; at the moment the possibility was very strong. Journalists coming out of Europe were already expressing that opinion. De Valera did not want a triumphant Germany regarding Ireland as an enemy and treating her accordingly. Nor could he afford to alienate Britain; not with six counties of his country still tightly held in her grasp. But he could not openly side with Britain either. That would mean surrendering the hard-won independence for which generations of Irish men had fought and died.

The word was quietly passed to the Irish newspapers. Nothing should be printed that might give offense to either Britain or Germany.

Every office in the secretariat was equipped with a radio. Broadcasting from Britain, Anthony Eden, who had returned to government as dominions secretary, said that after the war a new civilization must be built with peace, justice, and freedom as its foundations.

"He didn't mention the League, I notice," Seán remarked. "But that's what will be needed: the League or something like it."

The German Wehrmacht swept across Poland while the Luftwaffe pounded the railways and drove the Polish air force from the skies.

On the seventeenth of September the Russians invaded the reeling country.

By the end of the month Poland was shattered. Hitler and Stalin divided the land between them.

Russia was expelled from the League of Nations but did not bother to enter a protest.

. . .

THE World's Fair was held in New York City that October. To mark "League of Nations Day" on the twenty-first, speeches were broadcast from League members around the world. Henry Mooney was among those who heard Seán Lester on the radio. "The catastrophe of this war marks a collective failure for mankind," Lester told his unseen audience, "a failure in which all of us have some share and on account of which we must all feel a deep humility."[2]

That evening Henry said to Ella, "I wish Ursula would go back to Ireland while she still can."

"I'm sure she will, dear."

"I'm not. She rarely says anything personal in her letters anymore; all she writes about is the international situation. I suspect she'll stay where she is to view the excitement firsthand."

"Oh, Henry, it's going to be a lot more than just 'the excitement!'"

He replied somberly, "Yes, I'm afraid it is."

PRESIDENT Roosevelt issued a declaration of American neutrality similar to that issued by Woodrow Wilson at the start of the Great War.

How could the Americans, safe in the embrace of two broad oceans, begin to understand what was happening to the Old World from which the New had been born?

THE big Cadbury factory at Birmingham, England, covered itself with camouflage netting to fool German bombers, gave up the manufacture of chocolate, and concentrated on making gas masks. Thirty-eight million gas masks were issued to the British people.

ÉIRE would not be dispensing gas masks. "The simple truth," as Ursula wrote to Henry, "is that the nation lacks the ability to manufacture them. We still have so little in the way of industry. If Ireland gets sucked into this war, we do not have sufficient armaments to defend ourselves against invasion. For a long time I was furious with de Valera, but I am forced to acknowledge his foresight in insisting upon Irish neutrality. It is our only protection."

I keep having to rethink, she told herself as she sealed the envelope. *Once I believed the League of Nations was a fortress. But it has no more solidity than clouds that resemble mountains.*

Geneva was going about its business normally—except people were walking more briskly than usual, and French, the predominate language, was spoken even more quickly than usual. Shops sold out of basic staples almost as soon as they arrived.

The Irish newspapers that arrived in Seán Lester's office carried stern government warnings that stressed the unfairness of hoarding food, petrol, and other necessaries. The government also announced a new agricultural scheme to assure there would be enough grain and vegetables for the nation. Twelve and a half percent of all holdings over ten acres would have to be made available for tillage.

In November the Russians invaded Finland. Too little and too late, Britain agreed to send arms to defend the tiny nation.

The ax committee was taking up most of Lester's time. He was clearly exhausted. Early in December he fell ill and attended the Assembly with a raging fever. "As soon as I feel a bit better, I'm going back to Ireland for Christmas," he told Ursula. "Will you come?"

"It's too soon for us," she said.

Shortly before Christmas, Geraldine Dillon wrote from Ireland, "The newspapers are calling this 'the Terrible Winter.' We have dreadful ice and a black wind howling like a damned soul. The priests say it is God's punishment on us, but I do not know what we did wrong."

On Christmas Eve Ursula took Barry for a sleigh ride. Tourists were in short supply; the beautifully decorated sleighs drawn up in front of the luxury hotels along the Rive Droit were doing little business. One had a dapple-gray horse in the shafts. He turned his head toward Ursula as she approached and gave her a long look from between his blinkers.

She held Barry up to stroke the animal's soft nose. The baby reached out fearlessly, his eyes sparkling.

"Horse," Ursula told him.

He wriggled in her arms and made a quizzical sound.

"Horse," she repeated.

"*Oorse,*" Barry said clearly.

Ursula laughed with delight. "Oh, my little man!"

The driver tucked a heavy rug around his passengers to keep them warm and they set off with a jingle of sleigh bells. The air was crystalline with cold, the runners hissed over hard-packed snow. The steady rhythm of hoofbeats was music to Ursula's ears. "I used to have a horse," she told the child on her lap. "A gray horse very much like this one."

"*Oorse,*" said Barry again.

WHEN Seán Lester returned to Geneva from his holiday in Ireland he did not look rested. "On the way out it took me four days just to get to London," he told Ursula. "Civilian travel between England and Ireland will be suspended any day now. Members of the diplomatic corps will be given travel permits, of course, and so will accredited journalists. But that's all. Transport has to be kept available for the troops."

"British troops," said Ursula. "Remember that Éire's neutral."

"I expect many Irishmen will be joining British regiments."

She bristled with indignation. "How can they?"

Lester replied, "How can they not, under the circumstances?"

The Finnish army was making an astonishingly brave stand against the Russians in sub-zero weather. Ursula read the latest communiqué from Reuters aloud to Barry. Dressed in a bright red snowsuit, her son was sitting on the floor beside her desk, playing with a nest of Chinese boxes the Lesters had given him. He did not understand many of the words his mother spoke, but he looked up and gave her a toothless grin.

"Are you listening to the wireless?" Seán Lester asked from the doorway.

"Not yet, I was just—"

"Turn it on. There's something I want you to hear."

"What frequency?"

"Here, I'll get it for you."

Lester rotated the dial until, over the crackle of static, a nasal voice filled the room. "Germany calling! Germany calling!"

"Who on earth is that, Seán?"

"Fellow's name is William Joyce, but he's known as Lord Haw-Haw. When you hear the way he talks you can understand why. He's broadcasting Nazi propaganda from somewhere in Germany."

"He doesn't sound German."

"He's not, I'm sorry to say. He grew up in Galway."

She stared at Lester. "I don't believe it."

"It's true. His father was a naturalized U.S. citizen and Joyce was born in America, but he's spent most of his life in either Ireland or England. I just received a dossier on him from London. According to the information they have, he served as an informer for the Black and Tans and hates Irish Republicans. In England he got involved with Oswald Mosley's British Fascist organization and somehow obtained a British passport. Last August he went to Germany and offered his services to Josef Goebbels's Nazi propaganda ministry. Now he's Hitler's Irishman."

The sneering, supercilious tones of Lord Haw-Haw burrowed like worms into Ursula's brain. She was no longer neutral. "Damn the man and all he stands for!" she exploded.

ACCORDING to the *Irish Times,* the outbreak of war witnessed an increased surveillance of the IRA and a growing number of confrontations between them and gardai. In January 1940 a garda detective was fatally shot while trying to arrest Thomas MacCurtain, son of the Cork lord mayor murdered during the War of Independence. The government responded by introducing amendments to the Emergency Powers Bill and the Offences Against the State Bill specifically designed to facilitate the arrest and internment of members of the Irish Republican Army.

A British army camp in County Down was raided on the eleventh of February. The camp had so often been raided by the IRA to replenish their weapon supplies that it was known among Republicans as "the stores."

In Dublin's Mountjoy Jail a number of IRA prisoners went on hunger strike to protest the conditions under which they were kept. In the past the Irish government, recalling the agonizing martyrdom of Terence MacSwiney in a British prison, had given in to hunger strikers. This time de Valera let two men die. The strike was called off.[3]

When Ursula read about it in the Dublin papers she could hardly control her anger. "The rotten bastard!" she exploded. "The IRA put de Valera where he is today! How can he *do* that?"

"It's simply a different sort of war," Seán Lester told her. But she was not mollified.

IN March of 1940 the savage Russo-Finnish War finally ended. The peace treaty surrendered a large part of Finland to Russia, but it would prove to be a Pyrrhic victory. Stalin's purges during the thirties had emasculated his officer corps. As a result the Red Army had taken a frightful drubbing from the Finns for most of the war. Russia's military weaknesses were exposed to the world.

And particularly to Adolf Hitler.

With inexorable force Hitler's armies swept across Europe, invading the very countries that Joseph Avenol had hoped to combine into an all-European league. Denmark was overcome. British and French forces had joined the battle for Norway but the outlook was bleak. Belgium and the Netherlands expected to be next.

American journalists returning home from Europe were convinced Hitler would win.

Avenol felt the League of Nations should remove itself to France. "In order to save the Swiss government the embarrassment of being pressured by the Germans," as he explained in the Assembly. He even took the step of sending League archives to the quiet little spa town of Vichy.

A few days later he ordered Lester to France to bring them back. "The secretary-general received more opposition to the arrangement than he bargained for," Lester told Ursula. His eyes glinted with gentle malice. "Not everyone wants the League to become a French club."

Lester selected two male members of staff to accompany him to France. When they returned laden with file boxes, Ursula was seconded to help restore the archives to proper order.

Behind the scenes, the political infighting at the League continued.

In Éire a ramshackle old army camp on the Curragh of Kildare was assigned to hold IRA internees who had not been tried for any crime, but were being held as members of an illegal organization.

Curragh Camp was also the main camp for the regular army.

Louise wrote to Ursula, "We know there is a war on, but it really does not seem to have much to do with us. I think most Irish people feel the same. We have had enough of war in this country, we do not want to think about another one."

"God keep you," Ursula murmured as she read those words. "I hope you never have to."

The Lesters were a devoted couple. In spite of Seán's natural reserve, it was apparent to Ursula that he was very lonely without his wife. One morning she entered his office to find him staring at a photograph of Elsie on his desk. "You miss her very much, don't you?" Ursula said softly.

"Is it so obvious?"

"Down the country we would say it sticks out like horns on a pig."

Lester burst out laughing.

Ursula was not surprised when Elsie Lester arrived in Geneva at the end of April to visit her husband. The happiness of their reunion was somewhat marred by the general atmosphere. At the headquarters of the International Red Cross there was frantic activity, but elsewhere in Geneva a sort of paralysis had set in. People were waiting for the other shoe to drop.

Lester brought Elsie to the secretariat for a brief visit with old friends, after which they invited Ursula and her son to join them in Lester's private office for a quiet cup of tea. Barry amused himself by investigating the bottom drawers of Lester's desk. Ursula sought news of home.

"There are a lot of rumors about spies going around," Elsie reported.

"At least some of them are true," her husband said. "Éire's neutrality, added to her geographical location, makes her particularly attractive. The *Washington Evening Star* has even reported that Galway's being used as a U-boat base,[4] though I suspect that's a story leaked by the British to discredit Éire in American eyes. Churchill's furious over our neutrality.

"But I have no doubt there are people spying for Germany along the Irish coasts, both north and south. Now that the lads have returned from Spain, the IRA will want to take up the cudgel against the ancient enemy. How best to do that than by helping Germany? Remember the old axiom: 'My enemy's enemy is my friend.' "

Ursula said hotly, "Surely you can't think the IRA would . . ."

"I didn't say they all would. But a few of them, undoubtedly. And they'll believe they're doing the right thing."

Ursula started to say something else but was distracted by Barry. "Put that stapler back in the drawer," she said sharply. "It isn't a toy."

Elsie reached out to rumple the little boy's silky hair. "He doesn't know what a stapler is."

"He'll learn the hard way if he staples his feet with it."

"That's how children always learn," Elsie warned her. "The hard way."

Aware that he had touched a nerve with Ursula, Lester changed the subject—slightly. "The Americans have spies in Ireland too," he said to his wife. "They're well-placed and report only to Washington, but they send their intelligence through London."[5]

"How can you be so certain?"

"Oh, my sweet, this is the diplomatic service, remember? Everyone knows everything. War or no war, cable service from Dublin to the Continent remains available to German diplomats. Of course it goes through England.

In return the Germans are allowing the cable link from Switzerland to England to stay open. We're all busy deciphering messages and spying on one another. Espionage is a growth industry."

ELSIE had planned to stay for a month, but at Lester's insistence the date of her return to Ireland was moved forward. Then moved forward again.

MEANWHILE, the *Irish Times* reported that Aer Lingus was awaiting delivery of its first Douglas DC-3. The plane had been prepared by Fokker in Amsterdam and flown out of the Netherlands under the very noses of the invading German army.[6]

On Thursday morning, the ninth of May, Lester called Ursula into his office and closed the door. "You realize we're in the middle of both a Swiss crisis and a crisis in the secretariat," he said. "Six weeks ago I begged the secretary-general to let me make plans for a possible evacuation. Between our two offices we still have several hundred people, many of them women like yourself, with families.

"Avenol pooh-poohed it. He claimed adequate preparations were already made. When I told him no preparations had been made he gave a Gallic shrug and said that we must then share the fate of the Swiss people."[7] Lester looked thoroughly disgusted. "Whatever about that, yesterday afternoon I got return visas for Elsie. She'll go home Sunday, or Monday at the latest."

"Will you go with her?"

"My place is here. Whatever's coming, the League . . ." Lester broke off, unable to finish the thought.

He means the League, or something like it, will be very much needed. Brave men and women will have to keep it functioning while this thing runs its course, and try to rebuild when the war ends. However the war ends.

Ursula's heart leaped at the challenge.

Lester glanced at the photograph on his desk. "I'm going to take tomorrow afternoon off. Before she leaves, Elsie and I are going to have a picnic in the Versoix and I'll try to get in a spot of fishing."

That night Ursula went to bed fully prepared to stand shoulder to shoulder with Lester and the others at League headquarters who would be making a stand, however futile, for democracy.

.   .   .

SHE awoke in the dark. Barry was not yet awake; she could hear his soft baby snore as he lay beside her in the bed. The room retained warmth from the night before. The only sounds from the street were trucks making pre-dawn deliveries.

She could go back to sleep for at least another hour.

Instead she sat up in bed and threw back the covers.

The Irish in her did not trust the machineries of logic, in whose name so many terrible deeds were done. Life's truly great decisions should not be made cognitively. When it mattered most, Ursula Halloran relied on an intuitive certainty that occasionally rose within her like a rainbowed bubble, breaking the surface of a dark pool.

THE bubble rose. And she knew.

URSULA was among the first staffers to arrive at the secretariat that morning, but the tension was already palpable. Neville Chamberlain had resigned; later in the day Winston Churchill would be sworn in as the prime minister of Britain. A fresh crisis awaited him.

Before dawn the Germans had invaded Belgium and Holland.

The Dutch queen Wilhelmina delivered a stirring speech, urging her people to take up arms against the enemy. She ordered the Dutch merchant fleet to be placed at the disposal of the British, and made certain that the nation's gold reserves were taken aboard British warships. Then she and her family prepared themselves to depart for London, and exile.

When Seán Lester came in he found Ursula waiting for him with the news. He promptly telephoned Elsie to pack. "If you don't go now," Ursula heard him warn his wife, "you could be separated from the children for months. I'll have to keep you here because soon it won't be possible to travel."

When he hung up the phone Ursula said, "Can you get travel visas for Barry and me too?"

While she waited they received news of German attacks on French aerodromes.

RELUCTANTLY, Ursula left her beloved books behind. Lester promised they would be stored safely at the League. "You can retrieve them afterwards," he assured her.

Her one suitcase was stuffed with clothing, Barry's toys, and Saoirse's bridle. The Mauser was concealed among her underthings. If for any reason they were searched along the way, female lingerie might go unprobed. She had to sit on the case to make it close.

The envelope from under the mattress was not in her suitcase, nor in her handbag. Ursula remembered what war was like. Before leaving her room for the last time, she padded her figure with cash pinned to her undergarments.

On Saturday night she and Barry left Geneva with Elsie Lester. Because Europe's skies were no longer safe, they planned to take the train to Boulogne and cross the Channel on a passenger steamer, then fly to Ireland from London.

Ursula tried not to think about the boat journey.

Elsie was courageously cheerful. Dressed in powder blue with a new hat to match, she looked as gay as if she were going on the canceled picnic. But obviously it was not going to be a picnic. The train was packed. Every seat was taken. The passengers were, for the most part, tense and quiet. Many had brought an excessive amount of baggage. The areas around the doors were piled high, making it difficult to enter.

Ursula put her lone suitcase into the overhead above her seat. She did not want it out of her reach.

The night was unseasonably cold and the windows were tightly shut. The air grew stuffy while the train was still in the station. Ursula busied herself getting Barry settled. The adventure had excited him, he was laughing and waving to the other passengers.

Seán and Elsie Lester met one another's eyes through the window of the first-class carriage.

One last time.

THE rapid German advance caught up with the train as it raced across France.

Chapter Forty-five

THE lights had been turned down in the first-class carriage and pillows and blankets provided. Ursula and Elsie dozed fitfully. Barry slept with his head in his mother's lap. As usual, his hands were closed into tiny fists and pressed under his chin. He had never sucked his thumb.

An explosion shocked them awake.

The train shuddered but kept going.

Another explosion. Closer. Frightfully loud. A spray of dirt and gravel hit the window and a startled male passenger shouted a curse. The train hurled itself forward, roaring around a curve at dangerous speed. Suitcases piled in the aisles toppled over.

Barry sat up. "Mam?"

Ursula hugged him to her breast. "I think we're being bombed," she said in a surprisingly calm voice. To her own amazement she *was* calm, as if she had rehearsed for this all her life.

The engineer made a valiant effort but his train could not outrace the German bombers flying overhead. The track a mile or so ahead blew up with a terrible roar. Brakes squealed. Sparks raced past the windows in the night, staring in at the passengers with a terrible red malignance. The train stopped just in time to avoid being derailed.

Fighter planes promptly closed in to rake the stalled train with machine-gun fire.

Some of the passengers dived under their seats. Most swarmed into the aisle. Elsie Lester sat white-faced in shock.

Ursula set Barry on the floor below window level, slipped her feet into her shoes and put on her coat. How fast her brain was working! She seized the window sash with both hands and threw all her weight behind the downward push. The window did not budge.

"Where's your passport?" she shouted over her shoulder to Elsie.

The woman roused herself. "In my handbag."

"Handbags can go missing. Put your passport and your money down the front of your dress. Hurry!" Ursula tried the window again. Muscles and ligaments strained to tearing point, but the window remained firmly closed.

By now the aisle was blocked with hysterical passengers.

Ursula dragged her suitcase down from the overhead. Throwing it open, she retrieved the Mauser. With the butt of the gun she broke the window glass and knocked shards from the frame.

"Come on, Elsie, we're getting out of here." She thrust the Mauser into her coat pocket and helped her friend through the window, then handed Barry out to her. As Ursula scrambled after them a spear of glass lanced her thigh. She did not allow herself time to feel the pain.

"Under the carriage, quick!" she ordered.

As soon as her feet touched the ground she threw herself forward and began crawling under the train. Bullets spanged against metal close to her head. With knees and elbows she propelled her body further under the carriage.

Hot. Dark. Gravel cutting into knees and elbows. A strong smell of machine oil. The constant chatter of gunfire. Someone screaming.

"We're over here," called Elsie.

Ursula wormed her way toward them.

"Mam!" Barry cried out.

"It's all right, little man, just be still." Trying not to bump her head against the underside of the train, she took Barry from Elsie and did her best to cover his body with hers. *Thank God I'm thin, there's not much clearance here.*

Other people were crawling under the train now. Breathless, choking, crying. "Stop it!" a woman screamed at the guns. *"Stopitstopitstopit!"*

Invisible in the night, German fighter planes circled above the train. Seconds or centuries later there was a loud *"whoommmph!"* from somewhere up ahead. The planes roared off in search of other prey.

Within moments they could smell fire.

Ursula drew Barry from beneath her. "Elsie?"

"Yes."

"Hold Barry for me and stay right where you are. You should be safe enough for the time being. I'll find out what's happening." Ursula crawled out from under the train.

As she stood up, deferred pain stabbed her thigh. She took an involuntary half step and staggered sideways. The ground at this point fell steeply away from the tracks; Ursula found herself half-running, half-falling down the slope. When she regained her balance she saw that the engine was blazing fiercely. It was far enough ahead of the first-class carriage to represent no immediate threat, but the fire might spread.

Their attackers had gone, leaving an immobilized train somewhere in France in the middle of a cold night, with hundreds of terrified passengers and an unknown number of casualties.

But we're alive.

Against that fact, nothing else mattered.

Other people began to scramble out from under the train. They ran first in one direction and then in another, seeking they knew not what, their confusion as great as their terror.

Only Ursula stood still. Consciously organizing her thoughts. *One step at a time. No panic. Good warriors don't panic.* She stooped down and called to Elsie, "You're safest where you are for now. Stay there, I'll be right back."

"Where are you going?"

"To find someone in authority."

When Ursula reached the burning engine, what she saw—and smelled—convinced her its crew were past being able to help anyone. Sickened, she turned away.

By the light of the fire she noticed a railway porter sitting on the ground nearby, tightening his shoelaces. His face was blistered from the futile effort he had made to rescue the men in the engine. His uniform was badly scorched and he had lost his cap.

"*Pardonnez-moi, Monsieur,*" Ursula began.

"Eh?" Looking up, he cupped one hand behind his ear.

She raised her voice. "Can you tell me where we are?"

The man scrambled to his feet and replied in French, with frequent pauses to cough. He drew Ursula's attention to a few tiny pinpricks of light in the far distance. When he was satisfied that she understood he touched his forehead where the cap should be. Still coughing, he set off along the tracks.

Ursula hurried back to Elsie and Barry and called to them to come out. "The train's radio is destroyed," she told Elsie, "but one of the porters is going to follow the tracks to the next call box and summon help. He has no idea how long that will take, though.

"There's what appears to be a road some two miles north of here, and the porter thinks it may be the road from Dijon to Paris. So I'm going to try to flag down an automobile. Or a farm truck, anything."

"You propose to walk two miles in the dark? In those shoes?"

"Barefoot, if necessary," Ursula said. "Give Barry to me. I'll carry him."

Elsie shook her head. "We should wait here until help comes."

"Or until the German planes come back? No, Elsie. I'm going and you're going with me."

"I couldn't possibly . . ."

Ursula clamped a strong hand on the other woman's shoulder and propelled her forward. "You certainly can, and you are. Right now. You helped me when I needed it, I'm not going to leave you here in danger."

In Geneva, Seán Lester waited tensely for word from his wife. She had promised to telephone him as soon as they reached Boulogne. He spent a sleepless night, at last turning on the radio for company.

Radio Luxembourg was broadcasting a program of music entirely by German composers.

Ursula had estimated the distance to the road at two miles, but distance was deceptive in the dark. For a long time the moving lights seemed as far away as ever. Gradually the first few lights were joined by others, traveling fast and in only one direction. No one was going the other way.

The women's spring coats were insufficient protection against the wind that howled unimpeded across the fields. Deeply plowed furrows threatened to turn their ankles. They were unable to keep from crushing green and growing things beneath their feet.

After crawling over, and under, a succession of wire fences they eventually came to a huddle of farm buildings. Barns, sheds, outbuildings. No house. When they approached they found everything locked up tight. A solitary dog barked, then ran out to warn them off. He ran away again when Ursula scolded him in French.

Barry clung to his mother and sniffled but did not cry.

"If you're tired I'll carry him a while," Elsie offered.

"Not yet. I'm all right."

"You seem to be limping."

Ursula made herself laugh. "A blister on my heel. You were right about the shoes, maybe I should take them off."

"You'd take pneumonia, don't you dare!"

They kept walking.

Barry laid his head on his mother's shoulder, facing back the way they had come. Suddenly he gave a little start. "Boom!" he said.

Ursula spun around. A lurid glow lit the sky, a hot orange that pulsed and faded.

EARLY Sunday morning the radio carried news of the invasion of France. Without waiting to shave, Seán Lester hurried to League headquarters. "The trains!" he demanded. "Are they still running? Does anyone know?"

No one could tell him. Overcome by the swiftness of events, the communications network of the League of Nations had ground to a halt.

Lester spent an anguished day and another sleepless night. He was crouching over the radio again when the sun came up on Monday morning.

All the news was bad news. The German advance was unstoppable. Several civilian trains had been strafed; the number of casualties was not yet known. Lester went to the Palais des Nations, talked with overwrought colleagues whose conversations did not register on his mind, and eventually went home again to stare at the walls and wait.

On Monday evening the telephone finally rang.

"Oh Seán," Elsie said with a shaky laugh. "A great tragedy. My beautiful blue hat is all ruined with machine oil."[1]

"Thank God! I mean . . . is that all? Where are you?"

"We're at Dieppe. Boulogne and Calais are both closed. There are no commercial aeroplanes, of course, and no passenger steamers available at the moment, so we're taking the mail boat."

"I've been listening to the most horrible news. Was your train . . ."

"It was. Bombed and machine-gunned both. Oh Seán, Ursula was splendid! You should have seen her. She was injured herself but she got us safely away from the train and found a road. Everyone was racing west to get away from the Germans; I didn't think they would stop. But Ursula gave me the baby to hold and stepped right out in front of the cars."

"You said she was injured?"

"I hadn't realized until I saw her in the headlamps of the cars. Her whole skirt was covered with blood. She certainly did stop traffic, though! A man and his wife took us with them all the way to Paris and delivered us to your friend Seán Murphy, the Irish ambassador. He immediately took Ursula to hospital. The doctors removed a huge piece of glass from her thigh.

Half an inch further over would have cut the artery. They wanted to keep her in hospital overnight but she wouldn't have it.

"The ambassador's been wonderful to us. He's arranged everything. Our suitcases were left in the train but we'd put our passports and exit visas inside our clothes, so we have our documentation. In another twenty-four hours we'll be in London."

Lester felt weak with relief. "And little Barry, is he all right too?"

"Nothing seems to upset him much. He's like his mother in that respect, though when we were collecting our tickets for the boat Ursula began trembling. Reaction, I suppose."

"She's entitled," said Lester.

THE docks of Dieppe were crowded with people desperate to leave the Continent. They crowded onto the mail boat like so many cattle. Ursula studied their faces. Some looked relieved. A few seemed angry. Most appeared to be dazed.

Refugees, Ursula thought. *Leaving everything behind in order to escape with the most precious possession of all, life. What do you do when the familiar world turns upside down and you have to begin again?*

You just get on with it, that's all; and thank God there's something to be getting on with.

Ursula grimly endured the trip across the Channel. She carried Barry to the rail and let him feel the wind in his face and smell the sea. "Isn't this wonderful?" she said through gritted teeth.

He grinned his jolly toothless grin. " *'Derful.*"

She refused to infect him with her fear.

They arrived safely, disembarking in a driving rainstorm.

England. At once enemy camp and sanctuary. *How can it be both at the same time?* Ursula wondered.

The diplomatic network was waiting to enfold them. A motorcar with a crisply solicitous driver sped them to London, where they were already booked into a comfortable hotel near Marble Arch. A meal was brought to their room but the two women only picked at their food. Like Barry, they soon fell into an exhausted sleep.

The next morning Elsie made several telephone calls. "We can't get a flight to Ireland until tomorrow," she told Ursula. "We can go by steamship, but—"

"Let's wait for the plane," Ursula said quickly.

Elsie smiled. "I agree, we can all use a bit more rest. I do have to go out and pay a few calls later. If it stops raining, would you like to take Barry for a walk in Hyde Park? Or have you friends in London whom you'd like to see?"

Ursula shook her head. "We'll just stay here, if you don't mind."

After breakfast Barry fell asleep again. Ursula thought about doing the same thing herself, but could not. She was too tightly strung. Her brain was a kaleidoscope of recent images and future imaginings.

Me in England and thankful to be here. Astonishing. I keep being presented with the unexpected, like some giant cosmic test.

Ursula stood gazing down at the wonder of Barry; the human being she . . . and he . . . had created. The unexpected miracle.

When they got to Ireland she would have to explain him.

What did the Virgin Mary tell her family and friends—I was impregnated by God? Surely not. I'm amazed that Joseph believed that story. Or did he? Did he just love her so much he was willing to accept her even if she was a bit mad?

She drifted over to the window. Like almost every window in London it was fitted with blackout curtains. A fire extinguisher was mounted in a prominent place on the wall. When they checked in, the concierge had informed them that gas masks were available at the desk.

Looking down into the street, Ursula saw sandbags and metal barricades neatly stacked at the corner. Signposts pointed the way to the nearest bomb shelter. Men past the age for active military duty were patrolling the streets, dressed in the uniform of the home guard.

Britain was prepared to support her people in a bared-teeth defense of their nation.

Mary had Joseph to support her. I wonder how much carpenters made in Galilee two thousand years ago. Did they sell the gold and frankincense and myrrh to give them a nest egg? I would have done.

WHEN they reached Dublin they were warmly greeted by the Lesters' three daughters, who made a great fuss over Barry. "Ursula saved my life in France," Elsie told the girls. "Nothing we can ever do will be enough to repay her. I hope she and Barry will stay with us . . . well, forever, if they like."

Ursula was embarrassed. "You make it sound like more than it was, Elsie. I appreciate your offer more than you know, and we'll stay with you tonight, if that's all right. But first thing tomorrow I'm going to look for a furnished room that will accept a toddler. After that I must find a job. Your husband gave me an excellent letter of reference, but unfortunately it was in my suitcase. If he'll replace it . . ."

"I'm sure he will. When I cable him that we've arrived safely, I'll include your request," Elsie promised.

From the outbreak of war in 1939 a number of gardai had been temporarily transferred to Dublin and put on armed protection duty, though the basic principle of an unarmed police force was not changed.

Dublin itself was unchanged and unchanging. Everything looked the same as when Ursula left. The city had been frozen in time while the rest of the world fragmented and reformed itself in some new, desperate patterns.

Elsie Lester had contacts, and as always in Ireland, contacts were everything. Through them Ursula was directed to "private residential accommodation" in Molesworth Street; furnished flats that discreetly occupied the first and second floors above a row of professional offices.

The location was south of the Liffey and Ursula had always thought of herself as a northsider, but when she was shown the flat she had no difficulty changing allegiance. The bedroom and miniscule sitting room were freshly painted and papered. A toilet and washbasin occupied a small cubicle of their own. Ornamental ironwork outside the lower panes of the windows insured that no small child would tumble out.

There was no lino on the floors, no smell of damp.

The landlord was a plump little man with fat pink hands and a bald pink head. Ursula had been sent to him by Mrs. Seán Lester, Someone Important in his world view, so he was as ingratiating as a dog wagging its entire back end. He bustled about opening windows and pointing out amenities.

"Because we're close to government buildings we get a good class of tenant here," he told Ursula. "Staff from foreign embassies, even. The furniture and rugs are quality, you can see that yourself. And there's a fine hotel on the corner if you fancy a meal out, Mrs . . . ?"

"Halloran," Ursula said.

"Mrs. Halloran. Will Mr. Halloran be joining you?"

She told him the truth. The actual truth and nothing more. "Mr. Halloran fought in Spain."

"But the war is over and . . . ah. I see. My condolences, Mrs. Halloran, and may God have mercy on his soul. You and your wee lad are welcome here. I lost my father in the Great War. Now I manage his property for my mother, who is a widow like yourself. Only older, of course," he added with a self-conscious smirk. "You and I are about the same age, I should think."

I should think not! Ursula grasped her thumbs to keep from saying something that would cost her the flat. As soon as a month's rent was paid and the place officially hers, she installed a new lock on the door.

There was no unpacking to do. She hastily purchased clothes for herself and Barry, and Elsie Lester loaned her a few household necessities, including a gas ring and a teakettle, but the items that should have made the flat Ursula's home were lacking. No books. No bridle.

She had Barry, though. That made all the difference.

With the problem of shelter solved, the larger problem loomed. Ursula's savings would not last forever. The war was seriously interfering with postal services; Seán Lester's new letter of reference might take weeks to arrive. Meanwhile she must seek employment armed with only her nerve and her need.

THE French were doing all they could to hold back the Nazi tide, but it was apparent that while the Germans were in the war to win, the French were merely hoping not to lose.

On the twenty-eighth of May newspaper headlines screamed BELGIUM AND HOLLAND SURRENDER TO NAZIS!

Two days later British troops were fighting a desperate rearguard action on the French coast around Dunkirk.

In London, Sir Oswald Mosley was arrested and interned.

There was no work available in Dublin; not the sort for which Ursula was equipped. Any position that required intelligence or initiative was already filled by a man. The civil service was, of course, closed to her. An unwed mother had no hope there. She applied to every position advertised in the papers where it looked as if a woman could bring her child with her. In each instance she was told, "Stay home and tend to your baby, missus."

No one suggested how she was to support that baby.

URSULA banged the door knocker several times before Louise Hamilton opened to her with a mop in one hand and a dust cloth in the other. She stared at her caller as if seeing a ghost. "Is that really you?"

"The one and only. May I come in, Louise, or shall we talk out here on the stoop?"

"Come in, come in of course, and welcome, but..." Louise was plainly flustered. "But who is this?"

Straddling Ursula's hip was a child who looked to be around a year of age. Plump, rosy cheeks, eyes of storm gray, and a cap of silky red-gold hair gleaming in the morning sunlight.

Giving Louise one of his big grins, Barry reached toward her with a dimpled hand.

Louise melted as visibly as ice in the sun. She let him grasp one of her work-coarsened fingers with his own and gave him back smile for smile. "What a beautiful babby," she said without taking her eyes from his face.

"Meet Finbar Lewis Halloran," Ursula said. "My son."

SEATED beside his mother on the horsehair couch in the parlor, Barry was chattering to himself in a language all his own and playing with the tassel of a cushion.

Hector Hamilton was nowhere in sight. Five minutes before Ursula knocked on the door he had gone out to buy the morning papers, as was his habit. This always included at least an hour's conversation with acquaintances along the way.

Ursula had timed her visit very carefully.

"God between us and all harm," Louise ejaculated—for the second time in five minutes. "I just can't believe you have a babby, Ursula."

"I do, and there he is. Now are you going to offer me a cup of tea?"

"I will of course. But first you must tell me about your husband. I had no idea! Isn't it amazing that his name is Halloran too? Did you meet him as soon as you arrived in Geneva? Did he sweep you off your feet and marry you at once? He must have done. Is he—"

"I'm not married," Ursula interrupted to halt the spate of questions.

"But you told me the babby's name is..."

"It is. There just isn't any Mr. Halloran."

"You don't mean?"

"I do mean. Now what about that cup of tea?"

The color had drained from Louise's face. Tea was the last thing in her mind. "God between us and all harm! You have a...a..."

"An illegitimate baby," Ursula said calmly. "Though how Barry can possibly be called illegitimate escapes me. In the dictionary Henry gave me, the definition of legitimate is 'proper, regular, conforming to standard type.' Look at Barry. One head, one body, ten fingers, ten toes. Standard-type baby."

She had long since looked up the word in the dictionary to use as part of her arsenal; responses she had rehearsed while Barry still lay safely in her womb. Responses to spike the guns of any who sought to attack him.

Ursula believed in attacking first.

"Mr. Hamilton's going to be very upset about this," Louise warned. "If it was up to me, you'd both be welcome to live here, but..."

"We already have a place to live. It may not work out, but if it doesn't I'll find another one."

Barry doubled a little fist and punched his mother's arm, a new exercise he was mastering. She smiled down at him and rumpled the silky hair.

Louise's eyes were drawn to that hair. "The father..." she began. Stopped. Cleared her throat and tried again. "I mean to say, do you know who the father..."

"Of course I know who the father is. I'm surprised at you for even asking that."

"Then who?"

"He's out of the picture." Ursula thrust her chin forward in an expression Louise recognized of old. The older woman knew there would be no more information given on that subject.

Louise felt impelled to ask, "Was the babby, I mean, has he been..."

"Baptized? He has of course. By a genuinely Christian priest who had no qualms about baptizing an infant whose parents aren't married. That's why I went to Switzerland to have my child."

"You went to Switzerland to have him?" Louise echoed.

Ursula smiled. *I can at least give her that much.* "Barry was conceived here in Ireland."

The blunt words turned Louise bright red with embarrassment. As Ursula had intended, she stopped asking questions and hurried out to the kitchen to put the kettle on.

Over several cups of tea and a plate of sweet biscuits, the two women plotted the future between them before Hector Hamilton returned.

They would let him make the same assumption Ursula's new landlord had made. Widowhood was acceptable. "I won't tell an outright lie, though," Ursula warned Louise.

"You won't have to. I'll tell him you met a man in the Irish delegation in Geneva and were married at once, and then... well, something happened to him. That's enough to satisfy Mr. Hamilton, he never questions anything very much if it isn't about him."

"I don't like having you lie."

Louise gave Ursula the look women have exchanged between themselves for millennia when discussing the opposite sex. "I'm married," she said. "So it won't be the first time."

They arranged that Louise would keep Barry during the day while Ursula looked for work. It was obvious the two would get along. The older woman was charmed by the little boy and Barry liked everyone.

"You should leave now," Louise said regretfully, "before Hector comes home, so he won't have an opportunity to ask you too many questions. I'll tell him all he needs to know and let him settle it in his mind."

"You don't know how grateful I am."

It was hard for Ursula to tell Barry good-bye and leave him in the care of another woman for the day. Parting from her son was almost a physical pain.

My son. But not my possession, Ursula reminded herself sternly. *Barry belongs to Barry. He's a separate person.*

Louise accompanied her to the door, then exclaimed, "Merciful hour, I nearly forgot in the excitement! A letter came for you yesterday. I was going to forward it on to Switzerland, but since you're here, you can take it now."

"If you sent it to Switzerland the chances are I'd never get it anyway, under the circumstances."

"Wait here." Louise disappeared into the back of the house and returned carrying an envelope. Carrying it gingerly, as if it might be hot. "Please God it isn't bad news."

The envelope bore the return address of a legal firm in Ennis.

" 'We regret to inform you of the death of Miss Lucy Halloran, spinster, of this parish, on the tenth of May,' " Ursula read. " 'An accident suffered on her farm the previous evening proved fatal.' "

"I'm afraid it is bad news," Ursula told Louise. "Ned's sister Lucy has been killed."

"*Godamercyoner,*" Louise responded automatically, signing the cross on her bosom.

"Wait, there's more. Listen to this. " 'Some time ago, Miss Halloran left the enclosed with us in the event of her death.' " And then there's another letter."

Louise could hardly contain her excitement. "Read it out! I mean . . . unless it's too private."

Ursula stared at the sheet of paper she held in fingers suddenly gone numb. Lucy had written, 'To atone for a wrong I once did to Miss Ursula Halloran, I hereby leave her my farm and its income. I ask that she remember me kindly in her prayers.'

Lucy died on the tenth of May. The same day I knew it was time to come home.

11 June 1940
MUSSOLINI DECLARES WAR ON BRITAIN AND FRANCE
Confident That Germany Will Win, Il Duce Enters the Fray

14 June 1940
PARIS FALLS TO HITLER
German Troops Parade Up the Champs Elysees
Two Million Parisians Flee City, Roads Clogged with Refugees

22 June 1940
FRENCH SIGN ARMISTICE IN COACH USED FOR 1918 GERMAN SURRENDER
Hitler on Hand to Witness French Humiliation

Chapter Forty-six

BARRY loved the train. While Ursula read the newspapers, he alternated between babbling nonsensically to the other passengers and gazing out the window with rapt fascination.

One of Lucy's hired men met them at the railway station with a wagonette drawn by a roan mare. A cushion on the driver's seat indicated that this had been Lucy Halloran's personal transport as well as an all-purpose farm vehicle. The roan mare had a sway back and was seriously over at the knees.

"Oorse," Barry said when he saw her.

Gerry Ryan was a stubby, low-built man in his late forties, with a face, Ursula thought to herself, like a traffic accident. His weather-beaten complexion was blotched and mottled. His eyes were set at differing heights, half of his teeth were missing, and his huge nose sprawled across his face without any sense of discipline.

Lucy had hired Gerry and his brother George when she took ownership of the farm, and complained about them ever since. But never fired them.

On the station platform man and boy scrutinized one another. Barry with his head cocked to one side, Gerry unself-consciously scratching himself.

"Oogy," Barry decided.

"Short," Gerry retorted. Turning to Ursula he said, "This yours, is it?"

"He is mine."

"Call everybody ugly, does he?"

"It's a new word for him. He started to talk early."

"Didn't lick it off the ground though, did he?"

The exchange constituted Gerry Ryan's sole commentary on Barry. No questions were asked about the child's father or Ursula's marital situation. Gerry Ryan was a man who minded his own business.

The farm looked as Ursula remembered; as she had dreamed during lonely nights in Geneva. The contours of the forty-seven acres, the beloved land, were as familiar as the palms of her hands. But as they drove up the long, deeply rutted lane toward the house, she noticed that the walls on either side had gaps like broken teeth. In the fields beyond, bits of abandoned farm equipment lay rusting.

"Are we making any money at all, Gerry?"

"Just about hanging on."

"What crops are we growing?"

The hired man slanted a look in Ursula's direction. He was not accustomed to a woman taking interest in the details of agriculture. "Barley," he said, "and a few turnips. Ain't had a good barley crop for several years, though. We're too far away from the big buyers like Guinness and Murphys anyway. And turnips has got so watery it's hardly worth takin' 'em to market."

"Did the government include this farm in the compulsory tillage scheme?"

"Thought they would, but they didn't."

"Then what about livestock? Cows and pigs make money."

"Your aunt got rid of the livestock. She thought it was too much trouble."

She thought one old horse was too much trouble. "Are you the one who buried my horse, Gerry?"

He nodded. "Me and George."

"Was he ... did he ..."

"I don't think he suffered none," Ryan said gently.

AT the end of the lane the farmhouse came into view. *My house,* Ursula told herself. Still not quite believing. A small cottage built of local stone in an earlier century, the house had been added to and modified as the Halloran family prospered. It now stood two storeys high, with a steeply pitched slate roof bracketed by brick chimneys and a porch to shelter the rarely used front door.

Behind the house was the barn. *Saoirse's barn.*

"Could you show me where my horse is buried, Gerry?"

"Whenever you say."

Ryan drove the wagonette around to the farmyard. He handed Ursula the reins while he stepped down and opened the gate. A broad, sturdy gate made of thick iron pipes.

"Is that new?" Ursula asked.

"Your aunt bought it in the summer of '38. Old one fell apart completely, couldn't even patch it no more."

The heavy gate swung open with surprising ease. Ursula flapped the reins and drove the roan mare through.

"Your aunt had them special hinges installed," Ryan remarked as he closed the gate behind them. "That's what got her killed. She went to get the wagonette to drive into town, and a high wind slammed the gate against her and crushed her chest."

How strange the house was, unoccupied! Silent. Dusty. The remit of the hired men did not extend to housecleaning.

Carrying Barry, Ursula wandered from room to room, soaking up memories. Inevitably she wound up in the kitchen. She sat the toddler on the floor and glared at the big black iron range. One challenge she did not relish.

Barry pulled himself to his feet by hanging on to the leg of the big old table. He threw his mother a triumphant grin. "*'Tand!*" he announced.

"I see you standing." Ursula started to add, "Be careful," then decided against it.

With the choice of all the bedrooms, Ursula took her old one for herself and Barry. When he was bigger she would move him into Ned's room, she decided. Unless Ned came home.

If Ned ever comes home.

Once they were settled Ursula sent Gerry into town to buy the necessary supplies. Accompanied by his younger brother George, she began a systematic reconnoitre of the farm, field by field, building by building.

In the woodshed she found a neglected cider press bound to its base by a network of cobwebs. When she lifted the lid she caught a whiff of the faint, sharp sweetness of a long-ago autumn.

"George, were there many apples last year?"

George, who was as tall and gangling as his brother was short and squat, but no more handsome, shook his head. "Didn't bother to pick 'em."

"But they could have been sold in the market!"

"Trees 're too old, apples is small and wormy."

"All those trees need is care," Ursula replied, exasperated.

"Your aunt didn't tell us to do nothin' for 'em."

His words gave Ursula a clear picture of Lucy Halloran in recent years. An aging, sour spinster, increasingly self-absorbed. Without supervision her hired men did no more than they had to do.

Things will be different from now on.

Saw in hand, Ursula scrambled up into one of the neglected apple trees in the orchard.

George was alarmed. "What're you doing? You'll break your neck!"

"I'm going to prune these trees."

"Well get down and give me the saw. I'll do it."

"There's another saw in the barn," Ursula told him.

They worked in the orchard until dark.

The following morning, though her damaged thigh muscles were stiff and sore, Ursula loaded a wheelbarrow with well-rotted manure from the floor of the barn and spread it around the base of the apple trees. They would not produce much of a crop this autumn, but by next year the cider press could go back into service.

WITH the fall of France, the government of Éire had taken alarm. An official state of emergency was declared. Since the end of the Civil War the regular army had been largely stood down. Now the troops were called back and the force enlarged as rapidly as possible. Leading politicians of every persuasion urged the nation's men to prepare to defend their country if an invasion came.

Within twenty-four hours, teachers and students and laborers and professional men and shop owners and businessmen were joining the Emergency Army in their thousands.[1] The new recruits were known as "Emergency Men," or "Durationists."

Agricultural workers were deemed an essential part of the nation's wartime economy. Although not actively encouraged to enlist in the regular army, they were urged to volunteer for the newly established local defense force. George and Gerry Ryan dutifully signed up. They were issued green uniforms, outdated rifles of dubious reliability, and given a drill schedule. No matter what else was happening at the farm, Ursula saw to it that they never missed attending drill. "Always be ready to fight for Ireland," she told the brothers sternly. "And that's an order from me."

She was hugely proud of them.

She did not let herself think about how lonely she was. No one came to call. As far as Catholic Ireland was concerned, Ursula had done the unforgivable. She had borne a child while unmarried and dared to keep the baby. Her soul was damned.

The only friends she had now were those from the past.

Ursula began writing letters to give her new address to correspondents around the world. Felicity Rowe-Howell was the first to reply. "Congratulate me; I've joined the working classes. I'm now a factory worker at Cricklewood, helping to build a quite splendid bomber called a Halifax. When the shift is over we girls, still in our dungarees, jump on the underground and get off at Green Park. Within a few minutes we're in the Ritz Bar, being toasted by servicemen. This is the life, Ursula! Whatever did we do for excitement before the war?"

A few days later Madame Dosterschill popped unbidden into Ursula's thoughts. The gentle German language teacher with the twinkling eyes. What was happening to her in all of this?

Ursula wrote to Surval, hoping someone there would at least know where Madame was.

She never received a reply.

She never heard from either of the Florentine twins again, either.

MUSSOLINI'S decision to enter the war had dismayed many Italians, who traditionally regarded Britain as a friend. It also had the effect of virtually cutting off Geneva from the rest of the world.

"I still have not received your letter of recommendation from Seán," Elsie Lester wrote, "but am thankful that you no longer need it. Enjoy the farm, and please give Barry a big hug for me."

THE Ryan brothers had buried Saoirse in the field beside the laneway, where he had spent the last years of his life. Only one tree stood in the field, an ancient thorn tree that had sunk its roots deep into a strange low mound. At the foot of the mound was Saoirse's grave. One of the brothers had marked it with a slab of limestone.

Ursula rarely visited the cemetery on the hill where generations of Hallorans were buried. But she often visited Saoirse's grave.

KNOWING that experience was the best teacher, Ursula visited the markets to talk to veteran farmers. At first they were surprised that a young woman was showing any interest in agricultural matters, but she smiled and listened and smiled more, and eventually they warmed to her.

She was repeatedly told that the climate was colder and wetter than it used to be. Only one man disagreed. "Our climate is wonderful," he insisted. "Sure 'tis only the weather that spoils it."

The weather did seem to be causing exceptional difficulties for tillage farmers. The Halloran farm was not alone; throughout Clare yields had dropped drastically. Livestock, the old-timers claimed, could cope better. Damp, cold soil and a short summer season did not matter as much to them. In Ireland grass grew no matter what. Income per acre was lower with livestock farming than with tillage, but costs were lower too. There was no need to hire extra help at harvest time.

Ursula listened and learned.

"We're out of the barley business," she informed the Ryan brothers. "We're going to buy dairy cows."

George said, "Why not sheep? They don't need as much tending."

"They won't make as much money, either. There's a war on and there's talk of rationing. The prices for milk and butter are bound to go up."

"You know anything about dairy farming?" Gerry asked.

"I know how to *learn*," Ursula told him. "And I hope you do too."

As Ursula walked away the brothers exchanged glances. "What d'ye think?" George asked Gerry.

"Won't do no harm," the other replied.

In Europe Ursula had seen prosperous farms occupying land that appeared to be no more suitable than the wettest or stoniest holdings in Clare. Yet every acre was profitably put to work.

If they can do it, we can do it.

Once she had taken the farm for granted, but those days were well and truly gone. "Hard graft, that's what's needed now," she told Barry.

"*Grft,*" the little boy agreed. He was beginning to walk independently, toddling along behind his mother wherever she went. He did not want to be carried and did not even want his hand held.

Although publicly de Valera was unwavering in his commitment to Irish neutrality, on his instructions the Irish government quietly began supplying the British with intelligence information.[2] Finbar Cassidy helped collate the material. Sometimes he stopped in the midst of his work and thought of Ursula.

Thanks to his job in External Affairs, he knew she had joined Lester's staff at the League of Nations. He had heard nothing of her since. Once or twice he had started to write to her in Geneva, then decided against it. Finbar was not at his most persuasive in writing. Better to wait until she returned to Ireland.

Finbar knew how to be patient.

While he waited he lit candles for Ursula at Mass and prayed daily for her safety.

De Valera's determination to make Ireland self-sufficient meant new government agencies were being created to help the farmers. Ursula ordered every pamphlet available and attended every lecture in the Grange. She made a thorough study of those crops that were doing well in Clare; she toured local farms to see how the more successful farmers raised and fed— and culled, when necessary—their dairy herds.

Ursula did everything she asked her hired men to do except the culling. She could not kill an animal.

The work was unremitting but she thrived on it. What one did to a farm *showed*.

Ursula eagerly awaited the arrival of mail though she had no time to read it until the end of the day, when everyone else was in bed. Letters from abroad were very slow in coming. Many of her friends in Europe never responded to her change of address and request for news from their part of the world.

Some had vanished as surely as if the ground had opened and swallowed them up.

How strange it was to be so far removed from it all! Walking over a summer field starred with wildflowers while an armada of clouds sailed serenely overhead, it was easy to imagine that the world was at peace. *War? What war?*

That attitude was dangerous. Ignorance was dangerous; it left one unprepared.

The Ryan brothers, who lived on the other side of Clarecastle, walked out to the farm every morning. Ursula had them call at the newsagent's shop on their way and buy the papers for her.

The civil war in Spain was long since over, superseded by something worse. But in the pages of the *Clare Champion* and the *Limerick Leader* updated casualty lists containing local names still appeared from time to time. Ursula never found Ned Halloran among them.

That meant nothing. Many men went missing in war and were never accounted for.

In the pages of the *Irish Times* and *Irish Press* Ursula followed news of the war in Europe. She also listened avidly to the wireless in the parlor. Most farmhouses kept the wireless in the kitchen, but Ursula spent no more time in that room than necessary. She was learning to farm but she would never learn to cook well. The meals she prepared out of necessity could best be described as filling.

Fortunately Barry liked everything. Even eggs. So Ursula bought a rooster and a harem of hens.

After their evening meal she let Barry stay up for a while to listen to the wireless with her. Ursula treated the occasion as an event the way Henry had done so long ago when he read the newspapers to her, and gave Barry hot cocoa—until the cocoa ran out.

"We shan't be getting any more, I suspect," the shopkeepers said. "The war, you know."

URSULA listened alone to the last news bulletin on the wireless before she put out the lamps and went to bed.

She had not contacted Lewis during the stopover in London, nor had she seen Finbar while in Dublin. She did not want either man to know she was back in Ireland. All that was over now.

Yet in her dreams she could not escape her memories. Sometimes she awoke with a blurred sense of reality to find that the man in the bed beside her was a chubby little fellow with red-gold hair.

Chapter Forty-seven

"Y OU finally have a letter from Ursula," Ella told Henry when he arrived home one evening.

"Thank God. We've heard nothing from her in months and I was getting very worried. The situation in Europe . . ."

"You needn't worry anymore, dearest. The letter's postmarked 'Éire.' "

Henry almost snatched the envelope out of his wife's hand. While Ella hovered beside him, he read the letter aloud.

"We are safe at home," Ursula had written, "on the farm in Clare."

Ella raised her eyebrows. " 'We?' "

Henry read on. "So much has happened I hardly know where to begin. And yet nothing has happened here; not on the larger scale. People furtively pull back the curtains to spy on their neighbours just as they have always done. Their only interest is in the personal, not the global, and I am supplying a full quota of titillation.

" 'I am sorry to tell you that Lucy Halloran was killed in a farming accident this spring. From my point of view it was a blessing in disguise because she left the farm to me. I only learned this when I returned to Ireland, in need of a place to live and a way to support myself and Barry.' "

"Barry?" Ella echoed. "Who in the world is Barry?"

"Be patient, Cap'n, I'm coming to that. " 'Barry is the best news of all,' she says. 'He is my son, Finbar Lewis Halloran.' "

Ella looked around for the nearest chair and sank onto it. "Her son? I don't understand, Henry. When was she married? She never mentioned it before."

Henry's eyes were racing over the page. "She doesn't say anything about being married, Cap'n."

"Dear God."

"And she doesn't give any details about the boy's ... mmm ... father."

"Do you suppose she picked the child up in Europe as an orphan, a foundling? Like history repeating itself? Is that why his surname is Halloran?"

"Mmm ... no. Listen to this. " 'Barry was born in Geneva on the sixth of April, 1939. Ella will be glad to hear I had an easy birth. My obstetrician was one of the best in Europe. Afterward I was able to keep Barry with me while working at the League. In Ireland that sort of situation is not possible—unless one is running a farm, as I am now.' "

Henry put down the letter. He and his wife stared at each other.

At last he cleared his throat. "Little Business always was a law unto herself," he said.

TURNING a rundown tillage farm into an up-to-date dairy business would require a daunting amount of money. For the first time in her life, Ursula entered a bank to ask for a loan.

The Bank of Ireland on O'Connell Square in Ennis was an imposing structure by Irish standards, but Ursula swept through the doors as if she were accustomed to doing business there every day.

The bank manager, who recently had transferred up from Limerick, was amused by this woman with her audacious plans. She held title to a good-sized farm, but in the west of Ireland money was loaned as much on family reputation as on collateral. The manager narrowed his eyes to suspicious slits. "Who are your people, Miss Halloran?"

"Does the name Ned Halloran mean anything to you? He fought in 1916."

The man's expression changed abruptly. "Sure didn't I meet Ned Halloran when I was just a young lad? My da served with him in the War of Independence. He was a hard man, was Ned. His teeth were the softest part of him."

Ursula ignored the use of the past tense. "Ned Halloran is my father," she said.

That night the banker casually mentioned his new customer to his wife. Her face froze with outrage. "Do you not know that woman isn't married?"

"I do of course, it's on her loan application. But she has excellent collateral and the kind of attitude that—"

"She isn't married yet she has a *child*," his wife hissed. "How can you loan money to someone of such low morality?"

Part of the bank manager's business was to know everyone else's business—and keep it confidential. Over the years his wife's proclivity for gossip had caused him a number of problems, and was the principle reason he had been transferred from his last posting. "Her morality won't show on the balance sheet!" he snapped. "And that's all they pay me to worry about."

As soon as she had the money Ursula began buying cows. She hired builders to convert the barn into a modern milking parlor like those she had seen in Europe. The workmen argued with her over almost every detail. "You don't know what you're doing," she was told repeatedly.

"I know that I'm the one paying you. Do it my way or someone else will."

They were taken aback by her directness, but they did what she wanted. A job that paid in money rather than promises was worth keeping.

George and Gerry were put to work mending fences and reseeding pastures so the cattle could graze year-round. They were still hard at it when the cows arrived. Twenty black-and-white Frisians, a hardy breed originally developed in the northern Netherlands and valued for the quantity of their milk.

On the day they were delivered to the farm Ursula walked among them like a miser gloating over his gold. Stroking the spotted hides. Rubbing the knobbly skulls between the large ears. To take such joy in life when thousands were losing theirs as the war gathered momentum seemed like a betrayal, but she could not help it.

"Be careful, Miss," Gerry advised. "Dairy cows ain't pets."

"They won't hurt me," Ursula assured him. "Animals never hurt me." *Only people.*

ALTHOUGH America remained neutral Germany was threatening shipping in the North Atlantic. Yet mail continued to go through. Henry Mooney's letters attempted to discover, without asking outright, the circumstances of Barry's birth. Ursula's replies consisted of farm news and updates on the Irish political scene.

"She's not going to tell us," Henry told his wife.

"She probably thinks it's none of our business."

"But it is, Cap'n! She's family!"

Ella gave him a pitying look. "She's a grown woman, dearest. With a family of her own."

"Do you have any idea how much courage she'll need to raise a child when she's not married? It would be hard enough over here. In Ireland it must be ... mmm ... hell in a handbasket. People will be merciless to her."

MANY were—or tried to be. Ursula never actually said she was widowed but was willing to give that impression. No one believed it because Barry's surname was the same as her own.

As Ursula had written to Henry, curtains were twitched aside when she passed on the road. Hostile eyes peeked out at her; disapproving heads were shaken. The good women of Clarecastle made a point of avoiding her in the shops. Even in Ennis, the county seat, she was subjugated to stares and whispers.

From the very beginning she trained herself to act as if she did not notice. When the self-righteous treated her as if she were invisible, she responded by acting as if their bad manners were invisible. She went about her business with her chin up and giving everyone the same dazzling smile.

I have nothing to be ashamed of; I've given life to a child. You're the ones who should be ashamed, you vicious old harridans who profess to be Christians.

When, from the pulpit, the parish priest condemned "the invisible gas of moral turpitude seeping under Ireland's doors," Ursula stopped going to Mass. She sought a more compassionate God in the fields and meadows and whispered her prayers to the wind.

She was at work before sunrise and continued to work until dark. Aside from taking a long nap in the afternoon, Barry toddled along behind his mother or played happily nearby. The first time he fell down and skinned his knees he glanced toward Ursula. His crumpled face was on the verge of tears. Ursula made herself laugh. Taking his cue from her, Barry laughed too.

Until Barry came to the farm the Ryan brothers had had little contact with children. They considered them almost another species of animal, unpredictable and incomprehensible, best observed from afar. Barry changed all that. The two crusty old bachelors doted on him.

Barry Halloran did not cling to his mother's apron strings. Ursula did not wear an apron anyway. As soon as he was able to walk on his own, Barry wandered off by himself from time to time. " *'Sploring,*" he called it. Ursula gave him his head, though either she or one of the Ryan brothers was always aware of his location. "Call for help if you get into difficulties," he was told.

He never called for help.

Ursula was adamant that the cows and their environment be kept spot-lessly clean. The Ryan brothers grumbled aloud but began to take pride in their work. Without being told they sought out things that needed to be done, and did them. Every day brought some improvement to the place.

Neighboring farmers began nodding to Ursula when they met her in the road. Their wives continued to ignore her as if she were a bad smell in the air, but she did not care. She had the farm and Barry. She did not need the good opinion of other women.

THE wireless brought unrelenting bad news. The German Luftwaffe had increased aerial attacks on shipping in the English Channel. British losses were mounting up.

Mail boats and passenger steamers leaving Britain for Ireland were es-corted by British destroyers for much of the way, following a zigzag evasive course that invariably made them late for arriving. Boats leaving Irish ports for Britain were accorded the same service in reverse.

In France a little-known brigadier general and tank expert, Charles de Gaulle, urged his countrymen to fight on. "Whatever happens," he said, "the flame of the French resistance must not go out."

The British navy removed the threat of the French fleet falling into German hands by destroying most of the ships as they lay at anchor in Algeria. A thousand French sailors were killed in the process. The British government expressed regret at the loss of life and hoped it would not adversely affect Anglo-French relations.

"Britain is now fighting on alone," Churchill announced in a wireless program rebroadcast from the BBC. "Let us brace ourselves to our duty and so bear ourselves that if the British Commonwealth and Empire lasts a thousand years men will still say, 'This was their finest hour.'"

"'Chill," said Barry. "'Chill, Mam?" He looked at her questioningly.

She started to reply, "Our enemy." Bit back the words. "A brave man," she said instead.

THE war was moving closer to home.

On the twenty-sixth of August three women were killed when a creamery in County Wexford was struck by a German bomb. The Germans claimed the plane had been lost in fog.

At the end of the month Berlin was shaken by a British bombing raid. Royal Air Force planes struck back in retaliation for a massive air attack on London. In an exuberant report to Parliament, Churchill paid glowing tribute to the RAF pilots. "Never in the field of human conflict was so much owed by so many to so few."

Again Ursula was moved by his oratory. Because she was Irish she had an inherent sympathy for the underdog.

How odd to think of Britain as the underdog!

"Will America enter the war?" Ursula wrote to Henry, though she thought she knew the answer already. America had no territorial interests in Europe. It would do what de Valera was doing, stand aside and let the nations with imperial ambitions fight amongst themselves.

Some Irish people took the neutrality policy to the extreme by refusing to think about the war at all. They withdrew deeper into themselves; speaking softly, thinking circumspectly, narrowing their horizons to one small island, and within that, to county and parish and townland.

Ursula Halloran continued to follow the international situation as best she could. Elsie Lester kept her better informed about the League of Nations than any other source. The League had almost disappeared from the Irish consciousness.

After months of political intrigue, Joseph Avenol had resigned in August. Seán Lester was the new secretary-general. He dolefully predicted he might be the last. No one had faith in the League anymore. Even the Swiss government was withdrawing its support. The organization's presence in Geneva was seen as endangering Swiss neutrality.

At the end of September Elsie wrote, "I just had a rather upsetting telephone conversation with my husband. He was passing through London on his way back to Geneva. A committee including Seán and the president of the International Court of Justice had planned a meeting of the League's supervisory commission, and wanted to hold it in Lisbon to keep some presence on the international stage.

"Although both Spain and Portugal claim to be neutral, the Spanish government issued a barring order against the League. The committee members were turned away at the border—very unpleasantly, I gather. They considered themselves lucky to get away unharmed. Only the fact that Seán was Irish kept the matter from being worse than it was. Fortunately the Spanish still think of Ireland as a friend.

"I wish my husband would come home, Ursula, but I never say that to him. His integrity is too deep to allow him to run away. That is one of the reasons I love him."

.   .   .

IN October, harsh anti-Semitic laws were passed by the collaboratist Vichy regime in France, and the Germans prepared to use France's Atlantic seaports to shorten their own supply lines.

That same month, President Roosevelt denied that he had any plans to take America into the war.

But the battle for the Atlantic had begun.

Hitler had decided to defeat Britain by starving her out. The deadly German submarines known as U-boats and heavily armed German vessels masquerading as merchant ships had already sunk or captured thirty-six British vessels in the Atlantic. Britain's supply lifeline from America was seriously damaged.

TO her relief, Ursula finally received a letter from Heidi Neckermann. Originally postmarked Kenya, the letter obviously had passed through a number of hands. "I have been interned here as an enemy of the Crown," Heidi bewailed, "just because I am Austrian. My father and my husband are appealing the case but it looks very bleak. I fear I shall have to spend the duration of the war in a miserable internment camp with a lot of people who have fleas."

SEÁN Lester continued to maintain a doomed but courageous vigil in Geneva, holding up the flickering lamp of freedom against the approaching darkness.

I wish I were there with him, Ursula thought wistfully. *It would be like being with the Volunteers in the GPO when the British were closing in.*

Why must I always be torn between having the one and wanting the other?

IN November Franklin Delano Roosevelt was reelected by an overwhelming margin to become America's first three-term president. "Presidents and prime ministers need a war," Ursula remarked cynically when she and Barry heard the news on the wireless. "People are reluctant to change generals in mid-battle."

"*Jinrals?*" The little boy looked up at her quizzically.

"Men who lead other men in war."

"How?"

She paused to consider the question. Ursula always tried to give her son's questions a straightforward answer. "In olden times they carried a big sword," she told him, "and were better at fighting with it than anyone else."

It was simpler than trying to explain the machinations by which modern men rose to power.

THAT same month, Winston Churchill was back on the list of people whom Ursula despised.

Stunned by criticism over the shipping losses Britain was suffering, a furious Churchill blamed Ireland. The *Irish Press* quoted the prime minister as saying in the House of Commons, "The fact that we cannot use the south and west coasts of Ireland to refuel our flotillas and aircraft is a most grievous burden and one which should never have been placed upon our shoulders, broad though they be."

The British government further intimated that Éire was supplying fuel and provisions to German submarines. There were even suggestions that Britain should attack Ireland and reclaim the Treaty Ports.

There was no doubt that the ports were ideally located to facilitate communication and shorten supply lines for the Allies. But Eamon de Valera had no intention of allowing Britain a foothold in southern Ireland again.

His rebuke to Churchill in the Dáil was the confident retort of one nation's leader admonishing an equal. Radio Éireann reported it in full. "I would have refrained from making any comment upon Mr. Churchill's statement with reference to our ports, were it not for the fact that it has been followed by an extensive press campaign in Britain itself, and reechoed in the United States of America, that we should surrender or lease our ports to Britain for the conduct of the war.

"We want friendly relations with the people of Britain, as we want friendly relations with all other peoples, but naturally we want them with Britain because Britain is the nearest country to us on the globe. It was partly for that reason, and partly because I knew perfectly that it was a condition of neutrality, that I announced it would be our policy to use our strength to the utmost to see that this island was not going to be used as a basis of attack upon Britain.

"There has been no want of good faith as far as we are concerned. We have abided by our public as well as our private promises. It is a lie to say that German submarines or any other submarines are being supplied with fuel or provisions on our coasts. A most extensive system of coast observation has been established here since the war. *I say it is a lie, and I say further that it is known to be a falsehood by the British government itself.*

"Having said all that, these ports are ours. They are within our sovereignty, and there can be no question, as long as we remain neutral, of handing them over to anyone on any condition whatsoever. Any attempt to bring pressure to bear on us by any side—by any of the belligerents—by Britain—could only lead to bloodshed.

"As long as this Government remains in office we shall defend our rights in regard to these ports against whoever shall attack them, as we shall defend our rights in regard to every other part of our territory.

"I want to say to our people that we may be—I hope not—facing a grave crisis. If we are to face it than we shall do it, knowing that our cause is right and just and that, if we have to die for it, we shall be dying in that good cause."[1]

The pendulum swung. Ursula Halloran was once again cheering for Eamon de Valera.

IN a public statement the IRA quoted James Connolly: "We serve neither King nor Kaiser!"

WHILE returning to Canada after accepting the Nobel Prize for peace, the Canadian prime minister Lester Pearson spent Christmas 1940 in London. He subsequently related to the BBC, "I was awoken around midnight by a German bomb exploding outside my building. An air raid was in progress, and to block out the noise of guns and bombs I turned on the radio. It was tuned to a German station that only three hours before had been broadcasting Lord Haw-Haw, and now broadcast the most lovely Christmas carols. I was struck by their beauty. If only we could discover how these two divergent sounds could come from the same source we would be well on the way to achieving world peace."

Chapter Forty-eight

ON Christmas Eve Ursula tucked the Halloran family Bible under her arm and took Barry out to the barn. Wide-eyed with wonder, the little boy sat on a bale of hay while she read aloud the story of the birth in the stable at Bethlehem.

Ursula's attempt to cook the Christmas dinner was not a total success. At least it made the house smell wonderful. With no idea whether he was alive or dead, Ursula set a place for Ned at the table. It remained unoccupied.

Barry enthusiastically ate a portion of roast goose—burnt black on the outside and underdone on the inside—and asked for more.

ON the twenty-seventh of December, 1940, John Charles McQuaid was consecrated Roman Catholic Archbishop of Dublin.

THE public now referred to the conflict of 1914–18 as World War I. The horror of the trenches and the gas, the chivalry so often demonstrated by both sides—these were in the past, relics of ancient days.

World War II promised to be much worse.

As 1941 dawned, the skies were full of thunder.

On the second of January German bombs fell on southern Ireland following a line down the eastern side of the country. No one was killed but several people were injured. There was little doubt that the German pilots knew exactly where they were dropping their bombs.

De Valera's government issued a brief statement but did not condemn the attack outright. The newspapers speculated that the raid was a deliberate attempt to warn Éire not to abandon neutrality and gave aid to Britain.

Winston Churchill stated, "No attempt should be made to conceal from Mr. de Valera the depth and intensity of feeling against the policy of Irish neutrality. Juridically we have never recognized that Southern Ireland is an independent Sovereign State. Should the present situation last until the end of the war, a gulf will have opened between Northern and Southern Ireland which it will be impossible to bridge in this generation."[1]

JANUARY brought another threat to Ireland. There was an outbreak of foot-and-mouth disease in County Derry.

Britain immediately stopped all imports of Irish cattle. Soon all foxhunting and greyhound coursing was banned in Éire. Fairs, race meetings, and the St. Patrick's Day Dog Show were canceled. Cattle marts were closed. The government even banned walking in the mountains for fear of spreading the disease.

A siege mentality set in.

IN Éire the second great conflict in Europe within three decades was not called World War II. It was simply known as the Emergency.

Because Éire was a free nation, for the first time in modern history her citizens were free to enter or abstain from a British war. Tens of thousands joined the Allied Forces. Members of Fianna Fáil and Fine Gael found themselves united in their opposition to Hitler.

The nation's isolation from global affairs did not protect her from many of the war's effects. Previously de Valera had agreed to a British request that Ireland buy all its tea through the United Kingdom. In 1941 Britain cut the Irish tea ration in half.

The Irish also had been dependent on Britain for coal and oil, tea and candles, pots and pans and bricks and timber, nails and electric light bulbs and motorcars. None of these were available now. Britain continued to rely heavily on the importation of Irish foodstuffs, but the export of British goods to Éire had almost ceased entirely.

Many believed that Britain was punishing Éire for her neutrality.

The shortages proved to be something of a blessing in disguise. Thrown back on her own resources, Éire struggled in earnest to become the self-sufficient state de Valera had long desired. *Bord na Mona*, the Turf Board, set about developing the country's only indigenous fuel. Looking ahead to the end of the war, Seán Lemass, the government minister for supplies, initiated a project to build an oil refinery at Dublin Port.

People began to take pride in what they could do on their own.

Those who had motorcars put them up on blocks. Goff's, the bloodstock auctioneers, held a huge auction of horse-drawn vehicles. Hunters and children's ponies and aging racehorses suddenly found themselves between the shafts of cabs and sidecars.

"I think we should look into raising a few horses for sale," Ursula told Gerry Ryan.

"Breed the roan mare, you mean?"

Ursula laughed. "And pass on her faults to another generation? Indeed not. But I think we could find a couple of decent Irish draft mares if we shop around."

"War'll be over by the time you get the foals raised and ready to sell."

Ursula smiled. "Oh, there'll always be a market for a good horse."

By now Gerry recognized the look in her eyes. "Them mares is as good as bought," he told his brother. "Better build a shed for 'em in the high pasture."

WITH neutrality Éire had closed down. The only available entertainment was homegrown: theater and cinema and well-chaperoned dances. Dublin hotels offered "dress dances" every Saturday night for five shillings per person. Supper cost extra.

When the All-Ireland Ballroom Dancing Championships were held at the Gresham, female contestants arrived on bicycles with the skirts of their ball gowns tucked up.

As for books, Irish book publishers had virtually disappeared during the hard economic times of the thirties. What remained in the bookshops was mostly British-published and of limited variety. Censorship was in full flight. A book must win the approval of the Church if it hoped to find a readership in Éire—unless it was banned, which guaranteed it would be highly sought after and eagerly passed from hand to hand.

Ursula thought longingly of her favorite books, left behind in Geneva and probably lost forever.

At least she had the wireless.

The air was flooded with radio signals. Borne on invisible waves of power, messages arrived daily from the outside world. The German high command had trained thousands of wireless operators. Ireland was bombarded by Nazi propaganda programs in both English and Irish. The broadcasts often included music, humorous skits, or personal messages.

Irish-language broadcasts from Germany were not subtle. Attempting to destroy any sympathy Irish nationalists might feel for the British cause, they directly connected the colonial abuses of the English in the past with current events. The British were depicted as insatiable imperialists; the Germans as a valiant people fighting for their homeland.

Ireland was not the only country receiving German propaganda. Radio Berlin broadcast in fifty-four languages, reaching a wide international audience.

At first Ursula tuned in out of curiosity. When the hated voice of Lord Haw-Haw filled the farmhouse parlor she switched off the machine in disgust. Not everyone reacted that way. Many in Ireland enjoyed the German broadcasts. The music was catchy and modern and the jokes could be repeated in pubs and shops. One could ignore the blatant propaganda—or take pleasure in arguing with the wireless.

As a mainly agricultural country, Ireland in general did not suffer the food shortages other nations were enduring. Milk, eggs, bacon and pork were available—if one could pay for them. Prices went up as profiteers took advantage of consumer nervousness.

As always, the poor had the hardest time of it. Shortages reduced them to a basic level of subsistence as low as the oldest could remember.[2] Tough, stringy boiling beef was a shilling a pound; a stew made with a pound of beef and vegetables would feed a family for three days. The bread was called brown bread but was almost black, very coarse, with husks and sometimes even bits of hair sticking out of it. Boys claimed that if they kept a loaf until the next day they could play handball with it.

Ursula refused to be a profiteer. When local merchants learned she would supply butter at prewar prices, they bought all she could provide and quietly sold it under the counter to their regular customers. No talk now about unwed mothers and moral turpitude.

On April 15, 1941, the Germans dropped nearly three hundred bombs on Belfast. Seven hundred and forty-five people were killed and twice that number injured. Thousands of houses were left uninhabitable.

Forgetting about partition for the moment, Eamon de Valera sent all available fire brigades, ambulances, and medical personnel racing north across the border to the aid of the stricken city. "They are our own people, after all," he said.

GERRY Ryan wondered aloud, "How could the Germans bomb people who never done them no harm?"

In Ursula's mind a newsreel unrolled: The Black and Tans, Knockna-goshel, Ballyseedy . . . "There is a barbarian in all of us, Gerry, just under the skin," she said sadly. "We don't want to believe it but it's true. Fed enough carefully constructed propaganda, poisoned with enough emotive lies, any human being is capable of terrible things."

APRIL 30 saw the banning of private motoring throughout Éire. In Dublin the price of secondhand bicycles soared from a few shillings to ten pounds— more than a month's wages for the average worker.

On the fourth of May the bombers came again. This time they targeted the shipyards and Short's aircraft factory. Once again Éire was quick to offer help, which was gratefully accepted.

URSULA received a letter from Ella Mooney. It arrived in a bluish-gray envelope thinner than tissue paper, with a patriotically striped border and the words *V Mail* printed on it. The letter paper was equally thin and lightweight.

> Dear Ursula,
>
> Can you find out anything about my relatives in Belfast? We just learned of the bombing and I am worried about their safety. Enclosed is a list of their names and addresses. I also have written to my brother Edwin in Dublin, but I suspect you are much more resourceful.

Within a week Ursula was able to write reassuringly to Ella. "Everyone on your list is fine; no injuries, no property damage. I am told that the spirit in Belfast is tremendous."

•   •   •

URSULA stopped in her work and looked up. Aside from the ubiquitous clouds of an island at the rim of the Atlantic, the sky was empty. Silent except for the soughing of the wind. Yet elsewhere that same vast dome was crisscrossed with planes intent on deadly missions.

London writhing under the blitz. Refusing to give in.

Ursula admired their spirit.

But what of the spirit of the pilots flying the planes, setting out to kill people they would never see? They were probably just men who loved to fly.

The way Lewis Baines loved to fly.

It had been a long time since she thought of Lewis. The farm and the lives being lived there were too immediate.

ALTHOUGH Ursula put Barry first, the farm made endless demands. Cattle to milk, eggs to gather, customers provided with milk and butter, visits to the market to buy and sell. Brood mares to look at, decisions to make, accounts to balance.

The barn cat had seven kittens.

All life was here, filling Ursula to the brim.

Except... when she remembered the way the light fell on Lac Léman, or the coal-and-turf smell of Dublin, or the heady excitement of those days at 2RN and the League, herself at the heart of the action...

Or the warmth of a man's arms. And one extraordinary moment whose memory sometimes came to her entire, like a butterfly encased in amber.

ON the last night of May a 500-pound German bomb fell in the North Strand area. Two smaller bombs fell on the North Circular Road and on Summerhill Parade. Áras an Uachtaráin and the nearby American embassy were damaged when a 250-pound bomb landed in the Phoenix Park.

The air raid occurred too late to make the newspapers that the Ryan brothers brought to the farm. Ursula knew nothing about it until she went into the house to fix Barry's lunch, and paused as was her habit to listen to the one o'clock news bulletin on the wireless.

"Dublin this morning was a strangely silent town," the newsreader began. "Last night four or five bombs all told were dropped on this city, bringing the war to neutral Ireland. The North Strand and the Five Lamps district seem to have taken the worst of it.

"So far thirty-two are known dead, but that figure may rise. Many await identification at the morgue. In some cases this will be all but impossible.

"Over eighty people with severe injuries have been taken to Jervis Street Hospital and the Mater. The fire brigades and ambulance service have been stretched to their utmost. Upwards of thirty houses were completely demolished by the bombs and hundreds are left homeless. Areas of the city are covered with a layer of ash like fine dust.

"This morning shaken people were talking to one another in somber undertones, gathering on street corners to compare their experiences. A woman who lives in the North Strand relates that she was sitting in her kitchen having a last cup of tea well after midnight, when suddenly she heard a high, eerie whistle. A moment later the entire window came in on her.

"A man tells of seeing bloody clothing that had been blown onto the top of a lamp post, but there was no sign of the body it had clothed. Another describes seeing corpses on stretchers being loaded into a morgue wagon. Their torsos, which had been ripped wide open by the explosion, were held together with garden twine.[3]

"A North American bison at the zoo in the Phoenix Park took fright during the air raid and bashed his way out of his enclosure. The zoo's only elephant simply lay down and refused to get up, although it was uninjured."

Dear God. Ursula started to turn off the wireless but her hand froze in the act. *Did he say the North Strand?*

The bubble rose from its dark pool and she knew. Knew, and cursed the gift of knowing.

She ran out to the field where the roan mare was grazing and led her back to the farmyard. When she put Saoirse's saddle on the mare, the animal arched her swayed back in indignation. Ursula tightened the girth. The roan laid her ears back and tried to cow-kick her tormentor.

Talking around the straw he was chewing, Gerry Ryan remarked, "Yer one's not a saddle horse."

"She is now," Ursula told him, "because I've no time to waste with the wagonette. Mind Barry 'til I get back." Ignoring the stirrups, she vaulted onto the mare's back before the animal knew what was happening.

The mare valiantly tried to buck her off. Ursula's lips tightened over her teeth. She sawed the reins to pull the horse's head to the left, then right, then left again in quick succession. The distracted mare stopped fighting for a moment.

"Open the gate, Gerry!"

Ursula alternately bullied and cajoled her unwilling mount down the long lane. By the time they reached the road, the roan mare had surrendered to the stronger will. Ursula turned toward her Clarecastle and kicked her into a jarring gallop. Without shafts on either side to keep her going straight, the mare careened all over the road.

"I'm going to give you some proper training," Ursula warned the animal. "You're an embarrassment."

Someone else was using the telephone at the post office. Ursula waited with ill-concealed impatience. As soon as she had the Dublin Broadcasting Station on the line, she said, "I need information about the bombing of the North Strand."

An unfamiliar voice replied, "That will be on the next bulletin which is broadcast at—"

"You must be new," Ursula interrupted. "My name is Ursula Halloran and I worked there for years. When I request information I am always given it. This is *important*. I have to know the names of the casualties."

"The evening newspapers will—"

"Bugger the bloody papers!" Ursula exploded. "Tell me now or I'll have your job! I'm a personal friend of Eamon de Valera. Ask anyone there!"

"I'll get the casualty list for you right away," said the voice on the other end of the wire.

While Ursula waited, civilizations rose and fell.

THE ride back to the farm seemed very long, though in reality it was only a couple of miles. The subdued mare read Ursula's mood. She gave no trouble aside from trying to snatch a mouthful of weeds from the roadside. The warm, sweet air smelled of life and summer.

The sun should not be shining today. How dare the sun shine today? Finbar Cassidy. Oh, God. Finbar. I don't believe it.

I do believe it.

Ursula willed herself not to cry, but it was impossible. *As impossible as identifying some of the bodies? Maybe it wasn't Finbar after all. It might have been someone else.*

But she knew.

Her vision blurred with tears.

When they reached the farm lane the mare quickened her pace and tried to turn in. Ursula automatically tightened her grip on the reins. "Not 'til I tell you," she said to the horse.

An old man was hobbling down the road toward them from the direction of Ennis. He wore a pack on his back and was leaning heavily on a cane. Ursula roused herself from her grief long enough to feel a twinge of pity.

Poor creature looks destroyed. Turning the mare's head in the stranger's direction, she gave the reluctant animal a sharp kick in the ribs and rode toward him. *I'll bring him in for a cup of* . . .

Her mouth went dry.

The man was not old, and he was not a stranger.

"Papa!"

Chapter Forty-nine

IMMEDIATELY following the North Strand bombing Edouard Hempel, the German minister to Éire, went to the Department of External Affairs on behalf of his legation to discuss the incident. "I suspect the British dropped the bombs themselves to force Éire into the war," he said.[1]

Frank Aiken, who had been appointed as minister for defense by de Valera, already had information on his desk to the effect that the bomb fragments carried German markings. He replied to Hempel politely but noncommittally and sent him away.

Dear Henry,

*Buiochas le Dia,** Ned is home at last. I found him in the road on his way to the farm. It is a great relief that he is alive, though he is very changed. His hair has turned to pure silver. His face is sunburnt almost black, and as deeply lined as crumpled paper. The only features that are familiar are the cleft in his chin and those green, green eyes.

I have put him to bed and am feeding him all he will accept, which is not much at this stage. He is dreadfully thin and weak and suffers from occasional spells of blindness. They do not last long, but they are incapacitating when they occur.

He is very confused. I hope it is only temporary and will clear up when he regains some strength. There appear to be great holes in his memory. He cannot tell me where he has been since the Spanish war

---

*"Thanks be to God."

ended, he does not seem to remember Spain at all. Yet he clearly recalls
things that happened over twenty years ago. As far as he is concerned
the Rising is a recent event. He calls me Precious and does not understand about Barry.

"I don't understand about Barry either," Henry commented as he read
the letter aloud to his family.

"Hush," said Ella. "And go on."

"Well, Cap'n, which is it? Hush or go on?"

She laughed. "Oh you."

Henry read, " 'Síle is still alive to Ned. He calls her name every time a
door opens. His conviction is so total that I expect to hear her quick, light
step in the passage. You cannot imagine how eerie that is.

" 'He also asks for Frank and Norah and Lucy. When I tell him they
have passed away he does not hear me. I am going to bring Eileen out here
to visit as soon as he is a bit stronger. She will be so glad to see him. He
always was her favourite.' "

"Home is the hero, home from the hill," Bella trilled.

"You're misquoting again," said her father. "It's the hunter who's home
from the hill."

"What does that matter, you know what I mean. Isn't it romantic? Ned
fought courageously and was horribly wounded and yet somehow found his
way home to the bosom of his family to recover from his dreadful ordeal."

Henry replied, "I don't think Ned's spells of blindness are the result of
anything that happened in Spain. He took a nasty head wound during the
Rising in 1916 and it's affected him ever since, off and on."

"I wish I was in Ireland," Bella went on, enraptured with her vision. "I
would nurse him back to health myself. I would wear one of those starched
white—"

Her sister interrupted, "You hate sickness and mess, you wouldn't last
five minutes. Great Judas priest, Bella, how can you be so . . ."

"Language!" Ella snapped. "Hank, that sort of language is not used in
polite society."

"Pop-Pop says 'great Judas priest.' And besides, this isn't polite society,
it's Texas."

Henry Mooney spluttered with laughter.

Ella was not amused. "*We* are 'polite society' in Texas, young lady. I ask
you to remember that and behave accordingly. Your father has managed to
regain his position in the business world and your sister will be making her
debut at the Idlewilde Ball this year."

"She's welcome to it," said Hank. "Boring reception lines and wilting gardenias and a lot of sweaty boys stepping all over your feet. When I'm eighteen I'm not going to have a debut. I'm going to join the circus and be a trapeze artist. So there."

In the excitement of Ned's homecoming Ursula managed to keep thoughts of Finbar Cassidy at arm's length. Most of the time. But they were always there. Under the surface. Beneath the joy.

Taking care of Ned was almost like having another child. At first he required almost constant supervision. On days when the clouds hunkered down on the hills and the air was soft with rain, he was easy enough to manage. But when the sun shone he grew desperate and shouted orders to an army of phantasms.

Lucas Mulvaney finally had drunk himself into a permanent stupor and abandoned his family, so Ursula decided to ask Eileen to move back to the farm. She could help look after Ned and the little Mulvaneys would be company for Barry.

"I'm going to have to feed them anyway," Ursula told Ned, "so we might as well have them here."

"Why do you have to feed Eileen?" he asked. "Doesn't Norah do that?"

Ursula patiently explained—one more time—but he did not comprehend. To Ned Halloran, his Aunt Norah was still in the kitchen, cooking meals for the family on the black iron range.

When Ursula extended the invitation Eileen only pretended to think it over. The next morning she arrived at the kitchen door with her brood of unwashed, half-wild youngsters, all barefoot, and their few belongings wrapped up in a bedsheet.

Defeated by life, Eileen had long ago given up trying to teach manners to her children. There were five of them still living, ranging in age from two to seven. Her oldest two had died of tuberculosis, another had died in infancy, and one had been miscarried when Lucas beat his wife. *Thank God*, Ursula thought without a twinge of conscience. *There are quite enough already.*

"Training this lot," she remarked to George Ryan, "is going to be a lot harder than training the roan mare to saddle."

He sniggered. "Gonna use a whip on 'em?"

"I don't use a whip on anything," Ursula said frostily. "Except maybe on hired men who get above themselves."

After the bombing of the North Strand Ursula suffered from a sporadic but graphic nightmare. She was with Síle Halloran, but a very tall Síle, while she herself was small. Hand in hand they were running through a narrow laneway. Suddenly there was a whistle followed by a thunderous roar. The wall beside them exploded into a deadly rain of bricks and mortar.

Ursula always awoke at this point, bathed in sweat.

To everyone's surprise, it was Barry Halloran who had the most influence on Eileen Mulvaney's children. He was smarter and more self-confident than any of them, even the oldest. In no time the little band was looking to Barry for direction. If Barry wanted to play in the orchard, everyone played in the orchard. When Barry was hungry, everyone was hungry.

Throughout the summer Ned spent most of his time in bed. Eileen tended him lovingly, cooking special treats to tempt his appetite, putting cold cloths on his eyes when the blackness overtook him. From her busy schedule Ursula somehow carved out time each evening to sit with him, trying to find topics of conversation that would stimulate him. She shared her newspapers with him, but it was hard to know how much he understood of what he read. Again and again she found herself having to explain recent history. He would listen for a time, then just seem to drift away.

In August Churchill and Roosevelt proclaimed an Atlantic Charter to confirm the alliance of their two nations.

By September the foot-and-mouth crisis in Ireland was over. Britain began buying more Irish beef than ever before.

The *Irish Press* alleged that imported British cattle had brought the disease to Ireland in the first place.

At the Halloran farm three shaggy Irish draft mares slumbered in the autumn sun, up to their fetlocks in lush grass. Come spring, Ursula planned to take them to a stallion in Limerick, a slender, nervous, hot-blooded animal with a career on the racetrack behind him and a proclivity to jump out of paddocks, no matter how high the fence.

"I am a horse breeder now," she wrote to Fliss. "A serious one, hoping to make a living out of the business someday—not like the landed gentry who just play with their horses and do not care how much money they lose."

When she reread the letter she crossed out the last sentence before making a clean copy.

UNDER Archbishop MacQuaid's influence the diminution of the role of women in Irish society, which had begun with the 1937 constitution, accelerated. De Valera had been able to resist the more extreme blandishments of Cardinal McRory, but resisting John Charles McQuaid was a different matter. McQuaid was a close family friend. He and Vivion often went target shooting together—and the priest was the better shot.

He was also a dedicated social reformer who set about imposing his will on the whole of Éire. The highly devout Irish people had, for centuries, been taught to obey their clergy without question, but the new archbishop took that obedience to unprecedented heights. A great admirer of FBI Director J. Edgar Hoover, McQuaid emulated Hoover's technique of controlling through fear. He established a vigilance committee to amass files on politicians and priests, nuns and nurses and teachers and trade unionists and even housewives.

Within a short time Archbishop McQuaid was exercising enormous influence over almost every aspect of Irish life.

7 December 1941
JAPANESE ATTACK PEARL HARBOR

Chapter Fifty

SUDDENLY, violently, America was propelled into what could now truly be described as a global war. In one of his famous "fireside chats," President Roosevelt described America as the arsenal of democracy.

On the twenty-sixth of January, 1942, the first U.S. troops arrived in Belfast. Two weeks later the Northern Ireland military base at Derry was designated as part of the U.S. Atlantic fleet command.[1]

By that time Éire, with her regular army, army air corps, marine service, and local defense forces, had almost a quarter of a million well-disciplined men and women prepared to defend her neutrality. Army battalions sometimes bivouacked in ruined barracks that had been destroyed during the Civil War.

THE German U-boats stalking the Allied merchant fleet were condemned as heartless killers by their prey. But there was no denying the courage of their crews. Trapped below the surface in steel coffins, they endured foul air, intense claustrophobia, and depth charges exploding all around them for as much as twelve hours at a time. Eight out of every ten would be dead by the end of the war.

Neither sea nor air was a safe arena for warriors.

When Ursula mentioned America's entry into the war, Ned shook off some of the mists that enveloped his brain. "I was in the war," he said unexpectedly.

"You were, Papa. Both the Easter Rising and the War of Independence."

"I mean the war in Spain. Frank Ryan took some of us to fight for the Spanish Republic. With the . . ." He struggled for words. "The International Brigades."

"You remember that now?"

"I . . . think so. I know it was very hard. And at the end . . ."

"At the end?"

"They sent us home, those who survived. I must have been raving at that stage, I didn't even know who I was. Somewhere along the way my identification papers went missing. The next thing I remember, I'd been admitted to a hospital in Belfast—a British hospital; ironic, isn't it?—under the name of . . . MacNamee. Eoin MacNamee. I've no idea where the name came from."

Ursula was astounded. "How long were you there?"

"Weeks. Months, maybe. The hospital staff there were very good to me. One in particular. An English doctor with a bald head . . ." He closed his eyes.

Ursula waited. For a few moments Ned seemed to be asleep. Then he said clearly, "A decent Englishman pulled me back from the very brink of hell. He saved my life." He closed his eyes again.

"Dear God," breathed Ursula.

SHE was eager to ask him countless questions, but instinct warned her not to push too hard. He would tell her what he wanted her to know, in his own good time. He always had.

CONGRATULATE me, I am engaged to be married!" Fliss wrote to Ursula. "My timing is rather bad, as the most gorgeous American soldiers are flooding into England these days. You will be interested to learn that a surprising number have Irish surnames, though they speak with an American twang. They are all exotic and glamorous and of course they all swear they are single.

"My fiancé is a pilot in the Royal Air Force, which is glamorous too, especially since he's one of our own. I must be more conservative than I thought. We decided on the spur of the moment, but fortunately my parents approve of him. We plan to marry during his next leave. Is there any chance you could come over for the wedding?"

Ursula wrote back, "I am so happy for you, Fliss. I would come if I could, you know that. But the farm has me very tied down at the moment."

She did not mention Barry. In her letters to Felicity she had never mentioned Barry. She was not ashamed of him, quite the contrary, but as time passed she felt less and less inclined to explain him. She was not sure she could.

Eileen had taken over the cooking, for which Ursula was profoundly grateful, and developed her own domestic schedule. Monday was wash day; clothes and bed linen were boiled in the big coppers in the yard. George Ryan helped hang them on the clotheslines strung between house and barn. On Tuesday Eileen ironed. The house was aired, the rugs were beaten and butter was churned on Wednesday. Bread was baked every Thursday and stored in a large earthenware crock with an airtight lid. The kitchen received detailed attention on Friday; Eileen scrubbed the flagstone floor and blacked and polished the range until it shone. Saturday was general house-cleaning day. Evenings were reserved for sewing and mending, a never-ending chore. Sunday was for attending Mass, often twice in one day. But always without Ursula.

Once her routine was established Eileen never deviated from it. Bit by bit, Ned's baby sister was regaining her self-respect. Her hair was frequently unkempt and she would not even use cold cream on her face, but sometimes she hummed to herself as she bustled about the house.

"Perhaps the home is the right career for a woman," Ursula admitted to her one day. "For some women, I mean. It's wrong to try to force anyone into a box. Every person is unique."

If she needed proof she had only to look at her own son.

One February afternoon, when the light was blue and there was snow in the air, Ursula found Barry atop the mound in Saoirse's field. Standing with his sturdy legs braced far apart, his arms outstretched and his head thrown back. Letting the first snowflakes fall on his upturned face.

She smiled at the picture he made, but that particular hillock was sacrosanct. She called to him to come down at once.

Barry turned toward her. The child was alight from within, blazing with an intensity that made Ursula catch her breath. Fierce and totally adult, his gray eyes seemed to gaze upon her across a sweep of aeons.

He blinked. Laughed. Ran down the slope into her arms and was her little boy again.

HENRY Mooney had once said, "Children carry the history of their forebears like chapters in a book, if one knew how to read them." Ursula tried.

Were Barry's square shoulders inherited from my real father? Is his high-bridged nose my mother's nose?

In the little boy's long, flexible fingers, she recognized her own.

The signature of Barry's father had been obvious from the beginning.

Chapter Fifty-one

O<small>N</small> the sixth of May three million ration books were issued in Éire. On the following day a wireless broadcast by Seán Lemass outlined the details of their use to the nation. These came as a shock. For example, out of a total allowance of fifty-two coupons a year, forty would be required for a man's suit.[1]

The new Liffey hydroelectric scheme had made electricity available to an ever expanding range of households on the east side of the country, but now the Electricity Supply Board announced to its customers, "No Electric Heating! No Extra Electricity for Cooking!"[2]

Dublin traditionally had burned British coal, which was no longer available to the Irish. Gas supplies were severely diminished as well. Therefore turf, formerly despised by urban dwellers, was eagerly sought. The long road that ran through the Phoenix Park was banked on either side with sods of turf for use by the city.

Although Éire had enough food to survive, the nation was suffering from social and intellectual starvation. The stultifying effects of a repressive moral climate spread across the land like a mantle of pollution.

While millions of men and women around the world were dying horrific deaths, John Charles McQuaid was preoccupied with defending what he saw as the one true church. Efforts by organizations such as the Mercier Society to educate the people of Éire about other faiths were sternly dealt with by the archbishop.[3] High-minded sermons and savage condemnations were issued from the pulpit almost in the same breath.

"I was raised to be devout," Ursula wrote to Henry, "but I have come around to your way of looking at things. Ireland broke away from an oppressive Protestant empire only to install a repressive Catholic dictatorship. While I still believe in God, I now have more faith in the authority of experience than in the experience of authority."

In the straightened era of Archbishop McQuaid, clerics went striding across the fields, beating the tall grass to flush out courting couples. Priests marched onto dance floors to thrust a metal ruler between dancing couples to be certain that at least twelve inches separated their bodies, preventing any lustful stimulation.

Readers of the *Evening Press* were regaled with terrifying accounts of demons materializing amid clouds of sulphur. One priest claimed his hair turned white overnight after confronting the devil himself on some dance floor. A girl reputedly fainted after looking down and seeing that her partner had cloven hooves.

Disgusted, Ursula threw down the newspaper that had printed the story as fact. "It's not like this in other countries, Papa. We've become freaks; not people but terrified sheep."

"What do you know about other countries, Precious?"

"I've told you before, I went to school in Switzerland and—"

"Henry paid for it," Ned said.

She froze, waiting for an outburst that did not come.

"I'll thank him next time I see him," said Ned.

Ursula breathed a sigh of relief. "You won't see Henry again, Papa. He lives in America now."

NED was getting stronger. In late summer he ventured out into the yard and sat for hours on a stool beside the door. Unless the sun shone on him, in which case he went back inside.

Information seeped out of him in tiny droplets. Ursula learned that he had checked himself out of the Belfast hospital without permission as soon as he felt strong enough, and slowly, painfully made his way back to Clare using the old IRA network, or what remained of it.

"I left without thanking the doctor who saved me," he said with regret. "But I think about him. I think about him a lot."

"You could write to him, I suppose."

Ned gave a hollow laugh. "And sign the letter how? Eoin MacNamee? I think not, Precious. Best leave it alone. It could be dangerous to call attention to myself."

"But you have nothing to do with the IRA anymore."

He gave a snort. "Don't be daft. I'll be one of the Boys until I die."

"You can't be serious. Papa, your eyesight..."

"Sure I know I can never fire a rifle again. I wouldn't want to anyway. How could I shoot the British after one of them saved my life? I'm not that much of a bastard. But our lads will keep on fighting in whatever way they can until we have the Irish Republic, all thirty-two counties of it. And there are ways I can still help."

"What do you mean?"

The shutters came down. "Let's just say my experience is valuable. I know names, locations, who did what, who to trust...when I'm a bit stronger again I'll be useful. You'll see." His cleft chin jutted forward in a way Ursula recognized of old.

"Ned's stubborn look," the family called it.

Barry had taken a strong liking to Ned. Now when her son went missing Ursula usually found the pair together. There were times when Ned was still vague and unsure about Barry's identity, but on his better days he enthralled the little boy with war stories. Occasionally Ursula drifted close enough to overhear without being obvious. Some of Ned's tales were so wild he surely must be inventing them. But others sounded like they were from his own experience.

"Papa remembers more than he's willing to let on," Ursula remarked to Eileen.

"He always did keep himself to himself. And no harm either," Eileen added. "If I'd done that I'd be better off today."

Ursula could not help laughing, especially since Eileen was laughing too. A hint of her youthful beauty crept back into her careworn face.

"I think there's a curling tongs around here somewhere," Ursula volunteered. "I saw it when we were going through poor Norah's possessions. If I can find it, would you like to use it?"

In adulthood the two women had become friends. Eileen passed no remarks about the paternity of Barry; she could hardly afford to, with her own history.

By the autumn of 1942 Hitler's offensive against Stalingrad had developed into a brutal war of attrition. Twenty-two German divisions were being hurled at the Russians. Stalingrad no longer even resembled a city, but a monstrous cloud of burning, choking smoke.

•   •   •

IN Clare the autumn was crisp and frosty, painted in shafts of slanting, golden light. As the days grew shorter, Ned Halloran's energy level rose. One afternoon without telling anyone he sauntered into Clarecastle.

Ursula frantically searched for him. Barry watched for a while with his head cocked to one side, then volunteered, "Granda said he wuz firsty."

"Thirsty? Gerry, would you ever go down to the pub and bring him home? You can put my saddle on the roan mare, I think she'll carry double now."

Gerry was dismayed. "Ride her, you mean? I've never ridden a horse in my life."

Ursula rolled her eyes skyward. "Hitch her to the wagonette, then. But hurry. It's been a while since he had strong drink and who can say what it might do to him."

Within a couple of hours the two men returned together—both laughing. In Ned's cheeks there was a healthy flush of color not entirely dependent on alcohol. But the next day he stayed in bed, complaining of a headache.

ACROSS Eastern Europe drifted the smell of blood and broken dreams. The winter was bitter . . . but the thaw was on the way.

In January, the German forces besieging Stalingrad surrendered. Against impossible odds, the valiant Russians had held their city.

At the end of the month the Allies captured Tripoli, the last remaining Italian-held city of Mussolini's "New Roman Empire." Elsewhere his increasingly demoralized Blackshirts were fighting Italian partisans whom they called rebels and summarily shot when they captured them. Fellow countrymen.

Italy had descended into civil war.

EAMON de Valera delivered his customary radio broadcast on St. Patrick's Day. In the parlor of the Halloran farm everyone listened as he said, "Acutely conscious though we all are of the misery and desolation in which the greater part of the world is plunged, let us turn aside for a moment to that ideal Ireland that we would have. That Ireland, which we dreamed of, would be the home of a people who valued material wealth only as the basis of right living, of a people who were satisfied with frugal comfort and devoted their leisure to things of the spirit; a land whose countryside would be bright with cozy homesteads, whose fields and villages would be joyous with the sounds of industry, with the romping of sturdy children, the contests of athletic youths, the laughter of happy maidens, whose firesides would be forums for the wisdom of serene old age.

"It was the idea of such an Ireland, happy, vigorous, spiritual, that fired the imagination of our poets; that made successive generations of patriotic men give their lives to win religious and political liberty, and that will urge men in our own and future generations to die if need be, so that these liberties may be preserved."[4]

Ursula cut out a copy of the speech as it appeared in the *Irish Times* and sent it to Henry. He replied, "Frugal comfort indeed. That's just like de Valera, mouthing pious platitudes about the traditions of an impoverished people to persuade them it's good to be poor."

BARRY was getting old enough to notice that Ned and Eileen went to Mass but his mother did not. "Won't God let us come to his house?" he asked Ursula one day.

Ursula wrote to Henry Mooney, "I have decided to raise Barry as an Irish Catholic. When he is old enough he can make his own decisions about religion, but until then I want him to have the spiritual security I once felt. Perhaps I am mellowing, Henry."

From then on she attended Mass every Sunday, sitting in the pew with Ned on one side and Barry on the other. Eventually the most self-righteous members of the congregation stopped glaring at her. She was so indifferent to them that they were forced to fold up their hostility and put it away like an out-of-season garment, awaiting a more vulnerable victim.

ON June 22 a general election was held. Eight gallons of petrol were allocated to each candidate nominated for a constituency. Once again Fianna Fáil emerged as the largest party. Yet with only sixty-seven seats it lacked a clear majority. Although the Fine Gael representation was also reduced, a number of new parties were emerging and fighting hard.

Eamon de Valera remained as taoiseach, but the political future looked increasingly unstable.

SUMMER was the jewel of the year. Ancient, turbulent Ireland glowed in her mantle of green, crowned by the passionless stars.

Sometimes at night, when the children were asleep and Eileen was tidying up the kitchen and Ned had gone to his room, Ursula slipped out of the house to walk across the land. Just walk. From field to field. Pausing in the night to say a reassuring word to the drowsing cows; to stroke the nose of one of the horses—they all came to her when she approached—or merely standing still, breathing in.

I'VE had a letter from Louise," Ursula told Ned. "Hector's died of a bleeding ulcer. I didn't even know he had an ulcer."

"Hector who?"

"Hamilton. The man who married Louise. Barry and I will have to go up to Dublin for the funeral."

"Will Henry be there?" Ned inquired. Ursula noticed tension in his shoulders.

She said gently, "Henry won't be there, Papa. He's in America, remember?"

It might be her imagination, but it seemed that Ned's shoulders slumped in disappointment.

Wartime Dublin was every bit as grim as Ursula expected. Blackout curtains covered windows. Consumer goods of every description were in short supply. Department stores were advertising "men's utility suits," but they cleverly skimped on fabric by having fewer pockets. They still cost more coupons than most people could afford.

A few of the better butcher shops had signs in the windows that read WE WILL POST MEAT TO YOUR FRIENDS IN ENGLAND AND NORTHERN IRELAND.

Coffee was unobtainable at any price. Instead of butter, housewives were offered block margarine with a little packet of orange stain that turned it an unlikely shade of yellow. The result had the taste and texture of axle grease.

Sugar was currently the most elusive commodity.

One of Ursula's early improvements at the farm had been to install beehives in the orchard. She harvested their golden crop herself. At first she wore a long coat, heavy gloves and a veiled hat, but she soon discovered she could work with the bees barehanded. Gerry Ryan said he had never seen anyone with such a gift.

In her suitcase Ursula had six jars of honey for Louise Hamilton.

For the funeral she had brought her only black dress, the one from Geneva. It hung loose on her now. When she belted it around her waist the fabric bunched into pleats, but it would have to do.

Real silk stockings were only a memory. Small quantities of artificial silk were available if one had enough money and ration coupons, and time to search from shop to shop. Rumors were circulating about a miracle fabric called nylon, but it was not expected until after the war. Whenever that might be.

On the morning of the funeral Ursula did what most women were doing: she painted her legs with Miner's Liquid Stockings from Clerys' Department Store, and drew on seams with an eyebrow pencil.

Hector's funeral was a sober event. Louise was on the verge of tears but never quite let herself go. The other mourners held their grief in check. There was none of the pure, wild, quintessentially Irish keening Ursula had once heard in Clare.

No one would ever keen like that again.

The passions that had exploded into the Civil War had left scars on the Irish people. The children of those who had fought in the war were being taught to clamp down on their emotions, smother them, keep them tightly within bounds.

They must never forget that strong passions had cost Irish lives.

Yet the bitterness of the War of Brothers was not expunged. It was nursed in silence like some dark and poisonous fungus.

THE day after the funeral, Ursula told Louise, "I think Barry should see something of the city while we're here. Do you mind?"

"I don't mind. Just be sure you're back here for your tea."

Louise hated seeing them leave the house. The shadows in the corners were very cold and dark.

What Ursula had in mind was not a sightseeing venture. She took Barry directly to the North Strand. She had to see it for herself.

Although it had been two years since the air raid, a gaping crater remained in the street where a large object, eventually identified as a land mine, had fallen. The rubble had long since been cleared away but the destroyed houses were not being rebuilt. There were no building materials available.

Ragged urchins and mongrel dogs played on the savaged earth.

Ursula did not know where Finbar's house had stood. Redbrick; terraced. There. Or perhaps over there. *One of these blank spaces contained his walls and his roof. Sheltered that kind and gentle man. Please God it brought him happiness!*

She reached down and picked up an indignant Barry, who considered himself too old to be carried anymore. Ursula did not feel his weight. It was his living warmth she needed.

Time rushes on like a river in flood, speeding past treasures on the riverbank

*that we barely glimpse. We try to savor them in retrospect. We try to recapture
them in memory. But it's too late.*

It's too late.

IN the nearest shop she bought a sheet of toffee that came with a little
hammer. While Barry amused himself cracking the confection into bite-
sized pieces, Ursula spoke to the shopkeeper, a beefy, florid man with tufts
of ginger hair sticking out of his ears.

"Did you know Finbar Cassidy?" she asked. "I understand he used to
live in one of those houses over there."

The man gave a cryptic nod that could mean everything or nothing.

Ursula softened her voice; gave him one of her smiles. "Finbar and I
were . . . great friends, at one time." It was as much of an admission of
intimacy as any Irish woman could make; barter to elicit a response.

"I knew Cassidy. Nice lad."

"Were you here when the bombs fell?"

He nodded again. "We live over the shop. Heard it all. Saw it all too.
Bits of people blown about. The wife nearly lost her mind at what we saw.
Them damned Brits."

"The Luftwaffe bombed us, not the British," she corrected him.

"That what you think, is it?" He squinted at her over the counter. "I'll
tell you somethin' for nothin'. Everyone around here knows it." He tapped
the side of his nose with a finger as thick as a sausage. "We don't say nothin'
but we know.

"Them Nazis use radio beams to guide their planes. The Brits has learned
how to bend radio beams, and they bent the German beams so the Nazis
flew over Ireland instead of England and dropped their eggs on us. Killed
your Finbar, so they did. Killed a lot of us. Quicker'n'Cromwell."

Ursula felt violently sick. *It can't be true. Such a thing isn't possible.*

She grabbed her son and fled.

URSULA postponed her return to the farm for a few days. She told Louise
she wanted to visit some old friends. Leaving Barry at number 16, she went
first to the broadcasting station. Former colleagues were glad to see her and
she spent a pleasant hour reminiscing, but left no wiser about the North
Strand bombing. Everyone had heard the rumors; no one knew the facts.
All agreed, however: if there was any truth to the rumors then someone in
government must surely know.

Ursula spent the next day going from one government office to another, asking questions. She had no hesitation about using Seán Lester's name, intimating that she in some way was still acting on behalf of the League.

"The issue will require more investigation to avoid making unwarranted assertions," she was told at one department.

"Although we have the facts to hand we are not able to release them at this time," she was told by another.

Only one man went so far as to say, "A source claims the North Strand was bombed by a German who was lost and thought he was over Manchester."

"Has that been confirmed?"

"Confirmation of any sort is very difficult to obtain in wartime, Miss Halloran. But rest assured all possible steps are being taken. We are very mindful of our responsibilities to the people. In fact, if you examine the record of this government . . ."

On the following morning Ursula and Barry called on Elsie Lester. Ursula angrily related her experiences with government officialdom. "Do you know what I resent most?" she fumed. "The uglification of the language by a pox of politicians! De Valera's people babble out of both sides of their mouths at the same time but say nothing, they're totally unable to communicate. No one in authority will make a direct statement that might get him into trouble with either Germany *or* Britain. If nothing else, at least W.T. Cosgrave was a straight talker."

Elsie was sympathetic. "You said a close friend of yours was killed in the North Strand, so I can understand your frustration. If I were you I would want to know what happened too. But sometimes we simply have to let things go, Ursula."

I wish it were that easy.

Over tea and scones Elsie told her guests, "Seán's still in Geneva, but he's not very hopeful about the future. Although most of the staff at the secretariat is Swiss now, the Swiss government is keeping itself well clear of the League. Everyone agrees it's a moribund organization. I wish we knew where it all went wrong."

At last Ursula had to admit defeat. *"Sin é,"** she told Louise. "We're going home."

"Could you not stop for just a few days longer?" the old woman pleaded.

*"That's it."

"Yourself and the little fellow?" When Ursula and Barry left the life would go out of the house. The silence, like a reproach, would close on her and swallow her, and she was afraid.

Ursula read the fear in her eyes. "I'm afraid not, Louise. I have Barry and the farm, you see, and I must get on with things. You should too."

Louise gave a tremulous smile. "I will, don't worry."

They both knew it was a lie.

I'll find out what happened to the North Strand, Ursula promised herself on the train ride back to Clare. *I will find out. Someday. I owe it to him.*

Chapter Fifty-two

As it became increasingly apparent that America's entry into the war would bring about the final downfall of Germany, Irish cooperation with Britain in intelligence-gathering increased.

In spite of this Winston Churchill worked ceaselessly to drive a wedge between Washington and Dublin. One result was that the Americans requested de Valera to expel the German diplomatic legation from Ireland.[1] Minister Hempel and his family had been in Éire for years and had a number of friends in Dublin, where the children were attending school.

Precariously balanced on the tightrope of neutrality, which Hempel officially had recognized on behalf of the government of the Reich[2], de Valera refused to send any of them back in to the war.

By the autumn Barry's education was very much on Ursula's mind. With the exception of the youngest, Eileen's children were enrolled in the local National School. None of them had any academic ambitions. Like many children in rural Ireland they would leave school at twelve and never look back.

"I wish St. Enda's was still in operation," Ursula remarked to Ned one evening while she was fiddling with the radio dials and waiting for the news, "so Barry could have the education you did."

At the mention of St. Enda's a smile played over Ned's lips. "Do you mean courses designed to create well-rounded Irish men rather than imitation English men?"

"That's exactly what I want for Barry, Papa. He won't get it in the National School, though. They're still teaching English history as if Ireland never existed. And I'm reluctant to send him to the Christian Brothers because I've heard they can be very cruel. I can't bear the idea of having an education beaten into Barry. Mr. Pearse never hit you, or anyone."

"He did not," Ned agreed. "He made sure we enjoyed learning. His ideas were considered very radical but we boys who were lucky enough to attend his school positively devoured our studies." Ned's voice came alive with remembered enthusiasm. "After Mr. Pearse was executed his mother struggled to keep the school going but it wasn't the same without him. It finally closed in 1935."

A sudden idea seized Ursula. Pearse and St. Enda's were dead and gone—yet might they provide the doorway to bring Ned all the way back?

"Will you tutor Barry, Papa?" she asked. "Will you teach my son as you were taught?"

As Ned started to answer, static crackled and the newsreader's voice came on. Ursula hastily switched off the machine. "What did you say, Papa?"

"Barry. Your son. What about his father? Has he no interest in the boy's education?"

"He's not involved. He never will be."

Ned nodded to himself. *"Mar sin,"** he said. He sat quietly for a time, then cleared his throat. "Our Precious with a son of her own." He smiled again. "What does Síle think?"

"I . . . I'm sure she's pleased, Papa."

"If Síle wants me to, I'll teach Barry."

In the kitchen Ursula told Eileen, "Papa says he'll teach Barry himself. If Síle gives permission."

Eileen shook her head. "God love him. He'll never accept her death, will he? You'd best send your lad to the National School with mine."

The freight handler from the train station arrived at the farmhouse on his bicycle. "Ursula Halloran?"

"I am Ursula Halloran."

"We have a heavy parcel for you down to the station. Can you send a wagon for it?"

Gerry hitched up the roan mare and drove into town. He returned with a large, extremely battered box sent by *S. Lester, League of Nations Headquarters, Switzerland.* When she opened the box, Ursula found the precious

*"It's like that; thus."

books she had left behind in Geneva. Including Ned's textbooks from St. Enda's.

The hairs rose on the nape of her neck.

While Gerry carried the box up to her room she ran into the kitchen. "Eileen, you'll never believe what's after happening! Somehow Síle's sent Ned's old textbooks home so he can use them to teach Barry."

Eileen turned from the range and stared at her. "I don't believe it!"

"Funnily enough, I do."

THE Italian people had lost faith in their dictator. Mussolini, his inflated ambitions and his comic-opera army were swept away by the resistance movement. Il Duce was arrested and a new government set up to negotiate an armistice with the Allies.

In October 1943 Italy declared war on Germany.

BARRY was delighted with his lessons. Every morning as soon as he finished breakfast, he ran to his room and brought back his slate and box of chalks. While Ursula went out to tend the horses—her favorite part of the farmwork—two heads, silver and red-gold, bent over the books on the kitchen table.

Eileen's children begged to be allowed the same privilege.

"You'll have to work," Ned warned them. "No skiving off, hear?"

They all promised. And they all tried, though none with the enthusiasm of Barry.

At first Ned was short-tempered with the rowdy young Mulvaneys. As the weeks passed, however, by using Pádraic Pearse as a model he rediscovered a long-lost gentleness in himself.

When Ned found it difficult to deal with Eileen's children he summoned his memories of Pearse. Lowered his voice, smiled even if he did not feel like smiling. Repeated the lesson with infinite patience until it was understood. And always rewarded success with a bit of fun, a joke or a game or best of all, an hour's storytelling.

Somewhere along the way the edgy, irritable soldier Ned Halloran had become was replaced by a different man.

Ned did not allow his blind spells to interrupt the children's education. If he could not read the textbooks he quoted reams of material from memory, or assigned his students such tasks such as building a model windmill to demonstrate the principle of hydraulics.

When Ursula objected that they were too young, Ned disagreed. "Never underestimate how much a child can learn, Precious. Young brains are like blotting paper. Barry may not fully understand but he will take it in, and the knowledge will be there for him if he ever needs it."

"You would have made a wonderful teacher if you'd chosen to go that way," Ursula said.

"Perhaps. But what I really wanted was to be a writer."

"What became of that novel you were always going to write?"

"Och, it's up here." Ned tapped his skull with his fingers. "Some of it. Most of it's on paper. It isn't exactly a novel, though. More of a . . . memoir. History as I saw it."

"Does this book of yours include the war stories you tell Barry?"

"Still earwigging, are you? Well, they're part of it, but only one part. I've seen much more, Precious." A sly glint crept into his eyes. "I know secrets some would pay a fortune for; others would kill me to keep me from telling."

A chill ran up Ursula's spine. "What secrets, Papa?"

"They'll be in the book when it's published some day. It's important that people know."

"Are you certain? If telling could threaten your life . . ."

Ned adopted what Ursula thought of as his "professorial voice." "Think of the present as a thin film spread over a deep lake," he said. "The lake is composed of all the events that took place in the past. Our society, our economy, our politics, our culture—everything we are and have was created in the past. Today is only the end result. We're floating on top of history, we're created and supported by history. To be ignorant of history is to be ignorant of ourselves."

Week by week, month by month, Ned Halloran was coming back. Returning to himself. Working with the children relit the lamps in his mind. It was a cause for celebration when he essayed his first small joke in years.

One afternoon Ned sent Gerry Ryan to fetch a coat that he had left in the farmyard. When the hired man returned with the coat Ned said, *"Go raibh maith agat, Gearóid."* Here, have a drink on me." He tucked something into Gerry's pocket.

Thinking it was money, Gerry waited until he got to the pub in Clarecastle that night. He ordered his usual two pints. When the time came to

---

*"Thank you, Gerry."

pay, he took from his pocket . . . a desiccated tea bag from Ned's army back-pack.

An inventory of the pack's contents would almost constitute an inventory of Ned's adulthood. At the very bottom was a japanned black box with a lock. He wore the key on a thin cord around his neck.

EARLY in 1944 there was an American demand for the immediate removal of both the German and Japanese diplomatic legations from Ireland. The message was delivered to de Valera's office not by an American, but by the British representative in Ireland, a man who did not hold ambassadorial rank because Churchill refused to appoint an ambassador to what he still considered one of Britain's dominions.

De Valera made no immediate response to what was called "the American note." However, Robert Brennan, the Irish ambassador in Washington, did call on the U.S. State Department. He said he personally interpreted the note as an ultimatum, and feared that if the Irish government refused, Éire would be invaded by American forces.

The State Department vehemently denied there were any plans whatsoever to invade neutral Ireland.

In March de Valera sent a curt official refusal to the American request. Afterward, as Elsie Lester wrote to Ursula, Brennan quietly visited the State Department again. He stated that Éire was prepared to give prompt cooperation to any security safeguards the Allies wanted to take. He stressed that American officers who had visited Ireland the preceding year had expressed satisfaction with the measures already taken there.[3]

Publicly de Valera had stood firm against American demands. Privately he had made the necessary accommodations. Throughout the war he would continue to give unstinting aid to the Allies without ever allowing his actions to be made public.

WHEN Ursula read Elsie's letter to Ned, he asked, "What are your feelings about Dev?"

"Ambivalent. I despise him for putting women back in a box, for giving the Church so much power, and most of all for turning his back on the Republicans who put him where he is. Yet I admire his political adroitness. In spite of tremendous pressure from all sides he's kept us out of a war that would destroy this country. That takes a lot of courage."

"Och, Dev's not lacking in courage. Many people's lives are monuments to the cowardice of indecision, but not his. He always knows exactly what he's doing and is prepared to act on it."

"That's a quality you share with him, Papa."

"Do I?" Ned sounded genuinely curious, as if asking her to remember the self that he had forgotten.

"Your certainty is one of the things I most admire," she told him. "I envy you, knowing exactly who to love and who to hate."

"*Whom* to love," Ned corrected absentmindedly. "And a soldier should never hate because it affects his judgment. Remember Pearse's essay 'The Murder Machine'? He was writing about an educational system that cripples young minds. Well, a soldier who kills out of hatred is nothing more than a murder machine."

"Don't you hate anyone, Papa?"

He shook his head. "Not since I was in hospital in Belfast."

She would not mention the man who killed Síle; she was careful never to mention Síle to Ned. But there was an opportunity here.

"You don't even hate Henry?" Ursula asked carefully.

He gave her a quick, penetrating look. "Are you trying to manipulate me, Precious?"

Six hundred IRA internees on the Curragh were not alone in their incarceration. As a result of various plane crashes and forced landings, three hundred foreign airmen were also held there—both Germans and members of the RAF. Periodically the British government sent stiff demands for the release of the latter.

The de Valera government ignored them.

Ned was amused. "Dev may have been born in America, but he has the Irish character down pat," he said to Ursula. "If there's a problem, simply refuse to address it. Sooner or later it will go away. If it doesn't, try evasion, and if all else fails, a whopping big lie." He grinned. "Thanks be to God we're a creative race."

"I hope you're not teaching my son that philosophy."

Ned's grin deepened. "I won't have to teach him."

In response to de Valera's refusal to expel the German diplomats, the British government closed the border between Éire and Northern Ireland. Telephone services to Éire were withdrawn, the export to Éire of British newspapers was banned, and it was announced that London would censor all diplomatic bags bound for Éire.[4]

ÉIRE remained inward looking, obsessed with its own affairs. Domestic events dominated the headlines. ELECTRICITY SUPPLY BOARD ANNOUNCES FURTHER CUTS. RADIO ÉIREANN PROGRAMMES CURTAILED TO SAVE POWER. BALLINASLOE GROUP DISCUSSES FOUNDING ALL-IRELAND SHOWJUMPING ORGANISATION.

The last particularly interested Ursula Halloran.

IN early summer, Allied troops, including members of the Irish Guards, launched a breakout offensive at Anzio and formed a single Allied front stretching right across Italy. Sweeping aside German resistance in bloody hand-to-hand fighting, they entered Rome on the fourth of June.

HOLY CITY LIBERATED BY ALLIES! announced the Irish newspapers.

On the sixth of June banner headlines proclaimed, ALLIED TROOPS STORM ASHORE AT NORMANDY!

Nine days later America began the long-expected air offensive against the heartland of Japan.

The wireless crackled with excitement. 2RN brought in experts on air power to discuss America's campaign in the Pacific theater.

"The Pacific theater," Eileen remarked at the breakfast table. "Doesn't that sound exotic and far away?"

Ned reached for a piece of toasted bread. "It is far away. Are we out of marmalade?"

"There've been no oranges in years. You know that."

"Honey, then." He spread the golden syrup liberally on his toast and retired back behind his newspaper. "Damned war," he was heard to mutter. "A man needs marmalade."

"Isn't it strange," Elsie Lester wrote to Ursula, "the way everything comes down to the personal in the end? Millions have died and Europe lies in ruins, yet when I heard that the American army had smashed through the German lines, my first thought was for Seán. The war will soon be over. He will be able to come home.

"The League of Nations exists in name only now. Without the support of the great powers it is nothing. America has no interest and the Russians will never forgive their expulsion from the League in 1939. As Seán once predicted, a new organisation will be needed when the war finally ends. That is why he is hanging on in Geneva: to preserve the League's archives so they can be of use to whatever follows it."

Ursula read the letter to Ned. When she finished he commented, "You sound wistful, Precious."

"Perhaps I am. Part of me would love to be in Geneva with Seán Lester, waiting to see what will be born out of all this. Something like the League of Nations is desperately needed, but it must be given teeth."

Ned nodded. "You mean military might. That's what it always comes down to. Men can make as many pretty speeches as they like, talking about universal brotherhood and common decency, but in the finish-up it's the big brother with the hard fists who protects the little brother from the bullies."

"You're talking about the IRA now. And the north."

Ned gave a weary sigh. "I'm afraid the IRA's all but destroyed. Thanks to Dev, mostly."

"You don't sound very bitter," she noted with surprise.

"I told you, I don't hate anyone. Do you remember when the British hanged those two IRA men in 1940? I happen to know that Dev made personal appeals to both Eden and Chamberlain to spare their lives. He said the reprieve of the men would be an act of generosity a thousand times more valuable to Britain than anything that might be gained by killing them."[5]

Ursula said hotly, "Yet he's sanctioned the executions of Republicans himself!"

"Sometimes morality depends on circumstance, Precious. I've spent a lot of time in the north and I got to know some of the Unionists up there. Talked to them. *Listened* to them.

"Northern Protestants always viewed the British Isles as one great empire, social, cultural, and economic, in whose magnificence they shared. When Ireland opted out of the empire they were reduced to a minority enclave in the corner of a small island on the far edge of Europe. It frightened the life out of them, Precious; made them feel the way the Jews in the Warsaw ghetto must have felt. Doomed and desperate.

"The Unionists' fear has skewed their version of morality. It's driven them to do things that God-fearing men should never think of doing. That doesn't make it right, but it is understandable."

"I never thought I'd hear you saying such a thing, Papa."

His lips quirked. "If you live long enough, you'll hear yourself saying things you never thought you'd say."

.   .   .

LATER , long after she had gone to bed, Ursula found herself wondering, *How did he know about de Valera's personal appeal to Eden and Chamberlain? That wasn't in the newspapers.*

Chapter Fifty-three

On the twenty-fifth of August, 1944, French tanks led the Allies into Paris. A wildly ecstatic greeting awaited General Charles de Gaulle when he arrived in the city that evening. A towering figure as striking as Eamon de Valera, de Gaulle was reported as saying, "I wish simply and from the bottom of my heart to say, *Vive Paris*."

After that it seemed that almost every day another city was taken by the Allies. The German response was vicious. When an uprising was threatened by the Polish resistance movement, Nazi tanks razed the beautiful old city of Warsaw.

"I wonder if there is anything left of the Europe I remember," Ursula said to Eileen.

Up to her elbows in dishwater, Eileen glanced around at her own small kingdom. "Probably not," she said complacently. "But sure, you have this."

Foals in the field and calves in the pen. A blizzard of butterflies on an August morning.

I have everything I could possibly want.
Everything.
Of course I do.

Henry's despair leaped off the pages of his letter.

Dear Ursula,
We are heartbroken. After the latest in a long series of arguments with her mother about everything from her refusal to complete her edu-

cation to the amount of makeup she wears, our Bella has run off. As you can imagine, my dear wife is frantic.

For several years Bella has been corresponding with a young man she met in Saratoga Springs. His name is Michael Kavanagh and his father is employed by Paul and Kathleen O'Shaughnessy. I immediately telephoned them. Kathleen is in poor health, I am sorry to say, but Paul confirmed that the boy also had gone missing.

Young Kavanagh comes from a family of lifelong Fenians, which is why Kathleen hired his father in the first place. Ned's sister always supported the republican cause. But the young lad has got himself involved with the most extreme element of Irish-America. They are raising money to buy illegal arms for the IRA and agitating to "kick the Brits" out of Ireland. Britain is America's ally in the war, so the government here could consider these activities tantamount to treason.

Ursula, I don't want my lovely daughter charged with treason! She will be twenty-one this autumn and is technically free to do whatever she wants, but if she is with this boy—and both Ella and I fear the worst—anything could happen.

We do not want to bring the police into it for obvious reasons. With Paul's help, I have employed private detectives in New York to search for Bella and the young man. Unfortunately the war means that even the best detective firms are shorthanded. They have not been successful in locating either of them. I am at the end of my tether, I don't mind admitting.

I don't know how Ned feels about me now—probably he still hates me—but he is almost my last resource. He always was plugged into a wide network. Would you explain our problem and ask him if he can possibly find out anything for us? Not for myself, you understand, but for an innocent girl who needs his protection.

Ursula approached Ned with trepidation. He read Henry's letter impassively. Once he looked up. "So Kathleen finally married Paul," he said. "Good." When he finished reading he handed the letter back to Ursula. "And Henry has a daughter."

"He does, Papa. Two, in fact. I met Bella when they were still here in Ireland. She was a beautiful little girl and I expect she's a beautiful young woman."

"Who has run away with some man."

"So it appears." Ursula was watching Ned carefully. His face and voice gave away nothing, but his eyes began to take on a distant stare. "Papa? Is one of your spells coming on? Can you see me?"

"I can see Síle," Ned replied disconcertingly. "She ran away with a man once. Not me; long before me. If someone had intervened in time, perhaps she ..." He fell silent. Ursula waited.

Ned's fingers plucked at the knees of his trousers. "What did you say the boy's name was?"

"Michael Kavanagh. His father works for ..."

"My sister Kathleen. I know." Ned heaved a deep sigh. "Leave it with me."

"How will you ..."

"Leave it with me!" he roared. It was the first time since his return that he had showed any sign of temper.

The anger was still there, then. Simmering under the skin.

H ENRY Mooney opened Ursula's letter with trembling fingers. "I put your case to Ned," she had written.

> I cannot say if he will help or not, or even if he can help. You know how he is: secretive in the extreme. But he seemed touched by Bella's situation.
>
> He has told me that the IRA is all but destroyed. That "all but" is important. Obviously the IRA still has strong supporters in America and may yet be revitalised, because the situation in the north is as bad as ever. I am certain Ned knows a great deal about what is going on up there. He may also have connections in the States who would be willing to help find Michael Kavanagh. We can only wait and see. It would be counter-productive to push him, you know how stubborn he is.
>
> Last year I bought a bicycle for the farm. From time to time Ned takes it and peddles off for the day. When I ask him where he is going he either does not answer, or tells some vague story he knows I cannot verify. What can one do? My worry is that he might have a spell of blindness while he's on the bicycle.

Ella clasped her hands together. "Oh, Henry, is there any chance Ned's friends here can find Bella?"

"Don't get your hopes up, Cap'n. America's a huge country, and if some-one doesn't want to be found it's almost impossible to find them. That said, the Irish Republican network is very, very wide."

.   .   .

AT the end of August the Russian army captured the oil fields of Ploesti, depriving Germany of a third of her oil supplies, and swept on toward Bucharest.

A few evenings later, the newsreader on the wireless had a tone in his voice Ursula had never heard before. "We are informed that evidence of unsuspected Nazi atrocities has just come to light in Poland. Russian officers entering the Maidenek concentration camp have learnt that an estimated one and a half million internees were murdered there under conditions of what is termed 'clinical efficiency.' The bodies were stripped and burnt. Clothing and valuables were sent to Germany while the ashes were used . . ." His voice broke. "While the ashes were used as fertilizer."

Ned and Ursula stared at one another aghast. Suddenly the farmhouse parlor was too dark; the paraffin lamps could not assuage the gloom. Eileen was singing to herself in the kitchen but they did not hear her.

September, October. Nazi armies were on the run throughout Europe. Field Marshall Erwin Rommel committed suicide.

General Douglas MacArthur triumphantly waded ashore in the Philippines, saying "I have returned."

Harvest time. Saving the hay. Children studying at the kitchen table.

The spring foals were growing almost visibly. They had inherited the temperament of their Irish draft mothers, but lacked the athleticism of their racehorse sire. Plodding and good-natured, they did not measure up to the memory of Saoirse.

"I was hoping for reliable field hunters that could also do a bit of show jumping," Ursula told Gerry. "Once the war is over there'll be a good market for them again. I'm going to put our mares to a different stallion next year—and perhaps buy a couple more mares as well."

"We don't have enough pasture," Gerry warned. "Besides, I thought you was going to sell horses, not buy more."

"Only the colts. We'll keep the fillies to breed from."

"I'm after telling you there's not enough grass. We have dairy cows to feed, remember?"

"The holding across the road has been lying vacant for years," Ursula said. "It's only eight acres, but eight good acres. I always did think their grass was better than ours." Her eyes sparkled. "I'll have another little chat with my bank manager."

The bank manager had been one of those who scoffed when Ursula bought the first brood mares. "You'll find that horses are an expensive hobby, Miss Halloran. We don't eat horse meat in this country."

Yet he could not deny that the farm was prospering. Ursula planned every step carefully. No corner of the land was unproductive. On dry, stony soil at the far end of the highest field she had even planted a variety of herbs, which she gathered and dried and sold in bunches at the market. They were prized by local women who used them for homemade medicaments. The preceding year Ursula had borrowed enough money from the bank to reroof the house and install an indoor toilet. Within ninety days she had repaid the loan.

When other farmers came to him with excuses instead of repayments, complaining that the land would no longer provide a living, the banker invariably suggested they have a talk with Ursula Halloran. None of them did, of course. She was only a woman.

But if she was ready to expand her operations, he was willing to help.

Late in November Elsie Lester wrote to Ursula: "My husband feels that recent developments have vindicated him. As you know, there has been a four-power meeting in Washington, D.C., to discuss creating an organisation to insure worldwide security after the war."

"How would I know?" Ursula muttered to herself. "There's been nothing on the wireless or in the papers. We might as well be on another planet."

The letter went on. "Such an organisation will find the experience of the League of Nations invaluable. This is what Seán has been waiting and hoping for. The new body will be called the United Nations, with a special Security Council composed of the United States, Britain, China, and Russia. France is to join them later, and smaller countries will fill another six seats.

"It is a foregone conclusion that the British will vote against Éire being allowed to join, but Seán is hopeful. De Valera knows President Roosevelt personally. They met in 1919 when Dev was in the States on a fund-raising expedition,[1] and the two got along very well. Seán thinks Roosevelt may be persuaded, as Wilson was not, to consider Éire a separate and sovereign state deserving a position in world affairs."

Ned was in the farmyard, greasing the chain of the bicycle. He looked up as Ursula ran toward him. "What is the exact quote from Robert Emmet, Papa? You know the one I mean."

He smiled. " 'When my country takes her place among the nations of the earth, then and not till then, let my epitaph be written.' "

ANOTHER Christmas was approaching. The pudding was already made using honey instead of sugar, which gave it a rather gluey texture. In the yard the geese were fat. On Christmas Eve George would behead two of them with an axe. Eileen's children would pluck the birds—under protest.

That morning Ursula was up early, but not as early as Ned. When she passed his room she noticed that the door was slightly ajar. "Papa?"

No answer.

Ursula took a half-step inside.

The bed was neatly made. For a moment she was afraid he had vanished again, but his coat was still hanging on the back of the door. On the wash stand lay the cord he usually wore around his neck.

The silvery key on the cord seemed to glitter in the dim light.

Ursula picked it up and hefted it in her hand. An object so small . . . yet it must guard something very important. But what? Ned had few possessions. "Always travel light" was one of his axioms.

Her eye was drawn to his army backpack, wedged between the bed and the locker. Still holding the key, she stooped and hefted the pack onto the bed. It was heavier than she expected.

"What are you doing, Ursula?" asked a soft voice.

She whirled around. Ned lounged in the doorway, holding his shaving mug and brush. "I was out of shaving soap," he said, "so I went down to the kitchen to get a few slivers. What's your excuse?"

Ursula responded with the challenging, Ned Halloran look she had perfected for herself years ago. She could stand up to him now. In some curious way their roles had been reversed; she was the adult, he the child. "I was snooping, Papa, you know how curious I am." She held up the key. "I was wondering what you lock with this."

The tension went out of his face and he almost laughed. "How can anyone argue with such total honesty? Here, I'll show you." Ned stepped past her and took a black metal lockbox from his pack. "I keep the manuscript of my book in here," he said, setting the box on top of his locker.

"May I look at it?"

"Why? Is there something in particular you want to know?" His voice was soft again, almost a whisper. "Perhaps you're curious about other Christmases. Such as 1939, when the IRA raided the army arsenal in the Phoenix Park and got away with a million rounds of ammunition."

"My God! Were you there?"

"Och, I've been lots of places. Will-o'-the-wisp, that's me. Like my old friend Michael Collins."

Her words tumbled over one another. "Were you in the Phoenix Park raid? What happened to all that ammunition? Did it go to the north? Did you . . ."

Looking her straight in the eye, Ned said blandly, "I don't remember."

He took the key from her fingers and slipped the cord around his neck. She never again saw him without it.

But she knew Ned Halloran had come all the way back, as complex and maddening . . . and valiant . . . as ever.

Chapter Fifty-four

IN January the victorious Red Army sweeping through Poland discovered a German concentration camp at Auschwitz. By the time Russian tanks battered down the gates, most of the surviving inmates had been removed to Germany. The appalled Russians found five thousand living skeletons still within the camp, and huge mounds of corpses.

In February, Roosevelt, Churchill, and Stalin met at Yalta to agree on the final plans for defeating Germany and carving up postwar Europe. Meanwhile Allied bombers devastated Dresden and pounded German supply lines to bits.

On March 26 David Lloyd George died. Winston Churchill said of the former British prime minister who had negotiated the Treaty with Ireland, "Lloyd George was the greatest Welshman since the Tudor kings."

When Ned heard of Lloyd George's death, Ursula thought he would want to celebrate. But he seemed unmoved by the news. "Now he'll have to answer to his God," was all he said.

NORTHERN Ireland was preoccupied with the struggle against the Axis powers. Little energy was left over for fighting Catholics, though there were still some die-hard loyalists who could not resist the temptation to bully their neighbors. The situation was ignored by the government of Éire. Any action against British policy could threaten neutrality.

Beleaguered northern Catholics were not completely forgotten by their fellow Irishmen, however. As Ned had told Ursula, the IRA had been—

almost—emasculated by de Valera's policies. But it had not gone away.

From time to time there would be a knock at the door, or a whistle under the window, and Ned would leave the house. Sometimes he met one or more men in the laneway, talked with them for a while well out of earshot, and then returned. On other occasions he took his bicycle and went away for a few hours. He never announced where he was going or when he would be back, but he always returned by nightfall.

Barry was desperately curious. "Is Granda a spy, Mammy?" he kept asking Ursula.

"Of course not, don't be foolish."

"Then what is he? Is he still a soldier?"

She did not know how to answer that.

"I'm going to be a soldier like Granda when I grow up," Barry announced one day.

Ursula surprised herself with the vehemence of her response. "Under no circumstances!"

Hers had been a militant heart, but that was before Adolf Hitler had strode across the world stage, wreaking havoc. She had seen what the impulse to war could do.

She went straight to Ned. "I don't want you telling any more of your war stories to Barry. Or to Eileen's boys either, for that matter. Instruct them in history but don't glorify the army to them. *Any* army."

Ned raised a sardonic eyebrow. "This from a girl who used to carry a pistol under her clothes and talk about dying for the Republic?"

"That was then and this is now, Papa. No more war talk to Barry. I mean it!"

Hypocrisy is just one more item on my long list of sins, Ursula thought. *But am I being hypocritical—or just a mother? Mothers don't want their sons to be killed in war.*

What about fathers, is it the same for them?

Barry's father . . . don't go down that road, she warned herself.

IF Ned was no longer allowed to tell his stories to Barry, he could still put them on paper. The book became his obsession. Instead of listening to the wireless in the evenings, he went to his room and crouched over the pages of the manuscript with the paraffin lamp at his elbow. He worked at almost feverish pitch, as if trying to meet some unstated deadline.

"You're exhausting yourself, Papa," Ursula told him. "Surely the book will keep. Leave it be for a while. You can always work on it tomorrow."

But he would not, could not, leave it. There might be no tomorrow.

For Ned Halloran, the lights were slowly going out.

The spells of blindness were coming more frequently and lasting longer. Between them was the gradual blurring of normal vision. He could no longer tell if the sun was shining. Every day looked overcast. He turned up the lamp in his room as high as it would go and still it could not drive the shadows back.

The lessons Ned taught at the kitchen table were almost all from memory now. He made his way about the house and yard in the same fashion. If he had to go down the lane to meet someone he walked slowly, with his head down as if absorbed in thought. Someone watching from the house would not realize he was feeling for the ruts in the road with careful feet.

He rarely rode the bicycle into Clarecastle anymore, and never as far as Ennis. One day the light went out completely when he was halfway home, and he had to dismount from the machine and walk it the rest of the way back. By the time he reached the farm his clothes were soaked through with sweat, though the day was cold.

It was only a matter of time until Ursula realized what was happening.

She did not know how to broach the subject. Ned would hate pity. At last she took Eileen aside and said, "I think Papa's on the verge of being totally blind."

"Are you sure?"

"I'm afraid so. He's good at concealing his condition, but if you watch him closely you can tell. The children know; look at the way Barry takes his hand when they go outside together. And Barry never takes anyone's hand."

Eileen's lower lip began to tremble. "What can we do, Ursula?"

"Give him all the freedom he wants. He wouldn't have it any other way."

"But what if he hurts himself?"

"That's the risk of freedom," said Ursula.

WHEN Franklin Roosevelt died on the twelfth of April, 1945, the shock was seismic. He had taken America from the depths of depression, and the Allies to the threshold of victory. After the news was broadcast on the wireless Ursula spent a sleepless night. Before dawn she dressed and went outside.

A rising wind was blowing out the candles of the stars.

•   •   •

THE new president of the United States was Harry S. Truman, who had no connections with Ireland. He had only been in office for thirteen days when delegates gathered in San Francisco to make plans for the establishment of the United Nations.

No Irish representative was invited.

BENITO Mussolini was captured and shot by Italian partisans near Como on the twenty-eighth of April. Il Duce and his mistress were strung up by their heels for the crowd to jeer at and spit upon.

The following day in Italy twenty-two German divisions and six Italian Fascist divisions surrendered to the Allies.

On the thirtieth of the month Adolf Hitler committed suicide in his bunker in Berlin.

ELLA Mooney greeted her husband with flashing eyes as he came in from work. "What does your Mr. de Valera think he's playing at?"

Henry took time to hang his hat on the hat rack. "What's he done now, Cap'n?"

"Just look at the evening paper!" She thrust forward a copy of the *Times Herald* folded to an inside page. "De Valera's fraternizing with the Germans!"

Taking his reading glasses from his waistcoat pocket, Henry read the offending item. "Following the announcement of Adolf Hitler's death, Eamon de Valera, prime minister of Ireland, reportedly paid a formal call of condolence on Edouard Hempel, German minister to Dublin."

Henry turned to his wife. "You have the wrong end of the stick for once, Cap'n," he said mildly. "In the first place, he isn't *my* Mr. de Valera, but he is the taoiseach. Secondly, he didn't dance arm in arm down Grafton Street with Hempel. He simply extended the courtesy one head of state extends on the death of another."

"But how could he do such a thing!" she cried.

"Speaking personally," Henry replied, "I had just as soon he hadn't. But speaking objectively, I understand why he did. Dev wanted to show the world that Ireland—far from being the land of pigs in the parlor as our enemies would have us—observes international protocol. Anything less would have established an unfortunate precedent."

"At the very least," Ella sniffed, "I think he acted in bad taste."

Henry chuckled. "The ultimate condemnation, coming from you." His eye fell on the silver letter tray on the table beside the front door. The envelope on top of the stack had been torn open. He picked it up. "This from the detectives?"

"That's why I opened it without waiting for you."

"No good news, or you would have told me."

"No good news. Just this month's bill." Ella raised tragic eyes to Henry's. "Oh, my love, we're never going to see Bella again, are we?"

Her husband gathered her into his arms. "Sure we will, Cap'n," he said huskily. "Sure we will."

THE eighth of May, 1945, was declared as VE Day. Victory in Europe.

WINSTON Churchill used his victory speech to launch a bitter personal attack on Eamon de Valera. Presumably referring to the Treaty Ports, he said, "Had it been necessary, we should have been forced to come to close quarters with Mr. de Valera. With a restraint and poise to which, I venture to say, history will find few parallels, His Majesty's government never laid a violent hand on them, though at times it would have been quite easy and quite natural, and we left the de Valera government to frolic with the German and later with the Japanese representatives to its heart's content."[1]

Three days later Eamon de Valera entered the Dublin broadcasting station with the manuscript of his own victory speech carried firmly in his hand. The nation crowded around its radios, anxious to see how he would respond to Churchill.

As usual, the taoiseach spoke first in Irish then in English, thanking God for the end of the war and thanking all those who had worked so hard to preserve the nation during the difficult times just past. His listeners began to fear he would let Churchill's deliberate provocation go unchallenged.

They were wrong. "Certain newspapers have been very persistent in looking for my answer to Mr. Churchill's recent broadcast," de Valera said toward the end of his speech. "I know the kind of answer I am expected to make. I know the answer that springs to the lips of every man of Irish blood who heard or read that speech, no matter in what circumstances or in what part of the world he found himself. I know the reply I would have given a quarter of a century ago. But I have deliberately decided that is not the reply I shall make tonight.

"Mr. Churchill makes it clear that, in certain circumstances, he would have violated our neutrality and that he would have justified his actions by

Britain's necessity. It seems strange to me that Mr. Churchill does not see that this, if it be accepted, would mean that Britain's necessity would become a moral code and that, when this necessity became sufficiently great, other people's rights were not to count. It is quite true that other great powers believe in this same code in their own regard, and have behaved in accordance with it. That is precisely why we have the disastrous succession of wars—World War One and World War Two. And shall it be World War Three?

"It is indeed hard for the strong to be just to the weak. But acting justly always has its own rewards. By resisting his temptation in this instance, Mr. Churchill, instead of adding another horrid chapter to the already blood-stained record of the relations between England and this country, has advanced the cause of international morality an important step."

The taoiseach sadly referred to the way that partition had poisoned Anglo-Irish relations. He also remarked on the great pride Mr. Churchill had expressed in Britain's solitary stand against the forces of Nazi tyranny.

Then he concluded, "Could he not find in his heart the generosity to acknowledge that there is a small nation that stood alone not for one year or two, but for several hundred years against aggression; that endured spoliations, was clubbed many times into insensibility, but that each time on returning to consciousness took up the fight anew; a small nation that could never be got to accept defeat and has never surrendered her soul?"

EAMON de Valera's overriding passion had been that Éire would still be independent at the end of the war. He had succeeded and his people knew it. He had scarcely finished speaking when a huge crowd flooded into O'Connell Street to greet him as he emerged from the radio station. The cheer they raised rang through the streets of Dublin.

As soon as a full transcript of the text was published in the newspapers, Ursula clipped it out and sent it to Henry.

"At last we have something to cheer about," she wrote,

and people have gone quite wild with excitement over the taoiseach's speech. Granted, it was an able and passionate defence of the government's policy. But the national response seems to me to be out of proportion. I remember the aftermath of the War of Independence, when people truly believed Ireland had changed utterly and for the better and there was well-founded exhilaration.

Now, though—Ireland is the same self-righteous and repressive

Catholic state it has been since Mr. de Valera took office. Looking into the future, I see only more of the same. It is a sobering vista.

Thank God the Allies won the war in Europe. Given the nature of the Nazi regime, had Hitler won the war the best Ireland could have hoped for would be thraldom to Germany as once we were in thrall to Britain—and now are in thrall to the Church. What happened to the dream of Irish freedom? That is a rhetorical question, Henry, and one I had best not pursue. I get too angry, so I shall change the subject.

I am aware that the Americans are still fighting in the Pacific, but the papers here do not give that aspect of the war much coverage. What is your opinion of Japan? To the Irish, the Japanese seem as unreal as Mr. H. G. Wells's Martians. I would love to learn something about them. Oh Henry, there is still so much I want to learn about *everything*!

Elections were in the air. On the sixteenth of June Seán T. O'Kelly was elected as president of Éire. Seán Lemass succeeded him as *tánaiste**

"I disapprove of Lemass on principle," Ursula complained to Ned. "He used to have nothing but contempt for the wireless. He called it 'the hurdy-gurdy.' "[2]

Ned laughed. "You have to have a better reason than that for disliking someone, Precious."

"No, I don't. But the next time we have an election, I'll wager Lemass will be more than happy to campaign for office on the hurdy-gurdy!"

JULY saw the Labour Party win a landslide election in Britain. Churchill was out; the new prime minister was Clement Attlee. It was he who led the British delegation to the conference of the victorious Allies at Potsdam.

By the end of the month the unity of the Allies was shattered. Far from charting a safe course for postwar Europe, the Potsdam Conference, attended by Attlee, Stalin, and Truman, had seen the Soviet Union make a power grab of unprecedented proportions.

"An Iron Curtain has slammed down," Winston Churchill observed.

6 August 1945
UNITED STATES DROPS ATOMIC BOMB ON HIROSHIMA

*Deputy prime minister.

Chapter Fifty-five

TWO days later Joseph Stalin and the Soviet Union declared war on Japan.

On August 14 Japan unconditionally surrendered to the Americans.

VJ Day marked the end of a war that had cost at least 55 million lives and redrawn the map of the world yet again.

WAR'S end did not immediately make life easier in Ireland. The primary objective of the government was to restore the economy and avoid inflation. Wages were fixed; shortages and restrictions would continue for a number of months.

But great changes were literally in the air.

On the twenty-fourth of October Ursula shouted up the stairs, "Come down here quick, Papa, and listen to the wireless!"

Ned no longer hurtled down the stairs as he had done in his youth. By the time he reached the parlor the news broadcast was over, but Ursula was eager to tell him, "American Export Airlines just completed the first transatlantic passenger flight to Ireland! Do you know what this means?"

"I do," said Ned. "It means the Yanks are coming."

IN December Louise Hamilton wrote to Ursula, "It feels like all our Christmases have come at once. Oranges are on sale in Moore Street for the first time since the Emergency began. They cost thruppence ha'penny, but the pavements are already awash with orange peels and purple tissue paper."

"Soon you'll be able to have marmalade again," Ursula told Ned. "Provided that Eileen's willing to make it for you."

"And me with a clather of children to run after and a whole big house to keep?" Eileen interjected. "Chance would be a fine thing!"

That same evening she took Norah's old "receipt" book from its place on the dresser shelf and looked up the instructions for making marmalade.

Eileen Halloran Mulvaney considered herself very fortunate. By the end of the war half of Ireland's households were still cooking their meals on the hearth. The black iron range epitomized unimaginable luxury to women who spent their days bending, lifting, stirring over an open fire; wiping ash from their eyes and soot from their faces. Women who did the family washing and kept their children clean without running water in the house; women who endured the discomfort of an outdoor toilet in all weathers; women whose lives had narrowed to an endless round of exhaustive physical labor that was never acknowledged. It was what was expected of "the woman of the house," just as a baby a year was expected, no matter what her health.

But Eileen Mulvaney had been liberated.

ON the first of January, 1946, William Joyce, known as Lord Haw-Haw, was hanged in the Tower of London. He had been arrested by the British near the Dutch border the preceding May, tried and found guilty of treason. The British placed great stress on his Irish connections.

BY summer Eileen's oldest boy had turned into a gangling, acne-ridden adolescent who could no longer be persuaded to study. He much preferred to work outdoors; any sort of farmwork suited him. Had it not been for Barry, none of the Mulvaney brood would have continued to attend Ned's kitchen-table classes.

"Teaching those children is just about all Ned has left," Eileen said one day as she was clearing the table for the evening meal. "I'm amazed he can still cope."

"He's so maddeningly secretive!" Ursula complained. "He won't admit to being blind, so I'm not sure if he can still see anything or not. It's like everything else connected with him; we'll never know the whole of it." *At least, not while he's alive*, she thought to herself.

She had never told Eileen about the locked box in the bottom of Ned's army pack.

The mysteries of Ned Halloran's life did not end with that box. He had occasional visitors who knocked at the door, then waited in the lane until he made his careful way out to them. Ursula drew the curtains aside just enough to watch them out the window in the parlor. They talked while Ned listened. Or listened while he appeared to give instructions.

Ursula continued to read the newspapers aloud to him. He was avid for any story that involved the north. There were very few in any of the southern papers. "Éire forgets that those are our people too," Ned complained.

"How active is the IRA across the border, Papa?"

"What makes you think they're active at all?"

"Oh Papa. Do you really believe I don't know who those men are, the ones who call on you from time to time?"

"A man's entitled to have a few friends."

"Friends come into the parlor and talk and smoke and have a glass of whiskey. Those men never step inside the door."

He pretended not to hear.

IN July the Dáil agreed to apply for membership in the United Nations. The Union of Soviet Socialist Republics vetoed the application. Part of the price for Irish neutrality would be the exclusion of Ireland from the United Nations for ten years following the war.

THE winter of 1946 was one of the coldest in living memory. Fuel shortages caused business shutdowns; homeowners were urged to conserve paraffin oil. Ursula used candlelight and the long, bitter nights to write to her friends in Europe. In many cases she realized they were no longer at the addresses she had for them, but she posted the letters just the same.

The Irish men who had volunteered to fight with the Allies had returned home—except for those who were still in hospital, either in England or Northern Ireland. President Roosevelt had once dismissed the Irish army as "seven-hundred men armed with shotguns" but more men had joined up in the first days after the outbreak of war, than had joined the American forces immediately following Pearl Harbor.[1]

The twenty-year-old son of Ursula's nearest neighbor had seen action as a member of the Irish Guards. He had gone ashore with the first wave that landed at Anzio and been badly wounded. After more than two years in hospital he finally returned to Clare. His family gave a party and invited everyone within a five-mile radius to welcome the boy home.

Ned declined the invitation, but Ursula and Eileen went to the party. Whiskey flowed freely and there was enough food to use up a whole stack of coupon books. Everyone seemed to be enjoying themselves except the war hero. He kept his head down most of the time. When pressed, he answered questions about his experiences with a few mumbled phrases.

The horror of it was still in his eyes; the horror of floundering ashore through a sea of red mush and body parts.

When Ursula asked how it felt to be home, the young man replied, "It feels like I've never been away. I don't mean that in a good way. Has nothing changed in Ireland? Nothing at all? I thought everything would be different, somehow."

"So did we all," Ursula said bitterly.

WHEN they returned from the party Ned was waiting for them. "May I talk to you?" he whispered to Ursula.

"Of course. What is it?"

"Not here. Come upstairs with me."

Intrigued, she accompanied him to his room. He closed the door firmly behind her. "I have a message," he said, taking a folded piece of paper from his pocket.

"Do you want me to read it for you, Papa?"

"You don't understand," he replied. "This is for you. It was delivered this evening, while you were away."

Ursula eyed the folded paper with suspicion. "Delivered by whom?"

"Just read it."

Printed in block letters was a name and address. "That's Isabella Mooney," Ned explained. "She's married to Michael Kavanagh and they're living in upstate New York."

"Where did you get this?"

"From someone who knows someone who knows them. They're all right, the pair of them. Kavanagh's not a bad sort, I'm told. A bit hotheaded, but the Boys have promised to keep an eye on him to see that he gets into no trouble. And they always keep their promises."

"I . . . I hardly know what to say."

"Then don't say anything," Ned advised. "Just get word to her parents, will you? Tell them she'll contact them in her own time. I suspect she still has a bit of growing up to do." He laughed. "Takes a lifetime, that does."

Ursula wrote to Henry that same night.

His reply came by return post.

What extraordinary good news! We are more grateful than we can say. I will confess to you what I never dared say to the Cap'n. I feared our girl was dead.

Now that we know where she is and how she is, we shall wait for her to get in touch with us. It won't be easy. I want to hop on the next train to New York, but if you think it best, I can restrain myself.

You say they are renting a little bungalow in a small town and do not even have a car. I suppose she is embarrassed by her modest circumstances, which is why we have not heard from her before now. Bella was always such a snob. I cannot imagine what forces led her to such a complete turnaround. Love, I suppose. Love can do funny things to a person.

Time on the farm was measured by the seasons. Like the rituals of religion, they gave life a shape. Lent and Easter and Christmas. Summer and winter and spring. More colts on the ground, more customers for butter and milk, the children growing up, the adults growing older.

Determined to make the most of a bad situation, Ned accepted his blindness stoically. He had never had enough time for contemplation before; now he did. What did Henry call it? "Taking a walk around the inside of my head."

Henry.

The lost friend.

Looking back across his life, Ned examined its landscape. The moments of high emotionalism stood out like signposts. Loving Síle. The adventure of the Rising. The savagery of the Civil War.

Síle and Henry and the jealousy that had raged through him, making him mistake Henry for his enemy. What was that all about? he wondered now. Proving my manhood?

Retracing his steps, he began to see the pattern he unconsciously had followed all his days.

DUBLINERS had long been accustomed to electricity, yet in spite of the fact that airplanes were now crossing the Atlantic, people in the west of Ireland had continued to live as they had done for thousands of years. Everything was arranged around the availability of light. On the farms and in the villages, people went to bed with the sun. Before they retired they made certain everything was put away so there was nothing to stumble over in the night. Even a paraffin lamp made only a small pool of light.

Beyond that was the Dark.

Then in May of 1947, considerably after W.T. Cosgrave had once predicted, the Dark was pushed back in rural Ireland.

Ursula wrote to Louise, "Our lights have come on at last! A man came around weeks ago and installed a lot of fiddly equipment, then went away again. Yesterday an inspector called to the farm to announce, 'You're switched on, missus.' How lovely to have light whenever one needs it! Eileen is in ecstasy. She goes around the house turning on light bulbs just for the novelty of it. I thought nothing would ever change in this country, but this gives me hope."

That same month rubber hot water bottles, American lipstick, and nylon toothbrushes went on sale in Dublin. The stores were sold out in a matter of hours. "My girls were too late out of the starting blocks to get anything nice," Elsie Lester lamented in a letter to Ursula.

Some elements of Irish life were returning to normal. The Royal Dublin Horse Show had been canceled only once during the war years and was now predicted to be bigger than ever. Held on its traditional dates in August, it included an international show-jumping competition.

"That's our market—our future market," Ursula told Ned. "I'm going up to Dublin for the show this year and see what's on offer. Perhaps make a few connections for the future, when our horses are ready for sale."

"Is that so important?"

"Oh Papa! In Ireland it's not what you know, it's who you know. I've learned that much."

Leaving Barry at the farm, Ursula took the train to Dublin, where she stayed once again with Louise Hamilton. For several days she feasted her eyes on the glorious animals at the RDS grounds in Ballsbridge. In the evenings she paid long-overdue calls on old friends, some of whom, she was startled to see, *were* old.

At sixty-two, Helena Moloney was a matronly woman with gray hair and a sweet but sagging face. She could almost have been Ursula's grandmother. Kathleen Clarke, several years older, was as peppery as ever, her eyes still a piercing blue, but even Tom Clarke's indomitable widow could not hold back time. Her voice had taken on a querulous tone as if she were hard of hearing.

Louise Hamilton had become a frail old lady.

Ursula searched her own face in the mirror in her room. Thirty-seven or so; if she had been born in 1910 as people believed. Looked younger except for permanent windburn. Strong-featured, arresting but certainly not pretty. So familiar she never really saw it. Combed the hair, rubbed a bit of cold cream into the skin in a hopeless attempt to counter the effects of being out in all weathers, and occasionally applied a touch of lip rouge. That was all.

Looking at it now, she thought it might have been the face of a stranger. A stranger with lines around her eyes and threads of silver hair glinting through the rich brown.

Who are you that sneaked into me and took over my body when I wasn't looking?

Ireland might be unchanging, frozen in time, but its human inhabitants were not.

THAT autumn Irish bishops publicly condoned the boycotting of a divorced Protestant who was elected joint master of the Galway Hunt.

IN his blindness Ned could see Síle. She stood out brightly against the encroaching dark. His one and only love as she was when he first met her in a miserable hovel overpopulated with Duffys of every age.

A tall girl with creamy, freckled skin. Eyebrows and eyelashes of purest copper, rust-colored hair like raveled rope. Eyes slanted like a cat's. Those beloved eyes smiled at him. Those sensuous lips shaped his name.

"I'll be with you soon, *mo mhuirnín dílís*,"* he promised.

She shook her head until her hair tumbled around her shoulders just the way he liked. "There's no hurry. We're always together, living or dead."

His heart jumped. "You've always been with me? Even in Spain?"

"I was at your shoulder wherever you went."

"A ghost?"

Síle laughed; the rippling laugh so well remembered. "There are no ghosts, *a stór*. Only spirits. Every thing that lives or has ever lived has a spirit. You're surrounded by them like drops of water in the sea."

"That's my oldest nightmare," Ned told her. "The dark sea, waiting."

"Not dark, Ned. It only looks that way because human eyes can't see past the waves on the surface. The unknown frightens people and they call it death. But beneath those waves is the most wondrous light! Just beyond

*"My own true love."

your vision, all spirits are united in one immortal being."

The word triggered something in him. "United. In Ireland too?"

She laughed again. "In Ireland most of all. Can you not see it? Can none of you see it?"

"Not yet," Ned said sadly.

Síle melted into the surrounding darkness. He started to call her back, then remembered. *Living or dead, we're always together.*

Chapter Fifty-six

FOR Christmas 1947, the Mooneys sent Ursula an Eastman Kodak camera. "Please send some photographs of yourself and Barry. Take pictures of your horses, too," Ella urged. "Hank in particular would love to see those."

EARLY in 1948 Éire held a general election. The results saw Fianna Fáil's hold on government reduced to 68 seats in the Dáil; not enough for a majority against Fine Gael and a coalition of smaller parties. They held the balance of power now, and from their ranks the new taoiseach would be chosen.

Richard Mulcahy, the current leader of Fine Gael, had commanded Free State forces during the Civil War. He therefore was not acceptable to Seán MacBride, a former chief of staff of the IRA. The Clann na Poblachta party that MacBride had founded two years earlier had gained ten Dáil seats in the election and MacBride's individual voice carried weight as well. He was the son of Maud Gonne and the executed Major John MacBride, one of the heroes of the Rising. When he refused to accept Mulcahy a compromise was necessary.

On the eighteenth of February John A. Costello, a former attorney general in the Cosgrave administration, was named as taoiseach. To him fell the task of forming the first coalition government in the history of the state.

·   ·   ·

So Dev's out of power again," Ned commented, sounding bemused.

He and Ursula were sitting together in the parlor. The wireless and the electric light had been turned off for the evening. Ned did not need the light anyway.

The darkness that had claimed his eyes was slowly creeping over his spirit. As Ursula watched with a heavy heart, the boundaries of his world were shrinking. His physical condition was deteriorating day by day. He hardly ever went outside now, even when he had visitors. Soon, she suspected, he would not even leave his room.

Wild, reckless Ned Halloran, whose entire life had been one of action. Only his mind was still alert and alive.

"Do you think Dev will admit he's beaten and retire gracefully?" Ursula asked him.

"Not a chance. There's no way he'll simply disappear like an old soldier hanging up his rifle. We'll hear more from him, wait and see. In the meantime . . . who's this John Costello, anyway?"

"He's the Fine Gael lawyer who once boasted in the Dáil that the Blueshirts would be as victorious in Ireland as Mussolini's Blackshirts."

Ned chuckled. "He predicted more rightly than he knew, then. Where are the Blueshirts now?"

"Coming back, I'm afraid. Costello as taoiseach bodes ill for this country."

"Don't bleed before you're shot, Precious."

"Don't tell me you'd have any sympathy with a man who admired the Blueshirts!"

Ned gave a deep sigh. "It's a strange thing," he remarked. "When my eyes were good I saw everything in black and white. Now I can see all the shades of gray."

"You've become remarkably tolerant in your old age," said Ursula sarcastically. "I liked it better when you were a firebrand."

Ireland still had her share of firebrands. To the amazement of many, Costello appointed one of them, Seán MacBride, as minister of external affairs.

It was a shrewd move, coalescing radically diverse political philosophies within one cabinet. An apparently colorless man, Costello had a gift for springing surprises.

But no one thought of him as radical; indeed not, when his government sent a formal assurance to the pope: "We repose at the feet of Your Holiness the assurance of our filial loyalty and of our devotion to your August Person, as well as our firm resolve to be guided in all our work by the teaching of Christ and to strive to the attainment of a social order in Ireland based on Christian principles."[1]

"De Valera's brand of republicanism has been supplanted but the hold of the Church remains as strong as ever," Ursula wrote to Henry.

June 1, 1948
Dear Mr. Mooney,

Bella does not know I am writing this letter. For a long time certain friends of mine have been pressuring us to contact you, but she will not hear of it. She believes, sir, that you are dreadfully disappointed in her. Her pride will not allow her to say she is sorry. Once Bella gets an idea in her head she will not let it go.

I think you should know that you have a little granddaughter. Barbara Mooney Kavanagh was born on the third of May. She is very beautiful. Bella once remarked that she looks like Mrs. Mooney, which is the only mention she has ever made of her mother.

We are all three in good health. I am doing my best to provide a good home and keep my wife happy. Our current address is on this envelope. If it should change, I will inform you immediately.

                                        Sincerely,
                                        Michael Kavanagh

Ursula took countless photographs of her horses. At first the pictures were fuzzy and out of focus, and sometimes the animals lacked heads. But she persevered. When she had a dozen photographs she considered satisfactory, she announced she would take them to Dublin in August for the annual horse show. "I need to start advertising our stock to people who can afford really good horses."

Ned's sister laughed. "Buy some American lipstick for me too, will you?"

Ursula concealed the twinge of guilt she felt. "I'm not going on some frivolous shopping trip!" she insisted.

"And nylons," Eileen added wistfully. "I would dearly love to see a real pair of nylon stockings."

THE postwar prosperity that Henry Mooney wrote about in his letters to Ursula had not reached Ireland. Dublin in August of 1948 was, at first glance, little different from Dublin in 1938: shabby and curiously old-fashioned. Shop windows were fly-specked. Advertisements on hoardings were yellowed and peeling. Private automobiles were slow to return to the streets; many still used bicycles for transport.

But a few stirrings could be felt beneath the surface.

The Costello government was settling in and interest was focused on economic policy. The External Relations Act which had been part of the Anglo-Irish Treaty meant that the Free State retained strong economic ties with Britain. Some wanted to see those ties cut and the nation stand on her own two feet at last. Others were reluctant to cut the apron strings, no matter how onerous the relationship had been. "Stay with what's known," was their attitude.

Before attending the horse show Ursula paid a call on the Lesters. Let Eileen yearn for lipstick and nylons. She was hungry to discuss the changing political landscape with people who were knowledgeable.

Seán had returned from Geneva and he and Elsie were living at Avoca, County Wicklow. Ballanagh House was a spacious country residence, two-storied, L-shaped, embedded in rhododendron bushes and perfumed by newly-mown lawns. A pack of friendly dogs ran to greet Ursula when she arrived.

Elsie professed herself delighted with the rural life, but Ursula was curious to know how Seán Lester was adapting to a smaller stage. He seemed content, but admitted he was disappointed in the local fishing. "And how do you find life on the farm?" he asked her. "Is it dull after Geneva?"

"Dull?" Ursula laughed. "Hardly that. Every day is at least one new crisis. Working at the League prepared me admirably."

"I thought the new coalition government might find a place in its ranks for Seán," Elsie confided while her husband was at the other end of the room, fixing drinks. "But de Valera had no interest in employing his experience after the war and neither, it seems, does Costello."

Ann Lester entered the room carrying a tray of sandwiches. "I hate seeing my father ignored like that," she said hotly. "After all the credit he's brought to this country!"

"It's all right," Seán assured her as he passed the drinks. "I'm a man without ambition. Though I would like to think I make a good brandy and soda."

Elsie met Ursula's eyes. "At least the new United Nations appreciates him. Just this June the secretary-general, Trygve Lie, sent a long telegram asking Seán to lead a commission to deal with the India-Pakistan question."

"I thanked him most warmly," said Seán, "but explained that certain urgent personal affairs made it quite impossible to accept the commission."

Ann laughed in spite of herself. "He meant fishing season!"

The long afternoon was drowsy with the warmth of late summer but sparkled with conversation. Ursula hated to leave and promised to come back soon.

I have a foot in each of two worlds, she thought.

The grounds of the RDS were thronged with people. Several motorized horseboxes blocked traffic while sleek animals wearing head bumpers and protective bandages were being unloaded. The air smelt of dung and petrol and excitement.

This one, Ursula told herself. *This is the world I want. Isn't it?*

As Ursula joined the queue to buy her tickets, she found herself behind a stocky woman in a huge straw hat. For some reason the queue was hardly moving. Every time Ursula tried to peer around the hat, the woman shifted to one side or the other and blocked her view.

Ursula muttered irritably, "They'll be calling the first class soon and we're still going to be out here."

The woman in the hat turned around. "Ursula Halloran!" cried Felicity Rowe-Howell. "I'd have known you anywhere."

Ursula stared at the dumpy woman in the expensive but unbecoming print dress. Gone was the girl who once described herself as "jolly hockey-sticks." Only her voice belonged to the Fliss of memory. Her puffy face, slashed by dark red lipstick, was a campaign map of lost wars.

"You . . . you're looking very well yourself," Ursula stammered.

Fliss smoothed the front of her dress. "You're kind to say so, but I'm afraid I've put on a teeny bit of weight. They do claim it irons out the wrinkles, though." She gave a high-pitched, girlish giggle.

The queue at last started to move. The two old friends bought tickets together in the grandstand. While they waited for the first class to begin, Fliss asked a few personal questions that Ursula parried with the skill born of long practice. The other woman did not seem to mind. It was obvious that she really wanted to talk about herself.

"You didn't miss much by not coming to my wedding," Fliss said. "I married the wrong man anyway."

Ursula looked at her in surprise. "Did you now?"

"Oh yes." Very calmly. "I realized it when I was walking down the aisle and saw him waiting for me at the altar."

"Then why in God's name did you go through with it?"

"I had the dress and everyone was there," said Fliss, as if it were the most reasonable of explanations.

"Jaysus, Fliss!"

The other woman shrugged.

Ursula commented, "You don't seem very unhappy about it."

"Why should I be? He has his life now and I have mine. He lives in London and does the social rounds, or goes drinking with his old RAF pals. Drinks rather too much, really, but it's nothing to do with me anymore. I live in the country and do the sorts of things I like. Our paths almost never cross."

"Will you divorce?"

"Of course not, Ursula. Our arrangement suits us both just as it is."

"Have you children?"

"Two; a boy and a girl. Rather a miracle, really, considering their father never fancied me."

"Then why do you suppose he asked you to marry him?"

"Oh, I found out soon enough," Fliss replied. "He was in love with someone else but she threw him over." A shadow crossed her face; was swiftly blinked away. "He proposed to me out of bravado, really, to prove he could get anyone he wanted. He's still doing it."

Ursula gave a wry smile. "Proposing marriage to women?"

"Not marriage, no. Being married to me keeps him safe to make indecent proposals to others. He's quite successful at it, my friends tell me."

Ursula said, "If they tell you things like that, they're not what I call friends."

A bell rang. The two women turned toward the arena, where a big bay gelding was cantering toward the first jump. "Some think my husband is romantic," Fliss remarked while keeping her eyes on the horse. "A man who was spurned by the love of his life."

"Did he love the woman who threw him over?"

"Oh yes, I'm very certain of that." Fliss sounded so monumentally indifferent that she broke Ursula's heart. "My husband never discussed his 'grand passion' with me, but I once saw him reduced to tears by a piece of music that reminded him of her. We were at a dance and the orchestra played 'My Wild Irish Rose.' Lewis was so upset he left the hall. Left me standing in the middle of the dance floor by myself. I knew then there was no hope for us."

Ursula gaped at Fliss. "Lewis . . . Baines?"

"Of course. I thought you knew. Did I never tell you his name?"

· · ·

Ursula's world had rocked on its axis and left her momentarily stunned. She needed to reestablish contact with something solid—and Seán Lester was the most solid person she knew.

Ursula rang the Lesters and invited herself to Ballanagh House to say good-bye before returning to Clare.

"By all means come down!" Elsie told her eagerly. "Some other friends will be here for luncheon and you'll fit right in."

With her usual deft hospitality, Elsie set up a picnic under the trees. Two tables were covered with crisp linen cloths. Platters of cold ham and chicken were accompanied by bowls of salad and bread hot from the oven. Seán introduced Ursula to his other guests, four men from the Department of External Affairs. Ursula had met none of them before, but found them all intelligent and personable. To her disappointment, however, they were not forthcoming about John Costello and the new administration, though she asked as many leading questions as she dared.

When the meal was almost over it began to rain, and the party hastily adjourned inside. Ursula took the opportunity to visit the toilet. As she was returning down the hallway, she overheard raised voices coming from the library and halted in her tracks.

"I beg to disagree!" one of the guests was saying with some heat. "It would be a great mistake to repeal the External Relations Act. De Valera himself proposed an external association when drawing up Document Two, his suggested alternative to the Treaty. The idea was to avoid accepting an internal association that would require the swearing of an oath of allegiance to the king. If we were to set aside the External Relations Act it would mean leaving the Commonwealth and breaking the Treaty."

"Nations break treaties all the time," said another man. "Look at the war just concluded, for example."

"My point exactly. If we don't honor our commitments where does that leave us? On a par with Hitler?"

Ursula strained to hear.

"The act is a statute repealable by the legislature," Seán Lester pointed out in a dry voice, "not a fundamental law. It was a makeshift, a compromise, and I suspect that Dev was planning to repeal it eventually."

The first speaker said, "With Costello as taoiseach there'll be no repeal of the act, I assure you. Fine Gael's not a republican party."

The second speaker replied derisively, "You're right there, me lad. It's the party of the status quo."

Ursula gritted her teeth. *The status quo. Why is Ireland so damned predictable? Expect the worst and it happens, every time.*

As she was bidding the Lesters good-bye later, she leaned forward and asked Seán in a low voice, "Did de Valera really intend to get the republic back after all?"

He smiled a sad smile. "Did Michael Collins really intend to get the north back? Some questions can never be answered, Ursula."

*E*XISTENCE, thought Ursula on the train going home, *is made up of bits and pieces and unfinished stories. We're surprised by birth and thrust into life unprepared. We enter a world filled with beauty and horror; we want to live and we have to die. Every aspect of life is a paradox. How can we ever hope to make sense of it?*

A*T* a meeting of the Canadian Bar Association in Ottawa, Canada, in September of 1948, John A. Costello described the External Relations Act as being full of inaccuracies and infirmities. At a Canadian press conference a week later he confirmed a story carried by a Dublin newspaper, which claimed that his government intended to repeal the act.

He did not consult his cabinet before making the statement. They had no choice but to agree.

The world press was rocked by the unexpected announcement. Politically outmaneuvered, the British government could do nothing to keep Ireland in the Commonwealth any longer.

The apron strings were cut.

Chapter Fifty-seven

3 February 1949
Dear Henry,

If you can possibly arrange it, I hope you will pay a visit to Ireland soon. Papa is not at all well. The doctors say he has a brain tumor that has been growing very slowly for a long time. It might explain some of his bizarre behavior over the years.

The tumor is reaching dangerous proportions now. We discussed taking him to Dublin for an operation but he refuses to go. The medical consensus is that it probably would not make any difference anyway.

Papa never speaks of you by name, but like de Valera with Ireland, I believe I can read his heart. Come home, Henry, and make up the quarrel between you before it is too late.

How well he knew that quick light step! Ned turned an eager face toward the door of his bedroom. "Síle?"

"It's me, Papa."

"Oh. Of course."

Ursula heard the joy fade from his voice. "You have a visitor, Papa," she said. "Shall I bring him in?"

"Him?"

"Just a minute."

She ran back down the passage to where Henry was waiting. Behind his smile, his face felt stiff. "Will he see me?"

Ursula winced at his choice of verbs. "I think he will, Henry. His room's right down here, just follow me."

The walk to the bedroom door seemed very long.

URSULA had brought Henry from Shannon Airport in the farm's new motorcar. The black Ford was her pride and joy; something she could barely afford but had to have. The future.

"You drive a car like you ride a horse," Henry had complained, hanging on white-faced as the machine rocketed around curves and bounded over ruts.

When they reached the farmhouse he set his suitcase down just inside the door. "I want to go to Ned before anything else," he said. "Bite the bullet, so to speak." While Ursula took him upstairs, Eileen kept the children in the kitchen.

The door creaked open again. Ned felt a draft on his face. Someone entered. Heavy footsteps; strangely uncertain.

They stopped beside his bed.

"Hello, old-timer," said a deep voice.

The cracking sound in Ned's chest was that of the ice breaking around his heart.

Without saying a word, he opened his arms to his friend.

URSULA paced about the kitchen, picking things up and putting them down. Smoothing the oilcloth on the table. Moving the saucepans around on the range. "You'll ruin the dinner if you keep on," Eileen complained. "Would you ever sit down and calm yourself?"

"They've been up there together for a long time. I'd give anything to know what's happening."

"When were you ever backward about earwigging?" Eileen wanted to know.

Ursula grinned. Slipping off her shoes, she carried them in her hand as she tiptoed up the stairs. She could not hear anything until she stood outside Ned's room. The door was slightly ajar. She flattened herself against the passage wall and listened.

"We didn't really believe we could defeat England," Ned was saying.

"Not militarily. What we had to fight was the apathy of the Irish people. We had to arouse them to do whatever was necessary to take their destiny into their own hands. And we did. In 1916 the IRA gave Ireland her self-respect back.

"Then in 1919 Sinn Féin put political power in the hands of the people. What a weapon that was! Except we didn't appreciate it fully." Ned gave a weary sigh. "A man has a lot of time to think when he's sitting in the dark. Sometimes...only sometimes, mind...I think you were right all along, Henry. Perhaps after 1919 there should not have been a bullet fired in Ireland. We had leaders who were as clever as Lloyd George and his crowd; they just weren't experienced at political chicanery. Is it possible we might have won the Republic without any more bloodshed if we'd had the patience to learn the game?"

"That's what I thought at the time," Henry told him. "Had the IRA not kept fighting, the British wouldn't have sent in the Tans and..."

"And Síle would still be alive," said Ned.

"Yes," Henry replied in a choked voice. "Síle would still be alive."

The air was suddenly thick with pain. Even standing out in the passageway, Ursula could feel it. But whatever the quarrel had been between them, the anger was gone.

After a time Ned asked, "Could we have gained our independence your way, Henry? Would Britain ever have responded to anything other than physical force?"

"Did you read that speech W. B. Yeats once made in the Senate?" Henry responded. "He predicted we eventually would gain a united Ireland not through fighting, but through governing well. He wanted to create a culture that would represent the whole of the country and draw the imagination of the young."

"Draw the imagination of the young," echoed Ned. "That was Mr. Pearse's dream too." He fell silent again. Like Henry, Ursula waited.

Then she heard Ned say in a thoughtful voice, "If I had it to do over again perhaps I wouldn't be a soldier, Henry. Perhaps I'd be a teacher, a writer. A bard. Fight for minds instead of with bullets."

The woman listening in the passage was deeply shaken by his words. Battle had been Ned's creed. And through him, hers.

Ursula turned and went silently back down the stairs.

Later, much later, Henry joined Ursula and Eileen in the kitchen. The tracks of dried tears were still visible on his cheeks. "Ned's fallen asleep, I hope I didn't overtire him."

"He goes in and out of sleep a lot now," Ursula assured him. "Sometimes when he has bad headaches he sleeps all day. But in spite of the pain he could last for months, the doctors think. He seems determined to hold on as long as he can."

"Ned's always been stubborn," said Henry.

Eileen had prepared enough food to feed an army, or so it seemed, but a small army of children was waiting to gobble it down so none would go to waste. Henry was introduced to each of them in turn. Ursula saved Barry for last. At almost ten years of age he already came to his mother's shoulder. Long-boned and sturdy, he promised to be tall.

The boy held out his hand to Henry. "How do you do, sir. My mother speaks very highly of you, and I'm glad to meet you at last."

Henry chuckled. "So formal! How do you do, Barry." He shook the proffered hand, then reached out to rumple the boy's abundant red-gold hair. "You make me feel as old as God's governess, young fella. But where ever did you get those pointy ears?"

THE formal inauguration of the Republic of Ireland took place on 18 April, 1949. Easter Monday.

Because Ned was now too weak to leave his bed, Gerry had carried the wireless up to his room. Everyone gathered there to listen to the broadcast announcement. As Éire formally left the Commonwealth, Ned's hand groped across the quilt to find Ursula's.

The wireless crackled with magic.

Between one heartbeat and the next, the Republic of Ireland became official.

When the broadcast was over Ursula switched off the machine. "On Easter Monday thirty-three years ago," Ned murmured, "we marched out together for the Rising..." Exhausted by the excitement, he fell asleep in mid-thought.

His family tiptoed from the room.

Some time later, Ned Halloran awoke and lay listening to the sounds of life filling the old house. Counting his blessings.

He and Henry were friends again.

Síle was waiting in a place where the horizons were limitless.

And Ireland was a republic at last. Well, twenty-six counties of it. The Boys would win back the rest in time.

Turning his face to the wall, Ned Halloran went thankfully, peacefully, into the densely peopled dark.

FLAMING in the western sky were the banners of a salmon and gold sunset. Birds sang themselves to sleep in the hedgerows and shadows flowed like water across the hills of Clare.

The great fires that had swept the world and shaken its inhabitants to the core were over ... for a time.

Ireland Act, 1949

Be it enacted by the King's most Excellent Majesty, by and with the consent of the Lords Spiritual and Temporal, and Commons, in this present Parliament assembled, and by the authority of the same, as follows:

1. It is hereby recognized and declared that the part of Ireland heretofore known as Eire ceased, as from the eighteenth day of April, nineteen hundred and forty-nine, to be part of His Majesty's dominions.

2. It is hereby declared that Northern Ireland remains part of His Majesty's dominions and of the United Kingdom and it is hereby affirmed that in no event will Northern Ireland or any part thereof cease to be part of His Majesty's dominions and of the United Kingdom without consent of the Parliament of Northern Ireland.

3. The part of Ireland referred to in subsection (1) of this section is hereafter in this Act referred to, and may in any Act, enactment or instrument passed or made after the passing of this Act be referred to, by the name attributed thereto by the law thereof, that is to say, as the **Republic of Ireland.**

Source Notes

CHAPTER SIX

1. *The Victory of Sinn Féin*, p. 73
2. *Guns and Chiffon*, p. 42
3. *Forty Years of Irish Broadcasting*, p. 26

CHAPTER EIGHT

1. *The IRA in the Twilight Years*, p. 8
2. *De Valera*, p. 400
3. *Constance de Markievicz*, p. 349

CHAPTER NINE

1. *De Valera*, p. 405
2. *Rose and Crown*, p. 323
3. *Forty Years of Irish Broadcasting*, p. 44

CHAPTER ELEVEN

1. *Forty Years of Irish Broadcasting*, p. 59
2. *The IRA in the Twilight Years*, p. 154

CHAPTER TWELVE

1. *Soul of Fire*, p. 143
2. *Ireland This Century* p. 106
3. *Ireland's Holy Wars*, p. 303
4. *Women of the House*, p. 28
5. *Seán Lemass*, p. 55

CHAPTER FOURTEEN

1. *A View from Above*, p. 72
2. *A View from Above*, p. 53

CHAPTER FIFTEEN

1. *The Last Secretary-General*, p. 3
2. *The Last Secretary-General*, p. 13

CHAPTER SIXTEEN

1. *A View from Above*, p. 65

CHAPTER SEVENTEEN

1. *Ireland This Century*, p. 108

CHAPTER EIGHTEEN

1. *Women of the House*, p. 16
2. *The Last Secretary-General*, p. 24

CHAPTER NINETEEN

1. *Twentieth Century Ireland*, p. 20
2. *De Valera*, p. 436

CHAPTER TWENTY

1. *Ireland 1912–1985*, p. 176
2. *John Charles McQuaid*, p. 73

3. *Hanna Sheehy Skeffington*, p. 321

4. *Ireland; A Social and Cultural History*, p. 38

5. *The Eucharistic Triumph*, p. 22

CHAPTER TWENTY-THREE

1. *The Irish Counter-Revolution 1921–1936*, p. 327

CHAPTER TWENTY-FIVE

1. *The Irish Counter-Revolution 1921–1936*, p. 347

2. *The Irish Counter-Revolution 1921–1936*, p. 323

3. *Diana Mosley: A Biography*, p. 186

CHAPTER TWENTY-SIX

1. *Forty Years of Irish Broadcasting*, p. 91

CHAPTER TWENTY-SEVEN

1. *Chronicle of the 20th Century*, p. 436

2. *De Valera*, p. 473

CHAPTER TWENTY-EIGHT

1. *The Shelbourne Hotel*, p. 223

2. *A View from Above*, p. 75

CHAPTER THIRTY

1. *Ireland's Holy Wars*, p. 332

CHAPTER THIRTY-THREE

1. *Chronicle of the 20th Century*, p. 462

2. *The IRA in the Twilight Years*, p. 361

3. *Chronicle of the 20th Century*, p. 463

4. *The IRA in the Twilight Years*, p. 366

5. *The Irish and the Spanish Civil War*, p. 6

CHAPTER THIRTY-FOUR

1. *Chronicle of the 20th Century,* p. 478

CHAPTER THIRTY-FIVE

1. *Erin's Blood Royal,* p. 183
2. *The Last Secretary-General,* p. 151

CHAPTER THIRTY-SIX

1. *Irish Political Documents 1916–1949,* p. 218
2. *The Last Secretary-General,* p. 158

CHAPTER THIRTY-NINE

1. *The Chronicle of the 20th Century,* p. 502

CHAPTER FORTY

1. *The Irish and the Spanish Civil War,* p. 200

CHAPTER FORTY-ONE

1. *The Last Secretary-General,* p. 168

CHAPTER FORTY-TWO

1. *Chronicle of the 20th Century,* p. 507
2. *The Last Secretary-General,* p. 180

CHAPTER FORTY-FOUR

1. *Irish Political Documents 1916–1949,* p. 221
2. *The Last Secretary-General,* p. 182
3. *Ireland This Century,* p. 148
4. *The Emergency,* p. 122
5. *A U.S. Spy in Ireland,* p. 109
6. *An Irish Century 1845–1945,* p. 146
7. *The Last Secretary-General,* p. 187

CHAPTER FORTY-FIVE

1. *The Last Secretary-General*, p. 187

CHAPTER FORTY-SIX

1. *Step Together!*, p. 3
2. *British State Papers de-classified and released in 1999*

CHAPTER FORTY-SEVEN

1. *Irish Political Documents 1916–1949*, p. 224

CHAPTER FORTY-EIGHT

1. *De Valera*, p. 566
2. *The Emergency*, p. 36
3. *The Lost Years*, p. 128

CHAPTER FORTY-NINE

1. *Irish Times*, December 23, 1998

CHAPTER FIFTY

1. *A Chronology of Irish History*, p. 227

CHAPTER FIFTY-ONE

1. *The Lost Years*, p. 184
2. *The Emergency*, p. 11
3. *John Charles McQuaid*, pp. 175–192
4. *Irish Political Documents 1916–1949*, p. 231

CHAPTER FIFTY-TWO

1. *The Emergency*, p. 131
2. *De Valera*, p. 528
3. *Twentieth Century Ireland*, p. 152
4. *Ireland This Century*, p. 161
5. *De Valera*, p. 621

CHAPTER FIFTY-THREE

1. *De Valera*, p. 156

CHAPTER FIFTY-FOUR

1. *Eamon de Valera*, p. 413
2. *2RN*, p. 176

CHAPTER FIFTY-FIVE

1. *Step Together!*, p. 169

CHAPTER FIFTY-SIX

1. *Modern Ireland*, p. 565

Bibliography

Akenson, Donald Harmon. *Irish Catholics and Irish Protestants 1815–1922*. Dublin: Gill & Macmillan, 1991.

Andrew, Christopher, and Vasili Mitrokhin. *The Mitrokhin Archive*. London: Allen Lane, 1999.

Barrington, Brendan. *The Wartime Broadcasts of Francis Stuart, 1942–1944*. Dublin: Lilliput Press, 2000.

Bell, J. Bowyer. *The IRA; The Secret Army*. Dublin: AP Press, 1970.

Boylan, Patricia. *All Cultivated People*. Buckinghamshire, England: Colin Smythe Ltd., 1988.

Brennan, Robert. *Allegiance*. Dublin: Browne and Nolan, Ltd., 1950.

Brome, Vincent. *The International Brigades: Spain 1936–1939*. London: Heinemann, 1965.

Brown, Terence. *Ireland; A Social and Cultural History 1922–1985*. London: Fontana Press, 1985.

Capuchin Annual, The. Dublin: 1970.

Carey, Tim. *Mountjoy: The Story of a Prison.* Cork: The Collins Press, 2000.

Clayton, Pamela. *Enemies and Passing Friends.* London: Pluto Press, 1996.

Clear, Caitriona. *Women of the House.* Dublin: Irish Academic Press, 2000.

Coogan, Tim Pat. *De Valera.* London: Hutchinson, 1993.

Coogan, Tim Pat. *Ireland Since the Rising.* London: Pall Mall Press, 1966.

Coogan, Tim Pat. *Wherever Green Is Worn.* London: Hutchinson, 2000.

Cooney, John. *John Charles McQuaid.* Dublin: O'Brien Press, 1999.

Corbett, John. *A Time and Place for Mirth and Mischief.* Dublin: Lough Ree Publishing Co., 1998.

Dalley, Jan. *Diana Mosley: A Biography.* London: Faber & Faber, 1999.

De Valera, Eamon. *Peace and War: Speeches on International Affairs.* Dublin: M.H. Gill & Son, Ltd., 1944.

Doherty, Richard. *Irish Men and Women in the Second World War.* Dublin: Four Courts Press, 1999.

Dwyer, T. Ryle. *Short Fellow.* Dublin: Marino Books, 1995.

Elliott, Marianne. *The Catholics of Ireland.* London: Allen Lane, 2000.

Ellis, Peter Beresford. *Erin's Blood Royal.* London: Constable & Co., 1999.

Fallon, Brian. *An Age of Innocence: Irish Culture 1930–1960.* Dublin: Gill & Macmillan, 1998.

Fallon, Charlotte H. *Soul On Fire.* Cork: Mercier Press, 1986.

Fanning, Kennedy; Keogh and O'Halpin, editors. *Documents on Irish Foreign Policy Volume I.* Dublin: Royal Irish Academy for the Department of Foreign Affairs, 1998.

Farrell, Brian, editor. *RTE 100 Years*. Dublin: Town House, 2001.

Fischer, Joachim, and Myles Dillon, editors. *The Correspondence of Myles Dillon*. Dublin: Four Courts Press, 1999.

Fisk, Robert. *In Time of War: Ireland, Ulster, and the Price of Neutrality*. Dublin: Gill and Macmillan, 1996.

Fitzgibbon, Constantine. *Out of the Lion's Paw: Ireland Wins Her Freedom*. London, Macdonald & Co., 1969.

Forrest, Andrew D. *Worse Could Have Happened*. Dublin: Poolbeg Press, 1999.

Gageby, Douglas. *The Last Secretary-General: Sean Lester and the League of Nations*. Dublin: Town House Press, 1999.

Gallagher, Frank. *The Indivisible Island*. London: Victor Gollancz Ltd., 1957.

Gorham, Maurice. *Forty Years of Irish Broadcasting*. Dublin: Talbot Press Ltd., 1967.

Gray, Tony. *Ireland This Century*. London: Little Brown & Co., 1994.

Gray, Tony. *The Lost Years: The Emergency in Ireland 1939–45*. London: Little, Brown & Co., 1997.

Griffith, Kenneth, and Timothy O'Grady. *Curious Journey*. Cork: Mercier Press, 1998.

Harkness, D. W. *The Restless Dominion*. New York: New York University Press, 1970.

Haverty, Anne. *Constance Markievicz: An Independent Life*. London: Pandora, 1988.

Hegarty, Patrick Sarsfield. *The Victory of Sinn Féin*. Dublin: University College Dublin Press, 1998.

Jackson, John Wyse. *Flann O'Brien at War*. London: Duckworth, 1999.

Kearns, Kevin C. *Dublin Street Life & Lore: An Oral History.* Dublin: Gill & Macmillan, 1997.

Keogh, Dermot. *Twentieth-Century Ireland: Nation and State.* Dublin: Gill & Macmillan, 1994.

Kershaw, Ian. *Hitler 1889–1936.* London: Allen Lane, 1998.

Kiely, Benedict. *Counties of Contention.* Cork: Mercier Press, 1945.

Laffan, Michael. *The Resurrection of Ireland: The Sinn Féin Party 1916–1923.* Cambridge: Cambridge University Press, 1999.

Lee, Joseph. *Ireland 1912–1985: Politics and Society.* Cambridge: Cambridge University Press, 1989.

McCabe, Ian. *A Diplomatic History of Ireland 1948–49.* Dublin: Irish Academic Press, 1991.

MacCarron, Donal. *A View from Above: 200 Years of Aviation in Ireland.* Dublin: O'Brien Press, 2000.

MacCarron, Donal, *Step Together!: Ireland's Emergency Army.* Dublin: Irish Academic Press, 1999.

McCool, Sinéad. *Guns and Chiffon: Women Revolutionaries and Kilmainham Gaol.* Dublin: Government of Ireland Stationery Office, 1997.

MacEoin, Uinseann. *The IRA in the Twilight Years 1923–1948.* Dublin: privately published, 1997.

MacEoin, Uinseann. *Survivors.* Dublin: Argenta Publications, 1987.

MacLysaght, Edward. *Changing Times.* London: Colin Smythe Ltd., 1978.

McNamara, Maedhbh, and Pascal Mooney. *Women in Parliament.* Dublin: Wolfhound Press, 2000.

MacThomáis, Eamonn. *Me Jewel and Darlin' Dublin.* Dublin: O'Brien Press, 1974.

Marreco, Anne. *The Rebel Countess.* London: The Phoenix Press, 2000.

Mercer, Derrick, editor-in-chief. *Chronicle of the 20th Century.* London: Longmans, 1988.

Mitchell, Arthur, and Pádraig Ó Snodaigh. *Irish Political Documents 1916–1949.* Dublin: Irish Academic Press, 1985.

Moreton, Cole. *Hungry for Home.* London: Viking Press, 2000.

Nelligan, David. *The Spy in the Castle.* London: Prendeville Publ. Ltd., 1999.

Norman, Diana. *Terrible Beauty: A Life of Constance Markievicz.* Lond: Hodder & Stoughton Ltd., 1987.

O'Broin, Leon. *Protestant Nationalists in Revolutionary Ireland.* Dublin: Gill & Macmillan, 1985.

O'Callaghan, Fr. Jerome. *The Eucharistic Triumph.* London: Sands & Co., 1933.

O'Casey, Sean. *Autobiographies 2: Rose and Crown.* London: Papermac, division of Pan Macmillan, 1992.

O'Donoghue, David. *Hitler's Irish Voices.* Belfast: Beyond the Pale Publications, 1998.

O'Neill, Marie. *Grace Gifford Plunkett.* Dublin: Irish Academic Press, 2000.

Oram, Hugh. *The Newspaper Book.* Dublin: MO Books, 1983.

O'Sullivan, Donal. *The Irish Free State and Its Senate.* London: Faber & Faber, 1940.

Pakenham, Frank, Earl of Longford, and Thomas P. O'Neill. *Eamon de Valera.* Dublin: Gill & Macmillan, 1970.

Pakenham, Frank. *Peace by Ordeal.* Cork: Mercier Press Ltd., 1951.

Pearce, Donald R. *The Senate Speeches of W. B. Yeats.* London: Prendeville Publishing Ltd., 2002.

Pine, Richard. *2RN and the Origins of Irish Radio.* Dublin: Four Courts Press, 2002.

Quigley, Martin S. *A U. S. Spy in Ireland.* Dublin: Marino Press, 1999.

Regan, John M. *The Irish Counter-Revolution 1921–1936.* Dublin: Gill & Macmillan, 1999.

Ryan, Desmond. *Unique Dictator: A Study of Eamon de Valera.* London: Arthur Barker Ltd., 1936.

Saorstát Éireann: Official Handbook. Dublin: Talbot Press, 1932.

Share, Bernard. *The Emergency: Neutral Ireland 1939–45.* Dublin: Gill & Macmillan, 1978.

Skeffington, Owen Sheehy. *What Has Happened? 1916–1966.* Dublin: TCD Publishing Co., 1966.

Small, Stephen. *An Irish Century 1845–1945.* Dublin: Roberts Books, 1998.

Somerville-Large, Peter. *Irish Voices.* London: Chatto & Windus, 1999.

Spellissy, Seán, *The Merchants of Ennis.* Co. Clare: Ennis Chamber of Commerce, 1996.

Stradling, Robert. *The Irish and the Spanish Civil War 1936–1939.* Manchester: Mandolin, 1999.

Tanner, Marcus. *Ireland's Holy Wars.* London: Yale University Press UK, 2001.

Townshend, Charles. *Ireland: The 20th Century.* London: Arnold, 1999.

Van Voris. *Constance de Markievicz.* Massachusetts: University of Massachusetts Press, 1967.

Ward, Margaret. *Hanna Sheehy Skeffington: A Life.* Cork: Attic Press, 1997.